PILGRIMAGE

PILGRIMAGE

DIANA DAVIDSON

BRINDLE
& GLASS

Brindle & Glass Publishing Ltd.
brindleandglass.com

LIBRARY AND ARCHIVES CANADA CATALOGUING IN PUBLICATION
Davidson, Diana, 1976–
Pilgrimage / Diana Davidson.

Issued also in electronic format.
ISBN 978-1-927366-17-2

I. Title.

PS8607.A792P55 2013   C813'.6   C2013-902024-1

Editor: Leah Fowler
Proofreader: Heather Sangster, Strong Finish
Design: Pete Kohut
Cover image: CAP53, istockphoto.com
Author photo: Rachel Hummeny

Brindle & Glass is pleased to acknowledge the financial support for its publishing program from the Government of Canada through the Canada Book Fund, Canada Council for the Arts, and the Province of British Columbia through the British Columbia Arts Council and the Book Publishing Tax Credit.

MIX
Paper from
responsible sources
FSC
www.fsc.org   FSC® C016245

The interior pages of this book have been printed on 100% post-consumer recycled paper, processed chlorine free, and printed with vegetable-based inks.

1   2   3   4   5   17   16   15   14   13

PRINTED IN CANADA

This is dedicated to the woman in the well, who inspired this story, and to others whose stories are untold.

⇥ CONTENTS ⇤

Hibernation
DECEMBER 1891

Outside, the dogs bark and Mahkesîs looks at the door. The young woman finds herself easily startled now. Mahkesîs spends the winter days inside, in the dark closeness of her family's log cabin, trying to get used to the fluttering in her belly. It is the time of year when animals burrow and hide, the spruce trees are heavy with snow, and the naked poplars reach their spindly arms into the brutal, sharp northern sky. It is the time of year when it is hard to remember that, in summer, Lac St. Anne is a place of light, hope, and possibility. Mahkesîs quit working for the Englishman at the end of September so the baby will come in late spring or early summer. *At least it will be born when it is green and warm outside*, she thinks.

The barking gets louder. Mahkesîs's mother, Virginié, puts down her mending and says, in Cree, "Our visitors must be here!" Mahkesîs watches her small, slight mother go to the cabin door. Virginié's hands shake with nerves as she opens it.

"Tân'si! Come in!" Virginié exclaims as she greets her cousins. This late December afternoon, Virginié welcomes Payesîs Belcourt and Boots Mageau, along with Boots's husband, George, who have come visiting from St. Albert. Mahkesîs knows they have journeyed all day through the snow to get here, riding in a

1

Red River cart pulled by a donkey, to stay a few nights in this small cabin. Everyone will celebrate New Year's Eve at Lac St. Anne.

"It's colder than a witch's tit out there!" exclaims Boots in Cree as she shakes soft snowflakes from the shoulders of her woollen shawl and stamps packed snow and ice from her boots.

"Well, come in and have some warm tea then," Virginié says, smiling. Her mother gestures to Mahkesîs to take the kettle from over the fire.

Virginié tells George, "Luc and Gabriel are fishing down at the lake. There is hay for the donkey out back."

George nods and heads back outside without speaking or taking off his prized coat: the red, blue, green, and yellow stripes have faded over time, but the Hudson's Bay Company colours felted into white wool still stand out.

Virginié asks her cousins, "What is happening in St. Albert? You always have good stories."

Mahkesîs notices that her mother is fidgeting more than usual today; she wonders if Virginié is worried that Payesîs and Boots are here not only to celebrate New Year's Eve but also to assess her stomach for themselves. *There are rumours,* she thinks. *It is hard enough to keep people's eyes off me at Mass. Has the gossip really travelled to St. Albert? Or did the aunties stop somewhere else on the settlement before coming to our house?* Other women at Lac St. Anne may have noticed that Mahkesîs no longer tucks her blouse into her skirt to show off her small waist. Mahkesîs fears that some may chatter about her full breasts and hint of a belly to pass the time. But Mahkesîs has been told many times she is beautiful, and that she could pass for white and be married accordingly, and, once they know, she fears that some of the women will feel slightly vindicated that she is no better than any of their girls. She is sad that she is causing her mother so much worry and hates to think she will cause her shame. Her mother has not told Mahkesîs's father, Luc, about the pregnancy, and they will only be able to hide it for another month or so. Mahkesîs feels as trapped as the marten and muskrat that her father snares to trade at the Englishman's store.

Mahkesîs's grandmother, an elder whom everyone on the settlement calls "Nohkum" and whose Christian name is Angelique, sits in a chair near the fire this afternoon. The old woman wears her still-black hair in one long braid made shiny by bear grease. While Angelique has earned the right to speak her mind, this snowy winter afternoon, she listens: she chews tobacco and patterns a piece of hide with pink, white, and yellow beads as the other women sit on benches on either side of a long table and drink birchbark tea while they gossip in Cree.

Payesîs says, "I heard people in the South have no more buffalo. We've still got our moose and bears at least. And after four tough summers, we're bound to have a good one. Who knows though, things are changing. Harder to make a living just on fur now. We may all well have to start farming . . ."

Payesîs got her name because she chirps like a little bird; her Christian name is Florence. Mahkesîs knows the last years have been hard on her aunty: Payesîs lost her husband a few winters ago, and since then she has had to live with her sister Boots and George in a small house near the St. Albert Mission on the Sturgeon River. She had one child, a son, but he did not survive into adulthood. Mahkesîs has heard her aunty say, on more than one occasion, that her people have "scattered like fuzzy pussy willows blown away on a warm afternoon."

"Ah, Payesîs. No sense worrying about that. What can we do? Let's talk about something else, something fun!" says Boots.

Unlike her sister, who not only sounds but looks like a sparrow or waxwing, Boots is an angular woman who gets squarer even in lean seasons. Mahkesîs also calls Boots "Aunty," but she is fonder of Payesîs. Boots wears a pink blouse that pulls at the buttons over her pendulous breasts. She keeps a green-and-yellow scarf over her hair even though it's warm in the Cardinal home. When she was a girl, Boots got a pair of second-hand blue English galoshes from Sister Alphonse (before the Grey Nuns moved to St. Albert) and she wore them everywhere until her toes poked through cracks in the rubber. The name has lasted many more decades than the boots did.

Payesîs says, "What I mean is that it's not just the English and French who are coming here. That new train in Edmonton brings people from all sorts of countries and then they come north. Edmonton has just as many people as St. Albert and Lac St. Anne now. Heard they even got lights on the streets like they do in London or New York."

"I'd like to see the lights," Virginié says quietly. "I wonder if they look like Northern Lights, all green and blue dancing." She replaces a nearly melted candle with a new one on this dark December afternoon. Virginié tries not to use too many candles at once, but when company is visiting, she often tells Mahkesîs that there has to be light inside the cabin.

"Used to be that the North Saskatchewan River divided the Cree to the north and the Blackfoot to the south. There'll be none of us left soon," Payesîs continues.

"Pff. When was this a place of only Cree and Blackfoot? Two hundred years ago? Besides, everyone here, except Nohkum, is a mix of something: Cree, French, Scottish, Blackfoot, Dene, and Lord knows what else! Don't be so moody, Payesîs—the past is the past."

Mahkesîs notices that Payesîs does look sullen.

"But now that you mention it, I do believe your wrinkled-up face is two hundred years old," Boots teases.

"Assk. At least my ass doesn't hang over my chair," Payesîs says right back.

All the women laugh.

4

"Virginié, what's that handsome boy of yours up to?" Payesîs asks.

"Gabriel?"

Mahkesîs knows that her brother is an object of desire for many young girls, a potential prize for their mothers and aunties of families connected to this place. *He will have his pick of women to choose from*, she thinks.

"Emm-hmm. I heard he was going with Bertha Tourangeau," says Boots. "That true?"

"Oh, no." Virginié chuckles. "He was sweet on her this spring, but then he found work freighting on the Athabasca. When he came back this fall, they were done. I'm glad too. She's a bit funny, that one."

"Well, you would be too," says Payesîs, "if you had to skin rabbits all day to feed to a bunch of dogs. And your father built coffins!"

Mahkesîs knows that none of the women in the cabin like the fact that the Tourangeau girl gets Company money to feed perfectly good rabbits to a growing population of dogs that run wild and steal people's chickens at night. It is just one small example of how the Company's needs disturb the balance of things here. Mahkesîs especially dislikes Bertha: they are the same age and Bertha was often rude to her when they were children at the mission school. Bertha liked to pull hair and throw mud.

"It isn't good for a young woman to be around so much death. Everyone has to tan a hide or twist a chicken's neck now and then, but to snare rabbits day in and out and then skin them to feed bits and bones to a pack of barely tame dogs? Just doesn't seem right. She should be with Gabriel, making you grandchildren, hey, Virginié?" says Payesîs.

Flustered, Virginié says, "My Gabriel's only twenty. There is no rush for him to leave me yet."

"And how old was Luc when he courted you?" Boots chides. "He's a man. And he's plenty old enough to be making you a grandmother." She laughs and makes a lewd gesture with her hands. "Maybe Gabriel will find someone at the dance. Lots of people coming back here for New Year's Eve! My Elin is a good cook; she will make a good wife."

Mahkesîs knows that everyone here knows Boots would like Gabriel to pair up with her daughter, *but Elin is a plain girl who has inherited her mother's crass tongue and*, thinks Mahkesîs, *her father's face.*

"Gabriel's in no rush," Virginié says again. "It is different than when we were young. People need more now. More tea?"

Boots shakes her head.

Mahkesîs will be nineteen this summer. As the women talk, she has been standing at the fire stirring the rabbit stew she is preparing for their supper. It's the beginning of the winter, so the meat doesn't have to be boiled with the barley, onion, and carrots for many hours like it will in a few months. She has timed it so it will be ready shortly after the sun sets, when the men will return from the lake.

Payesîs changes the subject. "Mahkesîs, come sit down. That stew is just fine. I can smell that it needs more time."

Mahkesîs nods and sits at the table. She adjusts the long pins loosely holding her brown-auburn hair in a chignon at the base of her neck.

"Now, tell us about working for that Englishman and his wife. Did you help out at the store?" Payesîs asks.

Mahkesîs clears her throat. "I mostly worked at the house. I set up the Manager's Quarters for Mr. Barrett first and then his wife when she came over." She looks at her hands in her lap.

Mahkesîs knows she came to her position in Barrett's house because her father drank with Barrett at the store after hours. One night the trapper suggested his youngest child could help the Englishman set up his house at Lac St. Anne. Barrett, made amiable by local moonshine, agreed. Luc Cardinal told Barrett how he had christened his only daughter Adèle, after Sister Adèle Lamy, who came here with Father Lacombe and the other Grey Nuns from Quebec when he was a boy, and how she had learned most of her domestic skills at the mission school. Mahkesîs knew that her father needed the money she would make, and she knew that he hoped Barrett might arrange a church marriage for her with a young Company man. Mahkesîs heard her father tell her mother, "She can pass for white, and that's worth something." One spring afternoon, her father took her to the Company store. She stood there, on display like a fine beaver pelt, as Barrett looked her up and down and her father told Mr. Barrett, "Adèle knows what plants grow and won't grow, she knows just how much kindling is needed to start a fire and how many pumps of the long handle will fill a pail, and she speaks English, unlike some of the other girls here who go back to Cree or Michif after leaving school." Mahkesîs had the feeling, even then, that Barrett would have taken her just on looks. She started working for him the next day.

"That's all you're going to say?" asks Boots. "Must be more to tell."

What can I tell them? Mahkesîs thinks. *That at first Mr. Barrett and me settled into a comfortable routine? That I looked after a house made of thin, smooth logs painted white, its windows made of glass, not hide? That the first day I was alone in the house, I walked up and down its stairs with a smooth, white banister?* These women know that the Manager's Quarters are one of a handful of buildings on the settlement built by either the Church or Hudson's Bay Company. They know that the rest of the eighty or so houses at Lac St. Anne were built by the Métis families who have been here since the Church built its mission two generations ago. The women know the Manager's Quarters are different from

7

their own homes, different from the cabin they are drinking tea in this afternoon, this cabin that Mahkesîs's father and brothers built, on a plot that belonged to her grandmother's husband, by chopping down poplars and mixing clay and mud. *They already know all this. What more can I tell them?* she thinks.

Boots says, "He's a handsome devil, that Mr. Barrett. Never been too fond of Englishmen, with their bluish skin and long noses. But he's good to look at, that one, with his brown hair and dark eyes. Must have been fun seeing him in his long johns every morning." The older woman laughs.

Mahkesîs blushes at Boots's teasing.

Most mornings Mahkesîs arrived at the Manager's Quarters while Mr. Barrett was still sleeping. She would let herself in. He would wake up flustered, often with a headache from too much drink the night before, rush to get dressed in the clothes she had washed and pressed, run downstairs, and eat a breakfast of tea and porridge Mahkesîs had prepared. Mr. Barrett would leave for the store at around nine and return to a supper Mahkesîs also had prepared. After serving him, she would walk home across the creek and he would leave the dishes in a basin for her to do when she arrived early the next morning. Mahkesîs seeded a garden of potatoes, beans, peas, and carrots; the land at Lac St. Anne is full of clay and sand and the mossy underbrush of the boreal forest. Mahkesîs was taught to know that there is plenty to have and plenty to do here.

Mahkesîs thinks about how some days Mr. Barrett would leave instructions for her, but more often than not he wouldn't; Mahkesîs kept herself busy. The Cardinals' home has a dirt floor, which does not need scrubbing, but she kept the wooden floors of the Manager's Quarters clean and waxed and free of debris. One spring afternoon, Mr. Barrett came home early with a cart loaded with a wrought-iron bed that had come on the train from Toronto to Edmonton and then made it here. He had Mahkesîs help him assemble the bed upstairs. Mr. Barrett touched her hand as she passed him pieces; she didn't think much of it at the time.

Payesîs sees that the girl does not want to talk about Mr. Barrett and broaches another topic of much gossip. "Well, what was it like to work for Mrs. Barrett? I've heard that white woman is having trouble getting used to life here."

Mahkesîs knows the women are interested in Georgina Barrett because they don't know much about her. Mrs. Barrett does not go to Mass; the only church on the settlement is Catholic and the white woman is Anglican. Mrs. Barrett only occasionally helps her husband at the store. The only other white women any of the women gathered around the Cardinals' table know are nuns, and they are from Quebec.

"I've heard he'll have to send her back before she makes it through her first winter." Boots rolls her eyes and takes a noisy slurp of lukewarm tea.

Mahkesîs says, "Mrs. Barrett just needs some time to get used to it here. She'll be fine." She is not sure why she defends Mrs. Barrett.

Boots asks, "What's there to get used to? She lives in a nice house that you took care of, and now she has that other girl to do the work. She has wooden floors and a cast-iron stove. She has no little ones. She gets all her food from the store—probably without paying for it. What does she do all day?"

Mahkesîs thinks of how Georgina Barrett spent most of her days in bed. If she did come downstairs, she would sit for hours at her writing desk. Even on the rare days Mr. Barrett forced her to accompany him to the store, his wife returned home more miserable than when she left. Mrs. Barrett showed little interest in her new house and even less in its garden. Mahkesîs had to take in three of her dresses because the white woman had lost so much weight since coming here.

Payesîs chimes in, "We should take her squirrel hunting. That would help her get used to being here. I'd love to see that moniyaskwa drown and cook one of those little buggers."

All the women in the Cardinals' cabin laugh at the idea of the white woman out with them, trying not to get scratched or bitten by a squirrel, in her fine English clothes.

"And what about that housegirl of hers? The girl goes to Mass. And people say they talk differently. How can they be from the same country?" Boots wipes tears from her eyes.

Mahkesîs could tell that, unlike Georgina Barrett, the girl who came over with her, the one named Moira, is used to hard work. *She must be so lonely now that I've left*, Mahkesîs almost says out loud. They still see each other at Mass, but it is hard to have long conversations at church.

"Mahkesîs, why did Mrs. Barrett bring that girl? People who come out West don't usually bring servants," Payesîs says.

Boots snorts. "Well, why would they? They need us locals to survive, and we let them pay us nothing."

Mahkesîs says, "Moira is a hard worker. I think she likes it here. We should try to make her feel welcome."

Payesîs takes a drink of tea from a black metal mug that is part of a set Luc traded a silver fox pelt for when he and Virginié were first married and says to Mahkesîs, "Maybe. But she won't know how to get through winter here. And what about when the manager's wife has a child? You should go back and work for Barrett again then, Mahkesîs."

Boots adds, "Hmmph. They have that other pale girl. How much help does that Englishwoman need for one babe? Besides, that woman's too skinny to have a baby."

Mahkesîs's grandmother, who has been quiet up until now, spits her chewing tobacco into an empty tin can with jagged edges. She and Virginié are the only people who know what Barrett did to their girl.

Angelique says, "Assk. My girl's too good to work for that man. She's too good to wash and cook for a lazy white woman."

Mahkesîs gets up from the table carefully, with her back turned to them so they cannot measure the girth of her new stomach, and checks the fire. It is getting harder to hide. A few days ago, as she was getting dressed in the candlelight, Mahkesîs saw her mother looking at the purple marks appearing across her skin at her breasts and belly. Mahkesîs considers, for a moment, telling these women about everything: the day of the thunderstorm, the baby, the struggle, Barrett, Georgina. But she stops herself; they've probably heard it all before, and it wouldn't change anything for her. It would only enrage her father and maybe cause him to do something rash.

Mahkesîs spared her grandmother the details, but she told her enough so that the old woman knows it was not her choices that led to her situation.

The first time it happened, Mahkesîs was getting ready to walk back to her parents' cabin and the summer heat gave way to a violent thunderstorm. She had to wait out the rain in the kitchen. The Manager's Quarters are just behind the store, on the west end of the settlement, and it would take Mahkesîs a good half-hour to walk from the crossroads in front of it, across the creek, to her family's plot at the east end of the settlement. That stormy afternoon, she did not want to soak her English-style yellow cotton dress that she wore, as it was the only dress she could wear to work there. Barrett had not returned from the store yet when it had started raining; Mahkesîs had a supper of roast chicken, green onion from the garden, and new small potatoes with freshly churned butter waiting for him. It was enough food for a family, and he would eat it all. Mahkesîs didn't know how he was so wiry when he seemed to have an endless appetite.

She remembers how Barrett burst into the house, drenched

and drunk, after losing an afternoon game of cards he'd closed the store to host.

He called, "Adèle? You still here?" He shook water from his boots in the mud room. "I wanted to make sure you were all right."

"I'm fine, Mr. Barrett," she had answered. "Just waiting 'til it passes to walk home."

Mahkesîs sat at the table beading a piece of hide that her grandmother would sew into a moccasin. She quickly tucked it into her apron pocket.

"Well, you won't be going anywhere anytime soon. You'll never make it across the creek in those slippers. It's heaving out there! Let's have some tea, shall we?"

Mahkesîs nodded and got up to fill the kettle from the water pail. Barrett watched her. She placed it on the stove. She turned around to see him start to strip down to his undershirt and underwear.

"I best get out of these wet clothes. Now, be a good girl and hang them over that chair to dry."

Again, Mahkesîs did as she was told: she averted her eyes from Mr. Barrett and carefully placed his fine shirt and tailored trousers on the back of a kitchen chair.

Barrett came up to her from behind and placed his hands on her shoulders. He had whispered, "You know, you are different from other *half-breed* girls. You are quite lovely. You could actually pass for white."

Barrett turned her around and grabbed her face. He sloppily pressed his mouth against hers.

Mahkesîs will always remember his taste of cigars, whiskey, and vomit.

"No!" She tried to push him away.

"I like your father. Holds his liquor. Good card player."

Barrett held her by one arm. She could feel it bruising.

He reached around to the back of her neck and undid her

bun. He ran his fingers through her hair. "So pretty—like chocolate and ginger together."

He forced his tongue in her mouth again. He said, "I have been fantasizing about your bow-shaped mouth for weeks."

Mahkesîs tried to pull away.

"I'm a good girl," she begged.

"Stop pretending you don't want it," he had said. "Why else would you wear your dress so fitted, teasing me as you bend over to weed the garden? You know I watch you. You like that I watch you."

Barrett grabbed her other arm and pushed her down to the floor. Mahkesîs shivered as his undershirt pressed against her chest. He lifted her dress and forced her legs apart with his.

"Stop, please." Mahkesîs tried to push him off but knew she was trapped.

"Be nice," he had said through gritted teeth. "It will feel good."

Mahkesîs could not get up. Thunder clapped outside and rain pelted down onto the roof of the house and against the glass windows. All she could do was close her eyes and pretend it wasn't happening. She felt the crush of his torso against the beaded hide in her apron pocket. She felt piercing pain. The quill needle stuck into her belly. She heard him grunt and moan. That was the first time.

Mahkesîs wanted to quit working at the Manager's Quarters. She wanted to make Barrett pay for what he did to her. But there was no guarantee anyone would believe her—it would be her word against an Englishman's. Her family needed the four dollars a month she was earning; there'd been three lean hunting years in a row and the fur trade was slow. The day after that first time, Mahkesîs rationalized that she only had to stay until autumn, and then Mrs. Barrett would arrive from Cork and would know enough to keep the house. Hopefully the moose hunt would bring enough meat for the winter for her family.

Angelique says to Payesîs and Boots, "Mahkesîs has spent enough time working for people who are not ours. I'll teach her things she still needs to learn. We'll find her a nice boy, someone like us, someone she can make a good life with in the old ways."

Boots and Payesîs know that the talk about the Barretts is over. Angelique has as much said so. The old woman's strong hands, tattooed with charcoal and sinew the year she was first married to the most handsome man in her tribe, move quickly as she finishes a pattern on moose hide.

Payesîs talks about a scandal among one of the old Lac St. Anne families that connects them all. "Cain Joachim has gone missing from St. Albert. Been in the bush all fall. They say he's turned into a weetigo, that one."

"Oh, Payesîs, you shouldn't say such things," says Virginié, who is a devout Catholic and prefers to believe in the devil and his hellfire rather than the half-dead cannibals who feature in the stories of her mother's people.

The women talk and Mahkesîs checks the stew over the fire. She doesn't care too much for rabbit, but rabbits are easy to catch this time of year; some of them haven't turned completely white yet, and their mottled skin shows up against the snow. Virginié reaches up onto a shelf for some flour to make some bannock. She clears a spot on the big table. She dumps flour into the bowl and its dust billows into the air like falling snow. She cuts in chunks of bear grease to work into dough. Payesîs's hands dive into the bowl, like a northern pelican catching trout in its gullet, and they start to knead the flour and fat without the woman missing a beat of the conversation. Mahkesîs and the women who have raised her work hard and cannot imagine a life where they don't. Everything happens in careful cycles. Spring is for trapping thick winter furs and caring for the plants that come back to life. Summer is a time to pick berries, make pemmican, salt fish. Fall is when they skin corpses, stretch skins, carve meat away from bone and cure it to eat during these lean winter months. Winter is for resting and waiting.

The cabin door creaks open and ushers in a swirling gust of whiteness. The sun has already set and it is only four in the afternoon. The men shake off the cold at the door: Mahkesîs sees icicles in Luc's moustache and that George's cheeks are red on the verge of frostbite. Virginié gets up to take their coats and hang them to dry. Gabriel grins and holds up a string of five big jackfish he just caught through the ice on the nearby lake. Illuminated by candlelight, their green-yellow skins glisten under a thin layer of ice, their bellies shine a slimy white, and they smell of the deep freshwater. Virginié takes the fish from her favourite son and lays their bodies on the table: Mahkesîs knows her mother does this to stop the weight of hanging from a hook from further ripping their mouths open.

"Bonjour." Luc greets Payesîs and Boots as he stomps ice from his feet. He walks over to the table and assesses the mugs of tea and bowl of dough. Mahkesîs's father says to his wife in French, "Let's have a feast of fish for supper. George nearly fell through the ice getting us these jackfish. Cook them up for us."

Mahkesîs looks at him and says in Cree, "Papa—I've just made rabbit stew. And bannock will be ready as soon as we cook it."

"I didn't ask for your opinion, girl. I told you to fry up these fish."

"It's a waste." Mahkesîs stands tall, facing her father.

Everyone in the small cabin watches Mahkesîs and her father. Payesîs and Boots are quiet and Virginié nervously chews her nails. Tension hangs in the air like bait on a fishing line.

"How dare you speak to me like this in front of our guests." Luc moves toward her and grabs her upper arm. "Cook the fish or I swear I'll take a switch to you as if you were a child," he hisses in her ear.

15

Mahkesîs's grandmother speaks without looking up from her beading, "Don't you put a hand on my girl, Luc Cardinal. She is carrying your grandchild."

"Mama!" Virginié covers her mouth with her hand as the shock escapes.

Mahkesîs feels a flush of shame.

Her father looks at her with narrowed eyes. "Is this true?"

"Yes," Mahkesîs answers. Rabbit-meat juice drips from her spoon onto the dirt floor.

"Putain, whore," Luc says through gritted teeth. He spits at her feet, still holding her arm too tightly.

"Papa," says Gabriel, surprised but knowing he has to defend his sister. "Papa . . ."

Luc interrupts. "Who is the father?"

Mahkesîs answers, "I cannot tell you."

"Who is the father?" She feels him tighten his grip on her arm.

Virginié intervenes and gently pulls Mahkesîs away from the pot and away from Luc. She tries to calm her husband. "Luc, chérie, let's speak of this later, after supper, once we've all gotten over the surprise."

"Will this man take you in? Marry you? Will he raise this child?" Luc asks Mahkesîs.

Mahkesîs shakes her head from side to side.

"Well, you can stay here until you give birth. Only because it is winter and I am not a cruel man. Once this child is born, you will go to St. Albert Mission and repent and ask forgiveness. You cannot stay in this house." He looks at his wife. "Find a place for this child. Perhaps Thomas or Francis will raise it."

Luc looks at the old woman in her chair beading her hide and says, "We cannot feed another mouth."

Angelique raises her dark brown eyes to meet his; she reveals nothing else.

16

Virginié nods in compliance.

Luc says, "We will have something to eat and then we will leave. Barrett is hosting a card game at the store tonight. I'll take George and Gabriel. I can't look at this girl right now."

Virginié starts filling wooden bowls with stew. Payesîs puts the bannock she has been roasting on a plate.

Her brother looks at her as their mother places a piece of warm bannock on top of each bowl and sets them in front of the men. The men eat first, since there is only so much room around the table, and they hungrily finish their meal in silence. Then they dress for the walk to the Company store and leave. Mahkesîs wishes she could leave too, but she has nowhere else to go.

After the door opens and closes again, letting in another swirl of snow, Angelique, still in her chair, turns to Mahkesîs and says in Cree, "Let's us have some stew, my girl. Then we will clean up those fish and smoke them. Your father will probably drink enough tonight to forget all about them."

"He will not forget about the baby." Mahkesîs's throat is dry.

"No, he won't," says Angelique. "But you are strong. And smart; that's why I named you for a fox."

"At least he knows now," says Virginié, to no one in particular.

"We all know now," says Boots, trying not to reveal her excitement.

"And we can all help," says Payesîs. She gives a stern look to her sister and, smiling, places her hand on Mahkesîs's arm. "A baby is a gift!"

"A gift," Mahkesîs repeats softly.

⤖ *New Year* ⤖

"Would you like to dance?" a young man asks Moira. The Irish girl nods. Moira is a good dancer; she's confident enough to take the floor of any cottage kitchen. But tonight feels different. Moira's partner puts his right hand on the small of her back and takes her right hand in his left. Moira smells sweet tobacco on his breath.

The young man says into her ear, so she can hear over the music, "My sister tells me your name is Moira. I'm Gabriel."

"Oh, so you're named after an angel, are ya?" Moira lets him hold her even closer.

As the music builds, Gabriel whirls her out so quickly she needs to hold on tight to his hand so he can reel her back in to him. She feels that his palms are calloused. Gabriel leads her over roughly hewn floorboards made of spruce logs that are covered by a thin layer of dirt. Her cheek almost brushes against his jaw. They dance together, without speaking, for the rest of a song that misses his fiddle playing.

Gabriel bows and says, "Thank you. I hope we'll dance again." The young Métis man jumps back to his spot on the makeshift stage, with his two older brothers, Thomas and Francis, and picks up his instrument.

Moira stands in the middle of the little hall and tries to discreetly wipe sweat away from her forehead. She feels dizzy. She wants to look into his dark brown eyes again. Her friend Mahkesîs comes to her side and links arms with her to lead her to a bench against a wall.

"Who knew you were such a good dancer!" Mahkesîs teases. "You and my brother looked like waxwings drunk on mountain ash berries."

Moira does not understand her friend's comparison, but she does feel intoxicated. Her cheeks are burning. Maybe someone emptied a flask of whiskey in the cranberry punch. Maybe it is just the excitement: this is the first big social gathering Moira's been to since leaving her small village of Douglas, near Cork, and coming here, to Lac St. Anne in the Dominion of Canada.

Moira has lived at Lac St. Anne since September and knows quite a few families at the settlement. She goes to Mass and she spends the occasional afternoon helping Mr. Barrett at the store. She is trying to learn some Cree as not everyone here speaks English (and while she was taught some French at school, she understands little). Tonight, though, the hall is alive with all of these languages and full of people Moira has yet to meet, all come to the hall for the holiday festivities. She has learned that many families who used to live here, and left a generation ago to follow Father Lacombe to his new mission at St. Albert, still journey the full day to come back to this place for special occasions: New Year's Eve and the gathering in high summer for St. Anne's Feast Day. Tonight the mission hall bursts with men and women who greet one another with the goodwill of the season and the pent-up solitude of winter on the prairie. Water from the inside of the glass windows drips from the sills as the wooden building starts to warm from both the movement of bodies and a roaring cast-iron stove.

Moira's guardian and employer, James Barrett, has been

posted at Lac St. Anne to manage the small Hudson's Bay Company store. Mr. Barrett speaks enough Cree and French to do well here. Moira has learned from Mr. Barrett that he is more than a shopkeeper come all the way from London: part of his role is to decide what to do with this holding as the new Hudson's Bay Company store moves from the old fort into the new town of Edmonton to see if it is a success. Moira has overheard Mr. and Mrs. Barrett speak of how the Company needs to ascertain if these outposts are still viable or if they should concentrate their efforts in the growing commercial centres, such as the town of Edmonton, connected by a unifying new cross-country railway. Mr. Barrett has said that fur is not the commodity it once was and that this is a time of change and opportunity. The future is in land, developing, taming, and settling it, and in rumours of gold in the North. Mr. Barrett is a man who knows how to find opportunity. It seems to Moira that he is a man who makes the most of his situation.

Mrs. Barrett, on the other hand, is not happy to be living in Lac St. Anne. But then, she had not even been impressed by Halifax. Moira does not think Mrs. Barrett has changed since that journey from Cork to Lac St. Anne came to a close; Moira had assumed that Mrs. Barrett's sour disposition on the boat, train, and coach here was due to the fact that she was not used to travelling or perhaps because she missed Mr. Barrett. And since she was not impressed by the grand capital of Nova Scotia, Mrs. Barrett certainly was not impressed by the prairie town of Edmonton (even though it had street lights and a handsome new railway station). Mrs. Barrett argued and complained during the journey from Edmonton to Lac St. Anne, even though they all rode in a fine burgundy coach. Mrs. Barrett was not happy about sleeping in a moose-hide tent for the night—even if it was beside her new husband, whom she had not seen in many months. As Mrs. Barrett mentioned relentlessly, "I have never slept outdoors in my life, and I hope that this is both the first and last time I do so." She complained about the food they cooked over a campfire and about the bumps and ruts in the dirt roads as the wagon ventured north and west. Moira finds Mrs. Barrett sharp and sullen. Perhaps it has to do with why she brought her with her to Canada, but Moira does not feel she can ask Mrs. Barrett about it. In fact, the two women rarely speak unless Mrs. Barrett is demanding some task be done.

Despite having to live with Mrs. Barrett's temperament, Moira is settling into her new life at Lac St. Anne. Up until her journey here, Moira had spent her almost-eighteen years in her small fishing village on the Irish coast, and she'd thought she would live there all her life. The only place she'd been to outside of Douglas was Cork Quay, and that was only two and a half miles from her village. Since setting out on her journey here, Moira had seen ports and railway stations at Cork, Liverpool, Halifax, Quebec City, Toronto, Winnipeg, and Calgary, and, finally, the new train station in Edmonton. And while Lac St. Anne is small in comparison to some of these places, Moira is glad. In some ways, the settlement reminds her of Douglas: there are a handful of prominent families among the seven hundred or so residents, the Catholic church is the centre of social life, and the old ones pass the days telling stories about legends and mythical creatures. And there are many differences that Moira is still trying to understand: what a scrip is, why people are upset about trapping rights, why the Riel rebellions that happened six years ago changed the ways people talk to one another, and why the church is called "the mission." At home in Ireland, people call America and Canada the "new world," but there is a deep history here Moira wants to learn about, and she is unsure whom to ask. The Barretts are here to profit from this place. Even when she sees her friend Mahkesîs at Mass, the girl's mother hurries her out before they can talk. *Perhaps I can get to know the young man I just danced with*, Moira thinks, as she watches him play the fiddle.

Tonight, Moira sits next to Mahkesîs on a bench and watches her friend's brother perform on a makeshift stage. Gabriel is focused and intense; he creates music that is a mix of desperation and ecstasy. A red, yellow, and blue scarf wrapped around his torso swings against his beat. His left foot taps a rhythm to complement the hum of his strings and his brother Thomas's singing. The music the men play is different than the songs Moira knows from home: she does not recognize any of the tunes and cannot sing along but it is pleasant. She watches Gabriel play a birch fiddle that has two roughly painted round blue flowers on its body. His chin rests on the naked end and his hands caress its curves from neck to ribs. Moira is mesmerized by him.

"Moira, how was your Christmas?" Mahkesîs asks.

"Fine, lovely." Moira turns to her friend and smiles.

"Really?" Mahkesîs asks.

"Oh, Mahkesîs. I miss you so much." Moira cannot contain herself. "Mrs. Barrett is getting worse. Mr. Barrett hardly ever asks her to come to the shop and instead asks me to help him, which I don't mind, as I like visiting with the customers. But Mr. Barrett says business will be slow after Christmas and that he won't need me to come every day, and I do not want to stay in that house with her. I do all the work. She stays in her room all day and barely eats. When she does come downstairs, it's just to order me about."

Moira thinks about the man with the thin moustache who sat behind the long desk at Pier 21 in Halifax and listed her occupation as "Housekeeper" on the immigration manifest. *If only he knew*, thinks Moira. This post with the Barretts is the young girl's first job working in someone else's house, "in service" as Mrs. Barrett calls it, and Moira knows almost nothing about what is expected of her: she was not groomed to be a lady's maid. People in Douglas fish or cut turf. Some of the women work in the textile factories and spend dark days weaving wool shorn from sheep into yards of material that will become jackets, bedding, even the point blankets that will be shipped across the ocean and traded for beaver pelts at Fort Edmonton. Moira knows Mrs. Barrett's first husband was a factory owner and that the woman once had a house full of servants; she knows that this man was older and passed away shortly before Mrs. Barrett married Mr. Barrett but is unsure how that all happened or why.

Moira was nervous the whole journey over on *The Nova Scotian* that Mrs. Barrett would turn her out once the woman realized Moira did not know which fork went where (when there was more than one) or that plates are served from the left and cleared from the right. Moira paid fervent attention to dining details and to as many social interactions as she could on the ship to try to learn. Moira knows how to make a stew out of an onion, a few carrots and potatoes, and an already-stripped leg of lamb; she knows how to scrub bloodstains out of cloth; and, since she left school at ten to help at home while her mother, Deidre, took up shifts weaving at the factory, Moira knows how to quiet a colicky baby and convince a gaggle of toddlers to nap at the same time. It was Mahkesîs who taught Moira the particulars of serving in a lady's house—how to warm the china teapot with a swish of water before steeping the tea leaves and how to polish the silver with just a rag—as Mahkesîs was taught by the nuns at the Lac St. Anne mission school. After a few months here, Moira has relaxed in regard to these ignorances, as no one comes to the Manager's Quarters for dinner, or even tea. Mr. Barrett is usually so tired or drunk when he comes home in the evening that he gobbles whatever food Moira has made for him; he isn't one to worry about table manners. "Mahkesîs, I wish you came round still. You taught me well enough, but you're so good at handling Mrs. Barrett's moods. I never know what to say to that woman. She makes me nervous and grumpy all at once."

The Métis girl nods and listens.

Mahkesîs loves the way Moira says her name, with the emphasis on the wrong sound and skipping a syllable so it sounds more like "Mah-kiss." Moira is the only white person Mahkesîs knows who does not insist on calling her Adèle. Mahkesîs feels for her friend, having to be alone with that woman every day, especially since Georgina Barrett is unlike any other woman she knows. Mahkesîs thinks about how she grew up surrounded by women—her grandmother, her mother, her aunties, even the nuns—and how all these women know how to work hard. Even tonight, her mother is busy, along with Payesîs and Boots, working in the kitchen to make sure there is food for people to snack on and enjoy as they dance the night away to welcome in the New Year. By contrast, Mrs. Barrett sits in a corner by herself. She has no desire, or ability, to work, and that separates her even further from the other women who live at Lac St. Anne.

Mahkesîs says, "Do you remember that day Mrs. Barrett came down to the kitchen when we were baking?"

Moira laughs. "How could I forget? I've never seen anyone so upset about a wee little mouse!"

"Well, to be fair," says Mahkesîs, "it did jump right down her blouse as she leaned into the cupboard to get the sugar for her tea." She wipes tears from her eyes. "Has she come back into the kitchen since?"

"Aye, no," says Moira giggling. "Hardly! Well, I believe she's been harmed for good."

Mahkesîs thinks there is something missing in the white woman, something wrong. Mrs. Barrett seems to have no resiliency for change, and Mahkesîs wonders how she will survive here. Mahkesîs is heavier, softer, and rounder since leaving her job at the Barretts' house. She has resigned herself to this inevitability. It was a struggle to convince her father to let her come to the dance tonight. Angelique swayed him by saying her absence would cause further gossip and speculation, but Mahkesîs knows this rationale will only work for a few more weeks, maybe another month or so. So tonight she wants to enjoy herself, and she wants to be kind to Moira. She misses her: the Irish girl is one of her only friends. The last time the two girls talked, Mahkesîs was gruff and sharp. She had to be. She could not tell Moira why she was really leaving the Barretts' employment. She stood at the back door of the Manager's Quarters, at the end of the autumn day, as the sun started to set into the big, wide horizon, and told Moira she would not be coming back the next morning. Moira's sadness, and a shiver, made Mahkesîs want to wrap her arms around the Irish girl. Watching Mrs. Barrett now, and talking with Moira, she considers telling her. But Mahkesîs cannot protect Moira; she now has more than herself to think about. She prays that Barrett's cool blond wife is enough for him.

At the front of the hall, where the men are performing, a sturdy young woman with dark skin and a long, thin face moves to the centre of their group. Mahkesîs rolls her eyes. "Assk. I thought my brothers weren't going to play with her any longer."

"Why not? Who is she?" Moira asks.

"Her name is Bertha Tourangeau. She and my brother courted last summer. I was worried she would become family and I'd have to look at that sour face across the dinner table."

"But it did not last then?" Moira asks, trying not to sound as intrigued as she is.

"Bertha's an odd one. Collects rabbit meat for the Company dogs, and her father builds coffins. She's a good singer, but still, there are lots of girls who can carry a tune."

The Cardinal brothers start playing a lively melody. Bertha

starts singing in a pure, unornamented voice: "'Il faut donc tout y passer, Adieu! Je m'en vais en ménage, Ce n'est pas pur un an, C'est pour l'restant de ma vie, Aller dans la misère . . .'"

"Tell me what's she's saying," Moira asks. "It sounds so sad." She links arms with her friend.

"She's singing, 'Farewell, I'm getting married and it's for my whole life and I'm looking forward to hardship.'"

"Well. That's not very hopeful, is it?" Moira scrunches up her nose. "I am going to fall madly in love with the man I marry. Which I hope is soon as I turn eighteen this year!"

Moira stands and pulls Mahkesîs up to dance with her. They swirl and step and laugh as Bertha finishes her song.

Georgina, in her rigid corset, walks over to Mahkesîs and Moira. The white woman looks at Mahkesîs with disdain. She is glad the *half-breed* girl left of her own volition; she didn't like the way her husband looked at the girl. Georgina once watched James stand at the back door, smoking a pipe and staring at the girl as she bent over to harvest potatoes from the garden. Georgina did not like how the girl's faded yellow housedress stretched across her breasts as she hung wet clothes on a line. Moira is beautiful too: her slender body with the right curves, her deep black hair pulled into a bun at the nape of her pale neck, those wide green eyes, the way she laughs, tipping her head back with abandon. And she looks particularly lovely tonight in a cornflower blue silk gown that Georgina lent her for the party. The dress is too big for Georgina now. Still, it is a rare kindness Georgina's shown, letting Moira wear her castoff. Moira has yet to steal someone's husband, barter her marriage possibilities, or flirt with her husband's supervisor to help close a deal or gain a promotion. Both of these girls look so happy tonight as they dance and giggle. Georgina wonders if these two girls are mocking her.

"Moira. I need to speak with you." Mrs. Barrett grabs her by the arm and pulls Moira away from Mahkesîs (but not so far as to be out of earshot).

"People will talk—dancing so brazenly with that *half-breed*!"

Moira looks at Mrs. Barrett, puzzled. "Adèle?" she asks, careful to use Mahkesîs's Christian name.

"Don't be daft. The boy!" Mrs. Barrett snaps.

Moira is taken aback: the only person she noticed watching when she danced with Gabriel was the dark-skinned singer who sat in a corner with her arms crossed. She says, "Well, he seems a perfect gentleman and Adèle is his sister and . . ."

"Moira. You've heard of Frog Lake? Batoche? Do you know that the *half-breeds* here raided the store for guns in 1885! Did you? Do you know what his kind did to that British officer at Red River?"

Mahkesîs hears this exchange and recognizes Mrs. Barrett's tone. It is not one of embarrassment or even small-minded hatred despite her rattling off details of recent events. *She is jealous*, Mahkesîs thinks to herself. *Mrs. Barrett is jealous that Moira is the one who caught my brother's eye and danced in his arms.* Mahkesîs has even less respect for the woman now than she did a song ago.

Georgina continues, "Just because they hanged Riel as a traitor does not mean his supporters are not waiting and watching for their chance to strike again."

Moira knows vaguely about the places and incidents Mrs. Barrett speaks about but does not see how they relate to who she dances with at this party to bring in the New Year. Georgina has learned parts of the local history quickly and, unlike Moira, she believes she understands it well.

Georgina says, "Just because that boy is not full-blooded Indian does not mean he is not savage."

Moira looks at the floor and fidgets with her hands. She lifts her head to look right at Mrs. Barrett. "And who else would you have me dance with then? Besides Father Lizeé, we are the only people here who are not *half-breeds* of some sort. Would you have me dance all night with Mr. Barrett?"

Georgina leans closer to the younger woman and almost hisses. "Watch yourself, Moira. After all we've done for you. Mr. Barrett is involved in the election in Edmonton—a mere six weeks from now—and it does him no good to have you flirting with the *half-breed* son of one of his customers. People here have nothing to do but gossip. We can't have them saying you've gone savage now, can we?"

Moira thinks about an incident that happened on *The Nova Scotian*, the ship she and Mrs. Barrett took to cross the Atlantic. Mrs. Barrett spent much of her time inside their cabin, alone, sleeping or vomiting, and Moira tried to give her space by spending her days on the boat mingling with other travellers. Coming over on *The Nova Scotian* was an adventure: that was no famine ship. Although Mrs. Barrett was pouting that they were travelling in tourist class rather than first (an adjustment when Mr. Barrett had to pay for two tickets), Moira had never in her life experienced such luxury. Moira thrived on the boat: the motion didn't bother her and she loved the piano in the music hall, the chance to meet someone new every night at dinner, the dancing, and the card games people played well into the wee hours. During the day, the deck of *The Nova Scotian* was the place to meet people, though it was usually windy. Even when the sea was calm, the Atlantic waves stirred up a crisp breeze that made her eyes water. Moira had not imagined that the ocean could be so vast, so endless, so cold, and so grey. Over the weeks, Moira developed a friendship, a flirtation, with a young blacksmith who boarded *The Nova Scotian* in Liverpool. Daniel O'Connor was from Dublin, he was two years older than Moira, and he was headed to Toronto, where he would join his uncle and ply the family trade. Daniel and Moira would meet most afternoons on the deck. They tried to imagine what their new lives in the Dominion of Canada were going to be like. Once, their hands touched, and Daniel once gently brushed a strand of hair away from Moira's mouth when the wind was whipping, but that was the extent of their physical contact. One afternoon, out of the corner of her eye, Moira saw Mrs. Barrett try to steady herself on the damp deck boards. Mrs. Barrett came over and demanded that Moira help her dress for dinner. Humiliated, Moira excused herself and returned to the cabin to be chastised for her "unladylike behaviour."

Tonight at Lac St. Anne, Moira is surer of herself. She feels as if Lac St. Anne is becoming her home. And she knows more about Mrs. Barrett. Moira does not know or care to know all the details about the election in Edmonton or about Mr. Barrett's aspirations. She is starting to brush off Mrs. Barrett's frequent reminders that she is indebted to the Barretts for bringing her here. All Moira knows is that all she wants right now is for Gabriel Cardinal to hold her tight and reel her out again.

As Georgina berates their ward, her husband dances with a stream of pretty young women; he is careful to avoid the ones with feathers. Georgina does not want to be here. She leaves Moira with a question, but she does not really need an answer. "No more dances or encounters with that boy. Do you understand what I'm saying?"

Moira nods, feeling she has little choice to do anything else in this moment but determined to change how Mrs. Barrett treats her.

Satisfied, Georgina walks across the dance floor to interrupt her husband. "I am not feeling well and I would like you to take me home."

James, drunk, flustered, and out of breath from dancing, says, "Now?" and looks at his pocket watch. "Only ten minutes until we fire our guns!"

Georgina pouts.

Seeing he is in trouble, James nuzzles his wife's neck. "I want to kiss you at midnight to bring me good luck for the whole of next year." He tucks a stray blond curl behind her ear. Georgina concedes and lets a small smile cross her face. Her husband can charm her when he wants.

Father Lizeé's booming voice announces, "Everyone, it is time to go outside!" He makes this announcement in Cree, French, and, finally, English.

A flurry of activity begins in the hall as people put down their drinks and start piling on deerskin jackets and fur hats and slipping out of moccasins into fur-lined boots. People gather in anticipation; they don't mind that their breath will freeze in mid-air.

Mahkesîs is excited and she grabs Moira's hand to get a good spot outside: she wants to be close enough to see the flash of gunpowder in the vast dark sky but far enough away not to be choked by the smoke. Gabriel follows his sister and her friend. Once everyone is gathered outside, under a blue-black winter sky, Father Lizeé starts the countdown back from "ten" and people join in. Mothers urge their children to turn their eyes upward to watch for an explosion of white fire. When the men and boys shoot their guns in unison, the crowd of partygoers clap their hands and shout.

A group of men stand with their arms around one another and sing "Auld Lange Syne" in whiskey-fuelled harmony: "'We two have paddled in the stream, from morning sun till dine; But seas between us broad have roared since Auld Lang Syne.'" Some of the men have Scottish ancestry, mixed in with Cree and Blackfoot and French, and others have learned the song from the Scots who've passed through the area in search of their fortune. Moira recognizes the tune. She looks at Gabriel, who stands with his bandmates. He looks right at her and smiles. She wants Gabriel to come near her and lean in close. She wants his hands, the hands that stroke the fiddle with two blue flowers, to brush her cheek, to wrap around her waist. She wants him to kiss her lips. Moira wants him to show her this place before she learns too much from others. For now, she will have to be satisfied with their dance.

The dark-skinned girl who sang the lament about marriage, and glared at Moira when she danced with Gabriel, walks over to Moira and Mahkesîs. Snow crunches under her heavy boots that look like men's.

"He's mine, you know," Bertha says in Cree as she looks at Moira.

"Sorry?" Moira asks, confused.

"Bertha, that's not true. He ended things with you last summer," Mahkesîs interjects.

"I see her looking at him. And him at her. But he'll come back," Bertha says.

"Leave us alone," Mahkesîs says.

"He will."

"Awas!" Mahkesîs sounds angry.

"What is that all about?" Moira whispers to Mahkesîs as the other girl turns away, indignant.

"Ancient history," says Mahkesîs. "Bertha is strange some-times. I told you, she skins rabbits all day. Besides, my brother is free and, it would seem from your dance, very interested in you," she teases.

Moira smoothes the skirt of her borrowed dress. She likes the way the fabric rests again her skin. She has never worn anything made of silk, and she likes the way people are looking at her tonight. Some women are wearing crow feathers, beads, deerskin leggings, and woollen skirts they wove on looms in their cabins.

Soft snowflakes cool Moira's still-warm cheeks. The flakes swirl and tumble from the sky like the fairies in the stories

31

of her childhood. There is calm in the blackness of a night here; there is a quiet space where everything is frozen. It reminds Moira of the ocean at night. She thinks about the still vastness she searched for some early mornings on the boat coming here. She does not love the ocean, but she misses it. She misses its waves, its salty smell, the way it polishes rocks on the beach until they are shiny and black. Like all people born on an island, even if they fail to recognize it, the ocean and its changing tides are part of Moira's being. Just like the ice and snow are here.

As a young girl, Moira knew Ireland was surrounded by ocean but never knew what lay beyond the water. She thinks about a map that hangs above her family's kitchen table on a wall stained brown by peat smoke. It is yellowed and there is a corner missing but it is the most beautiful thing Moira's parents own. Two cherubs flutter in the top left corner and hold a banner proclaiming "Ireland" as a heaven on earth. Remnants of gold leaf carve the five ancient kingdoms of Ulster, Leinster, Meath, Connaught, and Munster into the page. Ships as big as counties travel along misty coasts, and sea monsters even bigger than the ships emerge from the depths of the water to splash across the page. Coarse-featured mermaids sit on rocks three times as big as Cork; they play harps and use songs to lure sailors to shore. Moira would often sit and copy the letters when she sat with her older sister, Bridgette, who was often made to copy Bible verses because she couldn't control her tongue or temper. On those rainy afternoons of map-gazing, Moira dreamed of exploring the whole island.

Moira sometimes imagined she would end up across the Atlantic: maybe she would go to Boston or New York. Being so close to the major port of Cork, Douglas was used to losing its young people to the boats that sailed for North America. On days when the loneliness, or Mrs. Barrett's moods, or the snow drifts, or the dark cold get to her, Moira makes herself think about her luck and how other girls in her village envied her the opportunity to leave and come to Canada. What the other girls could not know is that Moira is here because her mother is a quick-thinking midwife who saw opportunity in Mrs. Barrett's desperation. Moira was a last-minute addition to Mrs. Barrett's travel. Moira's mother wanted her youngest daughter to have something different than turf, rain, and struggle. This is the unspoken secret between them, the real reason Mrs. Barrett brought Moira with her to Canada, and it means that Georgina Barrett rarely speaks to Moira unless she has to. Georgina is afraid to tell, or show, Moira anything more about herself than is absolutely necessary.

Tonight, half a year and a world away from her family, Moira begins a new year with Métis musicians, English merchants, descendants of Québécois voyageurs and Cree women, those who believe they are here doing God's work, and those who have returned to this place because there is something magical and powerful about Lac St. Anne. Tonight, outside the church built just west of the lake named for Christ's grandmother, Moira stands in the darkness as black as the ocean at night. The nightly ritual of burning a candle in the window to light the way home for those in America made the Murphys' coastal village look like a blanket of stars fell on it every evening. Moira would just be one more star among many.

Moira catches snowflakes on her tongue. She laughs and encourages Mahkesîs to play her game. Moira hopes the handsome young man who plays the fiddle and led her across the dance floor is still watching her. Moira wants something, someone, who is just hers. This young man could be the real new beginning, the chance at something exciting, the chance for something different, the chance for adventure and romance. Moira turns in his direction and sees Gabriel staring back at her across the courtyard. He tips his cap to her and she blushes. Moira is glad it is too dark for him to see how hot her cheeks are, not with embarrassment at his attention, but with desire for more. Moira feels warm even though she can see her breath hang in the falling snow.

Misconceptions
FEBRUARY–MARCH 1892

"Moira," Georgina yells from her upstairs bedroom. "Help!"

Moira drops the potato she's examining for spots and wipes her hands on her apron. Skins fall into the sink; the potato is starting to sprout from being shut away in a crawlspace since summer. Moira rushes up the narrow wooden staircase that is still a novelty for her and finds Georgina hunched over, sitting on the edge of the wrought-iron bed.

"I can't stop it." Georgina's dyed-blond hair is matted to her forehead with sweat. Dark circles ring her eyes.

Moira walks past her, over to the porcelain wash basin on the dresser against the window, and sees that it is full of bloody water. She carefully pours clean water from a pitcher, painted with peonies, onto a clean cloth. "Let's wipe your face." Moira wordlessly encourages Georgina to lie down on the quilt. Blood has soaked through the back and front of Georgina's beige skirts. Moira sees a gold crucifix clutched in Georgina's hand; it is not something Moira has ever seen the Protestant woman wear. The necklace has left an imprint on Georgina's palm.

"How long have you been bleeding?"

"A day or two. Maybe more."

"Why didn't you say anything?" Moira asks, trying to assess the situation.

Georgina winces and doubles over in agony.

Moira says, "I'll go find Mrs. Letendre and Mrs. Cardinal— Adèle's grandmother and mother. They help women here deliver their babies."

"No. I want a doctor. No *squaw* is going to lay her hands on me."

"But the women here will know what to do, at least how to help stop the bleeding," Moira says with surprise.

"Go find someone to fetch Dr. Horace from St. Albert," Georgina insists, sucking in air against her teeth.

"All right." Moira nods. "I'll go see if Father Lizeé at the mission can send for him. I'll go tell Mr. Barrett at the store, and then I'll come back to be with you."

Moira thinks about the time it will take to trudge through the ice-crusted snow, the darkness in mid-afternoon, and the cold so brutal it will make her eyelashes freeze together. She thinks about the time it will take to find Dr. Horace and what will happen if he is not on the settlement today. She thinks about what might happen to Georgina if the bleeding doesn't stop. *God forgive me, but what if she dies?* Moira wonders. Mr. Barrett would probably marry again and might not need her as a house-girl. *Where would I go then?*

"Moira!" Georgina snaps. "Go! Go tell Mr. Barrett at the store first. Tell him to send for the doctor. Otherwise, if you go to the mission, by dinnertime the whole settlement will know I am losing this baby." Georgina is measured, even in pain.

Moira says, "All right. It will be all right," knowing from watching her mother work as a midwife that it probably won't be. Nonetheless, she tries to calm her mistress.

"Can't you . . ." Georgina asks in between pinched breaths. "Can't you do anything, Moira?"

"No. My mother didn't teach me enough. I'll say a prayer on my way." Moira crosses herself as she races out the door into the dead stillness of Lac St. Anne in February.

∞

Georgina sits at her writing desk. It's a warm early March day that simultaneously threatens snow and promises spring. It has been several weeks since she lost the baby, and she still sleeps most afternoons. Georgina sees Moira collect eggs from the small chicken coop that Georgina refuses to set foot in because of its stench. Moira shivers as she closes the door on the hatch. *Girls like Moira seem to thrive on physical labour,* Georgina thinks as she watches through a window. *Moira will make a good farmer's wife. Adèle actually had the makings of a decent lady's maid. She understood more about service than Moira; she intuitively knew her place.* But Georgina couldn't have her in the house, with James looking at her with such desire and knowing.

Georgina opens a letter from her mother in Cork, a woman married to an English merchant who wants for no material possession, and reads that her grandmother has died peacefully in Douglas. The letter has come from the Company headquarters in London and is dated December 31. Georgina regrets that the last time she wrote her grandmother was before Christmas. When Dr. Horace came back to the settlement to examine her again, weeks after his initial visit a day after she lost the baby, the old Scottish doctor assured her, "Many women go through this, Mrs. Barrett. I am sure you will go on to have healthy babies." Georgina had been waiting until she was with child again to write and share the good news with the old woman in Douglas.

If Georgina believed in ghosts, she would think she is being haunted: the spirit of the baby she lost across the ocean is wreaking havoc here on the prairies of the Northwest. But there is nothing supernatural about her situation, although believing in ghosts would be easier than her devastating suspicion that she wrecked her womb by taking those herbs. Georgina remembers the violent cramps and bright red blood from those awful nights spent writhing and trying to stay conscious in her grandmother's turf cottage in Douglas. And now, each month it is as if her body remembers the muscle spasms and the expulsion. The short time she was pregnant this winter was a relief, both for the promise of a child but also for the temporary respite from bleeding every few weeks. Georgina fears she may now not be able to give James the child she feels she needs to keep him.

The letter from her mother has taken Georgina by surprise. The woman has not spoken to her or had any contact since last spring, when Georgina's first husband, Bernard Adams, passed away from a heart attack. Georgina was not even sure that her mother and father knew she had moved to the Dominion of Canada, although she wrote them from the ocean liner that she had married a Company merchant named James Barrett and was moving to the colony. Georgina tries to write something in reply to her mother in Cork. She wants to write something that sounds sincere in her grief at the loss of her grandmother but that also shows her mother how well she is doing in this new world. But she has been staring at a blank sheet of paper, a quill in her hand, and has no idea what to write.

Instead of writing to her mother, Georgina starts writing her own story.

I am the proud wife of Mr. James Barrett, Manager with the Hudson's Bay Company, and I have known my husband for just over a year. We met at a ball in Cork, during the Christmas of 1890, at the Ambassador Hotel.

She imagines but doesn't write down that she had noticed him, and the gaggle of ladies surrounding him, early in the evening. Barrett saw her early on as well and, like most men, was intrigued by her pretty face, platinum hair, and slender body. Under the pretense of borrowing a cigarette, he asked a fellow clerk, "And who might that be?"

"Her?" the clerk quipped. "Why, Barrett. Don't you know? That's Mrs. Bernard Adams."

Another young Company man chimed in, "They were married the same summer the first Mrs. Adams was buried. This second Mrs. Adams is the same age as her husband's youngest son. Well done to both of them, I say," he had said with a laugh.

Georgina doesn't write down that she was already married when she met James.

I was living in Cork because I was married to Mr. Bernard Adams, an Englishman who had come to Ireland to set up a little weaving shop and turned it into one of the most important textile factories in the British Isles. The late Mr. Adams's factory was very successful, and he sold to many buyers. He also traded in London, British India, and even as far away as Australia. The late Mr. Adams had a small contract with the Hudson's Bay Company for many years, one of the multitude of places that wove the distinguished point material that was made into blankets and coats to trade with the Indians for their furs.

My second husband, Mr. James Barrett, is a Londoner who was sent to Cork specifically to negotiate a better contract with the factory on behalf of the Company. It was during this venture that we met and fell in love.

Georgina does not write that at the Christmas Ball at the Ambassador Hotel, James couldn't help but stare at her. James was instantly intrigued. The thought of this refined young woman with hair so blond it was almost white letting that old fat man writhe and sweat on top of her made James pity her. It also made him want her. James has always liked a woman in a difficult situation. That very evening, he became determined to have Georgina for himself. He wanted to show the girl with ivory skin what it was like to be with a real man. The challenge made him hard. The same shameless ambition that had allowed him to move up the ranks and become important within the Company gave James the resolve to relentlessly pursue her. Georgina does not write any of this on the paper because she does not know exactly why James pursued her so brazenly.

Georgina does remember how James sauntered over and asked, "May I have the honour of this dance, Mrs. Adams?"

She remembers the excitement and desire as she said, "Yes."

As they moved to the music, he introduced himself as "James Barrett, a man who does business with your good husband." And while James held Georgina inappropriately close, he asked, "And how would a man like me get to know a woman such as yourself, Mrs. Adams?"

Georgina does not write that she likely should have trusted her instincts and stayed away. But her curiosity, her boredom, and her vanity got the best of her. It was clear that this man desired her, and she liked the attention. Sensing she was being seduced, Georgina answered, "I suppose my husband could invite you to dine with us. How is Tuesday evening?"

Georgina had spent the time between their first dance and this moment planning every detail of a dinner party. She writes about the dinner party but leaves out the detail that she was married to Adams, who, at the time, was still very much alive.

In early 1891, I hosted a dinner party at my home in Cork at which Mr. Barrett was a guest. I had also invited Mr. Ernest McConnough, my first husband Bernard's right hand at the factory, his wife, Elizabeth, and their young daughter, Katherine.

She does not write about the pretense of inviting the McConnoughs to even the numbers and mask her desire.

After a four-course meal of pheasant and caviar and fine French wine and conversation about local mischief caused by the Fenians,

the talk turned to the wild Indians of Canada, a place Mr. Barrett
had been posted to through his Company work. Mrs. McConnough
regaled us with incidents from a book by a Mrs. Susanna Moodie,
who had moved from London to Canada. Mrs. McConnough asked
Mr. Barrett if Canada was really a place where "red Indians" still
live in tribes and wore animal skins and would attack white settle-
ments in the dead of night and steal the women. Mr. Barrett assured
Mrs. McConnough that while most of these tales were exaggerated,
and there were very few white women in the far West at any rate,
there had been a great rebellion in 1885 near the place he was posted,
Fort Winnipeg. He explained that the rebellion had resulted in the
kidnapping and murder of an Englishman named Thomas Scott.
Mr. Barrett assured Mrs. McConnough that the Crown had dealt
swiftly with this incident and that the rebellion's leader, a half-breed
Catholic zealot named Louis Riel, had been tried and summarily
hanged for his crimes. This story brought much excitement to the
party, and all in attendance agreed upon its fitting resolution.

Georgina does not write about what happened after this
conversation. She made eye contact with James and excused
herself to check on the kitchen staff while the rest of the party
retired to the drawing room for cigars, cognac, chocolate, and
chatter. James followed her, and she felt him behind her before
he turned her by the shoulders to dangerously kiss her on the
mouth. She remembers letting him take her hand and lead her
down a stairwell that led to the servants' quarters in complete
silence. Something else must have been said, exchanged, before
she let him pin her against a wall, open her blouse, and put his
mouth on her breasts. Before she let his hands search under her
skirts, the two were interrupted by footsteps at the top of the
stairs that threatened to expose them but ultimately did not.
In the period afterward, on the rare occasions her old flaccid
husband tried to exercise his rights, Georgina remembered the
way James's fingers and lips had made her gasp in ecstasy.

Georgina does not write that while their first dalliance was unconsummated, they rectified that by meeting frequently after that evening before James headed back to London. Bernard Adams never appeared jealous or suspicious of his beautiful young wife's affections. He was always working and paid little attention to Georgina's moods or activities. Indeed, on the night Bernard died, Georgina had just spent the afternoon with James Barrett in a room at the Ambassador Hotel. She had come home to have dinner with her elderly husband, who said he was feeling tired and went to bed early without touching a chocolate souf-flé. At first, when she crawled into bed beside him, Georgina thought it pleasant that Bernard was sleeping without his usual rattling snores and snorts. She quickly realized, though, that her husband was dead. And Georgina's first thought was, *I have my freedom now.*

Georgina does not write that it came as a nasty surprise to her when, a week after the old man's death from a heart attack right before Shrove Tuesday, the barrister read a will that specified that Bernard Adams's last wish was for his second wife, Georgina, to have no claim to his sizeable estate. Bernard's adult children from his first marriage were in attendance at the will's reading, so it was also a humiliation (and, for them, a delicious kind of apology for the shame they felt their father's marriage to Georgina had brought to their good mother's memory). Georgina was told she had a fortnight to leave the house in Cork and find somewhere else to live.

Georgina does not write about the feeling of desperation that overwhelmed her when she realized she had no one to turn to in Cork so she moved to a place she hadn't been since she was a child: she went to stay with her Catholic, Gaelic-speaking grandmother in the nearby village of Douglas. Her mother was ashamed that she had wasted the opportunity to become a wealthy widow and refused to have anything to do with Georgina, and her father did and thought whatever his wife told him to. Bernard had left Georgina exactly one hundred pounds—a decent sum but nowhere near what the house or a share in the factory would have been worth. But her mother's ma, an old, poor woman who had watched her own daughter deny her heritage and family to pass as Anglicized and marry a wealthy man, still had room in her cottage for a granddaughter she hadn't seen in more than a decade. It was the only place Georgina could go.

Georgina didn't think about James much after she moved to Douglas. He'd helped her make enough of a mess of her life and, frankly, she suspected her unattainability was a large part of her attractiveness. Now she was available, but she had nothing. She had to rid herself of that life and start anew somehow. But when James heard through the Company that Bernard Adams had died, he saw things differently than Georgina had suspected. He thought it was fate that Georgina had been widowed just as he was being sent back to the colony: maybe a white wife, a British wife, would keep him sane in the Canadian wilderness. When he first met Georgina, Barrett had been back in Great Britain on a Company-arranged transfer home. A dispute arising from an incident with a factor's daughter at Fort Winnipeg in the summer of 1890 had worried his superiors. There was concern that the stress of what had happened at Red River five years before and life in the Northwest since may have been turning him "savage." Barrett was an asset to the Company. They needed a man with his skills—cunning and experience—in this age of transition. So, after he had brokered the better deal with Adams and his Cork factory, James had been told it was time for him to return to the Northwest. He would be sent to Edmonton, not to Winnipeg, to appease the factor there. When he had heard about Bernard Adams's passing, James arranged to leave from Cork—and he set out from London to Ireland to find Georgina and tell her she must come with him. He found her in a cottage in a backwards village of Douglas just outside Cork. He promptly married her in a plain and almost-private ceremony in an Anglican church in Cork, and then he left, having arranged for Georgina to come out to Canada in the summer, when passage on the Atlantic was easier and the threat of ice had melted.

Of these truths, Georgina writes: *Little was I to know that a few months after that delightful dinner at my home in Cork, I would find myself as Mrs. James Barrett. My dear husband rescued me from early widowhood and arranged for me to join him for an adventure in the wilds of the Canadian colony. How surprising life can be!*

Her hands are stained with ink and cramped from the furious pace of writing, but, for the first time since losing the baby, Georgina feels exhilarated.

∞

Georgina is coming down the stairs after a nap to check on Moira's preparations for dinner when she hears the girl giggle in the mud room. Georgina stands up straighter and steels herself to investigate. She knows James is attracted to the girl, but flirting so out in the open, in her own kitchen, is really too much for her to take today. She will confront them. But as she walks into the kitchen, which is attached to the mud room, Georgina is surprised to find that it is not her husband who is the recipient of Moira's flirtation.

The *half-breed* boy who danced with Moira on New Year's Eve stands against the outside door of the mud room. He notices Georgina and tips his cap.

"Good morning, Mrs. Barrett. I'm Gabriel Cardinal. Adèle's brother." He is careful to use Mahkesîs's Christian name.

Georgina is surprised that his English is decent. "I know who you are. And I am sure you know that Adèle no longer works here. What are you doing in my house?" Gabriel is handsome, and Georgina knows that no good can come of his interest in the girl.

"I was at the Company store trading some furs with your husband and thought I would come call in on Moira."

"You have no need to do so."

Moira holds a basket of eggs in mid-air, stunned at Georgina's rudeness.

"Moira, put those down, go inside, and go up to your room."

"Georgina, we're just speaking about Adèle. There's nothing—"

"I told you to go up to your room. And you'll address me as Mrs. Barrett in front of strangers."

"I am not your child!"

"Do as she says, Moira. It's all right," Gabriel urges her.

"I'm sorry," Moira says to Gabriel and drops the pail. The brown-speckled eggs crack against one another. She avoids making eye contact with Georgina as she brushes past her to go through the kitchen to the bottom of the staircase. Moira climbs the stairs slowly and slams the door to her bedroom.

Georgina watches the young man watch Moira leave the mud room: she can see that he is filled with both desire and concern. Something in her shifts: Georgina thinks of this Cardinal boy playing the fiddle on New Year's Eve and is overcome by the memory of his hands, by the memory of him twirling Moira around the dusty wooden dance floor, by his youthful but mannish looks, and by the palpable desire between him and her housegirl. This man, boy really, standing in her mud room with such devotion and urgency makes her think of when she met James at the Ambassador Hotel in Cork. Gabriel makes Georgina want that feeling of heady desire and excitement of the forbidden. He makes her feel it again.

Gabriel says, "Mrs. Barrett, I am sorry if I have upset you or caused Miss Murphy to be in some sort of trouble. I was simply wanting to say hello to Moira. We have talked at Mass."

Georgina nods. She risks much by saying, "And what do you want with a girl, Gabriel?" She crosses the threshold between the kitchen and mud room to move closer to him. She has to stop herself from moving even closer, from touching Gabriel's smooth face, from whispering something in his ear that would render him helpless to her whim.

Gabriel is taken aback. "Mrs. Barrett, I would like to see Moira."

"You could see me." She tries to sound sweet and soft while fully knowing how bold her invitation is and what it could mean. "Mr. Barrett is at the store for the rest of the day."

Gabriel answers firmly, "I am here to see Moira. Please."

Embarrassed, Georgina steps back. Her eyes turn hard. "Moira doesn't need any *half-breed* suitors. And it is improper for a young man to call on a young lady without first asking permission from her guardians."

Gabriel refuses to let this woman treat him like a dog whining to be let in on a night when it is so cold that it won't even snow because he has rebuked her advances. He is young, but he knows what is at play here. Furthermore, he knows who he is and what he wants.

"Without my people, you and your husband would not survive long here. I will leave, but I will be back. And I will speak with Moira as long as she lets me. If not here, then at Mass or somewhere else."

"If you come back to this house, my husband will deal with you."

"I'd be happy to deal with your husband. I just did so at the store. He has dealings with many, many people—some of them would not leave your mud room calmly after being spoken to this way. And I am sure he would be interested in our conversation."

"Go!" Georgina stops her voice from quivering. "Leave my husband's property." She shifts her weight as her legs tremble underneath her petticoats.

"Good afternoon, Mrs. Barrett. And this is Company property." Gabriel tips his cap. He turns out of the mud room, goes outside, and mounts his mare and leaves the yard.

Moira watches him go from her bedroom window.

Georgina goes back inside the house. Her hands tremble from the confrontation and her cheeks feel as if they are on fire. *How could I be so foolish*, she admonishes herself, *to put myself in a position to be rejected by a half-breed boy? I would not have gone through with it*, she tries to convince herself. *He would not dare say anything to James.* Georgina is angry—with herself, with Gabriel's rejection, with James. And now she climbs the stairs to Moira's bedroom to play her role. Georgina opens the closed door without knocking. Moira stands at the window.

"You are not to meet Gabriel Cardinal again, Moira. Even at Mass. I do not want you speaking with him. Or doing anything else for that matter."

"But why? You can't possibly object to his race. I mean, everyone here is . . ."

"You will not speak with him again."

Moira is silent.

Georgina stands at the open bedroom door. "I am sure Mr. Barrett will feel the same way. You are young and under our care. I will not have you going about the settlement with a *half-breed*. I was under the impression that we had already had this discussion at the New Year's dance, and we'll not have it again."

"We might," Moira says, surprising herself with her certainty. "If Mr. Barrett became aware of certain things."

Moira looks right at Georgina.

Georgina asks, "What things?"

"Things from the past."

"Are you threatening me?" Georgina's voice is calm, belying her surprise. She hadn't thought Moira was capable of this kind of interaction. She thinks about the papers in her writing desk drawer. She must continue to write her story with the utmost care and discretion.

"I'm just saying. Women should keep each other's secrets."

Georgina pauses. "Yes, we should. But Gabriel Cardinal has not kept his desire for you secret. Men do not keep secrets the way we do."

"But . . ."

"You will not be seeing him again. Pull yourself together. Supper needs to be made soon."

Georgina closes the bedroom door and goes downstairs.

Later that evening, Georgina washes her face and hands at the blue porcelain bowl painted with deep pink peonies. She wants nothing more than to fall into a deep sleep and forget the day's events and the awkward, silent dinner with James and Moira. It has now been nearly three months since she lost the baby, and she is not yet pregnant. She needs to find the energy to perform and seduce. She pushes the desire for that *half-breed* boy and his quick hands out of her mind. This is about James: Georgina must continually assure James that his risk in making her his wife and bringing her here was worth the effort. She looks in a small, wavy hand mirror and pinches her cheeks pink. She makes sure there is nothing stuck between her teeth (not that she is eating much lately). It is hard to keep the red out of her hair here. In Cork, she went to a salon every fortnight and was served coffee and chocolate as the peroxide erased traces of Irish from her hair. It was something that her mother started arranging as soon as Georgina was of marriageable age. In Cork, they used peroxide and not the burning ash that girls in her grandmother's village resorted to to have angel-white hair. Here, at Lac St. Anne, Georgina has to do it herself with a pail of cold water and a tiny mirror in the kitchen. At least James can get peroxide in stock at the store. It is a small cost, all things considered.

Georgina slowly undoes her soft green woollen dress and slips out of its layers. She hangs her clothes on a dark wooden chair in the corner of the room. Georgina carefully takes off her corset, stockings, and bloomers and slips on a nightgown made of Irish linen. She crawls into bed with clean white sheets that she had brought with her and Moira had to scrub to get the bloodstains out and pulls the covers—a soft feather comforter she made James order from Montreal—up around her neck. She covers herself not out of modesty but because of a slight spring chill. She waits for James to finish a ledger he is trying to balance and thinks about Gabriel Cardinal: he is handsome and astute. Even though Georgina knows that there is no rationale to attraction, she wonders why a man like that likes a girl like Moira, and would risk coming here just to speak with her: it is not as if Moira has much to say. Georgina tells herself it is ridiculous to feel jealous of a *half-breed* boy's attentions to a simple Catholic girl from a family of tinkers and turf-cutters.

Georgina hears James's footsteps coming up the stairs, so she sits up and lets the blankets fall to her waist. She takes a deep breath. She sits up against the headboard, as straight as she can, to ensure that her breasts are visible under the stark white linen that becomes translucent in candlelight. She unpins her hair. She wants to look ready.

Georgina has learned the hard way that a wife needs to ensure her husband loves her and takes care of her. She has to make James's love and desire for her consistent and continual. There is no need for there to be anyone else. He has his flirtations and he likely visits the brothel next to Kelly's Saloon when he goes to Edmonton for business, but she is not going to worry about those whores: those women are not a threat to her. Georgina knows that, right now, James cares for her. Indeed, he needs her for some reason. He wanted her so badly that he made her his wife even though she was already his mistress. She needs to keep this balance of power. Georgina has to become pregnant again. This time, with luck, she will produce a son. It should be easy enough to do: she is good at getting pregnant. It is staying pregnant that is the problem now. Perhaps, Georgina thinks, she should confess her sins and seek absolution. Perhaps, she thinks, things will unfold as they should; she can only control so little.

"Good evening, my dear," James says as he enters the bedroom. He closes the door.

She smiles back seductively. "Good evening, my love."

⇥⇥ *Easter* ⇤⇤

On Palm Sunday, Gabriel walks out of the church to look for Moira. He sees her near a cluster of poplars at the edge of the mission grounds. She is surrounded by a small group of young children, including his little nephew, Thomas, and Ida's boy Pierre. They are all vying for her attention. Even though Moira barely speaks French or Cree, Father Lizeé has asked her to teach Sunday school to the young children who are still with their families at Lac St. Anne and have not yet been sent to school in St. Albert. It makes it hard for Gabriel to speak with her when he has been going to Mass just to do so.

Since they met at the dance on New Year's Eve, Gabriel has not stopped thinking about the Irish girl. He has never wanted any woman the way he wants Moira. It is now early April, and most of their relationship has developed in stolen moments after Mass (and the morning Georgina Barrett turned him away). *Finally*, he thinks, *the English that Pa insisted Mahkesís and I learn when we were small has come in handy*. He has heard that Moira sometimes minds the counter for Barrett at the store, but Gabriel has little reason to be there; he and his father are spending much of their days journeying out to check traps, hoping for even a skinny, mangy rabbit to supplement the dwindling winter stores. Church is his best chance of being near Moira. Father Lizeé thinks he has finally converted the young Métis man, and, in a sense, Gabriel has never been so devoted. But Gabriel is seeking something much more human and corporeal than the Saviour or Mother Mary can offer. He wants to kiss Moira's soft, flushed lips. He wants to lean in close to her ear and whisper again. When he is near her, Gabriel desperately wants to recreate their dance: grab her hand, feel her breathe, sense her nervousness at being so close to a man, echo her body's movements to the rhythm of the fiddle music.

Gabriel knows church is not the place for this exchange, nor for his desire. Instead, the two young people exchange pleasantries. Gabriel asks Moira how she is finding life here, she inquires about his sister, they speak of how much or how little snow has fallen the night before. Three Sundays ago he came to the mission and Moira was not even in church. Gabriel had to sit through Father Lizeé's sermon about Christ's forty days of temptation in the wilderness for nothing. He could have been enjoying one of the last days of ice fishing before the thaw. Moira's absence that morning was what prompted his uninvited visit to the Manager's Quarters (and Georgina Barrett's strange proposal and subsequent rudeness). Today, on Palm Sunday, Gabriel goes to church and knows he must speak with Moira. He has to have some time alone with the Irish girl before spring gives way to summer.

Gabriel has to know if Moira feels the same way about him; he needs to have a real conversation with her. In a few weeks, he will head north to Athabasca Landing and work as a freighter until the river freezes again in the fall. Gabriel and his older brothers, Thomas and Francis, all went last summer; a generation before, men would have gone on a buffalo hunt, but those days are gone. Francis is already at the landing now; he left as soon as the ice broke up because he's heading up a scow crew this year—"Good work for a *half-breed*," Gabriel has heard people say. And this work will mean Gabriel will be away from Lac St. Anne for months—except when the men are given time to come back for Feast Day—and in those months he will not be able to come to Mass to see Moira and Moira may find another suitor.

Moira looks up and smiles right at him standing outside the church door. This glance, this small acknowledgment, confirms for Gabriel what he already knows he wants. He approaches her and the group of children.

"Lovely!" he hears her say as a little girl hands her a fistful of brown-grey willow buds.

"We call these acimosihkanask," the child says.

Moira tries the Cree word. "A-see-mo-see-kanask?"

The little girl smiles and nods. "They look like the toes of a cat."

"Yes, pussy willows. The Lord had palm fronds, and we have pussy willows! Thank you, Margarite." Moira smiles back at the little girl as she kneels down to be at her level, not caring that the bottom of her woollen skirt is folding into the mud. Moira takes one of the fuzzy buds and rubs it across the top of her own hand. Margarite copies her and then takes one and rubs it across Moira's cheek.

"Mademoiselle!" Pierre says. "Il a un coincé dans son nez!" All the children giggle and Moira is at a loss for what is happening. She notices a small boy called Abelairde furiously rubbing his nose and ascertains what has happened. She gestures for him to come closer and gently extracts the pussy willow as the other children laugh and point.

Gabriel watches Moira give Abelairde a pat on the bum and send him on his way. "Good work handling that," he says.

"Abelairde may be a little embarrassed, but he is no worse for wear!" she lilts.

As the children disperse, off to their homes across the creek, or up to the church to find their parents, Gabriel moves closer to Moira.

He sees that she has collected a bushel of thin red willow branches full of the small fuzzy blooms in a basket. "For the service next Sunday," she says. "Father Lizeé only has old Sister Theresa to help him, and bless her heart, the Sister's aches and pains make it hard for her to be with the children. I think that is why he has asked me to help with the children on Sundays. I don't know how she manages during the week in that little schoolroom."

Gabriel thinks about when he was a child and Sister Theresa took it upon herself to tame the wildness in him. *At least Mahkesis and me were able to go to school just for the day and go home at night, unlike the children now being sent away after a few seasons with Sister Theresa*, he thinks.

Moira is nervous so she chatters. She looks in her basket. "At home we would put yellow daffodils the colour of egg yolks and tiny little bluebells all throughout the chapel on Easter Sunday. But spring comes a little later here." She smiles. Feeling a bit bolder, she says, a little flirtatiously, "But I am sure you haven't come to me to chat about flowers, have you, Mister Cardinal?"

"Call me Gabriel. No one calls me 'Mister.'" Gabriel's hands are sweating. "Moira, I'm hoping you'll come for a walk with me."

Moira smiles. "Now?"

"Yes."

"I can't, I'm afraid. I'm expected back at the Barretts to organize Sunday lunch."

"Oh, all right," Gabriel says quietly and looks at the muddy ground.

"But tomorrow," Moira says, realizing the risk of the invitation she's about to offer and feeling a flush come to her cheeks as she speaks. "Tomorrow morning Mr. and Mrs. Barrett are going

54

to St. Albert. I will be on my own for much of the day. We could go for a walk then."

∞

Gabriel's desire for the Irish girl is surprising and unrelenting. Even after being berated by the white woman, Gabriel risks going to the Barretts' house on Monday morning because Moira has invited him. He sits in the bush just outside the cleared land that surrounds the manager's white wooden house. Gabriel waits and waits. He hears a door opening and sees Mr. Barrett hold it open for his wife: the two leave, arms linked, for an outing. Gabriel does not mind waiting, but he hates sneaking up. He feels like he is hunting moose and has to be careful not to rustle fall's leaves underfoot, rather than someone trying to visit a girl he wants to court. But Gabriel does not want to cause Moira any more trouble, and Mrs. Barrett was clear that he is not welcome here. He watches the Barretts turn the corner, out of sight. Gabriel goes to the back of the house and steps into the mud room. He calls into the house, "Moira, Moira? It's Gabriel Cardinal." Moira comes through from somewhere into the kitchen and into the mud room. He smiles and his dark almond-shaped eyes sparkle. Moira has the same feeling whenever she sees him; she wants him to hold her close.

"Good morning!" she exclaims. Moira grabs her red knitted shawl from a hook in the mud room. She looks at what he is wearing to try to gauge where they are going on their walk: a long-sleeved shirt, an unbuttoned grey woollen vest, green thin woollen trousers, and worn boots. She is wearing a plain cotton dress with blue-and-white checks. She wished she had something finer to wear. She smoothes her hair back into its bun and puts on a straw bonnet. She feels excitement deep in her body. She dares to imagine holding his hand again and feeling his warm, tobacco-smelling breath on her skin as she did when they danced on New Year's Eve.

"Where shall we go for our outing?" she asks.

"I'd like to take you to the lakeshore," Gabriel answers. "It is quiet. We can be alone and we can talk."

Moira nods and lets her excitement push away her anxiety.

Gabriel takes Moira just south of the Barretts' house. They cross the creek, and Gabriel helps Moira navigate the muddy ground still marred in some places by dirty snow drifts. When he wordlessly takes her hand, Moira's palms are damp. She smiles and lets him hold her hand firmly.

Gabriel uses his other hand to point out a set of fresh deer tracks. "In Cree, a deer is 'âpiscimôsis' and tracks are 'miyânikwan.'"

Moira tries to repeat the expression, but her Irish accent makes the words unrecognizable to Gabriel's ear. They both giggle at her pronunciation.

On the way to the water's edge, Gabriel reaches down to pick a crocus that is more white than purple and holds the small, soft bloom up to Moira's cheek. She lets him. He says, "Feel how soft these are—they have a down like a duckling."

"Like acimosihkanask," she replies.

Gabriel leans in and kisses Moira. She lets him. She tastes like berries.

After kissing her just long enough to make her wonder what comes next, Gabriel pulls back. He wants to trace his hands along her neck and down to her breasts to trace their bluish veins that lead to rose-pink nipples. He wants to reach inside her and see if she is as pale on the inside as she is on the outside. He needs to put himself inside her and dilute his longing. But even if she would let him, he knows that he should wait.

"We should head to the water." He takes her hand and leads.

When they get to the grey-green sand that separates the bush from the lake, Gabriel takes his pack off his shoulders and puts the leather sack on the ground. He takes a tattered red-and-black-striped blanket out of his pack and lays it over the sand.

"Come and sit by me. Tell me something about Ireland. Tell me a story about faeries or banshees," he says. He sits down on the blanket, one leg bent, and pats his hand to invite Moira to sit with him.

"What's this now?" Moira laughs. "How do you know about Ireland?"

"I don't know much. But I do know that your people are good storytellers. So, tell me a story."

"About what?" she says playfully, lifting her skirts to sit down and join him on the blanket. They face each other. "And how do you know about my people now?"

"My father knew a Company man from Dublin once. He'd come here from Montreal, I think. O'Byrne was his name. Boy, could he talk. He told us about a hunter named Fionn who married a fawn, who was really a beautiful queen. They have a son who grows up to be a great warrior and a poet. It was one of my favourite stories as a kid."

Moira smiles. She knows the story well: the warrior Fionn McCool finds a fawn in the woods, but his dogs protect it and he cannot kill it. The warrior takes the strange animal back to his stronghold at Almu. He takes it inside. He awakes in the night to see a beautiful woman dressed in glittering white and silver standing at his bedside. She says, "I am Saeve and I was turned into a fawn by a dark Druid because I refused him. You saved me." Fionn and Saeve fall in love, they marry, and Saeve becomes pregnant with a son. It is a popular legend at home. Indeed, Fionn McCool is so ingrained in Irish mythology that Moira's brothers, Michael and Paul, have joined a group to fight the English that takes its name from this hero: the Fenian Brotherhood. Moira feels a pang of homesickness.

Moira asks Gabriel, "Ah, but did the Dubliner tell you the dark part of the story? Before Saeve gives birth, Fionn has to go away to war and a dark Druid captures her—pregnant belly and all. Saeve disappears, and it is only years later, while Fionn is out hunting, that he finds his son living in the woods and takes him back and makes him his heir."

"I don't remember that part," says Gabriel. "Maybe O'Byrne spared me and my sister some of those details. That Irishman was much better at telling stories and drinking than at trading. He gave us a good price on our furs though. One of the few who did. And he was kind to us even though we were just children."

Gabriel takes a wrapped piece of bannock out of his pack and hands some to Moira.

"Thank you," she says, taking a piece of fried dough from his hand. "Do you know that I have never been down to the water? It is beautiful. Even with the floes of ice still on it."

"You have never actually been to Lac St. Anne?" Gabriel asks. "Even though you have lived on the settlement since last fall?"

"No," says Moira. "I am either at the house or helping at the store."

"You should come here. It didn't take us long to walk to the shore," Gabriel says. He looks up. "So you've never seen the monster then?"

Moira rolls her eyes. "Now you're the one telling stories, to be sure."

"Well, when the French priests first came here, when my grandmother was a little girl, people called this 'Devil's Lake.' The elders say a creature lives deep in the water, near that island, Castle Island, at the east end. The monster causes storms that capsize canoes. My father says it's just a story that the Cree made up to scare the fur traders who overfished this lake to feed Fort Edmonton. Probably someone just saw a big jackfish one day; they will eat each other, you know, and once me and

Thomas caught one we figure was at least thirty pounds. But my grandmother swears that her older brother Norman once saw the monster's scaly brown tail appear and then disappear into the clear blue water—and what he saw was no jackfish."

Moira playfully puts her hands on her hips and feigns indignation. "Well, where I come from we also have mythical water creatures that are passed down in story and song. A map in my parents' kitchen shows mermaids combing their hair as they sit on rocks and lure sailors with their singing. But it is, all in fun now, isn't it?"

"Ah, but have you seen a weetigo yet?" Gabriel asks. "The half-man, half-animal that roams the edges of the settlement looking to feast on human flesh?" He growls and pretends to attack Moira as she giggles; he pins her to the blanket.

"I can tell the difference between story and truth, Gabriel Cardinal," she says.

"Can you?" Gabriel says softly. He raises his hands to stroke her face. He slowly undoes the cream-coloured ribbon under her chin and removes her straw bonnet. He slowly brushes her cheek with the side of his hand.

He pulls her into him and kisses her again.

Moira lets his hand finds its way over her breast and rest on her waist. She gives way to his lead and in to her desire. She feels like she could give herself to him right now, here, at the shore of a lake on a scratchy woollen blanket on top of spring mud and sand, but knows she cannot.

Gabriel has to have Moira, but he knows that now is not the time. He knows how to wait. This is a girl he wants to possess for longer than an afternoon of rutting in the bush. This is a girl he wants to introduce to his father, to be with, even to marry if she'll have him. Gabriel has thought about a way they could be together and a way he can show her off. He stops himself and rolls to his side, propping himself up with an elbow. He takes her hand.

"Moira, I want you to think about something. I am going up north for the summer to work on the Athabasca River. But in high summer, I will come back for a few days. Remember how people came here for New Year's Eve? Well, those same people, and more, will gather at the lake for St. Anne's Feast Day. This is a sacred place. Hundreds of people will come from all around—from Lac La Biche, Wabasca, Jasper House. They will camp and celebrate and fill the beach. We could be alone, for the night."

"How could we?" Moira asks, still lying on the blanket. She is not feigning modesty but, rather, is wondering about the practicality of spending the night with Gabriel. "The Barretts would never let me camp at the beach. And they will notice if I do not come home. I cannot even imagine what they will say if they find out I am here with you this afternoon."

Gabriel strokes her arm with his fingers as he speaks. "Go talk to Father Lizeé. Tell him you want to help with the pilgrimage. The Church baptizes people in the lake. People celebrate late into the evening and early in the morning. Tell the Barretts you will stay in the residence to help look after the travellers."

Moira nods.

Since their talk has turned serious now, Moira asks about her friend. "How is Mahkesîs?" She has heard things said at church.

"You don't call her Adèle?" he asks, a bit surprised. "I thought she went by her Christian name at work."

"She told me I could call her Mahkesîs," answers Moira. "One day while we were hanging clothes on the line she told me the story of how she was named for a fox. 'Tis a lovely name. Much more interesting than mine, which is simply 'Mary' in Irish. Although it is an honour to be named for Our Lady," Moira chatters, as she is nervous now.

"Mahkesîs is well." Gabriel protects his sister. "I would tell her you say 'hello,' but then she would know our secret. She would know I came to visit you."

Gabriel strokes Moira's cheek and kisses her again. "Don't be afraid. I know I am asking much of you. We will keep this a secret for a little while. At least until after we meet at Lac St. Anne. It's a way for us to be together."

He hopes Moira knows what he is asking of her. She lets him kiss her again and she kisses him back. Gabriel puts his hand under her blouse and close to her breast, for a moment, and ventures farther down to the waistband of her skirt. She pulls his hand away. He stops and regains control.

"I'd better get you back to that house before anyone knows you're gone."

∞

After delivering Moira back to the white wooden house, and riskily kissing her one last time in the mud room, Gabriel decides to ride out to check on the traps on the east side of the settlement. He is satisfied that he has been able to speak with Moira and thrilled that she let him kiss and caress her. Of course he wants more; he wants to quiet this unrelenting desire. But Gabriel learned something from his afternoon encounters with Bertha Tourangeau last spring: satisfying a need can lead to complicated consequences. And what he feels for Moira is so different. It is more than physical: he wants to make a life with her.

A promise can sustain him. Gabriel thinks Moira will come to him during the pilgrimage. Now, he has to think of a way to make enough money this summer to convince her that he really can make a life for her, with him, here. Gabriel had been saving up for a proper saddle and a bridle for his little horse, Trigger. Right now, he uses a piece of rope that he's fashioned into a bridle and keeps waxed so it doesn't chafe the little grey mare; most of the time, he rides bareback, sometimes using a red-and-black woollen blanket if he rides all day. Now, Gabriel will save his money to impress Moira and show her that his intentions are serious.

Of course, Gabriel will need to give some of the money he makes freighting to his parents. He will not waste his freighting money on drink and cards like some of the other men will, like his father wasted his scrip. *Maybe I can use this money to set up a farm*, he thinks. *Moira and I can homestead; we could grow things instead of trapping them. Maybe we can even build a red barn and a white wooden house like the Manager's Quarters.* Gabriel wants to offer Moira something that is more than what he came from, from what is here now. He thinks that maybe Moira will give him a chance to be something more than in between—something more than not Cree and not white.

As Gabriel gets closer to the trap lines and farther away from Moira, he thinks of his little sister, Mahkesîs, and how she waits for the birth of a baby. Gabriel tries to remember the boys he went to school with at the mission. Gabriel tries to think who the father could be but stops himself. He does not want rage to spoil his satisfaction at kissing the Irish girl. The last winter Gabriel was at school, the head nun, Sister Theresa, sent him home and told him he wasn't to come back. Sister Theresa told Luc and Virginié that Gabriel had a terrible temper and had beaten up a classmate. She said, "There is no room for such savagery in our school." Gabriel had fought another boy. The boys in Gabriel's class were starting to notice his sister. Both friends and enemies asked Gabriel about his sister: her golden skin and hair the colour of bulrushes in high summer, her laughter, her wit. One boy had made a comment about how he'd like to see if Mahkesîs's hair under her skirt had a tinge of red too. Gabriel's rage and frustration took over. He beat the boy so badly he cracked his ribs, took out three of his teeth, and made his eyes swell shut. It was after she whipped him with willow switches that Sister Theresa decided she couldn't tolerate such brutality in her school and sent Gabriel back to his parents before spring thaw. Even when Luc's beating left worse marks than the willow switches, Gabriel didn't mind being home. He hated school.

Angelique knew that Luc's beating would not teach Gabriel anything, except to resent his father, so that spring Angelique took her youngest grandson up into the bush and made him camp on his own with no supplies for a fortnight. She also wanted Gabriel to control his anger and not be tainted by it as his father, her son-in-law, was. Angelique wanted her grandson to learn patience and to ask for forgiveness from his ancestors. She told him, "You need to stay here until there is a new moon. Then you can come back." When he ventured into the boreal forest, Gabriel thought he knew patience: he had watched his father trap marten, he had watched his mother work all winter dyeing and tufting moose hair into patterns to sell to white people at the fort, he had watched winter ice melt into muddy prairie spring times. But those weeks of solitude in the bush when he was twelve taught him more about life here than anything he learned at the mission, about the fine balance between life and death, and the power to control both. It was a vision quest without the ceremony. Gabriel came back to his family's home knowing that lectures about redemption and scriptures about sacrifice paled in comparison to the realities of life in the North. Gabriel came back to his parents' cabin at the Lac St. Anne settlement thinner, darker, and calmer. He returned home a man instead of a boy.

This Sunday will be Easter. It is a celebration of resurrection and spring, but most importantly, it means Gabriel will get to see Moira at Mass on Good Friday and on Easter morning. Gabriel quiets his mind by watching the land unfold before him as he rides Trigger. The leaves of poplar trees rustle in a breeze and a chickadee calls to its mate. Gabriel looks up to see a cloudless blue sky hours away from sunset. When the end-of-day light streams through the clouds in a big prairie sky, Gabriel thinks it looks like heaven. And he knows what heaven looks like: Sister Theresa had an illustrated Bible that, on Friday afternoons, she would let the two best-behaved boys of the week come and look at. When he was small, Gabriel often got to look at the book and its pictures of Jesus talking to children gathered round his almost-bare feet. Once, Gabriel flipped to a picture of what looked like a summer sunset over Manito Sakahigan. The sun nearly burst out of the sky as its light streamed across the big blue horizon. Sister Theresa said, "That, my child, is the everlasting kingdom. Heaven." Gabriel remembers being excited to tell his grandmother that they lived next to heaven. Now, Gabriel tries to remember if he ever did.

This short ride to check traps makes Gabriel anticipate travelling to Athabasca Landing in the next few weeks. It will take him and Trigger three or four days to ride the hundred miles north. Trigger is a good little horse; Luc won her in a card game and gave her to Gabriel to ride. Luc said, "I may need her once and a while, but I'm an old trapper—I work alone." Gabriel suspects that Luc knew that if he kept Trigger as his own he would lose her in a future gamble, and he wanted to give his youngest son something. Their family home is on the settlement lot that Angelique's second husband took in the 1840s because his father has never been able to hold on to what he has, including his scrip. Gabriel knows his father has many faults, but he is also a man who knows himself and he is grateful to have Trigger. Gabriel has learned to ride the grey little mare steadily and slowly when he heads north. He has to try to keep Trigger as free of bites as possible. One man arrived at Athabasca Landing last summer and his poor horse's flanks were covered in dried blood as well as welts from painful horsefly bites. Gabriel loves the way that prairie gives way to boreal forest, how the big, flat horizons give way to tall, dense spruce and pine, how the ground beneath Trigger's hooves turns from yellow-green to blue-green the closer they get to the river. *Could we farm a plot near a river?* he wonders. *Would Moira like to live near the water?*

Gabriel rides along the river, to give Trigger an easier path, and sees the early evening sunlight sparkle in the water. The first yellow jacket he's seen this year buzzes around the blaze on Trigger's muzzle. She breathes through her nostrils to force it away and swishes her tail in nervousness. Gabriel pats her shoulder. "There there, girl." As he leans down, Gabriel looks at the moss and the leaves under Trigger's black hooves. He counts two, maybe three, shades of green poking through the dead fallow of last year. Spring and summer are the times of possibility.

Summer Solstice
JUNE 1892

As she helps her mother weed the rows of tangled bean vines in their small garden, Mahkesîs feels something trickle down between her legs. And then it breaks: so much liquid hits the black rich soil that it makes a dent in the soft dirt. It soaks her cotton skirt, pools around her feet, and dampens her moccasins before the young woman knows what it means. *People say a woman's "water breaks,"* she thinks, *but whatever liquid is coming from my body is not clean like water: it has a sweet and feral smell.*

"Oh, Mahkesîs!" Virginié yelps when she realizes what is happening. "Come in the house." Her mother holds her arm out for assistance while trying to keep a few small, ripe strawberries from spilling out from a fold in her apron.

"Mama, I'm fine," Mahkesîs answers. "I don't feel any pain." Her back has been sore most of the day. She's been hot and per-spiring all morning, but it is summer and it will be the longest day of the year soon, so Mahkesîs didn't think anything of it until now. Now, she realizes she's in labour.

"Let's go tell your grandmother," says Virginié nervously. "She knows what to do."

And Angelique does. She orders Luc out of the cabin, telling him in Cree instead of French, "Find a place to go for the rest of the day. And probably the night. But first, bring me some water and some firewood." Luc grudgingly obliges and then disappears.

Mahkesîs is not surprised that her father has nothing to say to her as he leaves. He has barely spoken to her or looked at her since that dark winter afternoon nearly six months ago.

Her grandmother puts her hands on Mahkesîs's belly and asks, "Do you feel any pain?" to which Mahkesîs shakes her head. The old woman says, "Emm-hmm. Tell me when it comes."

Angelique directs Virginié to get a kettle over the fire and tells Mahkesîs to come and help her knead dough at the table.

Virginié makes tea and prepares the only bed that is more than a mat on the floor with clean sheets from the line outside.

Apart from her water breaking, Mahkesîs's labour starts quietly, with a little cramping. At first the contractions are just flashes of pain every ten minutes or so, and she can lean against the wooden walls of the cabin and wait for them to pass.

During this first phase, Angelique tells her granddaughter stories as they wait. She speaks only in Cree. "When I first became a mother, your grandfather Mîstacakan and I followed the buffalo, the rivers, and the patterns of the seasons with our tribe. We lived east of here on the open prairie. We were happy. Everyone called me by my real name, Okinîy, for a rosehip."

Mahkesîs listens to the cadence of her grandmother's language, how the words build on one another and tell a story in how they fit together.

"Your grandfather and I had all we needed: food, shelter, love. I gave birth to your mother in a tipi, in the fall, deep in the bush when the trees are golden yellow but still full." Mahkesîs smiles, thinking of her grandmother as a young woman, going through what she is now. She breathes through a contraction.

Angelique tells her, "My husband's mother and sister helped me with your mother's birth. My oldest daughter, Kahkawiw, was four, and she watched it all. My son Amisk was just a babe and one of the women in the camp took him to play with her children nearby. The men were hunting wapiti and we were waiting for them to return. When your grandfather came back a day after your mother was born, he brought an elk for us. I showed him his new daughter. He was so happy he cried—and he was not a man to cry."

After hearing her grandmother's story, Mahkesîs feels that she can do this now. She has a bed, in a cabin, not a mat in a tent. She has her mother and grandmother to help her. She pushes the thought that there will be no proud husband to show the baby to from her mind.

Angelique doesn't tell her granddaughter the rest of her story about when Virginié was born. She doesn't tell her granddaughter that smallpox came in the winter when Virginié was still an infant and couldn't yet sit by herself. Smallpox took Mîstacakan from her, along with their little son named for the beaver they made their living on and their oldest daughter named for the raven because her hair was black-blue. She had to prepare her husband and her two small children for the next life while she had a baby at her breast. She and her baby Virginié survived; the older women in their winter camp told her that her milk had saved the little girl. *People now tell stories about the decimation, about how Manitou, God, the Creator abandoned the people on the plains. How else could you explain camps with burned-out fires and tipis full of the dead? The medicine didn't get out West in time for them.* Angelique thanks the Creator regularly that when the plague came again years later, the same year as Riel's first rebellion, her grown-up daughter, Virginié, and her grandchildren were living at Fort Edmonton and could get the white man's medicine. Luc proved himself in that situation: his bargaining and knowledge of English were worthy of something. Although there was a grandchild that did not survive and none of the Cardinals speak of this child.

Angelique tells her granddaughter, "You need to keep moving. It will help with the pains," and Mahkesîs listens. While her grandmother and mother boil water, prepare bedding, and make raspberry-leaf tea, Mahkesîs walks around the cabin. From a beam in the roof, against the wall farthest from the fireplace, hang twelve weasel corpses stretched inside out to dry. Mahkesîs thinks they look like a group of bishops—their snouts the pointed mitres—without clothes or skin. Underneath them rests a hoop made of willow branches propped against the wall nearest the fire; inside it, Angelique has stretched a beaver pelt. She punched tiny holes along its edges, tied with sinew, and showed Mahkesîs how to rub the skin with the animal's brains to make it soft. Holding another creature's brain is always a strange task, more so than holding its heart. It makes Mahkesîs wonder if an animal knows what's going to happen when it hears the snap of the snare or the pop of a rifle. Mahkesîs wonders, *Is childbirth making me think so strangely?*

Angelique watches. She is proud her granddaughter is being so strong. The girl will need this strength later too. She doesn't tell her granddaughter this. Instead, as she steeps the coarse green raspberry leaves that will help with what's to come, Angelique thinks about how, as a widow at twenty, she knew she would have to marry again to provide for her only surviving child—Virginié. That summer after she lost most of her family, while the men went hunting buffalo, she and her toddler camped with the women from her tribe outside Fort Edmonton so they could trade moccasins and gloves. She caught the eye of Frederick Letendre, a devout Métis trader whose father came from Red River and whose mother came from the Woodland Cree up north. Okinîy accepted Frederick's proposal knowing a church marriage would give her and her baby girl some security.

Her own sister had been left by the father of her six children. After a decade together, he returned to Quebec without her, and married a white woman in a church. Okinîy was baptized, married, and given the new name "Angelique Letendre" in the same morning. Frederick and Angelique settled at Lac St. Anne shortly after Father Thibault and Father Bourassa started the mission. Frederick and Angelique and Virginié lived on one of the first river lots. Gabriel and Mahkesîs's mother grew up going to Mass and speaking French as well as Cree. Angelique grew to accept her new name and her new husband. Life at Lac St. Anne was sometimes harsh, but Angelique was sure it was easier than it would have been on a reserve. She has heard the stories and is thankful that neither she nor her daughter ever had to spend fifteen minutes on her knees with a Department of Indian Affairs agent in exchange for extra rations of salt-pork. Or for too-thin blankets to keep children warm on beds of straw. Or for a pass card to leave the reserve. Angelique had made choices and given up many things—including her treaty rights—to make a life for her only child who survived the pox; as an old woman looking back, she did not think her compromises were as bad as some. She knew her abundance of love had made her daughter weak and scared, and that this weakness made Virginié unable to stand up to Luc, but she has done better with the girl. Mahkesîs reminds her of herself as a young woman.

Angelique does not tell Mahkesîs these parts of her story: the past will not change things or help her granddaughter now. Angelique knows her girl will have her own cruel introduction to motherhood and all its messiness because Luc insists she leave this baby here and go to St. Albert. Her daughter's husband is a drinker and a gambler and is foolish with money—after all, they live on Angelique's second husband's plot. Angelique has tried to fight him on this decision and it is clear she has lost. Luc has made it clear that he is head of their household.

For Mahkesîs, as the morning turns to afternoon, the pain moves from under her belly to just above her thighs. As afternoon turns to evening, the contractions spread like running hooves across her pelvis, and grip her lower back. Within eight or so hours of losing her water in the garden, Mahkesîs feels her whole body start to respond to the violent rhythms of a baby moving down and out into the world.

And for the first time since her water broke into the dirt outside, Mahkesîs lets out a yell with the waves of a contraction. Angelique knows she cannot be distracted now by thoughts of the past or worries about the future. She has to concentrate on helping to bring this great-grandchild into the world. It is time.

∞

Somehow, Mahkesîs has ended up on a red-and-black-striped blanket on the floor. Walking around the cabin, leaning against walls, squatting against the table is no longer possible with all the pain. She is on her side and her mother is rubbing her back. Her grandmother is at her legs. She moans like a moose calling and is embarrassed by the sound that comes out of her mouth. Her grandmother shakes her head and says, "Do what you need to, what you feel. It is just you and I and your mother."

Mahkesîs has no sense of time or even place: now she just knows the waves of pain and pressure. She holds on to the hope that with each clenching of her body, with each ripping of her hips, she is closer to being finished.

Her grandmother rubs a poultice of cloves and tobacco on her belly to help with the pain. Mahkesîs just wishes everyone would stop touching her.

When Mahkesîs says, through sweat and snot and tears, "This is hard, Nohkum, this is so hard," her grandmother assures her. "Ehâ. I know, my girl, I know."

Virginié holds her hand, wipes her brow, holds water to her lips, and takes directions from Angelique as to what to do although she knows as well as any other woman on the settlement. Angelique and Virginié have helped deliver many babies together. They have seen breech babies, stillborns, cords around necks, twins, girls born in the caul, babies born to a woman who didn't realize one was coming, even the child of a nun who had to be whisked away and taken in elsewhere before anyone suspected the truth.

Mahkesîs is relieved when she hears her grandmother say, "It's time to push, my girl. I can see the top of the little one's head."

When she feels that now-familiar rip of muscle and flash of hot pain circle her abdomen and back, Mahkesîs lets her mother help her sit up on her haunches. She bears down and pushes with all her strength. But she knows nothing moves, nothing comes through, not even blood.

"Am I closer?" she asks with a hopeful breathlessness and the taste of salt on her lips. "Can you see anything more?"

Angelique looks between Mahkesîs's legs and shakes her head. She does not tell her that she no longer sees the baby's head.

"Where do you feel it when you push, my girl?"

"My stomach, my legs, my hips, my back . . . everywhere . . ." Mahkesîs answers as her mother puts a cup of water to her lips. Her hair drips with sweat and tears stain her cheeks.

"Misôkan," Angelique says to her daughter, "the head is pushing against her tailbone. This baby's the wrong way round."

Virginié's voice trembles. "Should I send word for Dr. Horace?"

"No time," Angelique replies, shaking her head. "Mahkesîs, look at me. Next time you need to push, you tell me. I need to turn this baby so its scalp isn't pushing up against your back. I will do it when your body tells us it is time. I will reach in and do this so this baby can come out into the world. Âw mâka?"

Mahkesîs nods. "Okay."

Angelique speaks to her daughter. "Virginié, you stay beside her. Hold her hand, help her sit up when she needs to push, be strong for her." The old woman kneels back down on the ground and waits.

When Mahkesîs says, "I feel it coming . . ." Angelique pushes Mahkesîs's knees wide apart, reaches her old, tattooed hands inside, and cradles the infant's tiny shoulder-to-skull in her callused palm. When Mahkesîs's body pushes, Angelique gently but strongly twists the baby around. Mahkesîs screams out. When the contraction is done, she hears her grandmother say, "All right. Now, on your knees."

"My knees?" she asks, exhausted.

"It's the best way to bring a baby into the world."

Mahkesîs listens. Virginié helps her onto her knees and holds her up. Mahkesîs feels her mother's arms under hers and against her back. And with the next contraction, and push, her baby is born into Angelique's waiting hands. The old woman reaches into the infant's tiny mouth to clear out mucus and then firmly rubs its back until all the women hear it cry.

"Nâpesis!" Angelique exclaims.

"Oh, my girl, he's beautiful! Perfect!" Virginié exclaims.

Mahkesîs collapses on to her side. It is done.

Her grandmother places the vernix-covered baby on Mahkesîs's chest, in her arms, and gestures to her granddaughter to open her sweat-soaked blouse.

"Now?" Mahkesîs asks, a little stunned.

"He'll know what to do," answers Angelique.

Mahkesîs holds her little son to her breast as her grandmother cuts the cord and packs moss between her legs to absorb the blood. Virginié wraps a clean thin piece of cotton she purchased from the store around the little babe.

Mahkesîs holds her frantic, squiggling newborn to nurse for the first time and is in awe that her grandmother was right.

Both he and her body know what to do. As the baby gulps up milk, Mahkesîs drinks in his tiny nose, pink ears, and bow-shaped mouth. He has a cap of brown-red hair and translucent blue-grey eyes. The instant and devastating love for this baby dampens how he came to be: Barrett's whiskey breath and force that pinned her to a kitchen floor. Mahkesîs is glad this child is a boy as he will never go through what she has to create him and what she will give up to bring him into the world. She hopes that her brother and sister-in-law raise him to be a kinder man than his father. Or hers.

Angelique opens the cabin door and a smell of dew on grass wafts into the home. From where she lies, Mahkesîs can see the orange-pink glimmer of the sun in the sky.

"What time is it?" she asks.

Virginié looks at the family's pocket watch on the mantle. "It is three in the morning," she answers.

Angelique nods. "When morning comes, it will be the longest day of the year. We all need to get some rest now. For what's to come."

∞

Mahkesîs stands just outside the Cardinal family cabin with a bag at her feet. She has packed one of two dresses she owns (the other she is wearing), a pair of moccasins her grand-mother made, a pair of deer-hide gloves she made herself, a notebook with recipes for her grandmother's cures that she has kept under her sleeping mat since she was a little girl, the worn red-and-black-striped woollen blanket she gave birth on, and some pemmican for the ride. It is early morning on the first day of July. The sun is bright and prominent in the big blue sky: it may be a hot ride in the open cart all the way to St. Albert. Mahkesîs notices that a chokecherry bush will soon be heavy with swollen berries. Purple wildflowers and dark brown mushrooms are growing in a dense quilt on the edges of the bush.

The oldest Cardinal son, Thomas, readies their family mule to pull the cart, its two massive wheels, and its passengers all the way to St. Albert. Her father checks the wheel spokes. Angelique stands at the open door of the family cabin, arms crossed. Her mother stands beside her and Mahkesîs tries to nod in response to her mother's assurances that "The baby will be fine. Thomas and Ida will raise him well. Won't you, Thomas? And I will see him every few days. This is for the best." Mahkesîs is determined not to cry in front of her father.

It's been thirteen days since she gave birth to her baby boy, and her father has decided that it is time for Mahkesîs to leave Lac St. Anne for St. Albert. All she knows of St. Albert is that it is the place where the scrip office is and that it is the place Father Lacombe left St. Anne for when her mother was a girl. She knows it is the place where the beloved priest sat with another clergy three decades ago and ate pemmican and planted a poplar sapling in a snowbank by a little river and decided it would become a new settlement. She knows it is the place where her aunties live. She also knows that Luc has decided that Thomas will take her—along with some muskrat pelts Luc has directed his son to trade at the Company post in St. Albert "to make sure Barrett is giving them fair prices" here. Angelique named the baby Lucas, hoping to soften his grandfather, but Mahkesîs hopes her son will inherit little of his namesake and instead be wise and fair like the saint. Luc has still not spoken to his daughter.

Mahkesîs has always tried to understand her father, to forgive him for his boastfulness, and his temper. She knows that her father did not participate in the rebellions of 1885. He did not go to meetings in St. Albert where other men he called friends and cousins wrote letters, organized, mobilized. She knows he did not help raid the Company store that Barrett now oversees for supplies to help Riel's cause. Mahkesîs has heard her grandmother say that Luc did not think the rebellions would make a difference, that he thought most of the men at Lac St. Anne were too hot-headed, too Cree, too hell-bent on a fight. Mahkesîs knows little about his family except what her mother has revealed in pieces: he was born at Fort Chippewan to a voyageur father and Dene mother who died when he was small. He spent his life, up until he met Virginié, with men who travelled up and down the Athabasca District. Mahkesîs knows that her father has regretted his inaction ever since and that there are people on the settlement who will not let him forget it. Mahkesîs suspects that her father is boastful of what little he has and is willing to bet in all the card games at Barrett's store because he needs to prove he is something other than a coward. Mahkesîs has tried to understand him, love him even, and she was almost willing to forgive her father for sending her to Barrett—he couldn't have known. But this morning, Mahkesîs doubts she will ever be able to forgive him for separating her from her child.

This morning, Mahkesîs nursed her child one last time and then handed him to Ida and watched as her older brother Thomas's wife took her child away—to their cabin three plots west. Sleepy and happy and full of milk, the little one didn't cry or reach for her; he just settled into the arms of the woman who will be his new mother. Mahkesîs was devastated. She wonders if he will ever know she gave birth to him. *Will my son ever know that I love him so much that leaving makes my every breath feel like it is full of icy cold water, like I am drowning in the lake, instead of standing in a warm summer morning full of light?*

Angelique does not think that what is happening is best

for either her granddaughter or the new baby. There will be no one at the mission to rub the girl's bones back in place or know if the bleeding is subsiding. Luc is not even man enough to take his daughter to the St. Albert Mission himself. But Angelique knows she sometimes has to defer to the decisions of her son-in-law, a sometimes harsh but mostly simple man, because she is an old woman with only her daughter, Virginié, to care for her. At least she was able to give Mahkesîs some time with her child. Virginié thought it would be easiest if he went to Ida right away, as she was nursing her own baby anyway, but Angelique knew he should have a few days, a week or so, of his mother's milk, and knew Mahkesîs needed this too. Her daughter is not strong enough to stand her ground with Luc—he forced that out of her early in their marriage, before Frederick died and Okinîy had to rely on them. And there have always been the grandchildren to think of—Mahkesîs and Gabriel—the boy and girl that Okinîy lost came back to her in these children. And she has done her best to teach them the ways of her people, her language, of how life here once was not so long ago, in the hopes that they can keep a little of it alive somehow.

Going to St. Albert is something her Mahkesîs will just have to survive, at least for now. Angelique knows Mahkesîs will not stay long in that place. *She believes too much in the old ways, she is too much like her grandmother*, Angelique thinks. And Angelique also knows that Mahkesîs can't stay here. The Cardinals can't very well explain that the child is James Barrett's, and any other explanation leaves her granddaughter open to other scrutiny. Many people at Lac St. Anne are in debt to Barrett for supplies and through cards and many more simply pass through the store every day and might listen to what he has to say because he is a white man. Angelique knows the savagery of those with power—white men in particular. To see her granddaughter suffer this way breaks her heart. There is nothing she can say to change any of this or even make it better, so Angelique moves closer to her beloved Mahkesîs and simply takes her in her big, warm, tired arms and holds her tight.

When Mahkesîs pulls away, she sees tears on her grandmother's cheek.

"All right, all right," says Luc. "Thomas, get on early while the sun is out and not too high. At this time of year, you might even make it to St. Albert and back in one day."

Virginié kisses her daughter goodbye, not knowing how long it will be until she sees her again, and says, "You will be fine, Mahkesîs. You are strong and smart and know how to work. You will be of help to the priests and the nuns. Listen and be obedient. I will make sure the babe is taken care of."

"Call her Adèle, Virginié. She'd better get used to her Christian name again," says Luc as he checks the cart. "Time to go, Thomas!" he announces and slaps the mule's ass. The animal makes a sound between a whinny and a bray. Thomas nods and climbs into the driver's seat.

This is what Mahkesîs knows to be true: thirteen days ago, she gave birth to a baby on the floor of her parents' cabin while her mother held her hand and patted her brow with a soft wet rag. Nohkum's knowing hands guided the infant's head, twisted his shoulders just slightly, and pulled him out into the world. Nohkum turned him over and slapped his back to release the phlegm so he could breathe. Mahkesîs held him to her breast and he suckled, hungrily drinking in her milk as their hearts beat in rhythm.

She will go to Father Lacombe's mission at St. Albert. There is a new priest there, a young man named Father Bernier, who is expanding the school by taking in children from the surrounding reserves created by Treaty Six. Mahkesîs has listened to enough sermons about the heathens in the muskeg to know that the mission at St. Albert will be happy to have her to help with the children who come from the bush and only speak Cree. At least she will not have to see Barrett again: the Englishman would never set foot in a Catholic church, and he has no business in St. Albert, only in Edmonton.

Mahkesîs knows that moving to St. Albert will not give her a true new start: there are many connected families between Father Lacombe's old mission and the new one. Somebody will know who she is, where she comes from, and somebody will have heard she has had a baby out of wedlock. Mahkesîs thinks of Moira. *I wonder what it would be like to journey across an ocean on a boat, ride a train from Halifax to Edmonton, and come to a place where no one knows you and you know no one.* When she first met Moira, when the Irish girl first arrived here, Mahkesîs felt for her: she seemed like a deer who knows it is being stalked but can't smell the hunter. Now Mahkesîs envies Moira and her chance to start over again somewhere new, somewhere where her life can be reinvented as she sees fit. Mahkesîs has to forge ahead with the burdens of the past.

Mahkesîs climbs into the cart and places a folded blanket on the wooden slats. Still healing from childbirth, she carefully sits down beside her oldest brother, the one who will be the father to her baby. She takes a deep breath and does not look back at her mother, her father, or even her grandmother. She stares in front of her at the mule's long, coarse red-brown tail that it got from its horse mother.

Thomas grabs the reins of the little bay mule. "Ready, girl?" he asks the animal. He looks at Mahkesîs and smiles sadly. "Wawiyeh?"

She nods.

The cart groans and lurches forward. Mahkesîs winces as her now-full breasts push against her bodice and a dull ache pulses between her legs. The rawhide girdle her grandmother has told her to wear at least until she stops bleeding chafes against her thighs. The journey will take many hours.

The Red River cart pulls away from the Cardinals' cabin and the settlement where Mahkesîs has lived her entire life. The road out of Lac St. Anne disappears into the green spruce and black-and-white poplars ahead of them.

St. Anne's Feast Day

JULY 26, 1892

Moira has heard the stories: people come to Lac St. Anne looking for miracles. For generations and generations, people have called this lake Manito Sakahigan—Spirit Lake—for its healing powers. The Catholic Church christened it Lac St. Anne, after Christ's grandmother, and fifty years ago built a mission just west of the shoreline. Moira has heard Father Lizeé tell the story many times: a few years ago, the Oblate Council in Quebec told Father Lestanc, the St. Albert Superior, to close the mission here, since so many people had followed Father Lacombe to St. Albert. Instead, Father Lestanc had a vision of how to draw people back: he set up a shrine to Christ's grandmother and spread word of the healing waters. And people do come back. The children and grandchildren of families who used to live here return, even if it is just for a few days, and those who stayed welcome them along with others from all over the Northwest. All these pilgrims search and hope for change. This will be Moira's first Feast Day at Lac St. Anne.

This morning, Moira stands in a small wooden church that is packed with visitors. This "new" church is close to the residence. Both were built four years ago, the same year as the first formal pilgrimage, to accommodate the travellers that Father Lestanc had faith would come. While many people will stay on the beach, some will stay at the residence they have built at the mission, and Moira has volunteered to help Sister Theresa manage these guests. The wooden building was built by men who learned their skills from their fathers and grandfathers, men who built the York boats. These men know how to make wood bend and sway into arches and points. In the church at Lac St. Anne, the pews are short and made of wood. The bowl of water people use to bless themselves upon entering is made of clay, not silver. There is the large cast-iron stove, like the one in the Manager's Quarters that Mr. Barrett chops wood to feed, in the middle of the central aisle. A small upright piano with scratched sides is tucked into a back corner. It came here on the train from Upper Canada, and last fall a family of mice moved into it and jumped each time Sister Theresa played a hymn. The altar is sparsely decorated with an off-white cloth and one wooden crucifix. The windows have no stained glass; there are no brightly coloured pictures like in Moira's church in Douglas. This little wooden chapel hardly compares to the ancient stone cathedral along the cragged Irish coast Moira went to as a girl. This is just one of the differences in her new life here.

This morning, Moira watches Father Lizeé stand at the pulpit. His usually furrowed brow is relaxed. He seems happy to preside over his larger-than-usual congregation. Father Lizeé is a broad, tall man who does not need a footstool to reach the top of the pulpit. He stretches out his arms. This morning, he forgoes his Latin and speaks in a mixture of French and English, with the occasional Cree word.

"Welcome to new and old friends, and to the pilgrims who gather here on July 26, 1892, this Feast Day of St. Anne, the beloved grandmother of our Lord and saviour Jesus Christ. The relics of St. Anne are in the Church of St. Sophia, since they were brought from the Holy Land to Constantinople. But her spirit is here with us today."

Father Lizeé looks at the crowd. The Métis people he speaks

to find it hard to imagine where Constantinople is: most of them have spent their lives within a few hundred miles of here. But he is also speaking to the clergy and nuns who have gathered here today: Father Gabillon, who is well-respected by the Oblates; Father Bernier, the young priest at St. Albert; and Sister Ignatius from St. Albert, who has been in the West for most of her life and who is rumoured to have done unspeakable things in the name of "civilizing" the children here. Moira has noticed the clergy too, especially a young woman sitting beside the old nun who looks about her age and is fidgeting and perspiring in nervousness. Moira makes note to go introduce herself to the young sister after the service. This life out here is not easy and she has probably just arrived from out East.

Father Lizeé continues. "St. Anne is the patron saint of women in childbirth—the pain that is a consequence of Eve's original sin. She is also the patron of my home, Quebec. We have a shrine to her on the St. Lawrence River."

Father Lizeé pauses. He sees a mother fan air away from a coughing child's face.

"This morning, we faithful are here to walk in the healing powers of the lake named for her on these prairies far from Quebec. We will walk in the water and be cleansed, as our saviour Jesus Christ did with John the Baptist. We congregate as a community of loyal servants to the Lord. We will soon walk down to the lakeshore to show our devotion and to experience the graciousness of St. Anne, her grandson Jesus Christ the Lord, and God the Father. But first, I call upon Father Victorin Gabillon from the Hobbema Mission to tell us a story of St. Anne's healing powers he experienced here at St. Anne's lake last summer. Father Gabillon?"

Moira watches Father Gabillon rise from a front pew and take his turn at the pulpit. He is a smaller, older man than Father Lizeé. Moira has learned that Father Gabillon helped establish the Hobbema Mission of "Our Lady of Sorrows" to the east of Lac St. Anne. And like Father Lizeé, he came out West from Quebec when he was a very young man. Moira is still unsure of the difference between a settlement and a reserve, between scrip and a treaty. *I will have to ask Gabriel,* she thinks, *when we meet later.* Father Gabillon speaks with a softer voice than the man who introduces him but commands attention with persuasion.

"Friends, pilgrims, good people of this settlement. Last year I was an ill man, I was a dying man. The doctor at my mission told me I was not long for this world and that I should make my peace with God the Father. I felt as if a trap had been set in my chest—the pain was so great—and I believed the good doctor and started to reconcile myself to leave this world for the next. And, yet, I wanted to experience the love and graciousness of the gathering here, and so, with great help from Sisters Amory and Lavalle, I travelled to Lac St. Anne and entered her healing waters. Within two days, I felt like my old self, and by the time the leaves on the trees started to change colours, I felt like the man of my younger days. God has seen fit to heal me so I can carry on my work at the Hobbema Mission building a school for your children who need to know God. I am here this summer to give my thanks and share the news of the healing bestowed upon me by the blessed lady and our heavenly Father."

People in the little church listen, enraptured, to Father Gabillon's story. Many have come searching for their own miracles—a baby in an empty womb, an eye that will see again, a leg that will straighten, a dying child who will live to adulthood. This holy man has proven that what the elders have known for years is true: the lake can heal.

There are no relics here. There are no snippets of shrouds or pieces of bone or vials of sanctified blood. The appeal of this place comes from the testimonies of healing, the proof of real miracles, and generations of belief that this lake is special. It is a journey to the lake itself. People see the pilgrimage as a chance for change. Moira sees the gathering as her chance to be with Gabriel.

∞

It has been a hot day, and the heat shows no sign of abating into the evening. Moira learned last year that summer here can be as severe in its temperature as winter. She has taken off her indigo stockings, risking mosquito bites. Sweat gathers in the small of her back and in half-crescents under the arms of her light blue cotton blouse. The air is still. Round, flat poplar leaves shimmer silver in the early evening sun. Still blue water stretches into the vast prairie horizon.

It is easier than Moira thought it would be to slip away from the residence. Once Father Lizeé led his congregation to the lakeshore, the priest was so eager to get people into the water that neither he nor Sister Theresa nor Sister Frances Marie, a young woman from St. Albert who is paired up with Moira to cook and clean and look after the visitors, noticed Moira leave after evening Mass. Moira has to cross the arbitrary line between the part of the beach where the clergy gather and the part of the beach where the Métis and Cree families are camped in order to get to the trail she needs to take to meet Gabriel. He slipped her a map last time they saw each other at Mass on Easter Sunday, just before he left for the Athabasca Trail.

As she makes her way, Moira recognizes a group of children from Sunday school playing in the grey-green sand near the shore. She and Margarite and Pierre exchange smiles, and Moira stops and crouches down to join them; she asks the little group, "What are you building?"

Margarite replies in English, "We are trying to make a castle. But the sand is too slippery. Will you help us?"

Moira digs in, and the feel of sand between her fingers,

being on a beach so close to water, reminds her of Douglas, of home. The children watch her at first and then join in. It is hard to shape the fine sand into a tower, as they have no pail or trowel. They manage to make a structure that looks more like a long cabin rather than what Moira would recognize as a castle. She tries to use some tiny beige shells to decorate it, but the shells on this beach are from freshwater snails and are so fragile that they turn to powder as she picks them up. Margarite and Pierre gather tiny brown and grey pebbles instead to adorn their creation. But the little rocks are too heavy; they sink into the lake sand and threaten to crumble the structure from the outside.

"Where I am from, we have many castles," Moira says softly. "There is even one called Blarney Castle that has a magic stone. And people say, if you kiss that stone, it will give you the gift of eloquence."

"What is that—eloquence?" asks Margarite.

"'Tis the ability to talk well and tell stories," Moira answers. "And it is a gift for language. You have it already, my darling." Moira wants to tell the children about Ireland's grey-stone castles covered in moss and lichen that have stood for hundreds of years. She wants to tell the children about how tall and large these castles are, that they have names such as Blackrock and Clodah, and Ballincollig, and that they dominate the skyline for miles and miles. She wants to explain how many of the buildings have withstood invasions and wars and famine and still are beautiful to see, even in their defiant ruin. Moira realizes this is all as foreign to these children as their home was to her when she first arrived at Lac St. Anne.

One of the smallest children, a little boy whom Moira does not recognize, asks Margarite in Cree, "What is a castle?"

The girl answers, "Kihci-okimâwikamik."

Moira recognizes the word okimâw—"boss"—in the little

girl's translation. Margarite continues explaining to the other children in Cree. "A castle is a home for a king and a queen. A king and queen are like chiefs, and they rule a country, they own the land and sometimes other countries too. They live in castles, palaces. A castle is a towering stone building that protects them from the outside world."

The little boy asks Margarite, "Why would a chief have to protect himself from his own people?"

Margarite shrugs. She picks up a twig to dig a moat and explains how the water keeps people in and out. "A castle is like the fort at Edmonton or Lac La Biche," she says. "Only certain people can go inside. You will learn all about them when you go to Sister Theresa's school in the fall."

Margarite switches to English and asks Moira, "Miss? Are the castles in heaven made out of sand or stone?"

"That is a very good question. I think they are made of the whitest stone, called marble, and the brightest gold. And rubies and emeralds and sapphires. I imagine they are more beautiful than we can comprehend."

Margarite's mother approaches the group of children.

Moira recognizes the word "âstam" as the woman, who looks only a few years older than Moira, tells her daughter and the little boy to come back to camp for supper. Moira smiles at her, but the woman does not smile back. Moira stands up, brushes sand off her white-and-blue-checked skirt, says, "Goodbye" to the other children, and walks farther down the beach, looking for the break in the trees Gabriel drew for her.

Moira is filled with desire and fear as she makes her way into the poplars and spruce. She prays she does not get lost. She prays for forgiveness for what she is about to do, for the sensation in the bowl of her belly, for the urgency in which she wants Gabriel to kiss her and touch her and have her. She knows that what they are going to do is a sin, but her desire is smothering her common sense. Moira swats mosquitoes trying to bite her bare legs under her skirts and navigates poplar branches away from her face. Gabriel told her to meet him in the bush near the beach where the Métis and Cree set up camps. He told her, as he showed her his drawing, "Keep walking away from the mission, around the lake, and look for the moose-hide strings I will tie around spruce trunks. They will lead you to me." When she is almost ready to turn around and go back, Moira sees the ties, and she follows them to Gabriel. The young trapper sits on a tree stump carving a willow branch into a point with his pocketknife. She sees the small tipi he has set up. She has made her decision and no longer thinks about sin or forgiveness.

Gabriel stands. He thinks Moira's blue-black hair shimmers like a magpie's feathers. He wants to kiss the Irish girl again. He is nervous this time. He puts down his knife and wipes his hands on his trousers before taking hers.

"Moira, I'm so glad you came."

She nods and smiles shyly. "I am too."

There is still a soft pink glow in the big, open blue prairie sky; the sun will barely set tonight.

"Moira. We're alone. It is quiet. No one knows we're here. Do you still want to be with me here?"

"Yes."

"You're sure?" he asks.

"Yes."

"You want to spend the night with me?"

"Stop asking," she says tenderly. "I wouldn't have come if I didn't."

Gabriel listens to words roll off her tongue like she is singing a lullaby. He nods and gestures to the tipi. He starts to take off the jacket his mother beaded for him and unlaces his sturdy boots. Moira follows his lead and undoes the laces on her shoes. Inside, there is a new red-and-black-striped blanket; the young man spent some of the money he has earned freighting on the river so he could have this for tonight. Between the blanket and the ground is a brown bear hide that Gabriel took from his family's cabin: it was awkward to bring it here on his horse, but the young man wants this night to be perfect. He had to take it when no one was home and hide it in the bush. Gabriel kneels on their makeshift bed and she follows to face him. Gabriel undoes her hair and runs his hands through its blue-black sheen; he tucks a wave behind her ear. The two lovers look as if they are at an altar; they are both looking for something corporeal as well as spiritual.

Gabriel puts his hands around Moira's face and kisses her. They find each other.

She pulls away for a moment. "Gabriel, I have never, I am . . ."

"Don't be afraid."

He puts his mouth on hers. She tastes like berries. He tastes like sweet tobacco. Gabriel gently unbuttons Moira's blouse and kisses her where her collarbone meets the bottom of her neck. She softly sighs. He pauses, lifts his shirt over his head, and gestures for her to take off her opened blouse. She does. He charts his desire along her torso, kissing her breasts, stomach, and navel. Her skin is whiter than he imagined. He maps her body with his mouth. He undoes the back of her skirt and pulls it off. Gabriel's touch lingers for a moment and he thinks of pussy willows: their soft, fuzzy roundness at the end of red, naked branches. His callused hands become soft and swiftly find their way inside her. She wants to cry out but keeps quiet (she does not really know how far away they are from the main camp). She is glad when he kisses her mouth again. He slips out of his trousers. They are both naked. He enters her with both power and tenderness. Her hips arc to meet his rhythm. She is surprised that her body knows what to do. Gabriel makes Moira feel as if they are one. This is so different from the sticky fumblings her older sister,

Bridgette, confessed to her in whispers as they shivered in the rain walking along Cork's ragged coast. This is ecstasy. Love. A new way of being.

Afterward, Gabriel and Moira fall asleep for a while, her head on his chest. She wakes, starts to kiss him, and they make love again. This time she senses how to draw him deeper and give him more pleasure. They feel as if they are the only man and woman on earth. It is hard to tell the time of night, or day, in this time of year when the sun never quite sets, but they know they have a little time before the pilgrims at the water wake.

When it is light enough to see each other clearly, and the sun starts to heat up their tent, Gabriel says, "We need to pack up and head back to the beach." He starts to roll up the blanket and the bear hide, and once Moira is dressed, he gestures for her to go outside so he can dismantle the moose hide that made their tipi.

Moira asks him, "What happens now?"

"We will go to the lakeshore and eat breakfast," he says without meeting her eyes. "I want you to meet my parents and my grandmother."

"I have to go back to the residence. Sister Frances Marie and Father Lizeé will be wondering where I've gone," she says nervously, realizing she has not thought this part of the plan through.

"First, you have to eat breakfast. Then, we'll figure out how to get you back."

"I could just stay with you," she says, touching his arm.

"What do you mean?" Gabriel asks.

"Well, I could come back with you to your family, and live with you, and be your wife."

Gabriel smiles. He pulls her close and kisses her again.

"Yes, soon," he says. "I can make you my wife soon. But I have to go back to Athabasca Landing. I can only be a scow man in the summer; the work only lasts until the river freezes. And I have to head back north today. When I'm done the season, I'll come for you."

"But how can I go back to the Barretts now?"

"We'll think of something. It will be all right."

Moira feels panicked. "When? When will you come for me?"

"When I can. In autumn. Moira, I want to be with you. But I need you to wait. Until the beginning of winter."

Moira's cheeks burn. She wonders if he really will come back for her. Gabriel does not tell her that he wants to save some money of his own so they can start a life different from what they both know. And what Moira does know is that she has given herself to this young man with dark eyes and a kind smile and gentle hands without a ring or vows or blessing. She has given herself to someone who says she has to wait for him until he comes back from freighting on a river that is two days north on horseback and where she has no way to reach him. She thinks of her friend Mahkesîs and the rumours. She thinks of her own sister, Bridgette, in a convent in Ireland. Before the sun rose, Moira felt dizzy with love and passion and the ecstasy of all its newness. Now, Moira realizes how alone she is here at Lac St. Anne.

∞

Gabriel takes Moira's hand and they walk to the part of the beach where the locals camp. Moira follows him because she does not know what else to do. They weave in and out of the brush and what seems like a hundred people beginning their day. She sees men sitting on the sandy beach, smoking pipes, bouncing babies in their laps, and laughing at one another's stories about trapping and trading. Women unpack the supplies they have brought to make a morning meal.

On the grey-green sand, an old woman sits outside a small,

sun-bleached tipi. Her fingernails are stained purple from picking the season's first ripe saskatoon berries. She beads a small piece of hide with her signature pink, yellow, and white while she waits for her pot to heat up. The smell of animal fat frying over fire wafts through the air. Gabriel recognizes his grandmother's tattooed hands before he sees her face.

"Nohkum? Tân'si." He goes over and kisses her on the cheek.

The wrinkled woman looks up from her task and smiles at her favourite grandson.

"Where is everyone?" Gabriel asks her in Cree.

She answers, in Cree, "Your brothers are fishing. Your father, who knows? Sleeping off his drink or playing cards."

Gabriel touches his grandmother's arm. "Nohkum, this is Moira. She's from Ireland."

"Tân'si," Gabriel's grandmother says to the girl. She puts down her beadwork and spits tobacco into an empty can. Her dark brown eyes reveal nothing.

"Tân'si," Moira answers. Her Gaelic lilt makes the word sound like "dansang" instead of "dtansay."

"Moira came over with the Englishman Mahkesîs used to work for. You know, Mr. Barrett, the one who runs the Company store. Moira sometimes works there too."

"Ehâ. I know who she is and I know who he is."

Angelique is gruff with her grandson. She is old, not stupid. But she can't expect Gabriel to understand—he does not know who the real father of his new nephew is or the circumstances of how his sister's new baby came to be. Her sweet Mahkesîs, Gabriel's sister, could not come to the beach this year.

Angelique stands up to check the fire under her pot.

Gabriel's grandmother is bothered that Gabriel brings this ghost-white girl to her, to their camp, to this sacred gathering. She remembers her from the New Year's Eve dance; she was friendly with Mahkesîs. *But why this girl?* Angelique wonders.

What is special about her besides her difference? That Bertha Tourangeau, who was sweet on Gabriel last summer, is a fine girl and will make a good wife. She is sturdy, a hard worker, and comes from a good Métis family. She will keep a good house and knows how to tan hides. She will teach her children Cree. Could this pale girl from across an ocean do any of that? As if there are not enough beautiful Cree or Métis girls Gabriel could love. Even though people say Gabriel is handsome like his father, her youngest grandson reminds Angelique of her late husband Mîstacakan, so Gabriel's grandmother is polite to this foreigner he wants to introduce to her.

"Maskihkowapoy?" Gabriel's grandmother speaks Cree even though she knows enough English to ask Moira if she would like some tea.

Moira nods and Angelique pours three cups of birchbark tea. Long strips of black and brown fish dry on a wooden rack that looks like a headless dog. A pot whistles. Bannock, skewered with a branch, roasts in the belly of the fire. Gabriel's grandmother points to a patch of sand covered in a tattered red-and-black Company blanket similar to the one the two young people lay on together last night.

Moira nods appreciatively, sits on the blanket, and wonders what comes next. Pots and kettles hanging from hooks (on branches) remind Moira of the crook over the turf fire in her family's cottage. Moira wants to connect with Gabriel's grandmother. Gabriel is annoyed that his grandmother will not speak any English but is too respectful to show it. The Irish girl stays quiet.

"Pe mitso." Gabriel's grandmother is telling them to eat. The older woman takes some bannock off a burned willow branch and offers some to Moira and then to her grandson.

"Maskwawiyin," she says and points to a white mass of bear fat sputtering in a hanging pot. "Kinosew." She stirs the fresh fish as it fries. The woman rips out the fish's skeleton with the same agility Gabriel uses to separate fur and skin from the dark pink flesh of weasels and muskrats. Her elk tooth necklace shimmies as she works. Fat sizzles and spits. Flesh swims in grease.

Moira feels like she might vomit. She reluctantly takes a bite of fried dough and tries to picture cooking in a camp like this; her palms start sweating. She made a sacrifice to leave the rain, poverty, and hopelessness of life in Ireland. She got on a boat in Cork and left everyone she knew and loved so she would not have to spend the rest of her days trying to wash the bog out of her clothes, or praying to Mother Mary that her belly was empty that month, or struggling to feed a houseful of little ones hungry for food and love. She left that possibility of a life to come here. At home, Moira resisted boys' advances because it was a sin. Now she's given in to temptation—at a holy place.

Moira realizes that once Gabriel leaves again, to go back to his work on the Athabasca River, she will have no way to contact him, to find him if she needs to. She can't imagine what the Barretts will do to her if they discover this transgression. Maybe they will force her to leave their house—where would she go, what would she do? The only place she has ever lived besides Lac St. Anne is her Douglas, which is an ocean and a world away. Moira feels dizzy.

She thinks about the shame she would cause her mother if she knew about last night. She thinks about how her mother has prayed to Mother Mary for guidance every day since her father sent her older sister to a convent to conceal her out-of-wedlock pregnancy. For three years, Moira's mother, Deidre, nimbly pulled and twisted strands of wool on her wheel and hooked them into countless bonnets and blankets to give to newborns in the village. The more little items she made, the more Deidre hoped she would stop thinking about her first grandchild, the one she did not get to hold or see before the Sisters buried him in an unmarked grave. Moira knows pregnancy and babies can change—and end—life in an instant. After all, Georgina Barrett's loss, and Deidre's silence, had led Moira to the Dominion of Canada, to Lac St. Anne.

Moira looks at Gabriel's grandmother. She looks at Gabriel— the young man she let caress her body like it was a birchbark fiddle, the young man she loved and let love her, the young man she lay naked with all night, the young man who had brought her so much ecstasy that she had to bite her lip not to cry out. Moira looks away and can see pilgrims in the lake: clothed people stand with their arms in the air and their legs in the water. She watches Father Gabillon help people into the water from the shore. A brown-haired boy walks into the water carrying a roughly con- structed poplar cross, taller than he is, on his shoulders. Father Lizeé is also waist-deep in the lake; his robes are soaked. Moira can hear the priest chant in Latin as he blesses Manito Sakahigan with holy water from a swinging chalice.

Moira notices a middle-aged woman, much heavier than Gabriel's grandmother, standing deep in the lake with her eyes closed. Rosary beads dangle from her right hand. Her grey braid brushes the surface. She lets the lake lap softly at her sagging breasts. Water bleeds its way up to her heart, saturating her faded pink cotton blouse. She is wearing boots, but Moira cannot see this. The woman in the water stretches her arms up into the sky, calling out to Christ's grandmother. The old woman starts to sing the Lord's Prayer in Cree: "Nohtawinan Kihci-kisikohk Ka-yayin." People around her listen. They look to the sky and search for redemption and healing.

"Kinanâskomitin." Moira knows how to say "thank you" to Gabriel's grandmother. She stands up and brushes grey-green sand from the folds of her skirt.

Confused, Gabriel asks, "Where are you going?"

"To the water."

Gabriel does not follow her.

She feels Gabriel's grandmother watching her.

Moira walks away from her lover. When she reaches the shore, Moira bends down to unlace her boots and unroll her stockings. An upside-down pike carcass and tiny puff of muskrat corpse float at the water's edge, but they do not deter her. She places her stockings and boots in a pile and lifts her skirts to submerge her naked legs in weeds and water. For a moment, Moira thinks of a monster lurking deep beneath the surface of the water, but she brushes the thought away. She lets go of her skirt and clasps her hands to her chest.

Moira silently prays to St. Anne for guidance.

⇥ *Scowing* ⇤
AUGUST 1892

Gabriel wakes up to the sound of water beating against his caribou-skin tent; the rain sounds like pebbles being thrown at a stray dog. The ground underneath his mat is damp: water is leaking in and Gabriel wonders, for a moment, if the banks of the Athabasca River have given way. Today is his twenty-first birthday, but no one here knows this. He looks over to see that Muskwa's striped woollen blanket is already rolled up, which means Gabriel is alone in the tent. Gabriel reaches down and scratches at the mosquito bites on his ankles—the space between his socks and trousers that's sometimes exposed as he works or sleeps—and blood cakes under his fingernails: he knows better than to make the bites worse, but it is a momentary relief. Gabriel has spent the last five days travelling two hundred and fifty miles to Fort McMurray from Athabasca Landing with five other men. This morning, the small group of six will turn around with a freight of rich northern fur loaded onto a scow and follow the river back down toward Lac St. Anne but still a hundred miles away. Gabriel wonders what Moira is doing; he wishes he could have woken up beside her.

Gabriel knows many of the men who work as freighters in the summer because many young men from Lac St. Anne go up;

his older brother Francis is here, but they are not on the same crew. Gabriel's crew leader is a Scotsman named Sutherland who lives near Lac La Biche; other men come from around Slave Lake and Wabasca. When the railway between Calgary and Edmonton opened last year, more men than ever came north looking for work, and more have come this summer: and work on scows requires experienced men like Gabriel to show the others how deep to wade in muskeg and how to keep their hands from being bitten to a pulp by mosquitoes and horseflies.

When Sutherland's group of six journeyed up to Fort McMurray just a few days ago, the weather was fine: warm and dry during the day and cooling off at night, as is expected in August. The crew delivered supplies of tea and flour and paper from the south to the north, and Sutherland negotiated good prices for the muskrat pelts and black bear hides and especially for the caribou skins and antlers that would be turned into tools, which he traded again at Fort Edmonton for even bigger profits. The night that they reached Fort McMurray, it started to rain. And it has been pouring ever since. Heavy purple-black clouds swirl in the big broad sky, creating a depth of darkness that hasn't been felt since last winter gave way to this spring. This thick, angry sky is not the one that reminds Gabriel of images of heaven. But the rain is needed to put out the summer wildfires that are burning around Red Earth and Slave Lake. *Like Nohkum says, there is always a balance*, Gabriel thinks.

This is Gabriel's second summer on the river. Last summer, the other Métis men teased him and called him "nâpêsis" because he was the youngest there. Apart from the mosquitoes, Gabriel doesn't mind the work. He likes being outside. He doesn't mind chopping wood. He likes helping build scows, and he even likes dismantling them after they've been pummelled by the rapids. Gabriel doesn't even mind standing in the river all day loading freight to and from the wide, flat boats that look like splayed-open canoes. Scows are cheap, efficient vehicles for transporting materials between the landing and the sturdier, more sophisticated boats that travel up and down the river. The only job Gabriel doesn't enjoy is tarring the bottom of the scows when they are first assembled or need repair: collecting the oily tar from the sands just to the northeast of the landing is hot, dirty work that stains the hands.

When he is freighting, Gabriel keeps his mind busy by thinking about the places where these bales of fur, packages of soaps, bundles of Company point blankets, or boxes of new silver traps are headed. Fort McMurray, Lake Winnipeg, York: Gabriel wonders what it would be like to live in these places. He wonders what it would be like to live somewhere other than Lac St. Anne. Or Fort Edmonton, of which he has disjointed memories from his early childhood. He tries not to think about Moira too often while he is working, as there is no way to quiet his desire.

Working on the river, even at Athabasca Landing, can be dangerous—and not just because of the mosquitoes. Gabriel has heard talk about how the new men coming north from Calgary are not being trained properly. This is hard labour out here, and the rain and the wet will get to a man. The trail back to the Landing will now be a series of mud holes, deep crevices, and chewed-up earth, so the men have spent the last two days camped at Fort McMurray, doing nothing but playing cards in Sutherland's tent, waiting for a reprieve. Last night, Sutherland told them that they head back today, regardless of the rain. He said playfully at supper, in his thick north Scots accent, "I don't care if it rains, snows, or pisses gold tomorrow morning. We're headin' back with smiles on our faces and as much vigour in our step as if it is Hogmanay and we're going to see the bells. Each day we're here in this rainy swamp, I'm losing money paying all you bastards."

Sutherland's a decent man—a bit round considering that he spends his life labouring in the bush—but he likes his meat and he likes his whiskey and wine when he can get it, although he will make do with moonshine. One of the other men on this leg of the journey, Thompson, told Gabriel that Sutherland lives up at Frog Lake with a Cree woman. His first name is Gordon, but no one calls him that: it's either Sutherland or Pinky, a nickname he earned because his complexion turns bright red each prairie summer and any time he has a drink. "Now, mind ya, the water will be high, muddy, and fast. Deadfall and other debris will clog at the narrow points. We need to take care. Go slow and steady," Sutherland had added in a more serious tone.

The men trust Sutherland but know it will be a tough trek back to Athabasca Landing. They will not see families of women and children camped out on the banks to catch muskrats to sell and skin on this journey back as they did on the way north. They know that they will be fortunate to hold on to all their cargo against the rapids of a flooding river.

So, this morning of his twenty-first birthday, Gabriel pulls on trousers caked with mud and woollen socks that are only half-dried and gets ready to walk in water pulling a scow loaded with crates full of fur bales. He cannot help but think about how it has been two months since he woke up beside Moira. He had half-suspected that once he had been with her, at the lake, his desire might dissipate. That's what had happened with Bertha. And the first girl, the Yellowknee girl who married a Joachim boy, whom he had been with the whole summer he turned fifteen. As a trapper and a hunter, Gabriel loves the anticipation and the moment of conquest. Up until now, his pursuit of game and girls has been similar. But his desire for Moira is different: Gabriel still wants the Irish girl, even more than before, and being with her was so much more than a relief from arousal. Moira is much more than a fascination or even an opportunity now. He thinks about their night together over and over again: her soft, milky skin, her sighs and moans, her searching lips, the feeling of being inside her and looking at her green-grey eyes as he brought her pleasure. Gabriel thinks he really is in love with Moira. In the rain this morning, he questions his decision to be here, on the river, and has to shake away the gnawing thought that he should be on his way back to her now instead. *What I would have given to wake up beside her this morning,* he thinks. *But I am here for her, for us.* Gabriel knows he has to remember this.

∞

Gabriel knows his grandmother calls him a traveller because he's always wanted to be on the move, even as a child. Being a man gives him the obligation and the freedom to trap and hunt and roam and work. Unlike his sister, Gabriel has travelled miles away from his birthplace of Fort Edmonton; he remembers their early days at the fort in snippets and smells. Just as he does now, Gabriel's father travelled to find work in the summers when Gabriel was small. So as a boy, Gabriel spent the warm months surrounded by women and playing with children whose skin was a burned brown colour by the time the first winds of fall arrived. There were always other children to play with, and Gabriel remembers how he and his cohort would spend the summer travelling to York Factory in tiny birchbark canoes, a place their fathers had never actually been to but that loomed large in overheard conversations. Gabriel and his playmates would set out into the bush to set "traps," and they would hunt for giant buffalo and stealthy moose (which usually meant tormenting one of the many stray dogs roaming the camp for scraps of food). Mahkesîs was a regular companion in these games until she was about six or seven and had to spend her days helping their mother and grandmother. Gabriel remembers that she hated playing voyageur anyway because, being a girl, she was never allowed to paddle the imaginary boat.

Gabriel has heard the stories from his mother and grandmother about the year Mahkesîs was born: he was just a toddler and their mother was terrified of losing them both to either starvation or disease. The years around 1870 had been tough for the families at Lac St. Anne—the buffalo were quickly disappearing and Father Lacombe's dream of making it a farming colony had fully failed. Gabriel's father found work at Fort Edmonton in the spring, and so both he and his sister were born in the married men's quarters, at the time of the first of Riel's rebellions, famine, murders at the fort, and smallpox. Their two older brothers still bear the scars of that sickness they endured as little boys. A French trader named Gabriel LeBlanc helped the women in the camp near the fort protect their children by giving them medicine that came from York. Virginié has told Gabriel of his namesake and has said that she felt that if she named her infant son after this man, who was named after an angel from the Church's book, maybe he would be protected.

It was when they lived at Fort Edmonton that Gabriel first heard of a place called Ireland. His parents were still living in the married men's quarters, so Gabriel could not have been older than four or five, the night Luc invited the merchant O'Byrne from Dublin back for drinks and to practise his English. While his father could hardly read in any language, he could speak many and passed that trait on to him and Mahkesîs. The little room that Gabriel and his family lived in had a fireplace, one bed, cradles and hammocks, two chairs, a bench, a table pressed up against the wall so the door could open, and shelves made out of chunks of birch nailed into a wall of logs. In a place that cramped and small, it was impossible for Virginié to get Mahkesîs, Gabriel, Thomas, or Francis to sleep while Luc and the Dubliner drank and laughed. It was early winter and a snowstorm whipped and whirled outside the little room. The sky was an unrelenting dark. The men set in to their whiskey, and Virginié let the children sit on a blanket and play with jacks in the corner. It was this man who first told Gabriel about Ireland and about the story of Saeve and Fionn that he repeated to Moira that spring day at the water when she had first let him kiss her. Gabriel remembers, at one point in that night of his childhood, bouncing on the stranger's knee and listening to his stories of Saeve and Fionn, mermaids and faeries, and a wailing woman called a banshee. Gabriel had never seen, or heard, anything like the creatures this man with the singsong voice spoke of with such flair.

"Maybe one day you'll come across the ocean, me lad," the boisterous man said to the enraptured little boy. "Dublin is a grand city full of pubs and music and life. Beautiful women—with hair as black as a winter's night sky or fire-red as that sash your father wears round his waist when he plays the fiddle."

It amazed Gabriel that the man spoke directly to him, as if he was as important as an adult.

"Oh, but you'll also have to come out to the countryside. The real Ireland is in its country. People there still speak a language of ancient kings and queens—much like your ma's people."

The Dubliner paused and looked kindly toward a quiet Virginié.

"Oh, my lad. You'll see cragged coasts, kelly-green fields, and rolling hills in the countryside of my home. They call Ireland the Emerald Isle because there are so many shades of green to see. You know what an emerald is, don't ya? The most beautiful jewel in a crown is the emerald."

Gabriel remembers clearly what happened next. Luc started laughing, "This little one's never seen anything close to an emerald. Probably never will. Best we can hope for Gabriel is that he becomes a good hunter and that he doesn't get too savage-looking. He's already pretty good with a slingshot. Caught a squirrel a few weeks back, right, my boy?"

Gabriel remembers his mother wordlessly coming to take him from the stranger's knee. Gabriel also remembers feeling mad at his mother for pulling him away because his father was ruffling his hair and talking right to him. Gabriel decided that night that when he grew up he would find an emerald and bring it to show his father. Even as a little boy, Gabriel suspected his father would like to see one too. He wonders if Moira ever has.

∞

"Morning, men! Up and at 'em!" Gabriel hears Sutherland bellow outside his tent. Sutherland starts each day with the pronouncement "There's no better job than working in nature, boys!" and even this soaked-in morning is no exception. Sutherland likes to regale men around the nightly campfire with stories of working in the mines of Lanarkshire. The Scotsman truly believes he is lucky to be in the Northwest and not in the coal pits of Scotland. Sutherland has a fire going in his shelter so he can give the men their rations of tea and pemmican before they all set out.

When he came back from Lac St. Anne in late July, Gabriel worked hard to impress the other men working at Athabasca Landing. But when he looked at what he had made for most of a summer's work, it didn't amount to much: thirty dollars. That would get him a bigger sled or maybe a new trap, but Gabriel didn't need or want these things. He needed land, he needed a plot for him and Moira to settle on, he needed things to build a life with her. So, a week ago, when Sutherland stood at the front of the Stopping House, rang the dinner bell to get everyone's attention, and said, "I need five men for a dirty job.

I need some who know what's in store for them and some who have no idea." Gabriel raised his hand to ask, "Do we bring our horses?"

"No, boy. The trail's too torn up at the end of summer for horses. Especially a wee mare like yours. Any man who signs up can leave his horse here at the Stopping House and Mrs. McClaren will give them feed. We'll take it from your pay."

"And how much will that be?" an older man, who didn't end up joining them, had asked.

"A week's wages and one-twentieth of the commission we make on the fur we bring back," Sutherland answered.

Gabriel thought about it: having a bit more money in his pocket might help him when he goes back to Lac St. Anne and asks Mr. Barrett for Moira's hand. He didn't really want to leave Trigger at the Landing, but he wanted this work. Signing on for this trek would also mean he would not be back to Lac St. Anne until the beginning of September, and Gabriel had promised Moira he would come back in August. He had no way to get word to Moira about his decision to join Sutherland's crew. He could send a message with Francis, but judging from Mrs. Barrett's reaction in the spring, his brother would not be welcome at the Manager's Quarters. *But what if Moira thinks I am not coming back at all and decides to be with another man? She is beautiful, with her pale skin, blue-black hair, and green eyes*, he thinks. Gabriel knows Moira's difference gives her a world of opportunity here. Rumour had it that Barrett was going to fix her up with a Company clerk from one of the other posts—maybe Edmonton, maybe even Calgary. Gabriel couldn't compete with a white Company man for Moira. He has to make her his, and despite his worries, he rationalizes that he needs the money from this job to do it.

"I'm in," he had said to Sutherland. Gabriel was the first man to commit.

Now this motley crew of men trying to make their fortunes has spent the past five days together walking north and east, through the muskeg and mud of the boreal forest, up to Fort McMurray with their gear to bring back the scow. Besides Gabriel and Sutherland, the crew is made up of a sinewy man from Calgary named Ritchie, who had taken the new train to Edmonton and found his way up the hundred-mile trail because he'd heard a man could make it rich on the Athabasca; an older man named Thompson, who smokes constantly and speaks infrequently; Eugene from St. Albert, who, at twenty-five, has six children and had come north from Montana; and a quiet Cree who spoke little English and wouldn't use his Christian name. He calls himself Muskwa and, on different days, has told Gabriel he is from the Alexander and the Michael reserves. Gabriel knows it makes no sense for a treaty man to be here, but Muskwa doesn't seem Métis either. Sutherland doesn't care where any of the men are from; he really needed eight or ten men for the job they were going to do, but he was okay with working a little harder if it meant splitting the commission between fewer people.

This rainy August morning of Gabriel's twenty-first birthday, the men start travelling south, back to Athabasca Landing, pulling a scow loaded with twenty-five tonnes of fur from the north country. The men pull the fifty-foot-long scow by a rope, attached to their torsos with harnesses, and walk along the muddy, cragged riverbank. It is a more difficult and less efficient version of the voyageur work that one of Gabriel's ancestors on Luc's side had spent his life doing. *At least on this crew they carry hides to pitch tents*, Gabriel thinks. He has heard stories from his father that in his grandfather's time the men slept under overturned canoes, which they had sometimes had to repair with tar by candlelight to keep both the river and the rain out.

Sutherland warns them that the journey back may take longer than the four days it took to get here.

The scows the men pull are flat, open transports. Like the sail-less voyageur canoes that travelled from York Factory to Edmonton, these massive rafts are open and exposed to all the elements the northern summer can offer. The scows are made of timber cut from the surrounding boreal forest, ideally from tamarack because the reddish-brown wood's sap protects it from the oils that can float in the river as it moves north. It is challenging for the men to keep any momentum when pulling the lumbering beast of a boat; it is a feat to keep the scow from being pulled in an opposite direction by the Athabasca's current. Gabriel has heard that some teams have lost whole loads of cargo to something as simple as a shift in the river. If a man rode on a scow, his seat was a fur bale or box of supplies that had not been piled high on top of and against others. But the men on Sutherland's crew do not sit. All of them are needed to pull the scow, and they all have to keep a steady pace as they wade in and out of the water (against the current) and trudge on the slippery, muddy riverbank.

This morning, Gabriel feels like a dog pulling a sled: the work makes him appreciate them in a new way. To distract himself from the mud and the rain whipping at this face, Gabriel thinks of the thrill he gets when he is setting out on a winter journey with his dogs. He likes to pat them on their heads as they pace and whine, ready to get going. They know when something's starting, and they get excited to move, panting with their pink tongues, even on the coldest of winter days, and wagging their curled grey tails. Gabriel thinks about his team of four young mutts and their mother. For their first winter together, the mother led because she was the only dog with experience. Gabriel bred the pups by sending his father's strongest bitch out into a pack of wolves: if the dog survives, she comes home pregnant and often bruised, limping, and bloodied. His best dog came home once with a wound across her eye so deep that Gabriel thought she might lose her sight. Mahkesîs has told him that she thinks this common practice is cruel. Gabriel thinks it's worth the risk because these mixed puppies become the strongest sled dogs, able to endure.

Gabriel remembers how he manned his sled the night he met Moira at the New Year's Eve dance. He dressed his dogs in grey woollen coats that his mother had embroidered with small crimson roses (she also attached a fringe of small steel bells to jingle as they run)—a rare indulgence but a tradition. On the way back to the Cardinal cabin, Gabriel asked his sister if she wanted to go for a bit of a ride around the settlement and watch the sky. Really, he wanted to ask about the Irish girl away from Angelique's alert ears.

He playfully turned to his sister. "Tell me more about your Irish friend."

"Assk," scolded Mahkesîs. "What's there to tell? She's beautiful. And she's not from here." His sister was shivering, so he wrapped a dark brown buffalo-hide blanket around her shoulders. He remembers feeling that he did not know what to say to her now that her secret was known. He also remembers wishing that it was Moira in his sled and not Mahkesîs. The snow fell gently. Even though it was dark, the sky was luminescent.

Mahkesîs said, "Look—kîwetinohk kacakastek."

"Whoa!" Gabriel pulled his reins to stop his dogs. The sled crunched against the snow. They were near the frozen creek that divided the settlement.

Mahkesîs heard a faint crackling and looked up to see at least six shades of green and blue dancing, swirling in the night sky. Even the dogs turned their heads to the sky.

Gabriel said to his sister, "I dare you to whistle at them."

Mahkesîs shook her head. "Gabriel, you know if you whistle, they'll come down and punish you. Ancestors should be respected."

Gabriel pursed his lips to tease his sister.

"Gabriel!" She leaned forward to slap his arm.

"Oh, Mahkesîs," he laughed. "It's just a story."

"There's no such thing as just a story."

Gabriel wonders if she still believes this. He wonders what Mahkesîs believes now. He wishes he knew who the father of her baby is, he wishes she would tell him, so he could go set him straight and tell the man what he had done to his sister. Gabriel would never leave a woman in such a situation.

"Good God above!" A frantic cry brings Gabriel out of his daydreaming and back to the present moment. Gabriel feels a tug on the harness around his waist as he sees Sutherland lose his footing, his leg bending under him as he falls to the wet ground. Gabriel is pulled along with him and puts his hand out on the ground to brace himself in the mud. A huge wooden crate tips off the scow onto Sutherland's legs. Barley spills out from a ripped-open bag and scatters over the mud.

Sutherland screams out in pain, "Get this infernal load off me!"

"Stop!" Gabriel yells to the other men behind him. "Help me. Sutherland's pinned!"

The other men undo their harnesses and come to help their team leader. They try to heave the one-tonne crate off the lower half of Sutherland's body, but it has wedged itself into the mud with all its weight. It takes all the strength from each man to move it, and, when they succeed, it rolls down the bank and into the water.

"Aaaaah . . ." Sutherland moans and rolls his head to one side.

Ritchie jumps into the swollen, roaring river and tries to swim after the sinking crate.

"Get out of the water, man! We don't need two of us injured," yells Thompson.

"But it's a sixth of our commission sinking in that water," says Ritchie. "I've got to try to rescue some of it!"

Even through the sheets of rain that make everything black,

Gabriel can see a cragged white fragment protruding through skin and cloth.

"Sutherland," Gabriel says, leaning in so the Scotsman can hear him over all the commotion. "Your leg is badly broken. Don't try to move or stand up."

"We can load him on top of the scow," Eugene says. "If we can get him to the Stopping House at Athabasca Landing, we can call a doctor to come and sew up his leg."

"The Landing is too far away. He'll bleed out before we get there," Thompson says.

Dark red blood spurts from the man's punctured calf and pools underneath his motionless legs, now freed from the crate.

"I think the bone has hit an artery on its way through the skin," says Eugene. "We need to stop that blood."

Gabriel takes off his coat, kneels in the mud, and takes a knife out of his pocket to saw off the sleeve. He wraps the thick chunk of wool around the gaping wound, trying to create a tourniquet. The pressure makes Sutherland moan and, for a moment, lose consciousness.

"Take it off," Muskwa says in Cree to Gabriel.

"Why? It's the only thing soaking up the blood," Gabriel says in English so the other men can understand.

"Miskât," Muskwa says.

"What's he saying, Gabriel?" Eugene asks.

"He says we have to take off the leg," Gabriel translates.

No one says anything.

"Three summers ago, I guided a man who lost his leg on a field in North Carolina during that American war. He lived," says Eugene.

"I am not letting a savage cut off a man's leg right before my eyes . . ." says Ritchie, emerged from the river, dripping wet and holding only two fur bundles in his arms. He starts toward Muskwa.

Thompson stops him with his raised hand. "Stop. Leave the man alone. He knows what he's talking about. Someone has to make a decision, and quickly. This is what we will do."

The older man nods to Muskwa.

Sutherland moans.

"I can't believe this," says Ritchie, shivering from disbelief as much as from the cold of the river.

Muskwa rummages through his pack for his axe.

"Have you ever done this before?" Gabriel asks him in Cree.

"I've done it for a dog that got its paw in a trap," Muskwa answers in Cree. "Just have to make sure to do it at the joint. And that we leave enough skin to cover the wound. We need to heat up metal on the axe to stop the bleeding. We need to build a fire somehow."

"Gabriel, Thompson . . . Don't let him do it!" Ritchie yells frantically. He lunges for the axe and Thompson stops him. "Sutherland will surely die from this!"

"He'll die if I don't do it," says Muskwa calmly in clear English. It is the first time Gabriel has heard him speak it.

"Gabriel . . . Are you sure?" Eugene says, wiping rain from his brow.

"I trust Muskwa," says Gabriel. Even though they have shared a tent for several nights, Gabriel notices for the first time how young Muskwa looks—*he is probably younger than me*, Gabriel thinks.

Thompson nods. He quickly builds a small lean-to out of the pieces of broken crate to shelter a fire.

Ritchie turns away to vomit bile onto his boots.

Eugene and Thompson light a fire in the rain.

Gabriel kneels down beside the semi-conscious Scotsman and tells Sutherland, "I am putting a piece of wood in your mouth. You'll need to bite down and hold my hand in a moment."

Sutherland is barely conscious. Gabriel nods to Muskwa,

who tips his axe into the flames and steels himself for what he has to do.

Gabriel tells Sutherland to bite down.

The other men watch and listen quietly in shock.

∞

The next morning, Gabriel makes breakfast for everyone. Their group is leaderless; no one wants to replace Sutherland just yet, but Gabriel feels he should do this small job to try to keep the rhythm of their routine. Gabriel rations out the pemmican: the fried concoction of saskatoons, dried buffalo meat, and fat travels well but wears out its tangy taste after a few meals. The rain that has been pummelling the boreal forest for the past three days has finally abated, so Gabriel decides to fry up a bit of bacon rind for everyone and boil some tea on an outside fire. There is a slight chill left over from the days of storms. No one feels much like eating this morning. Muskwa spent the night out in the rain: he took his bloody axe and the crushed part of Sutherland's leg and went out into the bush. He left his gun at camp and hasn't returned. Gabriel barely slept, waiting for Muskwa to return to their tent, worried about what he would say to him when he did. Eugene and Ritchie debate whether or not they should wait a day or so to see how Sutherland does or if they should load him on a scow and start back to Athabasca Landing so they can get him medical care. The men don't want to admit that the Scotsman may well die still, even if he has made it through the night. They have all taken turns sitting with him during the night as he drifts in and out of consciousness.

Thompson takes a drag from his cigarette, stomps it out into the dirt, and says, "Well, Eugene must have fallen asleep in there. I guess I'll go wake him up and be the one to see if Sutherland made it into the morning."

Thompson goes into Sutherland's tent and the other men almost hold their breath.

Thompson comes out of the tent quickly and says, "Sutherland's alive, but he's not awake. What's left of his leg's still bleeding but not too bad. That dressing needs to be changed though."

Ritchie volunteers to gather new moss to pack into the dressing; Gabriel had suggested it, knowing that mothers use moss to line their babies' diapers. It should soak up the blood until they can get some proper bandages at Athabasca Landing.

Eugene emerges and volunteers to see if he can get Sutherland to eat and drink something. He takes a metal plate with a scrap of bacon, a lump of pemmican, and a cup of tea back into the tent.

The sun's been up for under an hour but the blood-hungry mosquitoes are already out in full swarm.

The men agree that they should try to get to Athabasca Landing but decide to wait a few hours before heading out along the river.

Gabriel cannot imagine the horror of losing a leg. The most pain he's been in was when he had to have his mother pull a tooth and pack the hole with cloves—he is lucky that way. *What will Sutherland think when he wakes up and sees a bloody stump where his lower leg was? How will he work and provide for his family near Lac La Biche?* Just a few nights ago, as they sat around a fire, Sutherland had told Gabriel, "The coal mines in Scotland are like a living grave, they are. My father was promised at baptism to the owner of the mine; he started working as soon as he turned four—for two pennies a twelve-hour day! I knew I had to leave that place, as I would not have my sons crawling on their little hands and knees through tunnels little bigger than they were wide, tunnels that are home to rats and damp and the bowels of the earth. I would not watch my wife work at the mines with a newborn strapped to her chest as my grandfather had. This new land, this Dominion of Canada, affords a man fine opportunities to make a life. I have a beautiful and kind woman, one of your kin, who knows how to treat a man, and, God willing, we will have some sons one day soon. But my point is this, young Gabriel, you make your life here, my boy. Even as a *half-breed*. And you can live your life above ground!"

Gabriel wonders if Sutherland is able to think about anything this morning or if he is still in too much pain to be awake. Will he blame Gabriel and the other men? Is that why Muskwa has not returned? Gabriel wonders if Sutherland misses his homeland, his family, if losing his leg in the bush will make him regret his decision to come here, not just to Fort McMurray and the Athabasca River but to Canada itself. Do men lose their legs in the coal mines? Gabriel vows that he will make sure Moira never regrets coming here—or loving him.

There may not be a monster in the Athabasca, thinks Gabriel, like the one the elders say lives in Manito Sakahigan, but this river is cruel. People worry so much about the snow, ice, and the brutal deep cold of winters in the North that they sometimes forget about the other realities of living here. The short summer months almost make the winters worth surviving, but they hold their own perils. Earning a living, and making a life, in the North is hard. Gabriel wants to say something, but no one talks. So Gabriel sits on a tree stump by the fire. He wonders what Moira is doing this morning, if she is making breakfast of eggs and bacon for Mr. Barrett or if today is a day she will help at the store. Only a short time and he will be back in Lac St. Anne. He won't make as much money from this journey now that a full crate has sunk in the river, but the extra will still help. He will ask Mr. Barrett for permission to marry Moira and he will be able to prove to the Englishman that he will make a good husband. He and Moira can homestead in the spring if he makes enough money trapping this winter. On his next birthday, he will ask Moira to make him an English-style cake with fluffy white layers and butter cream icing. He will have to make sure they have a cast-iron stove so she can bake it.

Gabriel draws lines in the muddy dirt with the sharp end of a broken poplar branch. The poplars are wet, so their black-and-white trunks shimmer green as if they are new—even the oldest branches in the boreal forest. The young man decides that he will never speak of his part in what they had to do to save Sutherland. Gabriel wonders if any of the shades of green glimmering off the poplar trunks are close to the colour of an emerald.

Trading

Georgina sighs. She stands behind a long wooden counter and rearranges an ink well and the ledger for no particular reason. This morning, James told Georgina, "I would like you to come to the store and help make it more welcoming." He explained, "The Company is focusing its efforts on making the first Edmonton store outside the fort a proper shop, like one might find in Toronto or Montreal or even London. We should do the same here." To this end he has brought back items from his recent trip to Edmonton to create a display: bars of English lavender soap that no one here will buy, copies of the Edmonton *Bulletin* newspaper that no one here will read, and five large glass jars that he told her to fill with bulk items. Georgina does her best to avoid brushing the lace cuffs of her cream blouse against the counter's surface. *As if he couldn't tell Moira to do this simple task*, she thinks. *He has trouble treating the help as he should.* Georgina is unsure why James even wants to try to beautify this dusty wooden store; it won't make any difference to his customers. They come here out of necessity and, if James is to be believed, he will be transferred to Edmonton by autumn. He owes this place nothing.

No customers have come in since they opened the door this

morning. People on the settlement are outside: women will be tending their meagre gardens and preparing supper while the men will be fishing at the lake or doing whatever they do in the bush. "Summer is the slow season," James has explained. He has told Georgina that fall is a time for real trade, when the men come in with their moose and elk hides, and late winter is when the furs of the martens and rabbits and foxes are best (and easiest to skin because the animals are thinner). Lac St. Anne: seven hundred people, dirt paths that pass for roads, and stretched animal carcasses displayed on the walls of this shack. *At least it has wooden floorboards, as rough as they are*, Georgina thinks. Moira has told her that most houses here have dirt floors. Even though James makes a commission, Georgina hopes no one comes in today. Georgina only speaks English, and most people here either know this and refuse to accommodate her, or they only speak Cree or some version of what they think of as French. Language differences are only part of the reason she rarely comes to the store. In Cork, when she was Mrs. Adams, Georgina was the wife of a factory owner and had house servants who did the household shopping for her; when she went shopping, it was for a new hat or a box of sweets. Now her husband expects her to come to his little store that smells of smoked hide and sawdust. James expects her to serve these backward people, these *half-breed* people, from behind a dirty counter.

It is hot inside the store today, so they are keeping the door open to the dusty outside. *At least the store has glass windows so there is decent light*, Georgina thinks. *Unlike most of the buildings here, which have animal hide for windows.* She has brought her journal and some letter-writing paper with her; since this spring, she has been writing nearly every day, keeping a kind of diary but also embellishing it with her observations about life in this place. Georgina has discovered that she can express on paper what she cannot speak—not that she really has anyone to speak with—and her scribbling is helping her to understand this place a little better. Right now she is too hot to do much of anything. Whenever she starts to be bothered by the heat, Georgina tries to remember the dark winter mornings with hot water bottles at her feet and layers of wool and fur bedding trying to stay warm as she calls for Moira to put more wood into the stove. Today, sweat trickles down her from the nape of her neck and settles in the ruffles of her collar. Georgina smoothes her moist hands along her pale pink-and-yellow silk top skirt.

"Only a few more hours," she mutters under her breath to no one in particular.

Georgina looks at the empty jars and thinks of the storefronts in Cork. Going from a city like that to a place like this is devastating. She misses the hurry on the cobblestone streets, the sounds of people bartering for fish and flowers at the market, the smell of gentlemen's tobacco as they discuss the day's *Punch* cartoon in the newspaper. What she wouldn't give for just one afternoon browsing St. Patrick's Street, to run her hand through racks of nightgowns made of silk, to covet jewel-coloured brocade jackets with velvet sashes, to spend an afternoon trying on shoes from France and Spain, to bring home an armful of waxy red and yellow tulips that arrived on a Dutch ferry. She can almost taste the sweet white scones served with clotted cream and big juicy strawberries that she would enjoy at high tea in a banquet room at the Ambassador Hotel. For the first time in as long as she can remember, Georgina feels hungry.

In her notebook, she has described the store as a "quaint and small little storefront in the wilds of the Dominion that is the centre of this little settlement." But that is not entirely true: the church and its hall seem to be the centre of Lac St. Anne, and she does not find the store "quaint." She despises the store. She despises that everything here is fur and leather and cheap bolts of cotton and wool smelling of a ewe's lanolin. She resents that her only walk today will be across the creek back to the Manager's Quarters and her shoes will be covered in dust and nettles and dirt. She has no appetite for Moira's soda bread or some old woman's bannock fried in animal fat dimpled with dried-up saskatoons that her husband accepts as some sort of payment. *Moira sometimes comments when I ask her to take in a dress, but it is no wonder I am becoming thinner*, she thinks, *when a craving for strawberries and scones has to be satisfied with bannock.*

Georgina does not like that when they arrived here this morning, James announced that Moira would spend the better part of the day working alongside him, sorting the new inventory that he had signed for at the Edmonton train station and brought here in Joseph's Red River cart. While Moira counts bags of flour, folds striped woollen blankets into small towers, and unpacks sinew-woven snowshoes and traps with sharp metal teeth, Georgina finds herself out front—exposed, bored to tears, tasked with filling five transparent jars, and alone. "Darling," James had explained, "what if you are already with child? I don't want you reaching up to the shelves and carrying stock. Mind the front. People will be pleased to see you at the counter when they come in." Georgina does not believe James; no one who comes in will be glad to see her.

James frequently promises Georgina that they will move to Edmonton before the year is out, assuring her, "I just have to put my time in at the store here and then I will secure a transfer to the new Company store in town." James tells her, "It will be a proper store in Edmonton, Georgina. On a boardwalk, with more inventory than soap and baking supplies, and it will have white clientele. The new railway in Edmonton has opened this country up to newcomers from all across the globe. If you can get to Halifax, you can get to Edmonton. And that couldn't be said even a year and a half ago." Georgina knows her husband wants to run for the newly formed town's council—he is close with some of Edmonton's first governors, who were elected in February, and sees them as his allies of sorts. James has told her, "Edmonton could again become the most important place in the Northwest—and not just because of its natural bounty of fur from beavers on the North Saskatchewan."

Of Edmonton, Georgina has written: *With its population doubling in the past five years, Edmonton needs to make decisions quickly. The new town is as close to a clean slate as possible, and all major decisions have yet to be debated: levels of taxation, liquor licensing, policing. My husband plans to have influence in all these arenas of civic life; his knowledge of the West and the Company will be an asset to the new town.*

Georgina often asks James when they will move, when he will be transferred. Her husband asks her to be patient. *As if I have a choice*, Georgina thinks. *Edmonton would be better than Lac St. Anne. But still, it is no Cork: electric lights were only installed in the past year.* When she left Ireland to come here, she had not thought that James Barrett would make her into a shopkeeper's wife on the wild frontier, but it is not as if she had other options. So Georgina does not ask her husband about his journey and he does not ask her about her feelings. They do not talk about what drew him to this colonial life, or what really happened with the factor's daughter at Winnipeg years ago, or how he moved between so many different worlds with such ease and, in some ways, seemed to thrive on that fluidity. They do not speak of any of this.

Nor do they speak of Georgina's fears or suspicions or monthly trials. James remains optimistic and Georgina focused. *If I had a baby to care for, James would not ask me to come mind this primitive little store*, Georgina thinks. Her husband is not particularly interested in the daily activities of his household, let alone the physical difficulties of womanhood as experienced by his wife. He spends his days here at the store, negotiating with locals over animal carcasses being exchanged for household goods, or closing the doors for an afternoon of gambling and drinking whiskey with the men he will squeeze money out of the next day. He is good at what he does: he speaks enough French and enough Cree to be amiable, and he has enough business sense and Company loyalty to make a profit. Much to Georgina's disappointment, he also makes the two-day trip into Edmonton every few weeks to meet with Factor Young at Fort Edmonton. *At least this is what he tells me*, Georgina thinks. A year ago, when she disembarked the train coming from Halifax to Edmonton, Georgina thought Edmonton was rustic, but now she finds the town, in comparison to Lac St. Anne at least, positively exciting. *At least there are places to go there other than the ramshackle cabin that is the Company store*, she thinks. When they first arrived here, James promised Georgina that he would take her to Edmonton regularly, so she could attend the Anglican church, but these promises have not materialized. Georgina's been begging James for weeks to take her to Edmonton, anywhere other than here, and each time she brings this up, her husband patronizingly kisses her on the forehead and says, "Next time, my darling. This trip is just for business."

Georgina suspects that when James travels to Edmonton, he spends his evenings at Kelly's Saloon. And Georgina knows that along with his taste for whiskey and cards comes a taste for women. *After all, James was so bold as to seduce me when I was another man's wife and in another man's home.* Georgina is not foolish: she was glad the Cardinal girl left, even if it meant that she had to admit she did not need two girls to help her in the house, when she saw how her husband looked at the girl. Georgina took some comfort in the fact that she had no real rivals here, only *half-breeds*. Sometimes, though, when he returns from town, Georgina wonders why James is unnecessarily rough with her. She wonders why he leaves bruises and forgoes her pleasure. Over the past few weeks, Georgina has tried not to notice James looking at Moira the same way he used to look at the Cardinal girl. She pushes from her mind that her husband looks at Moira with desire and evaluation as if she is a fur to barter over. *It is just my own frustration,* she tells herself, *at not being with child again.* Georgina knows she has to become pregnant again, regain the balance of power, prove her purpose, and become the wife James thinks he's married. She cannot let herself believe that she carries with her that history, that night in Douglas, instead of bearing James a son. Georgina does not write about any of this in her notebook.

My husband is a generous man. He makes sure to buy me a present when he travels to Edmonton without me. He likes to bring me something to make my life here a little easier, Georgina writes. Along with the stock and these ridiculous empty jars, James also brought Georgina a bottle of Graf's Hyglo nail polish paste in a soft pale pink the colour of tulips at a Cork storefront. Georgina wears her yellow and pink skirt today to match her freshly painted nails. For only this reason, she tries to feel glad she is not in the backroom. *Unpacking crates of flour, tea, and wool is just about the worst thing I could do to my freshly polished nails; even digging weeds out of the flower bed would do less damage*—she would have to set them all over again. *If I went to Edmonton, I could at least bring some peroxide home with me,* thinks Georgina. *I must be more careful to wear a hat when I am in the garden; the sun seems to bring out the red. There is no need to stock nail polish or hair dye here,* Georgina thinks. *The women at Lac St. Anne do not seem to care about their appearance, and they let themselves get fat and wrinkled.* She has been asking James to order the dye for more than a week, but he is distracted and has forgotten. Once he has fulfilled that request, she plans to ask him for a new pair of silk stockings.

She looks at the five glass jars on the counter in front of her. Georgina has filled one with black loose-leaf tea, which no one buys because they make their own with strong-smelling herbs from the bush, and one with bleached flour. She leaves three jars empty. She has spent most of the morning imagining them filled with items they can't get here: rhubarb and custard sweeties or potpourri made with tiny violets and flattened pansies and big fuchsia rose petals. Georgina dips her quill in the inkwell to describe them: *These three empty jars have something about them: their clarity illuminated by the sunlight coming through the open door, their clean, transparent beauty, their unrealized possibility.*

Moira comes out from the backroom carrying an armful of folded point blankets piled so high that they touch the bottom of her chin. "Where shall I put these, Georgina?" she asks. *The white wool against her face makes her black hair look even darker and her skin translucent,* thinks Georgina. *She really is a beautiful girl. No wonder the Cardinal boy desires her.*

"On the far side of the store, near the east window."

Moira nods, wary of Georgina's friendly tone.

Georgina watches her work, refolding the blankets as she shelves them, and notices the silver fox pelt that hangs on the east wall. *I had a red fox stole once,* Georgina remembers. *Bernard bought it for me shortly after we were married.* She wore the stole on the winter night she first met James at the Ambassador Hotel. The soft red fur stood out against the pale green silk dress she had commissioned for the Christmas Ball. *Pale colours look best against blond hair,* Georgina thinks. *How I would love to have somewhere to wear such a gift now. James could get me any fur I could like or want, but why? Where on earth would I wear it here?*

As Moira arranges the stock, Georgina says, "I think I'll come to the back and help you and Mr. Barrett catalogue stock. There is really very little for me to do out here . . ."

As Georgina speaks, an old Indian woman shuffles into the store with a pilled woollen bag full of beaded moccasins to trade. She wears worn slippers and smacks her nearly toothless gums.

"Tân'si, Mrs.Yellowknee!" Moira turns around and cheerfully greets the woman she sometimes sees at Mass; she is balanced precariously on a shelf. Georgina stays behind the counter.

"Tân'si, sweet girl." The old woman speaks in her best English. "Came for some flour. Some butter," she adds in a combination of Cree and French. "My Amos likes that cow milk taste in his bannock. Too spoiled to have it made with bear lard like when we grew up."

Moira comes down from the shelf to be closer to Mrs. Yellowknee. She catches most of what the older woman says and laughs while she replies in English, "Well, you are spoiling him then!"

"Ehâ, you will be a good wife, my girl." Mary Yellowknee slaps a bundled pile of moose-hide moccasins on the counter near the ledger book. The soft tan shoes are beaded in bright green, deep blue, and blood-red geometric patterns. They are lined with rabbit fur.

"Oh, Mrs. Yellowknee. These are so lovely—must have taken you days upon days. Perhaps you can show me to do this kind of work?"

Mary Yellowknee smiles at Moira. "Pff. This is winter work. You should be outside while the sun is shining. Look at you, your skin is like a wâpiski-wâpos."

Moira laughs at the comparison to a winter rabbit.

Mary Yellowknee turns to the shop manager's wife. "Your husband here?"

Georgina can barely understand the woman's accent.

"Sorry?"

"Onâpêmimâw? Husband?" Mary Yellowknee speaks as if Georgina is hard of hearing or simple.

124

Georgina looks at the plump, wrinkled woman with a mouth that's missing teeth, a long grey braid down her back, and dirty, worn-down fingernails. She says, "Yes. He's in the backroom. But I can help you with the trade."

"Namoya," says Mary Yellowknee. "I will talk to him." The women on the settlement know that Mrs. Barrett is stingy. Besides, her husband knows their men. He knows the bargains, the arrangements, and the deals that have been struck on other fronts.

"Fine." Georgina tries not to show her frustration. She notices the woman's faded pink blouse with buttons threatening to burst. *She must really need the money*, Georgina thinks. "James," she calls to the back. "There is a customer out here requesting to deal with you."

James comes through the backroom to the storefront and wipes his hands on his shopkeeper's apron.

"Well, hello, Mrs. Yellowknee. How are you this beautiful summer day?" He speaks in Cree.

"Âhâw."

Georgina hates that the old crone smiles at him with almost-respect.

"And Amos? Fine card player you've got there for a husband. Now, what have you brought for me today . . ." As James charms and negotiates with the old Indian woman, as he turns her wares over in his hands, Georgina is still behind the counter feeling even less useful than before. She watches as her husband, a man she has seen entertain the wives of Cork's most important businessmen, convinces an old *squaw* that he is giving her a fair trade. Georgina watches Moira, at her husband's side, act as if she is the manager's wife.

Georgina would like to be friends with other women, but she has a knack for creating enemies. Even at her grammar school in Cork, she was a quiet and clever girl who spent most of her time on her own reading or sketching, especially after it became apparent that she was becoming beautiful in a cool and porcelain way. Once she became Mrs. Adams, Cork's society politely tolerated her. But she knew she was a figure of fascination and fantasy for men in her husband's circle and a figure of scorn for the other wives, with whom she spent countless awkward dinner parties and social evenings during the four years of her first marriage. Georgina knew she reminded them how easily their own husbands might replace them if they happened to have a weak heart or catarrh that didn't dissipate. *Mistresses are one thing; second wives are quite another.*

"It's as good a trade as you would get in Edmonton," James says to Mrs. Yellowknee. "And it will take care of your husband's debts here."

Georgina thinks about the first time she took that days-long journey from Edmonton to Lac St. Anne. She writes:

The first time seeing the settlement at Lac St. Anne, I was shocked at how small it was. I remember the first time I saw the Manager's Quarters, the house my husband and I would live in, with its smooth, flat logs painted the whitest white. Behind it, there was a garden already growing vegetables, a water pump, a freshly painted outhouse, a just-cut pile of wood, and an open fire. Tall trees marked where the land had been cleared into a square the Company had claimed as property.

She remembers how James led her and Moira through a "mud room" into two large rooms on the main floor.

"Ladies," he said, gesturing. "I trust you will find everything you need."

She writes: *I looked around and I could see a lantern and a pair of what I later learned were shoes for walking on top of the snow. I noticed a long, thin rifle arched above the door between the mud room and the kitchen. In one of the two main-floor rooms was a long, freshly painted white table with six chairs that was the place we would eat our meals. Herbs I did not recognize hung drying from the ceiling. A huge black stove with silver detailing and ornately carved handles sat in the middle of the kitchen. The other main room had a bench that looked a bit like a settle-bed, covered in colourful cushions and folded woollen blankets. A sewing machine and letter-writing desk, complete with paper and an inkwell, were pushed up against perpendicular walls. This was my new home.* Georgina does not write that she felt as if she was stepping into some other woman's life. *No wonder I have never felt at home in Lac St. Anne,* she thinks. Georgina does not write about how she feels frustrated, trapped in this wilderness, how she has to work hard not to go mad. And she does not write about Moira. She has not mentioned Moira in all her pages and pages of thoughts and reflections.

"What are you scribbling away on, my dear?" James touches his wife's manicured hand and brings her into the present. Georgina notices that Mrs. Yellowknee has left. She can hear Moira rustling around in the back storeroom.

"Oh, nothing, James. Just a letter to my parents in Cork. I thought I could write and send it all in the same day since I am here." She smiles. "I am just telling them how fortunate I am to be Mrs. Barrett." Georgina knows her role here. She moves closer to him and whispers an attempt at seduction in his ear.

"Hmm . . . I can hardly wait until nightfall." He kisses her passionately.

Georgina learned the currency of sex while she was still a girl, and it still surprises her how far men will go, what they will do, and what it can cost them for a few minutes inside a woman. Georgina will never forgive her mother for bartering her to that old man Bernard Adams, when she was barely out of childhood, and for allowing her to arrive at the wedding night unprepared and therefore terrified and traumatized by what happened. However, Georgina is thankful to have learned the power she had with men early on in her life. Even that first, awful experience taught her something important about the nature of a man's desire and how it is bound to their feelings of entitlement.

"Georgina, darling. Why don't you head back to the house? You can finish your letter there. Moira can stay here and help me finish the inventory. I am sure no one else will come in today. Go enjoy the late afternoon in the garden."

"But I haven't yet finished with the jars, the decorating. And I am happy to come and help you in the storeroom," she replies, masking her suspicion as to why he wants her to leave.

"No, darling. Go home. All that can wait."

Georgina nods. She shivers even though sweat still trickles down her back.

Her husband returns to the backroom.

Georgina knows that her marriage, her relationship, is not one of lightness or play. Georgina is jealous of how that *half-breed* boy made Moira laugh and flirt at that excuse for a New Year's Eve ball, and how he longed for that simple girl at the threshold of the mud room and kitchen. Georgina knows that she and James are founded on something dark: reckless desire and the deception it necessitates. Georgina let herself be seduced by James when she was married to someone else—a fat, old, impotent man—but she still transgressed that convention and almost lost everything. The first time she let James kiss her or touch her breast underneath her gown or lift her skirts to put himself inside her, she was someone else's wife. Sometimes she wonders if a union borne out of such deception and thievery could ever amount to more than what it is.

Still, Georgina is not a spiritual or superstitious person. She is not even a religious person beyond what is necessary. But just as she has wondered if her womb is barren as some sort of punishment for the roots she took that landed her writhing on her grandmother's dirt floor, she sometimes wonders if her womb is not barren because she and James have not earned their partnership. Since losing the baby this spring, Georgina has been secretly wearing her grandmother's gold crucifix necklace against her skin, though she is careful to put it away at night to avoid her husband's questions. Right now, she can feel it against her damp collarbone. This simple act would be a kind of treason at home. She tries to push all these thoughts from her mind, push them down or away just as she has tried to forget Gabriel Cardinal's refusal of her advances, because she needs not to let herself own up to the truth that if James hadn't approached her that night at the Ambassador Hotel in Cork and ignited that possibility in her, she would have let someone else do so. It could have been anyone who led her down that path of all-consuming desire, that acknowledgment of being alive, that feeling of being wanted at all costs. Because Georgina cannot fully admit that it is only a series of accidents and poor decisions that have led her here, to this counter in an excuse for a store in the middle of a barren, primitive place an ocean and land mass away from civilization, to a marriage based on convenience and desperate decisions where she has no bargaining power. Georgina knows she cannot let that truth sneak in on long days of nothingness because then she will become hysterical.

As she gathers her letter paper and her notebook and prepares to walk back to the house, Georgina tries not to hear the sound of the rickety storeroom door close shut. She feels like screaming. Georgina knows she needs to do this because her husband is in the backroom with a younger girl who still doesn't understand how beautiful and desirable she really is; because her husband is in the backroom with the girl that a young, naive boy rejected her for out of some foolish notion of honour or commitment. Georgina has always been the kind of woman who thrives on being desired. And now she is not so sure that she is, or even that she is worth it: she has failed at this most basic of accomplishments for a woman.

She looks at the three empty jars on the counter. She feels a gnawing at the base of her pelvis and wonders how big a womb can really be, how far it can stretch. Georgina tries to ignore the memory of the clumps of flesh, the blood, the mess; she tries to ignore her foolishness, her violent sin, her fear that her wickedness may never be forgiven. Sweat beads along her darkening hairline and forms crescents under her arms. She feels as if she may vomit.

Because she needs to drive this image from her mind, Georgina calmly pushes one of the empty jars off the edge of the counter. It takes the inkwell with it and makes a satisfying clash as it hits the wooden floorboards and splinters into pieces. She comes out from behind the counter and kneels on the dusty floor. She doesn't think about how her silk skirt may be marred by ink. Before James comes rushing to her, red-faced and out of breath from what he was doing to Moira in the storeroom, Georgina has time with the broken pieces. Some are thin slivers and some are fat chunks. A few shards are wedged into the dirty space between the floorboards; others lie flat, glimmering in the sunlight coming in from the open door, as if on display. *They are like snowflakes, or diamonds*, she thinks as she takes a sharp shard and runs it against the palm of her left hand. The sting makes her wince and feel alive. She watches the skin open, the blood appear and flow, her palm darken. It is unlike the blood that comes as a monthly humiliation, or that stained the bedsheets Moira had to hang out in the cool March air, or that signalled such pain and distress on the floor of her grandmother's Irish kitchen. She is calm, watching, soothed. And this is how James finds her when he rushes into the storefront, too long after he heard the smash of the jar on the floor.

"Georgina!" James can see blood and ink all over her hand and wrist but cannot see where the blood originates from. He grabs a piece of sample fabric from the counter and wraps it around his wife's hand. The gingham fabric soaks through with bright red and indigo.

"What are you doing on the floor?"

"I was just filling the jars, as you asked," Georgina answers quietly. With her right hand she points to the two still-empty jars on the counter.

James presses on the cloth. "How did this happen?"

"I want to go home," is all Georgina says.

"Of course," James answers. "Moira . . ." he calls. "I am taking Mrs. Barrett home. She's made a bit of a mess. There's a broken jar. Please mind the store and clean up the glass. I'll be back before closing."

She hears Moira call out, "All right, Mr. Barrett."

Georgina smiles to herself as her husband tends to her. She decides to write of his devotion in her journal.

→→ *Missions* ←←

When she gets to the church at the St. Albert Mission, Payesîs Belcourt opens the doors and searches the log cathedral for any sign of Mahkesîs. Even though the community in St. Albert is devout, still loyal to the settlement's founder, Father Lacombe, many people will be fishing in the Sturgeon River or cooking their evening meal on an outside fire or hunting in the bush just north of here rather than coming to Mass this evening. It is the time of year when it starts to get dark a little earlier every evening and people feel an urgency as predictions are made about the first frost. And even though Payesîs has heard the priests and nuns here say that this church is not as big as the grey-stone and stained-glass cathedrals in Quebec, the cathedral at the St. Albert Mission will still not be full tonight.

Payesîs needs to speak to Mahkesîs about the rumours and about the girl's mother, Virginié. Payesîs stands in the church entrance and sees Sister Frances Marie chatting with the Dumonts near the cast-iron wood stove. The young nun and the elderly couple speak in French in hushed voices about reports that a man who went scowing up on the Athabasca River was attacked by a cougar and lost his leg. Mrs. Dumont says she suspects it was a river serpent since there are rarely any cougars in this part of the world. The young nun isn't sure how to respond, but she agrees it was an unfortunate accident.

Payesîs walks over and interrupts the conversation with a smile. "Hello, Ida. Harold. Pardon me, Sister."

"Hello, Mrs. Belcourt. How are you?" *Sister Frances Marie has only been here for a few months but she is good with names,* Payesîs thinks.

"Fine, Sister." She smiles. "I need to speak with Mahke . . . I mean, Adèle. I am her mother's cousin. Where can I find her?"

"I believe she's in the Indian schoolroom with the girls. And Sister Ignatius. If Adèle is not there, then you will find her in the Youville convent—the old Bishop's Palace."

Payesîs nods her thanks and makes her way out of the cathedral to walk toward the convent, where the mission's eight nuns and all the girl children sleep. It is a grand wooden building, four windows high, with tall staircases and a gabled roof. It is bigger than the Factor's Hall she remembers seeing as a child visiting Fort Edmonton at Christmas. She doesn't see any light through the windows and decides to try the schoolhouse, although she would like to avoid Sister Ignatius if possible. She feels the cool fall wind through her deerskin coat that is worn through under her arms and across her chest; she will have to figure out a way to patch it without ruining the smoothness of the hide. The woman relies on the kindness of her older sister and brother-in-law and will not ask George for a new coat. It is at times like these that Payesîs wonders if she shouldn't try to find another husband; she is only forty, after all. She pulls the scarf covering her head a little tighter under her chin.

It has been nine months since Payesîs last saw Mahkesîs in Virginié and Luc's cabin, right before the New Year's Eve dance in Lac St. Anne. The little bird-like woman walks round the wooden cathedral and enters the nursery school adjacent to it. Dry, brittle pine cones crunch under her worn black leather boots. Payesîs opens the schoolroom door a little, not sure whether she should have knocked, and the wooden door creaks on its rusting hinges. She sees Sister Ignatius standing at the front of the schoolroom, her back against a chalkboard covered in passages from Genesis, with her hands clasped in front of her waist just under her crucifix. *That woman must be a hundred years old*, Payesîs thinks. *And here she still is, tormenting children.* Payesîs sees Mahkesîs crouched down at a child's level, helping a little girl button up a light blue woollen cardigan with mismatched patches on the elbows. The girl smiles at Mahkesîs with big brown eyes. Payesîs sees a room full of brown-eyed girls with identical, roughly cut brown hair who look frightened and lost. *Probably most of these young girls have just arrived here in the past week or two*, she thinks. They are far away from their parents and families, and probably few of them speak English or French. Payesîs is glad these little ones at least have someone kind like Virginié's girl. Payesîs feels a pang of nervousness in her gut—maybe she should leave well enough alone—but, no, *I am here for Virginié*, she tells herself.

Payesîs watches Mahkesîs fasten the last button on the girl's cardigan and smooth down the ribbing. Virginié's daughter tries to reassure the child with a smile. She looks up to see Payesîs standing in the doorway. The old French nun, who has been at this mission for decades, curls a beckoning finger and gestures for the middle-aged woman to come inside the schoolroom. Payesîs nods. Just the sight of Sister Ignatius makes her shudder.

"Good evening, Sister. I need to speak with Adèle." Payesîs is conscious of her French, spoken with inflections of Cree, and resents having to be civil to this old witch of a woman.

"Make it quick; I need Adèle's help managing these girls at Mass."

Sister Ignatius has seen generations of native children come through this place and doesn't see what is special about Adèle

Cardinal. She's seen what these people are capable of: they may be able to become Christian, but being holy is another matter altogether. There are exceptions, Sister Sarah Riel, of course, who kept her piousness even as her *half-breed* brother incited rebellions and chaos across the West. And Adèle Cardinal is no Sarah Riel.

But the old woman is a serious nun who obeys her priest—even if he doesn't really know what he's doing or what to expect of these people. That much was clear during the conference of bishops the mission hosted this past summer. Father Bernier suggested including some of the local Métis men in the bishops' discussions with Ottawa about a new kind of school for the Indian children here. What he thought he would get out of these consultations, Sister Ignatius has no idea. These children need to become Catholic and educated and have the native driven out of them if the West is ever to become more than a collection of reserves and Company posts morphed into towns. But Sister Ignatius trusts that Father Bernier sees a reason for taking in this fallen heathen girl from Lac St. Anne as an extra pair of hands at the mission. It is handy that she can speak Cree (although Sister Ignatius would never admit this out loud). As for the *half-breed* girl's self-proclaimed wish to become a teacher here, which would essentially mean becoming a nun, Sister Ignatius will do everything she can to stop that. She wonders why this woman needs to speak with Adèle.

"Of course," Payesîs replies. She can tell that Sister Ignatius does not recognize her as a former pupil. The old woman's eyes are cloudy with cataracts. Even if they weren't, Payesîs imagines the old woman pays little attention to the individuality of her students; they likely form one ungodly, unwashed brown native mass to her. Payesîs feels slightly nauseated being back in this place and having to speak to this terrible woman face to face. She still has three milky white scars across her spine and against the small of her back, where, three decades ago, Sister Ignatius struck her three times with a willow branch—once for the Father, the Son, and the Holy Ghost—because the girl refused to stop speaking in Cree. Payesîs remembers how hard it was that year her family left Lac St. Anne to join Father Lacombe at his new settlement of St. Albert. She was ten that summer and was excited at the idea of living only nine miles, as the crow flies, from the Fort Edmonton she had heard so many stories about as a girl. She did not realize she would have to attend school and listen to Sister Ignatius tell the children how she was inspired by the three original Grey Nuns who went to Lac St. Anne and became the first white women that far west; how she travelled with a young priest from Gatineau, who started out at Fort McKay in the far North and is now west of there, at Fort St. John, and another young novice named Claire, who passed away after getting pox their second winter here; how she had to sit on a slight birch bench in an open boat, sweating from the shield to the prairies, sleeping in a makeshift tent in the rough bush, and squatting out of site trying not to soil her robe. *She spoke about her journey as if she had spent forty days in the desert tormented by Satan himself*, thinks Payesîs. The old nun looks smaller now, but it is hard to tell underneath her grey robe with black bib. Payesîs thinks she sees the crucifix shiver against the old woman's abdomen as her wrinkled hand trembles slightly.

Payesîs ignores Sister Ignatius if she sees her at Mass.

Mahkesîs stands up. She gently nudges the girl in the blue cardigan and points her toward a line of other little girls being inspected by Sister Ignatius. Mahkesîs is the one who nods now and almost whispers to Payesîs, "Let's go outside." The two women, who at the end of last year sat at the Cardinals' table with their hands kneading bannock in the same bowl, now stand outside a small Catholic church as the sun sets to make way for an orange harvest moon. They know that Sister Ignatius will demand that Mahkesîs report this conversation. They have both been changed by the hardship of being women under her watch.

Mahkesîs says in Cree, "It's nice to see you, Aunty."

"How's that old crone treating you? You okay?" Payesîs asks as she places her hand on the younger woman's shoulder.

"I'm fine. What do you want to speak with me about?" She tries not to show her emotion.

Payesîs drops her arm to her side. She rubs her hands together and tries hard to keep her composure. "Mahkesîs, I know that you've had a hard year."

Mahkesîs shivers. Her grey woollen smock dress is wrong for this climate: too hot in summer and not warm enough in winter.

Payesîs notices. "You're cold. Take my coat." The older woman starts unbuttoning her deerskin jacket.

"I'm fine. What else do you need to say, Aunty? I have to get back to the children." Mahkesîs feels her heart racing and her palms sweating.

"People are saying that the baby you gave to your brother and his wife is James Barrett's."

Mahkesîs feels like she can't breathe.

"I know he is not a nice man. If he forced you—"

"No," Mahkesîs lies. "He didn't."

"I care about you. Your mother misses you. She worries about you. I saw her just a few weeks ago when I went visiting at Lac St. Anne and, well, she doesn't seem herself. Your father is drinking a lot and she isn't trying to stop him. That Bertha girl has been coming round, looking for your brother Gabriel, and your mother isn't even discouraging her."

Silence rests between them.

"What I want to say, what I mean to say . . . You shutting yourself away here is not going to change that you have a son. I know what it is like to lose a child: my little one died in my arms before his fourth birthday. And I was never able to have any more. Now I am an old woman, widowed, and I rely on the kindness of my sister and George to keep me safe and fed. But you, you have a son still. You should go home. Be with your own people."

"Aunty, I can't go back to Lac St. Anne . . ."

"Adèle . . ." Sister Ignatius calls from the schoolroom's open door. "I need your help with the children. Father Bernier's ready to begin Mass."

Mahkesîs says to Payesîs, softly but with conviction, "My place is here now. If you see my mother, if you see my grandmother, tell them I miss them."

Mahkesîs goes back into the schoolroom.

∞

There is a lot of work at the St. Albert Mission to keep her busy, and for that Mahkesîs gives thanks. Today, on this early autumn afternoon, Mahkesîs sweeps and tidies the empty church before morning Mass. She thinks about Payesîs's visit yesterday and what it must have taken for her aunty to come find her, confront her, and ask her to go home. The young woman has thrown herself into work since arriving here a month or so ago. Inside the Youville residence, the wooden floors must be washed and waxed. There are twelve priests and eight nuns at the mission, and all the Fathers' and Sisters' robes have hems that need mending from dragging on the rough, dusty ground. The children's clothes need constant patching as they are passed from student to student. Outside in the garden that provides much of their food, potatoes and corn and onions need to be harvested before the first frost has a chance to discolour them. While St. Albert has a population similar to Lac St. Anne's, the mission here is so much larger than what she knew as the mission at home. In St. Albert, the mission is like its own village within the village:

there is the convent, the cathedral, a hospital, the residences for schoolchildren, and Mahkesîs has heard talk that there are plans to open one of the Crown's huge new red-brick schools to bring even more children here from surrounding reserves, settlements, and bush. It is hard to believe that this all started with two priests standing on a snowy hill planting a shivering sapling on a cold January morning a generation or so ago.

Mahkesîs's world here is small; she is confined to the mission and has not ventured into St. Albert to see its two hotels or shops or streets. She has heard that the stores in town are owned by the men who manage them—not by the Company—and that one of the hotels has a balcony as long as the width of the building itself. She hasn't seen it, but she would like to sometime. Mahkesîs is getting accustomed to the rhythm of the day here. When she first arrived, she was not ready for much more than just getting through the day. Now her breasts have stopped aching, stopped leaking, and her body is almost as slim as it was before (part of it is that she has no appetite and part of it is that the food here is bland). On first glance, no one would know that she gave birth to a baby boy at the beginning of the summer.

Inside, at the knave of the cathedral, stand two angels carved out of smooth pale stone called marble. Mahkesîs has heard many times how these statues were a gift to Bishop Grandin from a man named Brother Bouchard, how Brother Bouchard used his God-given talent to help makes this place beautiful and bring the finer arts to this fledgling mission. But it is a statue of Our Lady, carved out of pine, resting to the right of the altar, that Mahkesîs thinks is more beautiful than these white frozen angels. She likes that she can see the movements of the knife etched in the sculpture. Our Lady's body is little more than part of a tree trunk. Knots in the wood become blotches on her robe, and her splintering hood is far too large for her face. Her two sleeves come together just under where a bosom would be, giving the illusion that her hands have disappeared. Someone has tucked five straggly arcs of grain where her hands should be. But her face—her face is beautiful. It was made with detail and care, as her eyes, nose, and smile look to be carved by a different hand than the rest of her.

Small boxes depicting the Stations of the Cross decorate the walls of the cathedral. On her first Sunday here, sitting between Sister Frances Marie and Sister Ignatius, Mahkesîs could either look at Bishop Grandin, giving the sermon at the pulpit, or just past him at the box depicting Mary Magdalene at Jesus's tomb. The little wooden woman leans into a grave and lays her hand on the faintly carved body inside. Mahkesîs thinks about how this woman is said to have washed Jesus's feet with her tears and dried them with her hair when he was alive. It seems to her to be a strange act of love—one of subservience rather than affection. The nuns taught her that Mary Magdalene was a fallen woman. She changed her ways, repented, and Jesus saved her. But then she had to watch him die nailed to a tree, suffocating in the desert sun. Mahkesîs has wondered why God punished her in the end anyway.

Mahkesîs sits in this chapel and listens to Bishop Grandin tell his congregation, "Give thanks for this land that God has given us. We can enjoy and live a bountiful life here as long as we follow Christ's teachings and live holy lives."

That is as close as she gets to Bishop Grandin, or most of the clergy, for that matter. The one priest she has spoken to is Father Bernier. Father Bernier has taken her confession: he knows she has just had a baby, and that she has no husband, but he assures her God can forgive her. The young priest, so young he looks as if he hasn't yet grown into his own gangly arms and legs, has told Mahkesîs that he thinks a Cree-speaking Métis novice will help bring more native people into the fold. Mahkesîs understands this. She knows more and more people are becoming isolated as they sign treaties and move onto reserves. *Perhaps Father Bernier thinks my Cree will be useful in setting up such a residence here*, she thinks. Father Bernier speaks mostly in French, with some Latin, of course, all filtered through his heavy Québécois accent. Mahkesîs is happy to help Father Bernier in whatever he asks of her. She would like to be assigned to the hospital and plans to ask Father Bernier for his help in this once winter comes and there is less to do outside.

As hard as she works completing her tasks, Mahkesîs also works hard not to think about the baby boy. She can train her mind to be still as long as her body is busy.

She works hard not to wonder if he is eating well, she works hard not to imagine his new mother holding and nursing and cradling him, she works hard not to hum the Cree lullabies that may soothe him to sleep. She knows he is fine. Thomas and Ida have a new baby boy of their own, so her son will have a brother close to him. Virginié told Mahkesîs before she left Lac St. Anne that they were fortunate to have such an option.

Mahkesîs knows her older brother and his wife will be good parents to her child. But still, she worries that they may find it difficult to add another baby to their family that already has three other small children: one more baby means more moss-filled diapers to change and wash in a bucket outside, it means sharing the space in the birch cradle, it means another hungry little belly to fill in a lean season, it means one more precocious explorer wandering too deep in the brush when her son is old enough to toddle off while his other mother picks berries. Mahkesîs occasionally lets herself wish for the luxury of raising her child herself someday and then pays the price of being filled with longing. She takes a cloth and carefully wipes dust from the crevices in the wooden statue of Our Lady.

∞

One of the younger nuns, who has been here a little more than a year, is kind to Mahkesîs. She and Sister Frances Marie spend some of each day together, and Mahkesîs knows Father Bernier has asked Sister Frances Marie to train her. Sister Frances Marie is from Quebec, is learning English, and seems around the same age as Mahkesîs. Encased in one of the Grey Nuns' distinctive wimples, her face looks like a round and flat heart. Mahkesîs does not wear one of these head coverings, not being a true novice, and instead wears her hair in a tight bun and drapes a worn plaid shawl over her grey dress: it is just one of the differences between her and Sister Frances Marie. Mahkesîs knows Sister Frances Marie works hard: she is devoted to the Church, and, unlike Sister Ignatius, the younger nun shows affection to the Indian girls she helps teach sewing and needlework and butter-making. Something about Sister Frances Marie intrigues Mahkesîs: she doesn't seem to have chosen this path either and, rather, is here because she has nowhere else to be. She is kind to Mahkesîs even though she doesn't have to be.

Sister Frances Marie helps Sister Ignatius prepare lessons for the upcoming school year and helps serve Father Bernier. She is quiet and nervous, and most of their time together is spent either by Sister Frances Marie teaching Mahkesîs scripture or Mahkesîs teaching Marie the English translation for the Cree words the children whisper to one another some nights and are strapped for if Sister Ignatius hears them.

Sister Frances Marie has told Mahkesîs, "I am from a big family too and I miss mon père et ma mère, mon frère et mes soeurs. Where I am from, Île d'Orléans, not many people speak English. I learned a little to come out here but was relieved that most people here speak French."

Mahkesîs does not really understand this difficulty with language—she has always moved between Cree, French, Michif, and English with ease. Just as she tried to help Moira learn bits of French and Cree so she could speak to someone other than Mrs. Barrett, she is teaching Sister Frances Marie Cree, not only so the young nun can understand the children, but so that the two of them can speak in a language Sister Ignatius does not know. The woman has lived here for more than thirty years and refuses to learn a "savage" language.

Mahkesîs's real talent is in healing, which she learned from her grandmother. Soon after she arrived, Father Bernier caught a cold that forced him to bed for three days. Mahkesîs told Sister Ignatius and Sister Frances Marie that she would go pick some fireweed to brew into a tea to settle his rattling cough. Sister Ignatius told her, "We have no need for this kind of superstition at the mission, Adèle. If Father Bernier is not himself in a few days, we will take him to the hospital." When someone is sick here, they go to that whitewashed building at the edge of the mission, or one of the nuns sends for Dr. LeClaire to come with his black leather bag full of expensive medicine that came on the train from Calgary. Mahkesîs thinks sending for Dr. LeClaire is a waste of time and money when pink-purple fireweed, growing near one of the mission's outhouses, will soothe an upset stomach or salve a burn. Her grandmother taught her that willow-bark tea takes pain's edge away and calms a racing heart. She would like to learn more about healing at the hospital, and has asked Sister Ignatius if she could be assigned there, only to be met with a haughty laugh. "We cannot have a *half-breed* nurse, Adèle. Lord knows what you would do to the patients." That is why she will speak with Father Bernier in winter. He knows first-hand that she knows about healing.

Father Bernier is kind to her, but Sister Frances Marie is the closest thing Mahkesîs has had to a friend since she left Moira with the Barretts at the Manager's Quarters. Mahkesîs shares her name with Sister Frances Marie one afternoon as they pick early autumn's offering of red caps and morels in the brush around the mission.

"My family calls me Mahkesîs. You can call me that instead of Adèle when we're alone. As long as Sister Ignatius doesn't hear."

The Métis girl says this without making eye contact or breaking her rhythm of gently pulling the mushroom stalks out of the dirt. The soft gills of the red caps brush against her palm: the folds and waves do look like something you might find on a jackfish. The morels are taller and almost look like a black-grey honeycomb or even a small animal's brain. The shaggy manes are bell-shaped, and Mahkesîs likes their strong, meaty taste best of all. She collects the morels, the shaggy manes, and the larger red caps in a willow-branch basket.

Sister Frances Marie smiles and says, "It's a lovely name. Que cela signifie-t-il?"

"My grandmother named me for a fox."

The women find clusters of mushrooms underneath blankets of pine needles on the damp-smelling floor of the boreal forest. It takes a discerning eye to separate the delicacies from the deadly. Sister Frances Marie is nervous and checks with Mahkesîs each time she finds a new cluster: she has as much dirt in her basket as she does red caps or morels. They enjoy an hour or so away from the watchful eye of Sister Ignatius—this afternoon she is supervising the little girls who've just arrived as they prepare the meagre evening meal.

Sister Frances Marie is much quieter than Moira, Mahkesîs thinks. She would like to know more about her, about her life in Quebec, why she came here, why she is a nun. It is obvious she loves children, but she could have become a teacher in a schoolhouse or a nurse at a hospital—at least until she found a husband. But the young woman doesn't offer much and Mahkesîs is not going to pry. So they continue to pick mushrooms. The red caps exude a milky orange sap, the shaggy manes' inky juice stains the tips of Mahkesîs's fingers, and her nails are embedded with soil. Mahkesîs thinks about how when she was first pregnant, her grandmother caught her eating unwashed carrots from the cold storage shed that were still covered in dirt. Mahkesîs could have eaten handfuls of earth those first few months—it was her only craving. She and Sister Frances Marie have been picking for a good hour and have to bend down to reach into the ground. This afternoon, the young woman's back starts to feel sore and a twinge makes her body remember the pain of labour. She wonders, for a moment, what her baby is doing right now. Is he sleeping on Ida's back as she, too, works outside? Is he eating well and growing out of his newborn clothes? Is he smiling and cooing at the cousins he will know as brothers and sisters?

Saskatoons are Mahkesîs's favourite things to pick: they are sweet, thornless, and native to this place. Their bushes are not prickly like those of yellow-green gooseberries and deep red raspberries. She does not have to bend down to the ground to pick the blue-purple berries like when she picks low-bush cranberries and wild little blueberries: the berries fall into the cup of her hand with a little strip of the cluster. And saskatoons taste sweet and rich coming right off the bush; they are not like mushrooms, which have to be washed, boiled down, and cooked into something else to be edible.

Mahkesîs is starting to trust Sister Frances Marie. *It is nice to have someone my own age to talk to again.* She has not had that since she left Moira at the Barretts' house. And she grew up surrounded by women. *It is nice to have the chance to share stories.* Usually, she is the one listening.

"My grandmother used to tell me a story about a fox, a girl, and a weetigo," Mahkesîs starts. Sister Frances Marie listens; this is the most Mahkesîs has spoken since she arrived at the mission two months ago. "Nohkum tells a story about a little girl who is very sick with a cough in the winter. The medicine man in the village comes to listen to her chest and has a vision of a snowstorm inside her. He says a weetigo is causing the storm and will come to take her and eat her. He tells the men in the village, 'You must go and find the weetigo and kill it before it gets your child.' So, the father and three of the girl's uncles go hunting. The hunters start to get sick. They see a red fox against the snow and the fox is sick too. The fox says to them, 'A weetigo is causing all this. It wants to eat us all. I will let it chase me and then maybe it will stop chasing your little girl.'"

Sister Frances Marie is confused but is nervous to ask too many questions in case Mahkesîs stops telling the story. She has to ask, however, "What is a wee . . . a wee-ti-go?"

Mahkesîs tells her. "A monster. It's part human, but it eats people. It roasts their flesh on open fires. The only way to kill one is to cut off its head and bury it away from its body."

"Ah," says the young nun. She has heard of this creature from some of her parishioners and has tried to assure them that demon possessions are very rare. They do not seem reassured. Sister Frances Marie keeps picking mushrooms and listens.

Mahkesîs continues, "The girl's father says to the fox, 'We cannot let you do that alone. Lead us to the weetigo and we will kill it.' So the fox helps the hunters, these men who would usually be hunting her, and the weetigo falls for the trap. The hunters are able to catch the monster and cut off its head so it cannot put itself back together. The fox thanks the hunters for helping her and for not killing her too. She goes back to her den. When the hunters return home, they feel better and they see the little girl playing with her brothers and sisters. The fox saves the girl and the hunters."

Sister Frances Marie is not sure what to say in response. "Sounds very frightening. Have you ever seen one of these creatures, Mahkesîs?" the young nun asks, trying out the sound of Adèle's real name.

"My grandmother says that last time she knew of one for certain was the time just before Gabriel and I were born. It was a bad time with lots of sickness, lots of fighting, a murder at Fort Edmonton. The weetigo knew people were hurting and were not able to watch out for it. It managed to kill many people, many children, before it was caught."

"Do you believe this story?" the young nun asks tentatively.

"I think so."

"I do not know of any such creatures in Île d'Orléans. There was a story of a ghost in our cathedral. It was said that last century a young nun gave birth to a baby. The story goes that the father was a priest and that when the baby was taken from her, the young woman died of heartbreak. Her phantom is said to pace across the balcony of the transcept. I never saw her. Although sometimes there would be strange flashes of light on that side of the cathedral . . ." Her voice trails off. "Je suis désolée . . ."

"I am fine," says Mahkesîs. "I have not died of heartbreak." She pauses and looks into her basket. "The best place to pick mushrooms is around the lake at Lac St. Anne. You can also find saskatoons, low-bush cranberries, wild blueberries . . ." Mahkesîs thinks about how she didn't go to Manito Sakahigan this year, how she and her mother stayed in the cabin with the new baby, how Mahkesîs held his little, wiggling pink mouth to her breast for those first few wonderful weeks until she knew she had to leave with her brother Thomas in the Red River cart to come to the mission.

She asks Sister Frances Marie, "Did you pick any berries when you were there?"

Mahkesîs can see Sister Frances Marie wince but does not know it is because she feels a knot in her gut. Mahkesîs does not know that Sister Frances Marie feels terrible about telling Father Lizeé that the Irish girl who lives with the store manager disappeared to spend the night with Mahkesîs's brother Gabriel.

Mahkesîs does not know that Sister Frances Marie wonders why Moira told the truth about why she spent the night away from the Church camp when Sister Frances Marie confronted her. Why didn't the girl say she got lost in the bush? Mahkesîs does not know that Sister Frances Marie tries to make herself feel better by reasoning that Moira must atone for her sin and it was Father Lizeé's and her guardian's responsibility to ensure she didn't sin again. But something about James Barrett bothered the young nun. She couldn't quite say what, but she recognized a kind of cruelty in his calm demeanour—it reminded the young woman of Sister Ignatius. Sister Frances Marie did what she was supposed to, and yet she feels as if she has betrayed a young Irish girl she barely knows. Mahkesîs does not know any of this about her new friend and old friend.

Sister Frances Marie answers Mahkesîs, "No, I didn't. We were very busy with the services, and Father Lizeé asked me specifically to come help him at the water. He needed me at his side."

Mahkesîs smiles. She lets herself think of Manito Sakahigan and the families that gathered on the shore of that sparkling lake in high summer as she picks mushrooms in this valley. She wishes she could have gone to the sacred gathering place with her baby boy. If things were different, she could have taken him there to show him off to everyone, to let them see his bow-shaped mouth and bright, happy eyes for themselves. Even though Mahkesîs works hard not to think about the baby, she feels an emptiness, and a longing to cradle him in her arms and hold him against her heart. For the first few months she carried him, she was angry. She didn't choose this, and she certainly didn't want to bring a child of Barrett's into the world. Then, like her grandmother told her she would, she started to feel differently. When he was born, a boy brought into the world by her grandmother in her parents' house, Mahkesîs wondered for a few days if she could raise him. But the look in her father's eyes told her it would be best if she left. So she did. And now she is here, telling stories about foxes and weetigos to a young nun who seems as lonely and lost as she is. *How has it come to this*, Mahkesîs wonders. *How can people go to Manito Sakahigan and ignore the purple saskàtoons, the bounty of herbs and fish the Creator provided there, and instead spend the long summer nights reading and reciting texts about some ancient desert?* The more she learns and reads about this religion that she has spent her life believing in because her mother and father and numerous priests and nuns have said is the way and the light, the more she realizes how much like her grandmother she really is. Mahkesîs knows she is not going to become a nun, and it isn't just because Sister Ignatius tells her this multiple times a day. She knows that this is not her path. Now Mahkesîs has to figure out how long she will stay at the mission and where she will go once she leaves.

Sister Frances Marie adds, "But I like picking these champignons—mushrooms—with you. In fall, my mother and sisters and I would pick apples. So many apples. We were busy for many weeks making pies and jams and applesauce."

Mahkesîs lets herself imagine Quebec as Sister Frances Marie describes it: the blood-red and orange leaves this time of year that make the valleys look ablaze, the sight of tin pails on the maple tree as the temperature warms in late winter just enough for the sap to run. Mahkesîs has always thought of Quebec as the place where the nuns and priests come from, but, of course, she realizes now, it is also a place of families and traditions like those Sister Frances Maries now shares with her. Mahkesîs wants to know more about the young nun's life there, what she dreamed about as a girl, why she left and came West. But perhaps this conversation is for another day: she knows that there are no easy answers to these kinds of questions. And Mahkesîs senses she will have the chance to ask her another time because they are becoming close. There is something different about Sister Frances Marie: Mahkesîs is not quite sure what it is but she feels safe with her.

"We better get back," Mahkesîs says. "Sister Ignatius is probably wondering where we are. That woman scares me."

Sister Frances Marie pauses and says, "You know, perhaps she was not always this way, so hard. She told me how she came here when she was only seventeen. She came with a company of voyageurs transporting supplies up to York Factory and then headed out West. The journey took sixteen weeks of good weather."

Mahkesîs says, "Maybe it was that long journey, all that prairie sun reflecting off lakes and rivers, that now makes her face as wrinkled as a fallen crabapple shrivelled in the dirt." She expects Marie to laugh.

"Mahkesîs, this life of devotion is hard. We are all called to serve God in different ways." Sister Frances Marie touches Mahkesîs's hand. Mahkesîs lets her and feels a shiver of something unfamiliar.

Mahkesîs nods and says, "We should probably go back to help the new little girls with dinner." She knows that the shaggy manes have to be eaten, or at least cooked, the same day they are picked or they can cause people to have visions and nightmares. It is hard enough to understand the reality of this place without the threat of something like this. Mahkesîs needs to keep her wits with her if she is going to survive the mission.

Confessions

As the afternoon light fades outside, Georgina climbs up the curving wooden stairs in the Manager's Quarters and knocks on the bedroom door where Moira sleeps. Georgina feels she has been given an opportunity and she cannot waste it. Her stomach is in knots—she feels almost as if she is back on *The Nova Scotian* on one of the rough sea days from Cork to Halifax. Georgina can almost smell the salty waves in her nostrils as acid coats her throat. This is a delicate situation, and she has convinced herself that her future hangs on this encounter.

Georgina precariously balances a wooden tray with two cups of steaming black tea and a white china plate decorated with tiny pink roses. The plate holds three expensive, imported ginger biscuits that James sometimes has at the store. It took her a ridiculous amount of time to steep the tea—it has been months since she's done anything in the kitchen, and she couldn't easily find everything she needed. She would have to talk to Moira later about how she was organizing the supplies. Georgina also realized she has no idea what Moira takes in her tea, so she has brought it black, which is probably best considering the girl has an upset stomach. *My plan has to work*, she thinks. *It makes sense. I've written it down and thought it through. It will work.* Georgina uses her knuckles to knock loudly on the thin wooden door.

"Moira, let me in. I've come to check on you."

She puts her ear to the door and thinks she hears the wooden floor shift as the temperature outside drops. She thinks she hears the scrape of a chair being moved away. She sees the doorknob turn, the door crack open, and stands straight to face the ashen girl.

Georgina forces herself to smile and asks, "How are you feeling, Moira?"

Moira notices the tray and the good china. This is the first time Georgina has ever brought anything to her.

Moira answers, "Better. It must be the change in the season—winter coming and the chill . . ." Moira shakes as she speaks and has to sit down on the edge of the bunched-up quilt on top of the wrought-iron bed.

"Moira, stop. You're with child, aren't you?" Georgina puts the tray down on the night table, straightens the quilt, and sits down on the bed beside Moira. Their proximity mimics a kind of intimacy.

Moira nods. "Yes, I think so." Moira saw enough girls come in desperation to her mother asking for assurance and help, and sometimes a packet of herbs to steep into a barely drinkable tea, to know that she is going to have a baby. There is no point in lying about it.

Georgina has had her suspicions for a week or so. This morning, when she asked Moira to help her with some sewing, the girl had to race outside to vomit and narrowly missed the edge of the mud room floor. Georgina has also noticed that Moira has stayed home on the days she was to help that old nun with the children in the settlement's excuse for a school. The girl has also been unusually tired, retreating to her room as soon as she is done washing the supper dishes. Georgina could be angry;

indeed, she has every right to be furious. But she sees an opportunity in this situation. This autumn afternoon is one of the few times Georgina has felt any control or power since coming to Lac St. Anne.

Georgina says to Moira, with certainty, "You have all the signs I've had when I was with child. You are exhausted. You can't keep anything down. We can ask Dr. Horace to come from St. Albert to see you. We will not be able to tell him why until he gets here, and we will, of course, have to demand his discreetness."

Moira nods. She is surprised at Georgina's calmness and willingness to help. She does not say that there is no need to call the physician from St. Albert, that there are many women on the settlement who could confirm what she already knows and what Mrs. Barrett suspects.

Georgina says, "So, what are we going to do now that you are having my husband's child?"

Moira looks at her with shock, "What? I . . . no . . ."

Georgina interrupts Moira with calm and measured certainty. "Don't feign surprise. That day in the store this summer—that day I cut my hand—do you not think I know what the two of you were doing in the storeroom while I stood at the front counter?" Georgina rubs her scar with the opposite hand. "Do you not think I see the way he looks at you? It's the way he used to look at me."

Georgina takes a sip of tea from her china cup. The bell clinks against the saucer as she sets it down.

Georgina continues, "My husband has desired you since we first came here last summer. He admires a pretty girl." She thinks about, but does not speak to, her husband's dalliance with a factor's daughter in Winnipeg that sent him up here to this little outpost. "And he is a man who gets what he desires—at all costs. It makes him a successful businessman and a difficult husband."

Moira is silent.

153

"Have a biscuit, dear. The ginger will settle your stomach," Georgina says as she passes Moira the plate with the tiny pink roses.

Moira shakes her head.

Georgina wonders why Moira is so quiet—is she surprised, guilty, or just ill? *The girl should be thrilled that I am taking this so well, that I am not throwing her out into the dusty trails that pass for streets to make her own way on the settlement.* But Georgina knows she has to be present in this situation. She has to control its outcome.

Georgina continues talking without looking at Moira. "I will be frank with you, Moira. I know what kind of man my husband is. He had that *half-breed* girl to play out his wants for a while, but that can be expected. But you . . . I have long feared he would fall for you. He desires, and he thrives, on challenge. And before you snuck away to spend the night with that Cardinal boy, you were so pure and innocent. Now that it's happened, and now that you're having a baby, I feel strangely calm. I should despise you, but I do not."

This is the most candidly Georgina has spoken to Moira since they arrived in Lac St. Anne. She works hard to keep her voice at an even keel but it feels like the walls of the bedroom are closing in on her. The wooden floor planks seem to be rising and the arched ceiling seems to be narrowing its peak. She looks out the window, to the back garden, to ground herself. She recognizes a deep burning in the pit of her stomach, the same feeling of panic she had that day in the store when she smashed the jar. She tries to ignore it.

"Mrs. Barrett, you are wrong," Moira tries to intervene. She puts her hand on top of Georgina's and Georgina pulls her hand away.

Georgina clears her throat. "Moira, I have paid for my mistakes. I'm sure your mother told you the reason why I agreed to bring you with me. You know what I've done. And now, I know what you have done. But I think I have a way for both of us to redeem our sins."

"Georgina . . ." The name feels like the bush cranberries she has come to know on Moira's tongue. "All I know is that my mother helped you once, and then she told me I would go with you to Canada. I knew that whatever it was between you two could not be good; my mother is a midwife and you have no baby. But I am happy not to know the details."

Georgina looks out the little window at the frost-bitten remnants of the garden—black shrivelled pea plant vines and wilted brown potato bushes that were both green a few weeks ago. A deer munches a mouthful of brown grass on the edge of their plot; the animal has no antlers so it must be female. Georgina watches the little doe but doesn't shoo her away: in a moment of generosity, Georgina decides that the deer can have whatever is left for her here in this little cleared patch of land before it snows again.

Georgina continues to talk at Moira, wondering what kind of game the girl is playing by pretending to be naive and uncalculating. She ignores that Moira has called her by her first name for now.

"I grew up with a mother who erased any traces of her Catholic, Gaelic roots. She worked hard to get out of Douglas. She married an Anglican cloth merchant, changed the way she spoke, and left Douglas for Cork. I grew up attending the Church of England. My father was a successful businessman. My sister and I went to a fine finishing school to become ladies. Then, when I was sixteen, my mother told me I was to be married. Like any girl, I was excited. And then I discovered that I was to become wife to a man older than my own father. It was a business transaction. It had nothing to do with love or what was best for me."

Moira listens.

"And I was married to that horrible old man for almost a decade. It makes me shudder to think of how I had to let him lay on me with all his weight and hubris and pathetically pump and grunt away. Mercifully, in one sense, it didn't happen to completion very often—no wonder I never had a child. But I suppose if I had borne that old goat a child, he would not have written me out of his estate. Well, he still may have, since he obviously knew about Mr. Barrett."

Moira isn't sure what Georgina is telling her but feels as if she is hearing a confession.

"When my first husband died, I moved from my lovely house to my grandmother's hovel in Douglas. I really had nowhere else to go after it became clear I could not stay in Cork as the widowed Mrs. Adams. My grandmother took me in. Like you, I soon discovered that I was with child. I knew it was not Bernard's. And I was a widowed, disgraced woman. I could not have a bastard. I would never have a chance to start over if I had a child out of wedlock. And I had no inkling that James would find me. I didn't allow myself to imagine that he would come for me."

Moira wipes sweat from her forehead even though the bedroom is cool. She is nauseated.

Georgina says, "I had to take care of it. I took some herbs. But after a few days, I was still bleeding. And bleeding. It was far worse than what happened to me here this spring, and that was bad enough, as you well know. But my grandmother knew your mother could help. And she did. She came and took care of me. In my delirium and prayers, I told your mother everything—all my sins and secrets. Later, when she heard about my good fortune in becoming Mrs. James Barrett, she came to my grandmother's and demanded that I take you with me to Canada as a housekeeper. That was the negotiation for her discretion. To her credit, your mother saw an opportunity. For you."

Georgina thinks about Deidre's dedication to her daughter,

and she feels sorry for herself that her own mother could not show such love. She thinks about how when her first husband died, and shamed her for her infidelity, Georgina went to her parents' home in the same affluent neighbourhood of Cork where she and Bernard had lived. She stood in the rain, her hand on the red door with a Green Man's face for a knocker, and was turned away by her own mother. In fact, Georgina's mother told her, "You are a disgrace. Do not come back here again." She remembers the feel of water soaking into her boots and the now-familiar hot burn of shock on her cheeks. She knew, for certain, in that moment, that she had no one but herself to rely upon.

Georgina says, "By the time James came for me, by the time he found me in Douglas and asked me to be his wife and come to Canada, it was done. It was too late."

"I did not know." But Moira realizes that even though she hadn't known the details, she had, in some ways, known enough. Moira thinks back to the afternoon her mother told her that she had secured a position for her as a housekeeper to a woman going across the ocean. Moira remembers asking, "Ma, why would this woman take me all the way to Canada? We've never even met face to face. Why in heaven would she want me in her new life?"

Her mother looked at her and said, "Do you not think a woman who needs a midwife in the middle of the night and begs to keep it secret will do things out of the ordinary? Your journey is my price for keeping quiet."

After hearing other pieces of this story, Moira thinks she can understand now why Mrs. Barrett is so cold, so distant; why Mrs. Barrett resents her; and, maybe, why her womb is empty. But Moira, even in her panic at her own situation, cannot imagine being so desperate and selfish as to rid herself of a child. Surely Mrs. Barrett will go to hell for this sin; the Church is clear that life begins before a baby is born.

Georgina says, "I find it hard to believe you never suspected. You must have known."

Moira says, "I was happy not to know the details of what happened between you and Ma. I wanted a chance to have something more, something more than turf fires and hungry mouths to feed."

"And you have very nearly thrown that chance away. What will your life hold now that you've gotten yourself pregnant by another woman's husband—with the child of your employer?" asks Georgina.

Moira does not know how to answer.

Georgina's expression softens and she grabs Moira's hand. "We can give each other a second chance, Moira."

"What do you mean?" the girl asks, confused.

"I thought my barrenness, the baby I lost this spring, and my wandering second husband were my punishments. But now I see my prayers have been answered. I've been thinking all morning: you can have this baby and let me raise it as mine. Mine and James's. After all, it is his child."

"What?" whispers Moira.

"Listen to me, Moira. Some good can come of this. You have a baby you cannot want and I want a baby I cannot have."

Georgina thinks she is convincing the girl, but Moira is actually wondering if Mrs. Barrett is hysterical, losing her senses, to even propose this arrangement. She remembers the day in the store, the day she was thankful for Georgina's accident, as it stopped Mr. Barrett doing what he was doing to her. But perhaps it was the beginning of Mrs. Barrett's going mad.

Moira asks her, "And what will we tell people here, when I go to Mass or to the store, with this baby in my belly?"

"I have thought of that as well. We will tell them you were taken advantage of by a savage—that Cardinal boy who comes here looking for you. The one you disappeared with at the beach in the summer. I am sure that people in this place have been gossiping about that indiscretion for months. The timing works. We will tell people that James and I are going to take in the child out of the goodness of our hearts. James will be transferred soon to manage the new storefront in Edmonton and we will not need to tell anyone how this child came to be: people in our new place will assume he is our son. I have a feeling it is a boy—I do hope he looks like James. In a year's time, no one will know any differently."

"And what will become of me?" Moira asks, feigning anger to mask her fear.

"I am not a cruel woman, Moira. I will arrange for James to pay you a handsome sum and you can leave this place and start over somewhere new. Perhaps he can even find you a post in another Company man's home—somewhere far enough away that no one will know you've had a child. The child you bear us will want for nothing. We will give him every opportunity. I do believe that this is all fate, God's plan, if you will. This is perhaps why we all ended up here."

As she speaks, Georgina imagines writing all this down. *Yes, this makes sense*, she thinks. Of course, she will write this on letter paper rather than in her journal so it can be thrown into the fire if need be.

Moira steels herself to respond. "I do not think God has anything to do with this plan, Georgina. Gabriel Cardinal did not take me against my will. If you say he did, he will be hunted down and punished."

Georgina notices that Moira's expression has changed: her eyes have narrowed and her lips are pursed.

Moira believes that the child she carries is Gabriel's. It has to be. She feels that this baby was made in love not violence. She tries not to think about the possibility that Georgina is right and the child she carries is James Barrett's. She does not know if she could have become pregnant from what he did to her in the Company storeroom a few weeks after St. Anne's Feast Day; he was interrupted. She tries not to feel angry at the young nun from St. Albert who felt compelled to tell Father Lizeé, who felt compelled to tell the Barretts, that Moira had disappeared to the Cree and Métis part of the beach for the night. Georgina accused her, and James punished her. It happened just once, but Moira keeps a chair against her bedroom door as a precaution.

With a steady voice, Moira says to Georgina, "The only savage who harmed me was your husband. That day in the storeroom."

Georgina stands up from the bed and smoothes the front of her skirts. She turns to face Moira on the bed.

"You are lying," she says calmly. "If you were not carrying my husband's child, I would slap you for saying James is capable of such a thing. You've been tempting him since the day we arrived here. He could only resist for so long. He has broken his vows to me though, and for that, I am sure he is sorry. He will agree to my solution to your condition."

Moira decides she will not say any more. She will let Mrs. Barrett believe her husband is the father so she can stay in this house until she can find a way to reach Gabriel and leave Lac St. Anne with him.

Georgina's stance shifts and her voice turns sweeter. "Now, Moira, get some rest and try not to worry. I will take care of everything. Your job for the rest of today is to make sure this baby grows and grows. Next month, I am going to accompany James on a trip to Edmonton for a few days. When we return, we will all sit down at the table and you and I will tell him. News of this baby will be an early Christmas present."

Georgina motions for the girl to get back under the bed-clothes, and a frightened Moira cooperates.

"Everything will be all right. I will make supper this evening."

Moira does not respond.

Georgina leaves the room and goes downstairs into the living room to wait for her husband to return home from the store for dinner.

Georgina waits, and thinks, for many hours after her visit to Moira's bedroom. She writes of her success, and her excitement, in her journal. *I believe I have convinced Moira. I will finally become a mother. And I will not have to compromise my figure! Every challenge presents an opportunity.* Georgina is so caught up in her writing that her attempt to fix dinner results in a burned shepherd's pie. It does not matter: James does not come home to eat, so she throws out the wasted food and makes herself a fresh cup of tea. Georgina realizes she will have to keep her eye on Moira after their conversation. She will need to know where the pregnant girl is at all times and what she is doing. Georgina rarely pays attention to Moira's domestic work as long as meals are ready when James comes home, the floor is swept, and the water is waiting in buckets so she doesn't ever have to go to the pump herself. Georgina now sees Moira as a means to an end, like a prize heifer that will soon give birth and then go to market. This baby is a way to have everything she wants. Her husband may have wandering eyes and roving hands, but Georgina is determined to make the best of this predicament. Georgina knows that for her complicated plan to work, she cannot risk anyone finding out about the arrangement she is trying to put into place—not even that priest Father Lizeé hearing Moira's confession. The settlement is too close, too small, and too hungry for gossip. People here have so little to do.

Georgina writes at her desk until well after nightfall. She has to stop herself from calling out to Moira as she realizes she needs water for her evening toilette. She goes outside, holding a silver pail in one hand and a lit candle in the other, to pump water for her wash basin. The metal of the pump is cold to the touch. She ends up soaking her toes and the bottom of her skirts.

As she tries to avoid dirtying her skirts, Georgina notices the damage the deer has caused in trampling the remnants of the garden. She had been content to let the doe graze on remnants of summer, but the damage looks far worse at ground level than it did from the upstairs window. Georgina thinks, *I will ask James to shoot the animal and get one of the local women to do something with the hide. Maybe I can commission some soft warm booties for the baby; no beading though—I cannot have the baby look the least bit wild.* She hopes that James will be transferred to Edmonton soon and they will have to survive only one more winter in this small, backwards place.

She turns toward a rustling in the bush that edges the property. She thinks she can make out the shape of a large animal—the deer most likely—in the candlelight. Georgina decides she will write about this doe: she will make a beautiful moment out of something mundane, something tedious. Georgina imagines writing: *I shiver as a cool autumn wind lifts burned orange and golden poplar leaves off their branches; they fall to the ground in great piles under the falling darkness of ever-shortening days.*

⟶ Thanksgiving ⟵
OCTOBER 1892

Moira realizes she will have to bargain with Georgina if she is to leave the house on her own. After Georgina's bedroom visit, Moira trembled under her quilt. Her mind raced and her heart pounded. She tried to calm herself. Moira knew that afternoon that she would have to find Gabriel, she would have to walk to the Cardinals' cabin uninvited and find out how to reach him so she can tell him. Moira decided then and there that she would never let Georgina Barrett take her child.

On the third day after Georgina's bedroom visit, Moira wraps herself in her red knit shawl and tells Georgina, "I need to go to confession. I will not speak of the baby's father, and Father Lizeé has sworn an oath to keep my confession a secret. Surely you cannot object to this, Mrs. Barrett. Surely you trust a priest."

Georgina responds, "All right. But if you are gone for more than an hour, I will come to the church myself and find you."

Moira does not understand how fragile Georgina's control over her is. She is too distraught to realize that she still holds a secret that could destroy the Barretts' marriage. Moira is not conniving. She just wants to know where Gabriel is and if he will take care of her. She leaves the Manager's Quarters with a mission.

Moira does not go to Mass. She heads toward the chapel, as she sees Georgina watching her from the kitchen window, and goes through the mission grounds to cross the creek. Moira is in a hurry, so as to not arise suspicion in Georgina, but nausea hits her and she has to pause. She gently sits down on a fallen pine tree at the edge of the creek that divides the settlement. The log is covered with green lichen and clusters of tiny brown mushrooms but still smells of sap. A soft but cool wind rustles through yellow poplar leaves still clinging to the branches. The breeze carries the crisp, slightly damp smell of autumn. Clear water ripples over pebbles at the bottom of the creek. Douglas, the name of the village where Moira lived until she came here, comes from the Irish word for dark stream. But when Moira thinks about home, she thinks not about a creek but about the ocean; this body of water, and the lake named for Christ's grandmother, are both so small in comparison.

Moira knew when she boarded the ship in Cork for Liverpool that she would not return to Ireland. She knew she would become one of the candles lit in the window that made her village look like a map of stars at night. She often thinks of the song "Skibbereen," about a village in County Cork, and the lines where a boy in America asks his father, "I oft-times hear you speak of Erin's Isle / Her lofty scenes, her valleys green, her mountains rude and wild / They say it is a lovely land wherein a prince might dwell / So why did you abandon it, the reason to me tell." Although Moira didn't leave because of famine, or because of oppression, like those a generation before, she still left. Moira misses her mother. She wraps her red shawl tightly around her shoulders as she listens to the stillness at the creek.

Moira thinks of the map that hangs above her family's kitchen table, the table that fed many mouths with so little and held on to secrets spilled over cups of tea. Like other homes in the little village of Douglas, a peninsula jutting off the Irish mainland, the Murphys' cottage was made of turf and sheltered Deidre and Patrick, their children, and, when he was alive, Deidre's father. Hospitality, song, story, craic—these all came from living in a place with an uncertain future and a certainty of rain. The home and the hearth were central to Moira's life. No matter how cramped it was, no matter how many chickens ran loose inside in winter because it was too cold and wet for them to lay eggs outside, no matter how muddy the dirt floor would get from fishing nets hung on the ceiling dripping dry or the necessity of washing clothes inside when the rain had set in for days upon days, people were always welcome in her parents' home. Besides her grandfather, lots of people and animals lived there as Moira grew up: her oldest brother, Paul, and his new moon-faced wife; Michael, her youngest sibling, who was becoming a man; Moira's older sister, Bridgette, before she was sent to the convent; a black-and-white collie called Skib (because he always came running when the basket was brought down from the rafters to hold potatoes); two cats without names who kept the rats at bay; and, in the winter, a goat named Charlie, who didn't do much. Even though their cottage seemed full, the Murphys' family was small compared to most in the village. Four living children was a fraction of most broods. Moira knew that her mother had lost several half-formed, deformed, or stillborn babies and that the loss made her a sympathetic midwife.

As a child, Moira had little knowledge of how her home bore the scars of the Murphys' place in Ireland's history. She grew up in a house of love and song and laughter. By some miracle, she and her brothers and sister were all fed. Sometimes it seemed it was her mother's love alone that nourished them. Moira became aware of how much her parents struggled to make a life out of farming, fishing, spinning, and hoping there would be a good feed of potatoes and less rain that fall. It was a Sunday after

Mass, and after a too-thin mutton stew made in a pot hanging from a crook, that a family conversation changed the boundaries of Moira's world. Moira had just turned sixteen. Paul, Michael, and Pa argued about a notice in *The Times* that Paul had taken down from a bulletin board at the pub the night before. The newspaper in question was months old. It told how the Canadian government, "sympathizing with their fellow subjects of Ireland in their distressed circumstances, joins the Imperial Government in a well considered measure of relief by means of systematic emigration from Ireland."

Paul held on to the piece of newsprint as if it were proof of all problems.

"Can you believe it, Pa?" Paul sighed. "You can't blame people for going to America when they were starving to death, but to go to Canada? To willingly go to another one of that famine Queen's colonies? And not just West Britons, Pa. No, real Irishmen and their women and families. O'Neill said his sister and all her husband's family are packing up for a city called Halifax. A new life, they say. Traitors, he calls 'em. And so do I."

"Traitors." Michael almost spat the word out.

"Ireland is a wounded animal. A dog that's been kicked about so badly she is bleeding out her people. Well, if you beat a dog bad enough, one day she's gonna bite," said Paul. Paul's young wife looked beaten down herself.

Deidre intervened with a bowl of warm rhubarb pudding, which she set in the middle of the table. "Enough, Paul. Michael. Both of you. We're having a Sunday dinner and they'll be no more talk of traitors. Or bleeding dogs. Or that fellow O'Neill. He's nothing but trouble, as I've told you before."

Deidre wiped her hands on her skirt and turned back to the counter.

Pa put down his clay pipe and said, "Listen to your ma. We'll talk of this later."

Michael sulked. Paul threw the scrap of paper on the floor and started talking about the men at the fish market who weren't giving fair prices.

As Moira did the dishes, she repeated the words in her head and strung them together to make a bridge between two countries. This scrap of newsprint made her wonder what it would be like to leave Ireland, although she never really thought she would.

As she sits at the edge of this creek, Moira wonders, *Have I ruined my chance at a new life?* Each hour is filled with a hundred tiny self-flagellations and rationalizations of her situation: *Georgina cannot take this baby. My mother can never know that I have failed her so terribly. It will be all right if I can just find Gabriel.* Moira is frantic and tired—and nauseous. As she puts her head in her chilled hands and breathes to try to calm herself, Moira notices a tiny frog at the edge of the creek.

Moira remembers one autumn afternoon when she and Bridgette were small and her sister convinced her to sneak out of the house and go down the shore to look for mermaids. Their mother had gone to the shop and taken Michael with her, Paul was working with his father, and the two girls had been left to mind the house. They went down to the cliffs that looked as if God had taken a turf-cutter and carved out the green grass and clay to make bays and caves. Moira and Bridgette waited by the shore for hours, not noticing it was starting to become dark until it was. Moira built sand castles and Bridgette took off her stockings and shoes to wade into the icy water and call the sirens. Moira remembers how her sister held her hands out to the sea and let her golden-red hair out of its braid and into the wind. It seemed she stood that way for an hour, although in reality it was likely minutes. Bridgette seemed like the most beautiful girl in the world to Moira.

After Moira pleaded with her to come back to the shore, the girls finally made their way home to their by now distraught parents. Pa thrashed both of them for not making supper and disobeying their mother. Really he punished them for making their mother worry they'd gone too close to the rocks and been swept out to sea. Ma warmed water for Bridgette's feet, because even though she knew they had to be disciplined, she could not afford to lose any more children and was terrified her daughter would catch her death.

The girls' grandfather held a shivering Bridgette on his lap and whispered in Gaelic, "My girl, you must be careful—a woman with red hair who stands barefoot in the sea can cause a sailor to lose control of his ship."

Paul taunted, "So, girls, did you dance your toes off with the fairies?" It was then that Moira decided not to believe in fairies and the like, as it seemed that believing in them brought nothing but trouble. Punishment, however, did not deter Bridgette. She still snuck milk from the pail and left it on the windowsill for the fairies despite being disciplined over and over again for wasting food.

Thinking of milk in a pail almost makes Moira wretch, and she realizes she needs to get up from the log and make her way to the Cardinals' cabin. She needs a resolution. Mr. Barrett has a detailed map of the entire Lac St. Anne settlement, in case he needs someone to make a delivery, and in case he needs to settle an account, and Moira sometimes studied it on the occasional afternoons she would help at the store. In the giddy days that followed her first encounter with Gabriel at the New Year's Eve dance, Moira sought out where the Cardinal family plots were, so she knows now they are on the oldest part of the settlement, on the land closer to the beach and the lake. The creek bed separates the old land from the new land, with its mission and store and road, such as it is. Moira daydreamed that she may one day be invited there to meet his family, to share a cup of tea or even a meal, and be introduced as the girl Gabriel is courting. Moira has never received that invitation, but today that image of where the Cardinals' cabin is on the map has come in handy. She hopes she will not be unwelcome.

Moira knocks on the door. "Hello?"

The cabin smells a little like turf smoke—but sweeter—it is a mule deer hide that Angelique is tanning, but Moira does not recognize the scent.

She knocks again. "Hello? Is anyone home? Is this the Cardinals' residence?"

Moira is greeted only by a mangy-looking dog that appears part coyote or wolf. It searches for food and skittishly avoids her. Moira has a sense either that someone is inside and not answering or that whoever lives here has just left. There is a freshly chopped pile of wood and a kettle hanging over an outdoor fire that has just had its embers doused.

She tries knocking one more time.

Moira thinks about her friend Mahkesîs and how this is the house she grew up in. What would it have been like to be a child here? To know only this place? To have never seen the ocean? She thinks of Mahkesîs, stuck in a mission, like her sister, Bridgette, in the nunnery, punished or punishing herself for, she has heard, having a child out of wedlock. And after what Barrett did to her in the storage room at the store, Moira has no doubt that he did the same to Mahkesîs in those months before she and Georgina arrived from Ireland. She hopes Mahkesîs is all right. She wishes she could see her, but she has neither a reason nor the means to go to St. Albert.

"Hello? Is anyone there? I would like to speak with Gabriel, Gabriel Cardinal."

Moira is met only with silence.

As she turns to go back to Georgina at the Manager's Quarters, the enormity of her situation hits her and Moira decides to give her lie to Georgina some truth: she heads to the chapel before veering home across the creek. Evening Mass will not begin for another few hours, and at this time of year the congregation will be smaller than usual as people try to take advantage of the fading light and the animals rutting. This is the time of year that people need to make a kill that will last into winter, and they know that praying with Father Lizeé is not necessarily going to guarantee any success in that regard.

The empty chapel smells faintly of freshly cut poplar that waits in the cast-iron stove: this late afternoon, it is nearly as cold inside as it is outside. The chapel also smells strongly of incense. The perfume of ritual makes Moira more nauseous. It is quiet in the church. Moira sits in the third row on the right side. It is the same row her family still claims each Mass at the stone church in Douglas. A few years ago, Moira's family filled the length of the pew and her mother beamed with pride at the fact that she, her husband, her elder daughter, Bridgette, her younger daughter, Moira, her elder son, Paul, and her younger son, Michael, all attended Mass together. Then, everything changed: Paul married the moon-faced girl from the cottage down the road, Bridgette was sent to the convent, and Michael stopped coming to Mass altogether. In the months before Moira left for Canada, she and her mother and Pa sat in the pew on their own.

Moira thinks of her sister, Bridgette, shut away in a cold stone building, forced to launder clothes with lye that burns her hands. She imagines Bridgette's daily prayers to the Virgin Mary for forgiveness at her transgression while the boy she loved goes on with his life. She thinks of how Bridgette suffered and repented, only to deliver a dead baby she was not permitted to name or hold or love. She thinks of the letter Bridgette wrote to her shortly after the baby came: "In my mind I've named the baby Oisin—after the great poet from one of Grandfather's stories." Moira thinks of how her beautiful and clever sister, who loved to tell stories and believe in fairies, now lives a life of silence and penance, her long auburn curls shorn and her womanly body hidden under a black robe. Moira wishes she could have said goodbye to her sister before she left for Canada.

And, as she prays in this chapel at Lac St. Anne, Moira thinks about her mother's confessions that night she helped Georgina Barrett, the night that changed everything. Her mother grabbed her by the shoulders and whispered, "Moira. I will never forgive myself for letting Bridgette give birth to her child, my grand-baby, alone in that convent. I cannot do a thing to sway your brother Paul from joining the Fenians. But I can help give you something. You use that woman, her thankfulness to me, and her secret, to get on a boat to Canada."

"Canada . . ." Moira had said. "But Paul and Pa . . . what will they think of me moving to another of the Queen's colonies?"

"You never mind them," her mother had said. "Men seek out their conflicts and rebellions with little thought to the realities of living. Especially the truths of being a woman. Now, you go, my lovely. You take this turn of fate and you help her for a year as I agreed and then you leave her and make your own way—go to America, there are lots of people from Cork there. The new world is a place of opportunity. Tonight has given you a chance at a better life. If you go with this woman, you will not just survive, but you will really live, my girl." Moira was determined to learn from her sister's and her mother's mistakes, sacrifices, and pain.

Sitting in the empty chapel, Moira lets herself cry the first tears she has shed since Mr. Barrett forced her onto the floor of the storage room. Moira will never forget the pain and shock of what was happening. It hardly seemed to be the same act she and Gabriel sacrificed so much for to share at the lake. Moira knows that Mr. Barrett knows what he did to her is wrong. He has barely been able to look at her since. She cannot cry in the house. She does not want either of the Barretts to see her reddened eyes and streaked cheeks, or hear her sniffling. Here, alone in the chapel, she lets herself sob. She has a child on the way, no husband, and first-hand knowledge of what happens to girls like her, like her sister, Bridgette, like her friend Mahkesîs. *Where is Gabriel? Why has he not come back for me as he promised?* she wonders. Moira cries, uninterrupted. When she is out of tears, Moira wipes her cheeks and looks up at the altar. Women have decorated it with the last gifts of autumn: orange and yellow marigolds that survived the first frost drying out in a bundle, a basket of green zucchini from a well-tended garden and bouquets of red cap mushrooms from the wild sitting at the foot of the out-of-tune piano, and a glass jar full of blood-red juice squeezed from tiny high-bush cranberries are all offered to St. Anne. It is another week or so until All Saints' Day, but winter may come in the meantime, so people bring their gifts now.

Moira looks at the statue of St. Anne that sits at the altar in this small wooden church. The icon is one of the few things in this church that is made of stone; the saint's colourful paint is chipping away to reveal a white chalky surface underneath. Father Lizeé has told the story of how the three-foot-high statue came from Quebec when the Church renamed Manito Sakahigan for Christ's grandmother fifty years ago. Moira thinks about the journey this statue made, from a workman's shop in a town or city in Quebec to the settlement here, at this intersection of prairie and boreal forest. Moira thinks about this statue of Christ's grandmother wrapped up in cloth—maybe even a worn striped Company blanket like the one she and Gabriel had that night—stowed away in the bottom of a birchbark canoe. She thinks about what Gabriel has told her about freighting on the Athabasca. Moira thinks about this statue journeying all the way up to and down from Hudson's Bay, knocking against crates of supplies, exposed to the sun and rain and rhythms of the voyageurs' routines. She thinks, *It is a kind of miracle in its own right that the statue survived that journey.*

Moira wonders why this statue was chosen to make the

pilgrimage to her namesake: she is neither remarkable nor beautiful. This St. Anne's face is narrow and plain. The sculptor did not give her eyelashes or plump lips. She wears a bright green robe over a deep yellow dress and has a cream-coloured hood, almost like a habit, that covers her hair and much of her face. She looks like a tired, elderly nun. Her eyes are downcast and she places a hand on the shoulder of a young girl, about half her height, who reads a Bible. The girl has long brown hair and wears a blue robe. *Is she supposed to be Our Lady as a girl?* Moira wonders. Someone has placed a rosary around the young girl's neck. *Is this a statue of mother and daughter? What did St. Anne sacrifice for her daughter, the girl who bore the Son of God? And there is something else about this statue*, Moira thinks. Our Lady stands under a canopy made of hide decorated with pink and red wild roses made from tufts of dyed moose hair. Unlike the other local offerings on this altar, this canopy is not practical. Moira has learned that everything here has a use. *The hide canopy was probably meant to make St. Anne look like she belongs here, and yet it does the opposite.*

Moira prays to St. Anne—not to this statue but to the patron saint of childbirth. She does not ask Christ's grandmother for guidance as she did in the lake, because she knows now what she has to do. Instead, she prays for courage. She needs to find Gabriel and she needs to be with him. She has to trust that Gabriel will take responsibility and be a father. She will have to find a way to start a new life, again. She will have to have faith that what comes next is the real start to her new life, the life that her mother had hoped for her, the life she will make with Gabriel. Moira makes a promise to herself that she will not lose this baby to Georgina, to shame, or to her own complacency.

"I will not be shut away," she says out loud.

Moira hears footsteps behind her: the heavy certainty of Father Lizeé's gait announces his entry into the chapel.

"Can I help you, my child? Mass does not begin for another hour or so. Is there something you would like to confess?"

"No, Father," Moira answers. "I just came to pray."

Father Lizeé gestures to the space beside her.

She nods as he sits down.

"If I may offer some advice . . ."

Moira listens.

"I, too, came here from a very different place. The West, the North, this is not an easy place to live or make a life. There are deep histories here that you and I may never understand but that, in real ways, affect the present."

Moira has no idea how to respond.

"I hope I have not made things difficult for you at the Barretts. But I felt they needed to know about your night with the Cardinal boy. Sister Frances Marie only told me because she felt she had to. You may be lonely, my child, but you cannot give in to temptation and flattery."

Moira wipes her eyes with her shirt cuff.

"Gabriel Cardinal has courted girls before you. I thought I would be marrying him and Bertha Tourangeau."

Moira nods.

"This is a new place, Moira, and there is a world of possibility for you. I am hoping that you will continue your work with the children, on Sundays and in Sister Theresa's schoolroom. You have a patience and a kindness that they respond well to. And you have learned some Cree—that will be valuable. It is important that we keep our school here. I have heard that the Crown is building big schools to start a new kind of education for the Indians. I do not think our children would do well far away from home; it is hard enough that we send them to St. Albert after a few years with us."

Moira looks at the statue of St. Anne.

The priest continues, "Things are changing, my child. You do not have to take vows to be part of the mission, to be a teacher. There is a role for you here, and it does not need to include the Cardinal boy or the Barretts."

"Thank you, Father," Moira says.

"I will leave you to your prayers now." Father Lizeé goes to the altar to prepare for Mass.

After a few minutes, Moira gets up to leave. She crosses herself as she leaves the chapel. Outside, the sun is starting to set, and for some reason, for the second time this afternoon, Moira thinks of the Atlantic. She misses its waves, its salty smell, the way it polishes rocks on the beach so they are shiny and black. That water is so different than the lake here, or the creek she has just crossed, or, she imagines, the Athabasca River that Gabriel left her for. The ocean is deep and ambivalent: like a prairie full of new snow stretching out to the horizon. Like the prairie, men try to tame the ocean and learn its secrets: sometimes they succeed. Moira has to keep hoping that Gabriel will return for her.

✦✦ Rescue ✦✦

LATE OCTOBER 1892

Gabriel ties Trigger up to the post at the Company store in Lac
St. Anne. The first snow has fallen and then melted into the
not-quite frozen ground, and fallen leaves crunch underfoot.
Gabriel knows from the men on his scow team that prices for
fur are better in Edmonton, a man named Secord has opened up
a private store there with the trader McDougall, but Gabriel is
not here to barter or sell anything to Barrett. Gabriel has come
to the store to speak to Barrett, man to man, and ask permission
to marry Moira in a proper church wedding. He and Trigger
have just returned from his work on the Athabasca. Gabriel
pours water from his canteen and cups his hand under Trigger's
mouth; he will feed her properly after his other task is done.

Gabriel has managed to save some money—not as much as
he had wanted to, but he hopes it is enough to convince Barrett
that he will provide for Moira. Gabriel is returning from the
Athabasca River with experiences that have made him a man,
more so than his time in the wilderness when he was twelve,
and while he has vowed never to speak of these experiences of
sacrifice and loss, they will stay with him. Gabriel feels he has
earned the right to make Moira his wife.

Sutherland died of a fever shortly after the crew of five got back to Athabasca Landing, and Muskwa never returned to camp after what he had to do. The doctor who came to the Stopping House to examine Sutherland had quietly apologized. "There is nothing I can do. The toxins have spread throughout his body."

The crew buried the Scotsman by the river; the four remaining men on the scow team, the McClarens who ran the Stopping House, and a priest from the nearest church were his only mourners. Thompson thought that Sutherland had said his woman was camping with her family at Rossdale Flats, near Fort Edmonton. Mrs. McClaren said, "I will try to write to the woman, although there's no guarantee she can read." No one knew if Sutherland had been properly married or if it had been a "country marriage." "At least if it was a country marriage, it should be easier for the woman to move on," Mrs. McClaren had said.

Gabriel hoped for Sutherland's sake that the Athabasca grave was not dark and awful like the mines in Lanarkshire. They had buried Sutherland in early September and Gabriel decided he couldn't go home to Lac St. Anne, not yet. Even though he worried about Moira finding another suitor, he chose to stay north and help build boats for the next summer's work. Much of their commission was lost in the river and so, in the end, the extra trip to Fort McMurray did not bring in much money. Gabriel also still had Muskwa's rifle and was, in a way, waiting for the young man to come back and claim it. Gabriel needed some time before he went back to Moira. He did not want to taint her with this sense of death and loss that he could not wash away.

When the first snow fell, Gabriel felt ready to go home. And now that they have been apart for longer than he anticipated, and she is so close, Gabriel's desire for Moira is even greater than it was when they spent the night together on the beach three months ago. He has not yet gone home to see his grandmother or his mother in the Cardinals' cabin across the creek. Gabriel needs to do this first. He takes a deep breath, opens the door to the Company store, and hears little silver bells announce his entry.

Gabriel does not find Barrett behind the counter but Joseph Auger—a boy he went to school with years ago. The two men speak in Cree.

"Joseph. How are you?"

"Pretty good. How's that baby sister of yours?"

"Fine."

It surprises him that the boys Gabriel went to school with still ask about Mahkesîs. *She could have had any boy on the settlement*, he thinks.

"Heard Adèle's gonna become a nun at St. Albert," Joseph remarks. Gabriel remembers Joseph as a rough little boy, always covered with scrapes and bruises from fighting. His nose is crooked now, and he has a milky white scar across his lip.

"Far as I know." Gabriel tries to smile.

"She's way too pretty to be cooped up at a mission for the rest of her life. Huh. Never thought she'd turn to that. Well, I guess she's better off."

Before Gabriel can ask him to explain, the string of little bells, similar to the ones people put on their sled dogs, ring as the door opens again.

In walks Bertha Tourangeau.

"Hello, Mrs. Castor. How are you?" Joseph asks.

"Fine," says Bertha. She keeps her eyes on the floorboards and her chin tilted to one side.

"Mrs. Castor?" Gabriel asks in surprise. "Well, congratulations, Bertha. Which one of the boys did you marry?"

"Edward," says Bertha. "This summer. After Feast Day. I went to your house to tell you that I was going to marry him. Your mother told me you were on the river."

She raises her chin to meet Gabriel eyes. Bertha has a swollen lip and a cut above her eyebrow.

Gabriel starts to say something, but Joseph intervenes. "What can I get for you today?"

"Flour, please," says Bertha. "Can I put it on the account?"

Joseph pretends to look through Barrett's ledger, knowing full well that Bertha's new husband is banned from charging anything in the store since he has not paid his bill for several months and has a growing gambling debt with Barrett. The credit Bertha had left, from her time as the rabbit snarer, has been used up for many months. Her new husband doesn't want her out and around the settlement, so he saw to it that she was too bruised to do the job of snaring rabbits for dog feed. After weeks of her not showing up, Barrett had no choice but to replace Bertha with a young Callihou boy that he could pay less.

Gabriel looks at Bertha, who not only has bruises, but also a pregnant belly. He smiles, trying to mask his concern.

Joseph says, "Of course, Mrs. Castor. How much do you need?"

"Just a pound," she answers, her voice breaking a little.

"Well, we have a sale on just for today. You can have three pounds for the price of one."

Joseph turns to the shelf behind the counter and gives Bertha a cloth bag full of flour.

"You have just enough credit left in your account for it."

"Thank you," Bertha says humbly, knowing this is a generous lie. "Bye, Joseph. Bye, Gabriel."

Gabriel wants to say something, but Bertha leaves as quickly as she came in.

Gabriel looks at the rare silver fox hanging against the store's wall. There are two small holes where its eyes were. It has been on display in this store for many years, a dark stain near the haunches. a cautionary tale about taking care while skinning a catch. Hides that have been stretched on willow circles and rubbed with brains lie out on a bench. Rich brown beaver pelts will become top hats worn by gentlemen strolling down Fleet

Street a world away. White weasels become the collar on a monarch's robe. Skin away from bones becomes bread on the table.

Gabriel turns to Joseph. "That was decent of you."

"I'm a changed man." Joseph smiles, showing a gap where his tooth should be. "Not so wild anymore. Besides, I'll just take it out of my wages for today and say it was for my ma. Barrett won't care as long as somebody pays. And he won't know."

Gabriel asks, "Joseph—what did you mean before, when you said my sister's better off being a nun?"

Joseph pauses. "People talk about Barrett."

"What do they say?"

"Spends a lot of time at Kelly's and the brothel in Edmonton." Joseph snorts. "That's where he is right now—well, in Edmonton, I mean—but he might be at a brothel too. And they say he lives like he has two wives," he says more seriously.

Gabriel's mouth tightens.

"You know, I drove Barrett to Edmonton to meet them—his wife and the girl—when they came off the train. Thought it was odd then. That Irish girl, she's a beauty. And kind too. Not like the missus. You know the girl, right?"

"Yes," Gabriel answers.

"I heard you're sweet on her."

"Yes. I want to marry her."

"Well, if I know Barrett," Joseph says, looking down at the ledger book, "he'll want to marry her off to another Company man."

Gabriel nods.

"Look, Gabriel, I've always liked you. Barrett's gone to Edmonton today and taken his missus this time. Some Company event. All he's been talking about. That's why I'm here for the rest of the week watching the store."

"Really?"

"Yep." Joseph paused. "Moira's here. She's supposed to come

help me this afternoon. They got Mrs. Yellowknee to stay with her at the house. The Barretts will be gone the rest of the week."

Gabriel's mind races.

Joseph writes something in the ledger. "Too bad about that beautiful sister of yours. I was gonna ask you to tell her I have this good job here. I would make someone a good husband now."

Gabriel puts a coin on the counter. "That's for Bertha's flour." He reaches out to shake Joseph's hand. "Thank you."

"You're welcome." Joseph smiles and the scar on his lip widens. "One of us should get their girl."

Gabriel says, "If I see my sister, I will tell her about today, Joseph."

"I'd appreciate that."

Gabriel nods a goodbye. He leaves the store, slamming the wooden door behind him with enough force to knock the string of silver bells to the ground.

∞

"Thanks be to Mother Mary," Moira whispers. Moira's heart jumps when she looks out the kitchen window and sees Gabriel tie his small grey horse to a post in the fence that surrounds the Manager's Quarters.

Moira was just making a pot of tea for her and Mrs. Yellowknee, asleep in the sitting room with her beading on her lap. Moira has been learning some patterns from her, and both are making the best of the situation that their indebtedness to Barrett has put them in. Still, Moira knows Barrett asked Mrs. Yellowknee to watch her more than to keep her company, and she does not want to put the older woman in a difficult situation. She is glad she has dozed off. Moira wipes her hands on her apron, throws it off, grabs her coat to wrap around her belly, and runs outside.

"Gabriel—I've missed you so much!" Moira wants him to

embrace her, but she stands at a distance. She must gauge the situation before she tells him she is carrying his child. "Where have you been? I thought you'd be back a month ago. Why didn't you come back sooner?"

"Moira . . ." Gabriel puts his arms around the woman he loves and kisses her on the cheek. "I've been working hard. I took an extra job on the river trying to make money for us. Didn't you get my letter?"

"No." Moira is sure Georgina read any mail that came for her and would have destroyed such a letter from Gabriel.

"I wrote to my mother and I wrote to you, Moira. I wrote letters telling you both I would be home when it snowed. Didn't you get my message? I even had Thompson help me with yours to make sure the English was right . . ."

"It doesn't matter. You are here now." Moira's words tumble out. "James and Georgina are gone for a few nights so—"

"I know," Gabriel interrupted her. "That's why I'm here."

Gabriel kisses Moira softly on the mouth.

She lets him and kisses back. She says, "You have a beard . . ." and gently strokes his face.

Gabriel is not sure if her snow-white skin with freckles is a world opening up to him or a world closing in on him, but he knows he wants to try to make a life with her.

"I went to the store to speak to Barrett. I was going to ask him for your hand. When Joseph told me he was in Edmonton, I came to find you straight away. I haven't been home to see my family or clean up and shave."

"You were going to ask him for my hand? You really do want to marry me?"

"Yes, if you'll have me," he answers softly.

Moira blurts out, "I am going to have a baby."

He pulls back and instinctively looks at her stomach. "From the night at the lake . . ." He tries to sound pleased.

"Yes," she answers. "I am going to have your child." Moira hopes that if she says it out loud, it will be true.

"The Barretts did not want you to be with me before. I'm not sure if Barrett would have said yes when I asked his permission to make you my wife. What will he think if he knows this—does anyone know you're with child? Does Barrett know?"

"Oh, Gabriel . . ." Moira fights back tears. "Mrs. Barrett knows. She scares me. She's gone mad, I think. She wants me to give her the baby to raise as her own."

Moira knows that if she tells Gabriel what Barrett has done to her, Gabriel may doubt that he is the father and perhaps won't rescue her. She also knows Gabriel could try to hurt the Englishman. And Gabriel would be caught. Moira knows she has to keep quiet. It is just something she needs to put out of her mind and forget ever happened. Now that Gabriel has come for her, maybe she can.

Gabriel is calm. "Go pack a few things. Just things you can't leave behind. We'll be on horseback. We'll leave right away."

"Why can't we stay at Lac St. Anne?" Moira asks. "Father Lizeé would marry us tomorrow if we explained. We can live with your family. I'm sure your mother could use extra help now that winter's coming. I'm a hard worker."

"I know," Gabriel says. "But Barrett could protest it. He could come and take you back. And he's friends with Mounted Police."

Moira looks at him, her head titled, confused.

Gabriel thinks, but doesn't say, *To be a Mounted Police, a man has to be a British citizen and has to be unmarried. How would such a person understand that I love you and you belong with me, not at Barrett's house? Those men are like priests, but with better guns—they will side with an Englishman over a trapper and scowman.* There is no love lost between them and the Métis since the rebellions. Gabriel knows that he and

Moira have to leave. He needs her to trust him and follow him.

"We need to leave here today," Gabriel announces. "We will have to stay away for a while. Maybe until after the baby is born. Will you come with me?"

Moira nods but her hands tremble.

Gabriel moves to her. "Do not be afraid, Moira." He holds her around the waist and kisses her cheek again.

Moira closes her eyes and sighs. She lets herself be in his arms. She will leave with Gabriel. She will let him take her away from Lac St. Anne. She does not really understand why they have to leave this place, the second place she has ever lived, but she knows she cannot risk Barrett stopping her from being with Gabriel.

Gabriel sees the sadness in her eyes. He reassures her. "I love you, Moira. I want to make a home with you. It just may be a while before we can do it right."

Moira nods.

"Let's get on our way. We need to make good time while the weather is mild." He kisses Moira's forehead. "Go back into the house and pack what you need."

Moira does as he says.

Gabriel finds himself in the Barretts' mud room. He remembers last spring when all he wanted was to be invited inside. Moira raises her fingers to her mouth. "Ssh." She motions to him. She needs to check if Mrs. Yellowknee is awake or asleep. Gabriel waits in this room that separates outside from inside. He wonders if this is the kind of house Moira wants to live in with him.

Gabriel's father and brothers built their home by chopping down poplars and mixing clay and mud. The Englishman was given this house by the Company and it was built by other men. Someone else painted it white. This floor is made of wood, not dirt. Looking into the kitchen, Gabriel sees china dishes displayed in a redwood cabinet that probably came from England, pots hanging on hooks, and a sewing machine on top of a long table near the cast-iron stove. Gabriel thinks of how the windows in the married men's quarters at the fort were stretched animal skin that yellowed the light. His mother spent the winter in there with babies and toddlers, preparing meal after meal of greasy pemmican, and hoping her husband's traps were full. Gabriel remembers the dogs begging and scavenging around the fort's edges. As soon as the snow started to melt, their smells filled every corner.

Like the world of the buffalo to the south, this world has disappeared, and sometimes Gabriel thinks it's for the best. He wants more and he wants to have more with Moira. But the land the Crown's offering the Cree and Métis is swamp and unfit for planting anything. Eighty-three dollars is not enough to start a life. Gabriel knows he will have to keep trapping, and probably go back to the river for a few more summers (which makes it hard to farm), to make enough money so he can build a white wooden house where Moira can have a garden to grow things like purple lavender and yellow daffodils just because they look nice. But right now, he knows he just needs to take Moira away.

With her few possessions in a small bag, Moira leaves the Manager's Quarters with Gabriel.

"Are you ready?" he asks.

"Yes," Moira answers. She almost wishes that the old woman had been awake so she could talk with someone about what she is about to do. *But it is for the best, really*, Moira thinks, *seeing as I am leaving and do not want to put her in more of a difficult position than she will already be in when she wakes up and I am gone.*

Gabriel looks at Moira's cloth bag with flowers on it and realizes she has no idea how to be outside or in the bush. He says, "We need to stop at my parents' home. We need to get you some warm leggings and gloves that will withstand the cold."

Moira nods. Gabriel helps her onto Trigger and they cross the little creek that divides the settlement.

When they reach the Cardinals' cabin, Gabriel ties Trigger up to a post and gestures for Moira to dismount. She shakes her head. "No, it is better if I stay outside."

It is Gabriel's turn to nod. "You'll be all right? You are warm enough?"

Moira replies, "Yes," and makes an effort to smile.

Part of Gabriel hopes that no one is at home, as it would be easier to pretend and write his mother that he had decided to stay up at Athabasca Landing for a few more weeks. He carefully opens the cabin door and, of course, his grandmother is here, sitting beside the fireplace in the rocking chair with a blanket over her legs. A kettle boils water over the fire. Gabriel can see that Angelique is beading a pair of deerskin gloves with her signature rose. She chews tobacco.

Gabriel sees how his grandmother looks at him. She will see a man with a sense of urgency, an unkempt beard, and worry. She will see that this is not a homecoming.

"Tân'si, Nohkum," he says, kissing her on the cheek. "I'm just here to get a few things." He speaks in Cree.

"You've been gone for months. Where are you off to now?"

Gabriel doesn't answer. "Do you know if Mahkesîs still has any of her winter clothes here?"

"Ehâ. Why? Are you going to St. Albert to see your sister?" The old woman keeps her eyes on her handiwork. She creates a circle of yellow beads for the centre of a deep pink wild rose.

"Maybe," Gabriel lies and feels a pang of guilt. "Can you tell me where I could find a pair of deerskin leggings, some good gloves?" He looks around the cabin, assessing what he can take that will be of use and will not be too missed.

"Wait and you can take these gloves I'm beading to your sister. I was going to trade them, but she will need a new pair for winter."

"I can't wait, Nohkum," Gabriel says this softly. He moves closer and kneels at her feet. "And I am not going to see Mahkesîs."

His grandmother looks at him.

"I am going away with Moira."

The old woman says, "The one you brought to me at the lake. Let her be."

"I can't, Nohkum." Gabriel takes the needle out of her tattooed hand so he can enclose her hand in his. He knows it is a risk, but he has to explain to his grandmother why he is leaving the same day he returned, why she will not see him for a long time. "I have to take care of Moira. I love her. I am going to make her my wife."

As he sits close to his grandmother, Gabriel can smell that she has just put bear grease in her braid.

"Moira is going to have my child."

Angelique chews, spits, and looks sternly at her youngest grandson. "Emm-hmm. I see. Stay here. Make her your wife here. Go to the priest today."

He shakes his head. "We need to leave, Nohkum. Moira lives with Barrett. He brought her over here from Ireland. He has a say in who she can marry—and I don't think he'll want it to be me."

The mention of Barrett's name makes Angelique wince. She thinks of her sweet Mahkesîs and the baby being raised by Thomas and Ida. *One man has caused my family so much pain*, she thinks. *He has driven both my favourites away from Lac St. Anne.*

"We have to go away from here for a while, but we'll be back. Once the baby is born and we are married."

"You come back for the next gathering at Manito Sakahigan. I want to meet this child. I hope it looks like you."

"Nohkum, don't tell anyone I came home. Moira's guardian may look for us, and we need to get a head start." He stands up and adds, "I have a gun."

Angelique stands up and goes over to her bed.

"Take this point blanket," she says, handing it to him. "Take that cradleboard up in the loft." She points. "You'll need these things." She shuffles to the cupboard near the table. "Take a pack of pemmican. It lasts a group of six men a hundred miles. If you don't eat it all, you can trade it," she says as she gestures to a block of dried moose meat and saskatoons.

"But, Nohkum, you need to sell that."

Angelique touches Gabriel's face and sighs. "You need it more. You cannot go off into the bush with a pregnant girl and no food." She does not think she will see him again. Angelique has always loved Gabriel and his sister the most.

∞

"As it snows, their fur changes. White ones make more money."

Gabriel splits the skin and hair from a grey-brown weasel and exposes the rodent's soft pink muscle. The young trapper throws the carcass into a bucket, carefully places the fur on a worn piece of moose hide to protect it from dirt, and uses a rag to wipe the blood from his fingers. He reaches into his pack and picks out a new body to flesh. Gabriel's hands move over the little weasels with the same precision he uses to play the fiddle. His hands move with the same care as when he made love to Moira, months ago at the lake. Moira sits on a tree stump and watches him work. Gabriel has taken her deep into the brush. He figures they have until nightfall until Mrs. Yellowknee confides in someone about Moira's disappearance. He skins the weasels now because he does not want to travel with the little corpses. Moira pulls her red shawl tight around her shoulders.

An autumn frost has turned the grass brown, and the first snow has melted into the dirt; blood from the weasels splatters the ground like juice from a summer cranberry.

Moira decides that now is as good a time as any to ask. "Is it true that Mahkesîs had a baby?"

Gabriel pauses and turns to look at her. There is no reason to keep secrets now. "Yes," he answers. "She had a little boy. He is being raised by my brother Thomas and his wife, Ida. They have a child around the same age."

"Oh," says Moira. She cannot reveal why she suspects Barrett is the father of Gabriel's nephew, so she asks, "Did she tell you who the father is?"

"No," says Gabriel. "She knows Papa and I would go after him. And, for some reason, she doesn't want to be with him. She left Lac St. Anne for the mission at St. Albert. Maybe she was not ready to be a mother."

Moira feels a slight, on behalf of her friend, but also feels she should reassure Gabriel. "I am ready," she says. "I will be a good mother to this little one. I think it is a boy." She places her right hand on her small belly.

"I have no doubt," Gabriel says softly. He thinks about Moira's ease and lightness with the children at Sunday school and knows he really has no doubt she will be wonderful with their baby. He feels guilt for not preparing for this possibility, for convincing and seducing Moira at the lake, and relief that this did not happen with Bertha or the first girl. He turns to her and says, "I am sorry I did not come back sooner. I just wanted to earn some extra money and . . ."

"It's all right," says Moira sweetly. "We are together now. That is all that matters." And again, Moira hopes that if she says this out loud it will be true.

The two leave the little clearing as soon as the sun sets. Gabriel and Moira ride the small grey horse and try to get as far away from Lac St. Anne as quickly as they can before the Barretts return from Edmonton and discover Moira's absence. Moira quickly left them a note, before she thought it through, when she was gathering up her small bag of belongings. She has not told Gabriel she did this. *He has enough to worry about*, she thinks. Moira is not used to riding, and the growing baby in her belly makes it uncomfortable. Still, pure exhaustion lets her sleep sitting upright for part of the night. Trigger leads Moira and Gabriel east across the bush until the sun comes up.

Gabriel stops Trigger and dismounts. He puts out his hand for Moira to help her dismount. He says, "Let's set up shelter here and rest for a few hours." The young man cuts down three young trees to make poles. Gabriel shows her how to unroll the moose-hide canvas. Moira does as she's told and wonders how many days they will camp like this. Gabriel looks around. He sighs. "We can start a fire and it will be warm inside."

Moira agrees. "We are together."

Once inside the tent, Gabriel lays out his sleeping mat. Moira lies down and pulls a red-and-black-striped blanket over herself. Gabriel lies down beside her. He kisses her shivering lips. He remembers her clean, sweet taste—like berries and soap. She lets him put his cold hands underneath her woollen winter jacket and her thick linen blouse. He strokes her neck, her breasts; his hands are now warm. He maps his desire on her body with his fingers. He puts his lips on the skin that shows through an opening in her blouse. She reaches down and touches him. He moans. He works hard not to lose control. He carefully pulls up her skirts and arranges to gently put himself inside her. "The baby?" he asks, and she answers, "It's all right." It is too cold for them to lie naked together, as they did at Lac St. Anne, and Gabriel feels the layers of clothes between them. He is careful not to kick her with his boots. He is careful not to press too heavily on her belly. Still, her body remembers, and once again her hips arc to meet his rhythm. There is now a hint of sadness in their lovemaking; it is less innocent and less careful than at the lake. Gabriel thinks it is because Moira has missed him, and he is partly right.

Afterward, Gabriel pretends to sleep. His mind whirls with questions and keeps him awake. If he knew what he knows now when he met Moira ten months ago at the New Year's Eve dance, would he have pursued her so relentlessly? Gabriel remembers how Moira watched him play the fiddle with a group of other young men. He remembers how his left foot tapped against the uneven floorboards covered in a fine layer of dirt. He longs for his birch fiddle, how his chin rests on the naked end and his hands caress it just as his hands caress Moira's body. *Can we go back?* Gabriel wonders. *Can we really start again somewhere new? Will we be able to travel far enough away, and fast enough, that Barrett will not find us and take her away from me?*

Gabriel kisses her cheek and gets up to leave the tipi. Moira does not stir and she does not hear his footsteps on the frozen grass—he's used to trapping and he knows how to move without being heard.

It is snowing now, and Gabriel recognizes the difference between early spring and late fall on the prairie. New snow means winter is coming, but it also purifies, covers, whitens. It brings change, even if in that change, everything seems still. Everything he has is in that small tipi. Gabriel knows he has to keep them safe from the cold.

⤞ *Discovery* ⤝
NOVEMBER–DECEMBER 1892

Mahkesîs sits on the edge of the bed in the small room she shares with Sister Frances Marie and Sister Ignatius at the Youville convent. Sister Frances Marie is fast asleep. It is half-past six, according to the brass pocket watch Mahkesîs has borrowed from Father Bernier's trouser pocket to time her escape, and Sister Frances Marie will soon be getting up to wake the children and join the other nuns to lead them in morning prayer before breakfast. Sister Ignatius is in the children's room tonight; the women take turns sleeping in the big communal room with their wards. If Mahkesîs does not leave the mission tonight, she will have to wait another three days before she is out of the old nun's sight, and by then it will likely be snowing. It is surprising that it hasn't yet, since yesterday was All Saints' Day.

It is not the best time to travel, but Mahkesîs needs to leave now or she will have to wait until spring. The days are getting shorter; the sun crests over the hill a little later each morning. Mahkesîs has made preparations to travel on foot: she has been able to take some old cheese and bread from the pantry without Sister Ignatius noticing, and she has taken a pair of brown woollen trousers and a man's white cotton shirt while doing Father's laundry and mending. She has also packed some of the willow-bark tea she made to soothe aches and pains. She is using the small moose-hide sack that she came here with to carry these supplies.

Mahkesîs was ready to leave before daybreak, but for some reason she couldn't. She has already sat on the hill and stared out into the dark eastern horizon. She sat on the frosted brown-green grass outside the mission and watched her breath form smoke-like rings in the cool fall air. News of Gabriel's leaving Lac St. Anne with Moira has stirred something in her; it has led her to this morning and her decision to leave St. Albert. But something has also called her back inside the residence before she can start her journey.

"Sister," Mahkesîs whispers as she gently shakes the other woman's bare foot under a woollen blanket. "Sister Frances Marie."

The young nun opens her eyes, confused. "Mahkesîs, what is it? Are you all right?"

"I'm fine."

"It's so early . . . barely morning . . ."

"I want to say goodbye."

"What?" The metal bed creaks as Sister Frances Marie sits up.

Mahkesîs will not miss these hard beds—the same kind as in the children's rooms. Sister Ignatius ordered them from a catalogue and they came on a canoe from the York Factory. They are thin; it's as if they're designed to make it difficult for children to cuddle and sleep two or three to a bed as they would have at home. Mahkesîs doesn't know why the mission doesn't have wooden beds, beds someone local could make for the children.

"I'm leaving," says Mahkesîs.

"Where are you going?"

"West."

"To Lac St. Anne?"

"No. Lac St. Anne is north. I am going west to the mountains."

"Where? What do you mean?" The young nun rubs her eyes.

"I heard Father Bernier talking about this new mission in the mountains. People there are mostly Métis, Cree, and Iroquois. And some explorers from the East. I've heard my father talk about a post called Jasper House."

"Why do you want to go there?"

"I'm going to learn from the people there before everything changes there too. There are lakes with healing powers, lakes like Manito Sakahigan, lakes with blue-green water found nowhere else. Lakes that haven't been renamed yet."

"It is practically winter. How will you travel by yourself? It's not safe for a woman!"

Mahkesîs looks at Sister Frances Marie: her brow is wrinkled and her eyes are wide with concern. She hears the worry in her friend's voice. But Mahkesîs is not scared of her planned journey. When she thinks about danger, she remembers being trapped inside Barrett's house and trapped under him on the kitchen floor. She thinks of this little room—a former married men's quarters Father Lacombe salvaged a few years ago as a living quarters for him and Sister Ignatius, one each, when the fort started to be dismantled—and how the walls are haunted by past and present desperation and resignation. She thinks about the mornings she has woken up here and been disappointed not to have died in her sleep. Mahkesîs isn't scared of the land, the snow, the wild, the bush. She knows how to navigate, how to survive winter, how to work with nature—even when it is harsh or ambivalent.

She looks at Sister Frances Marie.

"I took these clothes from Father Bernier when he gave them to me for mending," she says, trying to assuage her friend's worry.

The young nun's eyes have adjusted to the dark and she can see that Mahkesîs is wearing brown woollen trousers, a tartan woollen vest with patches, and a buckskin jacket. On her feet are the high moccasins she came here with that Sister Ignatius took away. Mahkesîs has tucked her dark hair into a bun rather than a braid and is wearing a man's tartan county cap. Sister Frances Marie could cover for Mahkesîs for a day or so, but Father Bernier will notice if one of his hats, or his prize buckskin jacket he received as a "welcome" present from women in his parish, goes missing. He values his few possessions. The young nun does not think Mahkesîs's disguise will fool anyone: her face is far too beautiful to pass for a man's.

Sister Frances Marie feels panic rise up in her chest. She can't lose Mahkesîs.

"You can't leave," she says.

"Your calling is to God. Mine is not. I came here because I thought I had nowhere else to go. I don't belong here."

"Don't leave today, please. Let's think this through. You don't have to stay here, but you need a better plan."

"Like what?" Mahkesîs asks, surprised that Sister Frances Marie is not telling her that what she is about to do is wrong.

"I don't know yet, but I'll come with you. I can ask to be transferred to this mission in the mountains, to where you are going."

"Really?" Mahkesîs is surprised. "St. Albert is the only place you have been since leaving your parents' home in Quebec. Why would you be willing to leave?"

"I don't want to be without you." The young nun does something she has never done before but something she has thought about doing since the day she and Mahkesîs went mushroom picking. Marie kisses Mahkesîs. On the mouth, on the lips.

Mahkesîs doesn't pull back. The kiss is sweet, soft, and right. For the first time in her life, a kiss comes without expectation, demand, or a veiled threat of violence.

"All right," Mahkesîs says. "I'll wait."

∞

Mahkesîs has always known winter as the time of year when her father, uncles, and brothers spend their days reliving fall's moose hunts and waiting for a mild day to ice fish. This winter Mahkesîs finds herself still at the mission, and yet it is a winter that is more like spring because it is full of possibility and newness. She has not abandoned her plan to leave St. Albert but realizes that travelling will be far easier in the spring. She returned Father Bernier's buckskin jacket, gloves, and woollen cap the same morning she took them. She has stored the trousers, shirt, and vest, pretending to be mending them. She again wears the same grey pinafore that Sister Frances Marie wears (but over her own fraying yellow-and-green calico dress). Since that chilly autumn morning a few weeks ago, when Mahkesîs almost left and Marie's mouth made her stay, everything has changed and Mahkesîs is willing to wait. She no longer feels trapped. She no longer feels that if she stays here she might die. Nor does she wish to any longer.

Every third night, Mahkesîs and Marie are alone together. They plan and dream and explore. In these quiet hours, Mahkesîs and Marie speak of what life will be like west of here, in the mountains. Mahkesîs wonders if she really can claim the two-hundred-and-forty-dollar fortune that scrip would bring and what she would do with the money. She cannot imagine having so much and yet knows that the costs of things—a rifle, a hide to make a tipi, blankets, some pemmican, silk thread and beads and other supplies to make moccasins and gun cases and gloves and buckskin jackets to sell—could eat up much of that, let alone if they go without Father Bernier and have to find a place to stop at until they decide if they are going to stay. They talk of what they will do in this new place, how they will make a living and a life together. They imagine how high the mountains will be—higher than the hills of Île d'Orléans, Marie imagines—but neither woman can quite comprehend what it will be like to live on cragged rock, on a crèche for curly horned mountain goats grazing fireweed in late summer. Mahkesîs knows there are elk and bear in the mountains. She knows what to do with both of these animals, how to slice the hide from the carcass and still preserve the fur and tan the skin, and she was a decent shot with a rifle when she had the chance to practise with Gabriel but she would not call herself a hunter. *Will there be red caps and shaggy manes and saskatoons and low-bush cranberries there?* Mahkesîs wonders. How will she learn which mushrooms and berries are safe to eat? She can imagine the lakes. *What kind of fish swim in the mountain lakes said to be a blue unlike any other, more beautiful even than the water of Manito Sakahigan?*

Every third night the women allay each other's fears about the future between kisses and sighs of pleasure. They assure each other that they will be all right if they can be together. Mahkesîs has started to live each day for every third night. What happens every third night is possibility—the possibility of a life that is more than just survival. It may be a chance of living a life with love.

And this possibility has made Mahkesîs feel again. When she first arrived at the mission, she was numb. She had kept her body busy. She tried to will herself into forgetting: what Barrett had done to her, the weight of her baby in her belly, and, for a few strange weeks, his little body curled in her arms, at her breast, as he made himself even smaller. Most of all, Mahkesîs had tried to forget the love that had taken her by surprise: after all, considering where the baby had come from, and all she had to give up for him, Mahkesîs had no reason to feel anything but resentment for this child. But the moment her grandmother put him to her breast, Mahkesîs was in love. He was hers, and in spite of the hundred reasons not to love him, Mahkesîs knew in that instant that she would never love anyone as much or with so much conviction as she did this squiggling baby.

A few weeks after arriving at the mission, after it took up too much energy to be numb, to feel so little, was when the desire to die slowly emerged. Mahkesîs knew that taking her own life was wrong. The priests and nuns said it was a sin and would result in an eternity in purgatory. Taking her own life would cause her mother and father shame at not being able to bury their daughter in consecrated ground. But it wasn't only religion that taught Mahkesîs how precious life is. It was her grandmother's stories of her life as a young mother, watching her children and husband die of a disease with no name in her language, and wandering the camps hoping to find someone to help her and finding only abandoned gatherings or tipis full of corpses. It was this same knowledge of life's intransigence that kept Mahkesîs from eating green potato peels or drinking raspberry-leaf tea when she suspected she was carrying a child from James Barrett. Mahkesîs could not help but imagine, indeed hope, that she might come down with the coughing illness that sometimes affected the children here, or that one of Sister Ignatius's blows to the back of her head might knock the life out of her, or that eating an old piece of improperly cured moose meat may lead worms to lay eggs in her gut and eat her from the inside out. Being dead seemed like an easier alternative. It was easier to imagine these horrors than face the truth: Mahkesîs was suffering from heartbreak at the thought of never being able to hold her son again.

Now, every third night, she experiences love and hope and light even though winter is not a time for this kind of love. Mahkesîs knows winter is not a time for abundance. This is the time of quiet solitude in the darkness, days sitting next to other women but not always speaking, muted candlelight, rationed whiskey, and the pungent scent of burning spruce in the stove. This is the time of year to be still and careful, and love is the antithesis of both. Winter is the time of year that fits in the palm of the hand—like your own breath warming the fingers, like the body of a tiny black wren fallen from its nest, like the tear-stained cheek of a small Métis child missing her home. And yet it is in these darkest, deepest, shortest days of winter that Mahkesîs falls in love with Marie.

And with Marie, there is so much to discover—her childhood milking cows and picking apples near the plains of Abraham, her thoughts on God and morality and what it means to be good, her excitement to see the mountains' tall peaks and deep valleys. This is a different love than when Mahkesîs held her baby and it is different than when her older and younger brothers' friends would try to catch her eye or stare at her body or tell lewd jokes for her to overhear. What she and Marie share every third long night seems different than what she has heard happen between her mother and father in the muffled darkness of the Cardinal home. As Mahkesîs goes about her tasks at the mission—scrubbing floors, peeling potatoes, making stew out of a small cut of moose meat, and hemming and mending clothes—she counts down the hours until she can again lie next to Marie. She thinks about Marie's mouth and how her lips feel against her skin as they kiss her collarbone. Mahkesîs wants to feel Marie's skin against hers, she wants to hear her sigh and murmur with anticipation, she wants to taste her pleasure, she wants to know her rhythms so well that they become her own. She wonders, *Is this the love I have been waiting for? Or is this just the way to survive right now?* For Mahkesîs, survival has been about not letting in pain, and this, whatever this is between her and Marie, is teaching her what pleasure is, what desire means. But it also risks a whole new world of pain. It is a love that could break her wide open.

Mahkesîs knows what is happening between her and Marie is dangerous. To lie together like man and wife, and share the pleasure they share, is a sin. There will be terrible consequences if anyone discovers them. *In this place, maybe any kind of freedom, any chance at happiness, is dangerous,* Mahkesîs thinks.

It was Sister Ignatius who told Mahkesîs the rumours about Gabriel running away with her friend the Irish girl. Sister Ignatius has told Mahkesîs, "Adèle, I am praying that your brother will come to his senses and turn himself over to the Mounted Police. He will hang if anything happens to that girl. I hear her guardian, Mr. Barrett, is a Company man. Any Company man has powerful friends."

Mahkesîs does not have faith in any prayer that comes from a woman who lines little girls up against the side of the schoolroom and whips them with a willow branch when they say "Manito" instead of "Our Father." From a woman rumoured to once, years ago, have driven nails through a little boy's hands to teach him of stigmata. From a woman who left Payesîs Belcourt with three milky scars across the small of her back for more than thirty years. *What does this old nun think will happen to a Métis man who has taken a white girl away from her English employer? What does she think a man hired to represent the interests of the Company on a Catholic Métis settlement will do if Gabriel "turns himself in"? Who—or what—could Sister Ignatius possibly be praying for in this situation?*

In the past, Gabriel could have left and no one would have followed him. But Mahkesîs knows from both of her parents that relationships between anyone who was native in any way and anyone who was white changed after Riel's rebellions. Mahkesîs was just a little girl then, but she remembers her father and mother arguing after he returned home with a black eye, a missing tooth, and a recently acquired rifle. Mahkesîs couldn't control that world of power, men, politics. But she has learned that as a woman she does have control over her own body. She has promised herself that she will never be in that position again— ever. Her brother Gabriel had courage and conviction—not only to take the risk of leaving and being caught by the Mounted Police or, worse, Barrett himself, but also to make sacrifices to be with the woman he loved. And it gave possibility to the fantasy; it made Mahkesîs dizzy to think that maybe she could run away too and, even, run away with Marie.

At Mass this past Sunday, Father Bernier spoke about the difficulties of birth—which was a little surprising from a priest. He connected what was happening in the nation with scripture leading up to the Holy Season. He said to his congregation, "Birthing anything is always painful, and messy, and our new country is no exception." He read from one of Mahkesîs's favourite Bible stories: the angel Gabriel's visitation to Our Lady. She knows it word by word because Virginié used to tell it to her and Gabriel when they were children to explain her brother's name. Mahkesîs has always liked the part where the angel Gabriel tells Mary, "Do not be afraid, Mary, for you have found favour with God." She knows how frightened Mary must have felt with the responsibility of bearing a son without a husband, and the Son of God at that. And she thought it was probably true what the Bible story said, that Mary accepted the angel's explanation and told him, "I am the handmaid of the Lord. May it be done to me according to your word." What else can women do? Mahkesîs believes the part of the story that once Mary accepted this, the angel Gabriel left her alone.

From her own experience, she knows that pregnancy is a hard and lonely time. She knows her situation was particularly difficult, but she also has memories of aunties and sisters-in-law throwing up into a bucket beside the stove or struggling to skin hides with a bulging belly while being kicked from the inside. How she felt a gush of water trickle down her bare legs as she worked in the garden. How she gave birth to her baby on the floor of her parents' cabin while her mother held her hand and patted her brow with a soft wet rag. How she held him to her breast even before Nohkum cut the cord connecting his little body to hers.

On one of their nights together, as they lie together in the single bed with their bare legs intertwined under a woollen blanket, Marie says to Mahkesîs, gently but firmly, "Tell me about the father of your child."

Mahkesîs shakes her head.

"Who was he? Did he love you as I do?" Marie asks playfully as she strokes the inside of Mahkesîs's thigh with her gentle fingers.

"No," she whispers. "He did not love me at all. He forced me."

Marie pauses and Mahkesîs pulls away a little. She tells Marie about the thunderstorm and the beading needle in her apron. She tells Marie about the time after that first time, and the times after that. She tells Marie about how she could tell no one, first because her family needed the money she was being paid to cook and clean and then because she feared her father or brothers would get themselves in trouble by hurting Barrett. The words tumble out like berries spilling from a basket. And Marie listens until Mahkesîs is done.

Then Marie holds her closer and lets her sink into her arms. She says, "Mahkesîs, I am so sorry this happened to you."

And for the first time, Mahkesîs knows that what Marie says is true: she deserves forgiveness and grace and compassion. The tears come without permission, and Mahkesîs cries silently in the gentle arms of the woman she loves.

Marie's love, and her faith in her, has made Mahkesîs strong again. In the days after her confession, she decides that in the spring, before they go west to the mountains, she will go home to Lac St. Anne. She will thank her brother and his wife for taking in her child and tell them that she is ready to be a mother to her son. Her grandmother will help her. And her baby will be all right as long as he is with her. And Marie.

She and Marie will be able to love each other differently in the spring—in the light and the hope and the world's affirmation of newness.

∞

Mahkesîs dreams that a crow is sticking its sharp orange beak into her shoulder blade. She shrugs to push it away. It keeps poking. She opens her eyes and turns her body around to face something black, something still, in the doorway. It is Sister Ignatius.

Marie, whose back was against her front and whom she had her arm around, sleeps deeply beside her. Mahkesîs wordlessly jolts her awake.

"Quelle est cette abomination?" asks Sister Ignatius in a flat caw.

Mahkesîs puts her feet on the floor to stop her head from spinning. She stands up, and the wooden floor creaks underneath her bare feet. She is only wearing a thin nightdress and is aware that Sister Ignatius can probably see through the cotton with her candlelight. It is icy cold.

"Why are you here? Why aren't you with the children?" Mahkesîs asks the old nun, her voice wavering. She has to think to find the words in French.

The two women are usually more careful than this—putting a chair against the door and moving to separate beds afterward in case Sister Ignatius comes by—but today is December 24 and both women have been run off their feet with preparations and comforting homesick children. They fell asleep in each other's arms.

The old nun glares at Mahkesîs. "I came to ask for one of your remedies, Adèle. One of the girls is coughing up blood and I don't want to send word to the hospital until morning unless absolutely necessary." She pauses. "Answer my question. What is happening in this room? Why are you sharing a bed with Sister Frances Marie as if you are husband and wife?"

"Sister Ignatius, I . . . we . . ." Sister Frances Marie, who is now sitting up with the blanket under her chin, stutters.

"Someone answer me!" the old nun growls.

"Don't say another thing, Marie," says Mahkesîs. "We don't have to explain anything to this woman."

"Yes, you do. I am the head nun at this mission and I will not have this depravity on my watch. Both of you need to go to Father Bernier immediately and ask for confession."

"We have not done anything wrong," says Mahkesîs.

Ignoring her for the moment, Sister Ignatius speaks to Marie. "Your weakness is your downfall. We all have temptations of the flesh, but we must not give in to them. We are married to Christ—he is our husband, our love, our saviour. The devil is in you, Marie, much more so than I realized. I can help you overcome this." The old nun almost sounds kind.

"Now, as for you." She looks hard at Mahkesîs. "You will leave in the morning. Your wildness has corrupted Sister Frances Marie. It was a mistake for Father Bernier to welcome you here in the first place. I feel shame that you share a name with that wonderful Sister Adèle who came here years ago with Father Lacombe. Go back to your kind. Go back to the bush of your little settlement that God has all but abandoned. Devil's Lake."

Mahkesîs knows she should hold her tongue, but something about that name, Devil's Lake, enrages something deep.

"It was never the Devil's Lake. It was—still is for many—called Manito Sakahigan. It is a sacred place for my people. Your kind didn't understand that. You may call it Lac St. Anne, but it was a gathering place long before you ever came here. And it will be long after you are gone."

The old nun starts to speak, but Mahkesîs interrupts her, "And Sister Frances Marie is coming with me."

"Is this true?" The old crow turns to Sister Frances Marie.

The young woman stutters as sweat beads at her temples. "I . . . I want to be with Mahkesîs—that's her real name, not Adèle. I am going to leave with her."

"You cannot," says Sister Ignatius smugly. She clasps and unclasps her wrinkled withered hands. The movement of her hands underneath her grey robe makes her arms seem to flutter. "Sister Frances Marie, if you leave, I will tell Father Bernier myself about everything I saw a moment ago. I will have him write your family in Quebec about what you have done here. I know your father is ill—what do you think news of his daughter's depravity will do to him?"

Sister Frances Marie looks ashen. Mahkesîs knows from the look on her lover's face that things have now turned.

The old nun knows too that she has power over the scared young woman.

Sister Ignatius purses her wrinkled lips. "Adèle, you will leave in the morning and you will not speak of this to anyone. Think up another reason for why you have left. You are obviously skilled at deception."

Mahkesîs says, "I will keep silent over what you saw this morning because I don't want to cause Marie any pain or shame."

The old nun narrows her eyes.

"And in exchange for my silence, you will lend me an axe and one of the moose skins that Father Lacombe left so I can make fire and a shelter. I will also take a point blanket. There are many new and unused ones left over from the bishops' conference."

"Fine." The old nun realizes she needs Adèle's silence in order to retain her control over Sister Frances Marie. She continues, "Sister Frances Marie, if you stay and repent then I will not write your family. You and I will deal with this ourselves and not involve Father Bernier. Unless you need to confess to him, and that is between you and Our Holy Father. May God forgive you both for this unspeakable sin." Sister Ignatius crosses herself and points at the door of the bedroom.

Marie turns to Mahkesîs. She is pale and shaking. "Oh, Mahkesîs. My parents . . . My father . . . I can't leave now . . ."

Mahkesîs says, "Are you sure?"

"Not when my father is ill. A letter from Sister Ignatius would break his heart."

Mahkesîs turns her eyes to the floor and says in Cree, "I will wait for you. I will go home to my family, and collect my son, and I will wait at Lac St. Anne until St. Anne's Feast Day in high summer. If you come to the lake, like you did last year, I will have everything ready. We will be able to leave together, go west into the mountains and—"

"That is enough. It is time for you to leave, Adèle." Sister Ignatius grabs Mahkesîs's arm.

"Until St. Anne's Feast Day then," Marie whispers.

"Yes," says Mahkesîs.

This promise of summer will have to be enough. Marie's promise will have to sustain her.

"Until St. Anne's Feast Day."

She thinks the journey from this one place named for a saint to another place renamed for a saint will take a few days on foot. Unlike her brother and Moira, no one will be following or tracking her. Her parents and grandmother will not know she is coming—even Sister Ignatius's wicked tongue will take more than a few days to relay information from St. Albert to Lac St. Anne. And the old nun is likely to respond to questions about Adèle's absence with a curt, tight-lipped "Gone." Perhaps people will be too distracted with Christmas to notice. Mahkesîs has often thought about the solitude of travelling on her own but has always known that this is something men can do, not women.

Now she will experience a different kind of aloneness than the debilitating loneliness and heartache she carried with her when she first arrived here this summer. But she is angry not to be leaving on her own terms.

Mahkesîs pulls away from Sister Ignatius's grasp. The old nun waits for her to walk through the door and follows her to the supply room. Mahkesîs will leave the St. Albert Mission before the sun rises. It is Christmas Eve day and it is snowing gently.

Winter Solstice
DECEMBER 1892

Prohibited by law and by her own sense of dignity from entering Kelly's Saloon, Georgina walks up five wide wooden stairs and waits on the establishment's front porch. A few days ago, when James announced that he needed to go to Edmonton before the New Year for some urgent business, Georgina convinced him to take her with him so they could spend Christmas here. "After all, there is no Anglican church at Lac St. Anne, so if we spent Christmas in Edmonton, I could attend a proper Christmas Eve service," she had persuaded him. The red brick of the Jasper House Hotel is a welcome change from the whitewashed wood of the Manager's Quarters at Lac St. Anne. But, still, *I will not be treated this way*, she thinks. Georgina has left the dining room at the Jasper House Hotel and walked half a mile to the saloon to collect her husband.

It is a shame that she is driven to this after such a pleasant day. *James should know better*, thinks Georgina. *Moira's disappearance has unsettled and upset me, especially all the gossip around it*. Georgina cried for a day after discovering the note the Irish girl left, stating only, *I am leaving to start a new life with Gabriel Cardinal. Thank you for what you have done for me. Moira Murphy*. Georgina was devastated that her plan to mother Moira's baby would likely not come to fruition. She was equally frustrated that her husband felt no compunction to report this situation to the Mounted Police. In his words, "Moira is a housegirl. We will hire someone else, someone local who does not require room and board. Or, surely, you could manage on your own until the transfer is arranged." In the month or so since Moira left, Georgina has been debating whether or not to tell her husband about the child and compel him to go after the girl. Tonight, at dinner, she was going to, but then James failed to meet her in the dining room of their hotel. After waiting for more than an hour, angry and humiliated, Georgina has come to collect her husband and tell him what needs to be done. For what seems like hours but is only minutes, Georgina waits, shivering, on the steps of Kelly's Saloon until someone approaches.

A round, burly man with a ginger beard and sausage-like fingers ties up his large brown workhorse, gives it a pat on the haunches, pulls up his falling-down trousers, and spits phlegm onto the ground.

Georgina politely asks him, "Excuse me, sir. Would you mind telling my husband, Mr. James Barrett, that I am here and would like to speak with him? He'll likely be playing cards. He's a tall man with brown hair and a trimmed moustache." She feels so much more at ease here in Edmonton, where she knows her English will be understood.

The heavy man nods and wordlessly obliges. She can smell the manure on his boots, but from his expression, Georgina can see it is he who pities her. He disappears through the saloon's batwing doors and Georgina's anger grows. There is a bench against the building, but it is covered in a fine layer of snow and Georgina does not want to get her brown woollen skirt wet. She stands and waits. Georgina can hear men's laughter inside.

After several minutes, James wanders outside, swaying and

squinting his eyes to adjust to the darkness. He is wearing only a cotton shirt and trousers with drink spilled all over them. His suspenders are exposed. He had left the hotel this afternoon properly dressed in a grey waistcoat and jacket.

"Georgina, what on earth are you doing here?"

"James, we need to talk."

"Darling, I am so sorry. I've missed dinner, haven't I?"

Georgina nods. "Yes, but that is not really why I came, I want—"

"Oh, my lovely wife, I will make it up to you." Drink makes James particularly affectionate to Georgina. He protectively puts his arm around her but realizes there is no place he can lead her. She cannot come inside the saloon.

"This is no place for a lady. And it is snowing! Whatever brought you out here can wait until I get back to the hotel. Did you walk here?"

"Yes, I walked." Georgina shivers but not from the cold: James's touch can still ignite desire and need in her. "We need to talk. In private, proper husband-and-wife talk."

James sighs and smiles. "Right now I'm three hands away from winning a considerable sum. I promise you when I win you can order whatever you like from the catalogue at McDougall's. Maybe we can even send for a new hat or such from a proper millinery in Toronto, even London. I will go ask Kelly if one of his men can walk you back to Jasper House and I will be along shortly—"

"You must lay your claim to your child before it is too late," Georgina uncharacteristically interrupts her husband.

James sees his wife, really looks at her. He recognizes her fragility now. That day in the store, when he was with Moira in the back, when Georgina cut her hand on the broken jar—he has tried to be better since that hot August afternoon. Now he feels as if something has crashed inside him. James knows that the right thing to do now is speak the truth.

"Georgina, I had no idea you suspected. I've had the rumours relayed to me and it is indeed possible. I am sorry." He steadies himself against a beam on the saloon's front porch. "But surely you can't be serious about claiming the child."

"I have never been more serious in my life."

Beads of sweat start to freeze in James's moustache.

"Georgina, my sweet, why on earth would you want me to claim a *half-breed* bastard?"

"A *half-breed*?" Georgina asks in a voice lower than usual.

"Yes, my dear, a *half-breed*: that's what any child of that girl Adèle's would be, wouldn't it? I suppose technically a *quarter-breed*, but still. I've heard that she had a child that her family is raising and went to the mission in St. Albert. Why would you want to mother a child with that history, that savage blood, those propensities? It simply isn't done."

Georgina is silent. She wrings her gloved hands. She, too, had heard rumours that the Cardinal girl who had briefly worked for them when she first arrived had had a child, but Georgina hadn't suspected her husband was the father. With girls like that there was no telling how many men could make such a claim. She had no doubt her husband had had relations with the girl before she arrived at the settlement, but a child? The fact that James knows about this situation, and has brought this up, must mean he has some guilt. Georgina feels bile rise up in her throat. Her husband has two bastards with two different girls and her womb remains empty and hostile.

James says, "Now, I know it is hard to adjust to life out here in the wild. Things will be better once you're with child again. I'm sure you'll bear me a son yet." James tries to tenderly take his wife's hand.

Georgina is silent.

The drink makes James keep talking to fill the quiet. "You're upset. Understandable. And I can see that Moira running off has disappointed you, but, really, what can you expect? From what you've told me, the girl had no proper upbringing or education. I still don't understand why you insisted on bringing her here as help."

In a strange way, Georgina misses Moira. And not just because of the baby. Moira was the closest thing Georgina had to a friend here, and now she has left her and ruined Georgina's plan. Georgina realizes she is alone.

A nearby streetlight illuminates the snowflakes as they start to get heavier, quicker in reaching the ground.

James continues. "While I can see Moira provided you with some company, is her loss really that substantial? Does it matter if she runs off with some local boy? If she'd stayed in Cork, she'd probably be spending her days in a turf hovel birthing little *paddies*. She is lovely and I'd hoped to marry her off to a junior clerk or some such when I needed an extra bargaining piece. I'm the one who should be upset—I paid for her passage and can't even get anything out of her now that she's run away. Well, I can see now that my ideas were a tad arcane, I suppose."

If there is ever a time for Georgina to confront James, about Moira's pregnancy and his serial unfaithfulness, it is now. If there is ever a time to tell James the truth, about what happened in Douglas, about why she brought Moira to Canada, and about the slim probability she'll be able to bear him a child, it is now. If there is ever a time for her to tell him that she is profoundly lonely and deeply unhappy and is unsure what can be done to change any of this, it is now.

But Georgina says nothing. She cannot take the risk that James will leave her. She has no one else to provide for her and she knows how that feels. There is no grandmother in Douglas here.

Georgina thinks of the first time she let James put his mouth on hers, and let his hand force its way under her petticoats, in that fine, tall house she was mistress of in Cork. If only she had paid less attention to James's foot on hers under the table or his intense eyes staring her down and making her feel naked in front of her old flaccid husband and listened to the dinner conversation on that night two years ago. If only she had paid more attention to the details in the stories exchanged about the Dominion of Canada and all its wild savagery. She had thought it little more than a reflection of the lack of activity in Mrs. McConnough's life when the woman had taken a little too much pleasure in listening to James's account of the Red River rebellions. Georgina remembers how she had asked, right after the main course of pheasant had been served, "Mr. Barrett, is it true that these red Indians want to capture white women and have their way with them?"

James had coyly answered, "Only the prettiest white ladies, such as yourself, Mrs. McConnough." And the fat, middle-aged woman had blushed and gulped half the Bordeaux in her Waterford crystal glass.

Georgina had wondered at the time how James could stomach flirting with that woman.

But he had continued, enrapturing the homely, skinny McConnough daughter as well. "It is a sight to see when there is a Company ball on the prairies. Nothing like the lovely evening we had a few nights ago at the Ambassador Hotel, mind you. No, in the Dominion, the Factor's House at a fort is the site of a party, and the Indians, they get all painted up and whoop and beat their drums, feathers, skins, and all."

And tonight again, nearly two years later, even after all that has transpired in this conversation in the lightly falling snow, James continues to believe he can charm any woman with flattery and promises. Georgina realizes she is, in some ways, the same as plump old Mrs. McConnough. And she can see that James thinks she is.

Her husband continues, "I have some exciting news for you that I was saving until the details were finalized. But telling you now may snap you out of this melancholia and irrationality. The Company has offered me a new post."

"Edmonton?" Georgina asks, thinking of how she amused herself today while James met with the factor at the fort and with his contacts on town council whom he wanted to help him run in the next town election. While her husband paved their future, Georgina walked along the boardwalk streets, looking in the shops, and finding little trinkets to send her sister for Christmas—although the gifts likely wouldn't reach the British Isles until well after the holidays now, but that couldn't be helped. There was nothing she could have gotten in Lac St. Anne that would be appropriate to send. Georgina bought herself two fresh, yeasty white bread buns at Lauder's (how she loved to eat something other than the bannock local women brought to the store or that flat, basic soda bread Moira made). She spent a good hour gazing at the jewellery and china in Raymer's store. The man at the counter kept asking her if he could help her, if she was looking for something in particular; Georgina was content just to look for now. She needed something to distract her from Moira's disappearance—and all the gossip on the settlement about it. Georgina had enjoyed a day away from all of that, taking high tea (with strawberry jam rather than fresh berries but still better than bannock). *I could live here*, thought Georgina. *I could be an alderman's wife.* Once she got back to the room and the inkwell, she had spent a good hour or so detailing all of this in her journal.

"No, darling, not Edmonton. Vancouver. Seems like our time in this backwater has paid off—they've punished me enough for that misunderstanding in Winnipeg. So, they have offered me Vancouver. A proper city on the coast. It's a port—you can get real black tea and silk for a reasonable price, and the mail is far quicker than here. Vancouver has more than the handful of electric lights in Edmonton and there are streetcars. An opera house. It is a proper city—well over thirteen thousand people— with societies and organizations."

"And an Anglican church?" Georgina asks.

"Yes, of course, my dear. Many."

It is starting to snow with conviction but without sound. James is too drunk to notice as his wife's shivers turn to trembles.

"I'm sure Vancouver's no London, or even Cork, mind you, but it's far closer to that life than anything in this place. One big advantage is that there are no natives in Vancouver. The Company opened a store there ten years ago and it is a proper store—no trading for beads or bartering hides and the like. The natives have all gone back to their villages on the coast. Being a port city on the Pacific, I'm told they do have a lot of Chinese, but the Orientals are happy to keep to their own part of the city."

Georgina remembers the docks at Cork: the masses of humanity desperate to leave the British Isles for this new land. Georgina had never had occasion to go the docks before: she had lived a sheltered life as a lady in Cork's anglo society. She remembers the smells and sounds of other people's bodies pushing one another. There didn't seem to be any room for any more people on the dock, but more and more kept coming. Men smoked and waved tickets of paper in the air. In futile gestures, women straightened out children's collars and buttoned up jackets. Servants counted trunks and crates. People descended on the boat like maggots devouring a rotting carcass. A battering of languages filled the air. Every kind of colour and kind of dress assaulted the eye. Even the ocean there was ugly: steam, coal, garbage, scavenging gulls, muggy stink. Georgina hopes the port at Vancouver is different.

"There are plenty of lovely shops there, darling. I could give you things you deserve, things you need." James takes his wife's shivering hands. "And it rarely snows there. Well, not like here. The climate is similar to what we were used to in Britain."

Something changes in Georgina's expression. "I could buy proper clothes, and have somewhere to wear them."

"Yes, my darling." James smiles.

He thinks of the day he met his new wife at the train station in Edmonton. That was only a year and a few months ago. She had looked both beautiful and ridiculous as she stepped down from the railcar in a cornflower blue silk dress. Barrett had come to fetch her and the girl she had brought with her in a fine burgundy stagecoach he had borrowed for the day; he wanted to take Georgina straight to the fort to show Factor Livestock what a fine wife he had. Of course, Barrett did not drive the coach himself. He had hired dark-skinned Joseph Auger to drive the vehicle and take care of the two Company horses that pulled it. Georgina had looked so vulnerable, and so beholden to him. James had thought then that Georgina's white skin might have kept him sane in the wilderness. But it hadn't. It was this place; it skewed his judgment. It was too wild, too new, too untamed for a man of his weaknesses and desires. He could start again in Vancouver—a proper town—he could start again with Georgina and give her a life more suited to her tastes and expectations. James was good at starting over. The unattainable could always be attained.

"Do you remember the day I met you at the train station? You looked so beautiful in that blue gown and hat with an ostrich feather. You stepped from one world into the next and trusted me that we would have a new life here, together. Well, it may have taken me a while, but I am making good on that promise."

Georgina remembers that day like it is a scene in a novel. At least that is how she has written it:

Months after our wedding in Ireland, I have to admit that, while I was thrilled, I was also nervous to reunite with my new husband. I saw the sign "Edmonton" hanging over the doorway of a humble wooden building. The train station was a rough imitation of the station I knew in Cork. I had to carefully and deliberately negotiate the metal steps and make my way onto the platform made of planks. I allowed a young train steward to help me so as not to trip over my bustled lace overskirt that I had carefully chosen for this disembarking. Engine steam lingered in the surprisingly warm air. The train gurgled and rattled. It was much hotter, and dustier, here than I had expected. Why, everything I had heard and read about Canada warned how frightfully cold it was! People in the station admired my cornflower blue silk dress and hat that I had bought with money James gave me as a gift before he went on ahead to sort out our living arrangements. Likely most people in the station were not used to such finery! My dear husband pushed through a small crowd to get to me, took of his hat, grabbed me around the waist, and twirled me in his arms as if I were a young girl at a dance.

"Darling!" he exclaimed. "It is so wonderful to see you! You look as beautiful as ever." He kissed me on the lips and I was full of excitement about our new life.

Tonight, even after so much has happened, and not happened, in two years, Georgina again stands in Edmonton, although this time in front of a tavern rather than at a train station, and listens to James's plans for the future.

Georgina crosses her arms and rubs her gloved palms together in an attempt to stop shivering.

James, feigning sobriety, says, "Now, I can't leave you out here, can I? Ah, well, wait here and I'll fetch my hat and coat. I really was winning that game. You'll make it up to me when we get back to the room, won't you, darling?"

Georgina has to make a decision. She thinks of Moira,

pregnant with what is possibly James's child, running away into the bush with that *half-breed* boy. And Georgina thinks of that night in Douglas when she thought she would bleed to death in her grandmother's cottage, and Moira's mother, Deidre, took pity on her and saved her with ancient secret knowledge. Georgina thinks of her grandmother—the only person who truly loved her—buried in some Irish coastal cemetery she would never see, a pile of rocks on top of a shallow grave, salt settling in the air. Georgina thinks of the luxury of never again having to work in that claustrophobic little store at Lac St. Anne, handling a beaded slipper passed to her by some old crone who wants to trade it for butter or trying to explain to an old man who speaks Cree and French but not enough English why it is not in his best interest to exchange a crumpled two-dollar note for a crisp one-dollar bill.

She also thinks about yesterday, at the hotel, when James had shown up with whiskey on his breath. He didn't bother with romance or compliments or affection; he took her from behind. The burgundy carpet left a rash on Georgina's cheek that she's had to use too much rouge to cover up. After he had left, telling her he would be back at dinnertime, she thought about the factor's daughter in Winnipeg. She thought about Adèle in the Manager's Quarters and Moira in the store. Times like yesterday afternoon make Georgina wonder, if only for a moment, if Moira had been telling the truth.

But she pushes those thoughts from her mind. This transfer to Vancouver will offer Georgina a chance to have a life like the one she knew as Mrs. Adams, but this time with James—a man who despite all his faults and wandering and occasional roughness is still someone who can make her gasp in ecstasy. *It is not him*, she thinks, *and it is not me. It is this place, this backwards, wild, hard place.* She will do things her way once they move to Vancouver. *It will be just us: no Moira to remind me of my past or to tempt my husband. We can start again.*

"I will be right back," James says as he goes into Kelly's to collect his coat, hat, and, he hopes, winnings.

In Vancouver, Georgina will no longer have to think about her secret: the secret Moira held about why Georgina has not been able to carry a child since coming to Canada, the secret Moira has now carried away with her into the bush. *If I let Moira go*, Georgina realizes, *some of the burden of the past goes with her.* Georgina thinks of the chance to start over again, to be a proper wife, to attend balls in grand Vancouver hotels made of marble and stone rather than jigs in wooden halls built by the men who dance on their floors. Perhaps there would even be a grand hotel like the Ambassador—the place where she first met James—with gilded chandeliers and a mirror-polish dance floor. Georgina thinks about the chance to be charming and witty and make James proud. Perhaps this could be enough, this could make up in some small way for not being able to have a child for him. And she will write. Georgina is determined to become the next Mrs. Moodie, the next chronicler of life in the bush, with tall tales for all those at home who wish to read about her adventures and triumphs in the wild West of Canada. She will tell James about this plan when they are settled in Vancouver.

Georgina looks at the horse that the man with the ginger beard has tied to a post. It's been patiently waiting for the burly man the entire time she and James have been talking. The animal has smooth cocoa hair and a cream blaze on its forehead. It must have cost its owner a considerable sum. It is calm and obedient. The horse barely moves. It scrunches its muzzle as snowflakes land on its face, in its eyes. An occasional switch of its tail is its only sign of resistance.

"Right then," James says as he reappears. "Ready, my love?"

Georgina straightens her shoulders and smoothes a snow-damp chunk of dyed-blond hair away from her face. She asks her husband, with expectation but without emotion, "When can we leave?"

→→ Birthday ←←

Snow falls in cruel wet clumps in late December. It is getting hard for Trigger to carry all three of them every day, along with pulling the sled with the pack of pemmican and other supplies, and make good distance. Trigger's hooves sink through the crust of ice forming over the snow. Gabriel and a visibly pregnant Moira have been riding, and camping, for nearly two months now. Gabriel is keeping to the bush to hide them from the Mounted Police that Barrett has probably set on their trail.

Gabriel thinks they could reach Cypress Hills in a day or so more of riding. His grandmother's people are from Cypress Hills, an area the Cree call Munatoubgow. He has never been there. Gabriel has never been east of Athabasca Landing until now. They need to settle somewhere soon. It is getting too cold to camp in a moose-hide tipi, even with a fire going day and night, and Gabriel spends hours each afternoon setting up shelter and finding and chopping enough wood as Moira melts snow into water and rations their pemmican and Trigger's oats. They haven't eaten anything but the buffalo meat, fat, and dried saskatoons for weeks; they ran out of the other things they brought with them soon after leaving Lac St. Anne. He has Muskwa's rifle still but few bullets, and those he wants to keep for defence rather than hunting. Trigger is getting worn, and Gabriel can see that Moira is tired. All he knows about Munatoubgow is that his grandmother talked about the bergamot there, which you can steep into headache-curing tea.

All Moira can do is think when they ride. Occasionally she falls asleep, out of pure exhaustion—*the baby must be growing quickly*, she thinks—but mostly she stays awake. When Gabriel rides with her, and the wind isn't howling, they can talk. But Gabriel often walks so he can lead Trigger through the drifts. Moira tries to talk with him, but it is hard for him to hear her—their language is diffused by snow. Gabriel asks her numerous times a day, "How are you feeling?" and she replies, "Well. Now that I am with you." And it is partly true. They do not speak about where they are heading because they do not know—except that they are going east, away from James Barrett and the Mounted Police who may be looking for them. They do not speak about how many days or weeks their journey may take them: they do not know. There is no point in speaking about the future beyond each short day. It is just the two of them, Trigger, a place to rest each night, and the falling snow.

But they can talk at night. As Gabriel makes a fire and Moira rations out the pemmican and the occasional small jackfish caught during a detour on the day's ride when they see a small pond, they talk because they can hear one another in the closeness of the little tipi.

"What is your favourite part of Christmas?" Moira asks Gabriel one night as they hold each other under woollen blankets and try to keep warm in their temporary shelter.

"Hmm . . . I don't know," he answers. "I suppose it would be the dances. The music. How everyone takes time to celebrate and visit."

"Was it the same when you were a little boy?" she asks, stroking the lines of his face.

"Yes," he says. "Except the dances at Fort Edmonton were much larger than at Lac St. Anne. The factor would open his house up to the people who lived at the fort, like we did for a time, and everyone he traded with. Grand chiefs of both Cree and Blackfoot tribes were invited; people came not only from Lac St. Anne and St. Albert and Strathcona, but from as far north as Fort Chip and Wabasca and around the Peace River. People would travel for days to come for Christmas at the fort. Sleds full of fish would come from Lac St. Anne to feed everyone. I loved the cannon, on its two great big wheels, and I wanted to figure out how it worked, how it made such a big noise at midnight. I remember how huge the Factor's House seemed to me when I was a little boy. Now I hear the Company's sold it off in pieces."

Moira caresses Gabriel's arm as she listens.

"We could see the outside of the Factor's House, its balconies and glass windows, when we played on the fort grounds. In Cree we called it okimawwaciy—the boss's house. The Christmas dance was the only time we would go inside. One year, I think it was the last Christmas we spent there before we moved to Lac St. Anne, Mahkesîs took my hand and led me out of the great hall where people had gathered. She was small—she must have been only three or four that winter—but she was the one who wanted to explore other parts of that great wooden house, to see how long the hallways were, to know what was behind all those doors in all those rooms."

"And what did you find?" Moira asks.

"Snowshoes that had never been laced hanging on the walls, pristine Company blankets sitting folded on the ends of beds already covered with other quilts, paintings of green rolling hills in places I had only heard about: England, Scotland, and . . ." Here Gabriel looks Moira in the eyes and smiles. ". . . Ireland."

She kisses him and asks, "What else? Tell me more."

"There were all kinds of animals hanging on display. A red fox, a whole black bear with its mouth stretched open, its teeth bared, the mounted head of a young elk with velvet still on its antlers. I remember thinking, as young as I was, that the fox pelt would have fed us for weeks or meant a new kettle for Mama. The whole place was like the most beautiful store I could imagine but bigger and grander, and for nobody but the factor and the Company men."

"Didn't the adults notice you had disappeared?"

Gabriel laughs softly. "No, no. At Christmas, my parents would see their friends and family from Lac St. Anne and St. Albert who they hadn't seen since summer probably. All the adults were too busy drinking and dancing and feasting to notice that a couple of kids weren't underfoot. Besides, Mahkesîs could have explained it if we had been caught. She was always the clever one and the one who felt she had to protect the rest of us from my father's hand."

Moira hears Gabriel's voice change as he talks about Mahkesîs, so she tries to shift the tone. "Christmas in Douglas was always a happy, happy time. Even though my family has never had much, Ma would save and scrimp and work miracles in her own right to give us a feast." Moira thinks of the table in her parents' home and, hanging above it, the curled map of Ireland with its sirens perched on top of the rocks.

"Mass on Christmas Eve has always been my favourite part of the season. It was always a flurry of activity during the day. Ma usually burst into tears at some point over something that wasn't getting done or some shortcoming with the meal that only she knew of, but by the time we were all sitting in our pew in the church, none of that mattered. We chanted and prayed and sang carols until our voices tired."

Moira takes a breath and starts to sing softly, almost in a whisper, "'In Bethlehem upon that morn / there was a blessed

Messiah born. / The night before that happy tide / the noble Virgin and her guide / were long time seeking up and down / to find a lodging in the town / but mark right well what came to pass / from every door repelled, alas / as was foretold, their refuge all / was but a humble ox's stall.'"

"What's that song called?" Gabriel asks.

"'The Wexford Carol.'"

"It would sound nice on the fiddle. Maybe I can learn to play it for next Christmas," Gabriel says. He stops himself from pointing out that they are a bit like Mary and Joseph, wandering the wilderness and seeking refuge.

"It is my mother's favourite carol. She would often sing it as we walked home to have our feast after the service. The water always seemed calmer, the stars a bit brighter, Ma and Pa just a bit more loving. That's what I think of when I think of Christmas."

"I am sorry you won't have that this Christmas," Gabriel says.

"I have you. And our baby. I will sing hymns to the baby next year."

Gabriel runs his hand through her undone hair.

"You are keeping me safe. That—this—is all I need." Moira means what she says.

Since suspecting she was with child early in the fall, Moira has had a lot of time to think about the choice she has made and what has brought her to this place. She has thought about her mother's quick-thinking desperation in using Georgina's pain to her benefit. She has thought about the physical journey by boat and train and wagon to get from Douglas to Lac St. Anne. She has thought about the night on the beach and how her life could have been like her sister's if Gabriel hadn't come back for her as he promised. And she has thought about her own foolishness and the risk in giving in to desire. Everything has brought her to this place of a love so authentic, so encompassing, so intense she thought it only possible in stories. But none of this matters now, none of this matters when Gabriel holds her in his arms. Gabriel and their baby inside her are everything.

Moira kisses Gabriel passionately and they fall into the rhythm of becoming one.

But that is the night. In the daytime, she has to push away her doubt and worry. The solitude of riding a horse in the snow sometimes leaves Moira wondering, *Is this the future?* There is no housework to distract her, no needlework to concentrate on, no strained silence between her and Georgina to negotiate. She should feel happy: she is with a man she thinks she loves, their child grows inside her body, and they set up camp and hold each other every night in the bush. In Lac St. Anne, this is what Moira thought she wanted. All those nights hoping she would not hear Barrett's heavy footsteps, Gabriel was everything she thought she needed. Moira thought that having to wait for Gabriel, and not knowing if he would come back, was her punishment for wanting too much.

For most of her life, all her prayers have consisted of wishes of protection for her mother and sister and a request for a better day tomorrow. These requests came as she bowed her head and knelt on the stone floor of her family's church or the turf floor under the bed she shared with her sister until their father sent Bridgette away. Moira's hopes for the future were entangled with rock and peat; she kept her eyes firmly on the ground while her thoughts carried up to heaven. In her prayers, Moira never dared to specify what that tomorrow might look like, so she thought her prayers were answered beyond what she could hope for when her mother told her she was going on a boat to Canada. Moira left everyone and everything she knew, the shores of the ocean, and the songs of her culture to come here. In recent months, Moira dared to imagine she would one day have a proper house with separate rooms, like the one she lived in with the Barretts. Maybe a church wedding in a new dress made of soft silk and a bouquet of lush purple flowers, several small laughing children running in and out of a kitchen while she chooses what to make them for dinner, a husband who shows affection and tempers his drinking. And here she is—surrounded by nothing but flat, ambivalent whiteness and her trust that Gabriel will protect her and love her. This uncertain future will have to be enough. Gabriel will have to be enough. She has to trust him when he tells her, "Do not be afraid." Moira has to trust that he will lead her through this.

Moira wants to bury her face into Gabriel's back to stop snow hitting her eyes, but her belly is in the way. She wonders if he feels the baby moving through her and his thick hide jacket, which she now wears instead of her woollen one. When she does look up, she sees pine, spruce, and poplar trees stretched out before them in endless rows, their branches swaying under the weight of the storm. Moira's hands dig into Gabriel's torso as her stomach rips open with pain from the inside out. She feels wet between her legs.

She cries out, "Gabriel!"

Moira has to repeat herself so he can hear her, but Gabriel feels her hands clench him through his coat. "I'm going to stop up ahead. Hold on. Whoa, Trigger." Gabriel jumps off and extends his hand to Moira, who is bent over and moaning. He speaks softly. "Come down off Trigger and lie flat on the ground. I'll set up our shelter. Maybe we've been riding too long today."

Moira nods, clutching her belly.

"You just need to rest." Gabriel reaches up to help her off the horse. When she inadvertently lets out a short, sharp scream, the young man senses that the girl he loves needs more than a reprieve from riding.

"It is too early," Moira says.

Gabriel nods and rolls a mat onto the snow for Moira to lie on. Moira is in too much pain to walk, so he lets her fall from the horse into his arms. Gabriel looks like a bridegroom stepping over the threshold as he places her on the mat. He works quickly to set up a lean-to and start a fire beside it. Gabriel doesn't know how to stop whatever is happening to her. He decides he must leave Moira and see if there is anyone nearby who can help. Some of the land they rode past today has been cleared for farming, so there may be a homestead nearby. It will be faster if he goes alone and it is best if she can lie still.

He tells her, "I am going to be right back. I am going to go get help."

Moira whispers, "All right. Hurry."

A farmhouse is his best bet. It is the Christmas season and people will be gathered together. He has no idea how far away they are from a settlement or reserve. The Cree may be more likely to help him once he speaks than settlers would be, but the reserves are probably farther back from the river into the muskeg. *Besides, he thinks, what if Barrett has sent word through the Mounted Police to Indian Agents who patrol the borders of the reserves? Those agents may be looking out for a half-breed and a pregnant white woman heading east.* And Gabriel does not know exactly where they are. He has never been this far east of Lac St. Anne. He panics. *Are people here still Cree? Are there any Métis settlements nearby? What countries do the homesteaders come from? What languages will people know? Will they understand one of the three I speak?*

Gabriel travels for an hour or two and cannot find signs of anyone. As the sun starts to set, and the grey-pink light of the shortest days of winter stretches across the endless horizon, it still snows. Gabriel does not want to get confused or stuck in a storm, so he heads back to Moira. He rationalizes that he just has to get Moira through this day, this night, and then they will be all right. If he can get Moira to ride a bit tomorrow, in daylight, maybe he can find them some help.

∞

Moira wanted to beg Gabriel to stay but knows she needs a woman's help for the baby to survive whatever is happening to her. Besides, pain makes minutes seem like hours and hours seem like minutes, so what does it matter how long he is gone? It just matters that he is not there. She is glad to be off the horse and finds the pangs easier to bear on her hands and knees. In between contractions, she lies curled in the fetal position. She tries, and fails, not to vomit. She feels like she is back on *The Nova Scotian* that brought her here from Cork.

Suddenly Moira knows where she is. She is no longer sheltered by a lean-to but inside a tent made of hide, and there is light from a small fire. She is warmer. Gabriel must have come back, cut down some trees, and put up this tipi. They must be staying the night here. It is dark outside. There are shadows on the animal skin walls. She is covered by a striped woollen blanket; it itches her. Gabriel kneels at her side and holds a metal cup of melted snow to her parched lips. He wears a beard of ice crystals. Moira thinks, *He looks like an angel.*

The only thing Gabriel can think to say is, "Do not be afraid, Moira. I am here with you. It will be all right."

Between the now-familiar waves of hot pain, Moira takes a drink. Her body is on fire, but she knows it is cold because her breath hangs in the air. Her lips are chapped from dehydration not just a result of the dry cold. Her blue-black hair, the colour of a raven's feather, is matted with sweat against her face. She tries to take deep breaths in and out to stop the baby from coming.

Moira thinks of the ocean. She remembers how it crashes. *The ocean is not full of peaceful pulses and gentle rocking; it is a cold, wild, wind-whipping place. Now I understand why poets and singers talk about it as the womb of the earth.* Moira thinks of her mother, Deidre. She thinks of her sister, Bridgette. She thinks of her friend Mahkesîs and her baby that she had to leave behind. She even thinks of this spring and Georgina and how Moira didn't know how to stop the blood seeping through Georgina's skirts and how Georgina was horrified at the thought of Angelique Letendre's hands on her body. Moira remembers the tiny clump of tissue in the mess of the bedclothes that Dr. Horace said would have been Georgina's baby. How Moira wishes Gabriel's grandmother was here with her now. How she wishes someone was helping her. *This baby, my baby, is much bigger than that one Georgina lost. Isn't it?* Moira thinks of Our Lady. *If she gave birth in a manger in the desert with ox and lamb, perhaps I will have to give birth in a moose-hide tent in a snowstorm with Trigger standing guard outside. But December is too early for my mortal baby to come,* Moira thinks, and she mutters the beginning of a prayer to St. Anne, the patron saint of childbirth, to help her. *Surely St. Anne will stop this. The first time we made love was on the shores of a lake named for her—that must mean something,* Moira thinks. She feels as helpless as Our Lady was when her child died on the cross. *Where was St. Anne, Our Lady's mother, Christ's grandmother, then? Where is St. Anne now? Others are here: the weetigo that people say roams the edges of the settlement, the dark Druid who took Saeve from Fionn, the angel who looks like Gabriel, the monster in the lake, the ghosts of the baby her sister lost in the convent and even the one Georgina lost in the white wooden house. But where is St. Anne?* In and out of consciousness, Moira tells Gabriel she loves him, she hates him, she has to get out of the tipi, she needs to go back to Ireland. She hears snippets of songs in her head. She can hear that strange girl, Bertha Tourangeau, and her plain, pure voice singing, "C'est pur l'restant de ma vie / Aller dans la misère . . ." singing at the hall on New Year's Eve. That was almost a year ago. She thinks of the line, "Your mother, too, God rest her soul, lay on the snowy ground," from the song "Skibbereen." *That woman in the song who is buried in Ireland could not have seen as much snow in her lifetime as we have seen just in the last few days*, Moira thinks.

Moira tries to will herself to stand up. *If I can just stand up, I can leave and find a better place, a safer place, a warmer place to have this baby.* But, of course, she cannot stand. She cannot leave. She cannot even stop her body from betraying her. She tries not to push, but her hips and belly take over. The baby is small, but her hip bones make creaking noises anyway; they rip and stretch out of instinct rather than necessity. Blood and fluids soak the striped blanket Gabriel has placed under her; its wool itches the backs of her now-bare legs. *What did Dr. Horace use to stop Georgina's bleeding last spring? What was it?* Moira thinks, *If I could remember, I could tell Gabriel and he could go find it. What would Ma do?* Moira cannot remember. *Why can't I remember?* The wind howls like a council of hungry, determined wolves. Her body betrays her with one final contraction. The baby is too early. Its lungs cannot fill with air. It cannot wail. It cannot suckle. This baby did not have a chance.

Gabriel does not know what else to do but cut the cord with his skinning knife and wipe the blood from his hands. He wraps the quiet little body in the piece of softened hide that encased his knife.

He asks Moira, "Would you like to see our daughter?"

Moira shakes her head.

He says, "Moira, she's perfect. Our baby. She's just too small."

Gabriel looks at the body in his hand.

Moira gives in and lets Gabriel hand her their too-little daughter. The baby does not fill her arms. She tries to memorize the tiny features: nose, lips, ears, fused-shut eyelids. She wants to be able to recognize her child in the afterlife. It is all too much. Moira starts to moan and keen like the old women in her ancient village who held day-long wakes for their dead. She makes a sound like the wailing banshee—the ghost of a woman who takes other women's children to try to fill her own loss. Moira's grief straddles the realms of the living and the dead.

Gabriel whispers to Moira, "Calm down, save your strength, ssh."

He gently takes the dead baby from her and kisses their child's tiny forehead.

Moira sees him leave through her tears but does not know where he goes.

When Gabriel comes back, Moira is quiet. She has stopped crying and has closed her eyes. Gabriel kneels beside her and strokes her hair. He tells her, "The Northern Lights are out. Green and blue. The same green as in your eyes. My mother's people believe they are our ancestors dancing—kîwetinohk kacakastek in Cree. Maybe that's what they are. Maybe the lights will look after our little girl."

Moira's eyes remains closed as she speaks. "There is something I need to tell you—"

Gabriel interrupts her. "You need to rest. In a day or so, we'll set out again. There has to be a farmhouse or settlement nearby. I didn't travel far enough earlier today. I didn't want you to be alone too long. Once we get to a town or a settlement or even a camp, the women there will know what you need and how to take care of you. I'm sorry I don't know how to help you."

Moira sighs as if she were a child herself. She can wait to tell him about Barrett, about how, perhaps, this child didn't survive because it was conceived in violence. *After all*, she thinks, *how could St. Anne let our baby be born too soon?*

"Do not be afraid," Gabriel says. "It is going to be all right."

Her eyes still closed, Moira smiles at Gabriel's generous lie.

Gabriel decides he also needs sleep so he can think clearly once morning breaks. He lies down beside the Irish girl, the woman he wants to make a life with, and wonders where they will go from here. He thinks that if he holds her tight, he can keep the chill away and keep her safe. He thinks that if he keeps breathing, if her body can feel the rhythm of his heart and lungs, he can make her breathe too. The movement of her chest rising up and down means she is still with him. That is all that matters now.

After a few hours of rest, Gabriel wakes up. He listens for the sounds he fell asleep to: the wind, the wolves and coyotes, Moira's breathing. Gabriel hears nothing. He puts his head to Moira's chest. He grabs her cold hand. Gabriel realizes that he's failed and he has lost her. The night the Irish girl gives birth to their too-early daughter, she silently bleeds to death in his arms.

Gabriel dresses the mother of his child in her layers of clothes. He gently puts her back in the madder-red skirt she had let out early in the fall to make room for her belly. He refastens the blouse she tried to rip off in the throes of confusion and delirium. He winds her in the now-soiled blanket they first made love on at Lac St. Anne and carries her out of the tent. There is so much snow.

Gabriel does not know what to do with Moira's body. The ground is frozen and the wind is cold. His grandmother's people used to give their dead to the trees in winter and then bury them when the dirt thawed. *Do they still do that?* he catches himself thinking. Gabriel decides he cannot leave Moira in a tree, not here, so he will have to take her with him, at least for a while, until something makes sense.

Gabriel drapes Moira over a nervous Trigger. The little horse gets antsy when they go out hunting and Gabriel has to sling a deer over her back to get it back to the cabin. The animal can smell and sense death, and it spooks her. She paws the ground and whinnies. He strokes Trigger's muzzle. Gabriel does his best to keep the blanket wrapped around Moira as he positions her over Trigger.

Besides Muskwa's rifle and a few bullets, Gabriel only has a small axe and a small shovel. He needs to find a place where the snow is partly cleared so he can build a fire to thaw the ground and dig a shallow grave. *If I leave her exposed, wrapped only in a blanket, it will be far too easy for coyotes or wolves on the ground or ravens and magpies in the air to pick her apart. If I wrap her in a hide and secure it with sinew, then I will have nothing to build a shelter with and I will freeze to death.* So Gabriel rides for a while with Moira; he is not sure how long, hours, days maybe. He stops only to let Trigger rest.

As Gabriel starts a little fire to melt some ice for them to drink, he notices the afternoon sunlight hits a patch of white differently than it does the drifts around them. He goes over to where the light hits the ground and sees a collection of logs nailed into a board. He carefully nudges it with his foot in case it is a trap. Gabriel finds the opening to a pit, what looks like the beginnings of a well, but there is no visible homestead for miles around. He wonders why the people who dug this hole decided against setting up a life here. In this moment, this makes sense.

Gabriel places Moira's body, as gently as he can, down the empty well.

He stands at this makeshift grave and promises Moira he will come back for her when the snow melts and give her a proper burial. He sets up a shelter and has a bit of pemmican. He sleeps. When he wakes up, it is morning and it has stopped snowing. The sky is clear. The sun hangs in the sky like bait on a fishing line. He and Trigger keep heading east.

Gabriel does not realize it, but it is Christmas morning. The people he fears are chasing him are sleeping under a goose-down duvet in Edmonton's Jasper House Hotel and a chambermaid is stoking a fire in their room to keep them warm. James will give Georgina an expensive bottle of perfume that smells like spiced oranges that he took from the store in Edmonton and neglected to record in the ledger. Later, the Barretts will enjoy a feast prepared by others. They will dine on roast goose with dried apples, fruitcake that has come from London, and chocolates that come from France via Quebec. After dinner, James Barrett will get drunk on expensive brandy while his wife daydreams about her life in Vancouver. Gabriel's parents have gathered everyone in their cabin, but it is not the usual festive celebration because Angelique has not gotten out of her bed for two days and everyone fears the worst. They will still have whitefish and pickled carrots and canned raspberries with a bit of sugar to cut the tartness, and the children will still delight in receiving hand-carved toys Luc has been whittling over the past few weeks—including a small canoe for his namesake grandson. Virginié will think of her two absent children and pray they are safe. Gabriel's sister, Mahkesîs, is outdoors too—farther west and north—making her way home to Lac St. Anne after leaving the St. Albert Mission. Unlike Gabriel, she does not have Trigger to help with her the journey; she is alone. And unlike Gabriel, Mahkesîs keeps warm under a moose hide that was skinned by Father Lacombe himself and a striped Hudson's Bay blanket that she took from the mission. Gabriel's sister is at peace in her solitude as she journeys home, while to Gabriel his loss seems like a cruel nightmare he hopes to wake from soon. Gabriel does not know where he will go now.

After he puts out his fire, rolls up his canvas, and feeds Trigger a ration of oats, Gabriel hears rustling in the snow. He looks up to see, only a hundred or so yards from where he slept, two young deer burying their muzzles in the cleared area looking for grass, however dead and dry it may be, to nibble. They may be two does or they may be a young buck and doe—hard for Gabriel to tell from this distance—and they pay little attention to him.

Gabriel could try to kill them—he could use the meat—but the thought of putting another limp body on Trigger's back is too much for him to bear this morning. The snow covers the deers' spines as they munch and rummage. One of them pauses, looks up at Gabriel and Trigger, and continues her foraging.

⇥ Requiem ⇤
LATE DECEMBER 1892

On December 27, Mahkesîs crosses the wooden footbridge over the creek that runs through the Lac St. Anne settlement. The little bridge is covered with ice and snow, and although it is probably more dangerous to cross it rather than the creek underneath it, Mahkesîs does so out of habit. The packed snow crunches underneath the worn soles of her high moccasins lined with warm rabbit fur. After three days of travelling the sixty miles northwest from the St. Albert Mission, she is home. She has gotten used to the feeling of an axe at her hips and the ease of moving in trousers. She has also eaten all the bread and cheese she took from the pantry at the mission and has ripped a hole in her gloves while chopping wood for a fire that resulted in a burn on her right hand. Her lips are badly chapped, her shoulders are sore from bearing the weight of the rolled-up moose hide and blanket, and her toes are numb from negotiating the icy snow in moccasins. While Mahkesîs has always envied the freedom her father and brothers have in working outside—going out to check trap lines or hunting moose or scowing on the Athabasca—and having a world outside the rooms of a cabin, travelling has been harder than she expected. Being out on the road, even for only three days, took more resilience than she had anticipated.

The solitude of her journey has given Mahkesîs time to think. She knows she is ready to be a mother to her son, she is ready to face her family, and she is even ready to see Barrett if she must. While Mahkesîs is not glad that Sister Ignatius discovered her and Marie together, and she worries about Marie being beholden to that cruel woman's knowing, Mahkesîs is glad to be away from the mission. She is glad to be home. She takes a deep breath and approaches the door of her family's cabin. The Cardinals' sled dogs bark, announcing the young woman's arrival, and her mother opens the door that creaks on its hinges and shifts in the deep winter.

"Oh, Mahkesîs," says Virginié, her small, thin face red and puffy from sobbing. "You are too late."

"Mama . . ." Mahkesîs stretches out her arms to hug her mother. "I am not here for Christmas. I'm here for good. I've left St. Albert."

"Oh, my sweet girl." Virginié wipes her nose on her sleeve. "You are too late to say goodbye. Nohkum passed away last night."

"What?" Mahkesîs whispers.

Virginié wraps an arm around Mahkesîs and pulls her out of the cold. "Come inside now. Quick, we don't want the cold air in."

"Oh, Mama . . ." Mahkesîs pulls the door closed behind her.

Virginié is glad to have her youngest daughter home, but it takes a few conversations to clarify that Mahkesîs did not return to Lac St. Anne because of the letter Virginié wrote explaining that Angelique was very ill—a letter that Luc sent through Barrett's store a week or so ago to be delivered to Sister Ignatius at the mission—but because Mahkesîs has left her post. Virginié hasn't been sleeping much and there is much to do. Mahkesîs can tell that her mother is distracted by her grief.

"I don't know why that letter didn't reach you. I should have written Boots to bring you home," is all Virginié can say. "She and George, and Payesîs, came up here five days ago."

Her first night home in Lac St. Anne, Mahkesîs's mother and father argue about where to bury her grandmother.

Luc says, "I will not let you put your mother in a tree for the crows to pick at her just because it is what her people used to do. The old ways are gone, Virginié—they have been for a long time. Besides, we called Father Lizeé to give her last rites. He is waiting for me to tell him when we want the funeral Mass."

Virginié rarely raises her voice to Luc, remembering that the few times she did it resulted in a black eye or bleeding lip, but she knows her mother would not want to be buried next to the church. "You know how she felt about that graveyard. My mother thought it was an invitation for bad spirits, for weetigos to prowl, to have bodies so close to where you pray." Virginié fidgets with her hands. "She told me she wanted to be buried up north, near Lake Wabasca. That is where my father was from." Virginié tries to make herself small.

"Superstitions," Luc says as he chews a gristly piece of rabbit meat, its salty juice lingering in his moustache. "It's barbaric to leave the woman's body in a tree and wait for spring thaw to bury her in supposedly sacred ground somewhere out in the bush. Do you even know where she wanted to be put? And how am I going to get her body up to Wabasca? Besides, your mother was baptized at the mission in Lac St. Anne when she married Frederick Letendre. She should be buried in consecrated church ground next to him."

"But that is not what she would have wanted," begs Virginié. "My mother wanted to be buried in the old way."

"Mama's right—"

"Adèle," Luc says, turning to his daughter, "this is not your decision. Furthermore, I don't know why you are here if you didn't know about your grandmother. I don't know why you left the mission and what you think you are going to do now. But I do know this: if I ever see you in men's clothes again, I will beat whatever possessed you to dress like that right out of you. I hope you haven't done anything else to further disgrace your mother and me. I am glad your grandmother did not live to see you like this."

Mahkesîs is not frightened. "Nohkum thought it was a sign that Father Lizeé's sled dogs would steal the crosses from the graveyard and chew on them—"

"Enough of this!" says Luc, slamming his fist on the wooden table, causing some onion and carrot to spill out of the bowl. "Virginié, I took your mother in when Frederick passed away. I tolerated her insistence on traditional ways and even speaking Cree to the children. But I will not compromise on this. Angelique will be buried at the church."

"You did not take her in," Virginié says in rare defiance. "You gambled your scrip away and she let us live on her lot, her settlement."

Luc raises his hand to his wife and Mahkesîs grabs his wrist to stop him.

The three of them stare at one another in surprise. "I don't know what my family has come to." Luc lowers his hand, frees it from his daughter's grasp, and shakes his head. "My youngest son a fugitive with a foreign girl and my pretty daughter travelling by herself, dressed like a man, leaving the mission with no explanation. Not to mention the baby being raised by your brother."

He looks at his daughter. She is thinner, of course, since she left in the Red River cart, but she also seems stronger. Mahkesîs does not seem to be affected by his outbursts or pronouncements.

Luc points menacingly at his wife. "This is your doing, Virginié—you were too soft with the two youngest. When Thomas and Francis were sick with pox at the fort, it scared you. It made you love the little ones too much."

"Stop it, Papa," Mahkesîs says calmly. "Mama's been through enough. She has just lost her mother."

Luc does not know how to respond.

Virginié weeps quietly at the table, her stew untouched.

Mahkesîs says, "I am not the same girl who left here months ago. You do not scare me. I came home to get my son, your namesake, and then I am leaving. And I will give him all the love I possibly can, all the love I have not been able to give him these first months of his life. I will teach him to be a kind and loving man. Unlike that man you made me go work for. Before I came home with a child on the way."

Her last statement lingers unpacked and defiant in the cabin.

Luc stares at his daughter. He does not know what to say. He sighs. "I'm going out," he says. Then he turns to Virginié. "I will see if Father Lizeé can do the funeral later in the week. People have come for New Year's Eve at Lac St. Anne, and Father Lizeé could combine the two services."

Virginié nods. She averts her eyes to the dirt floor until her husband has got his coats, gloves, boots, and hat on and she feels the cool air swoosh in as he slams the door.

"I can't even tell your brother about your grandmother," Virginié says. "I don't even know where Gabriel is or when he is coming home."

Mahkesîs gets up and goes to her mother. She holds her hand.

"I guess it does not matter now, does it?" Virginié asks her daughter. "Mama will be buried next to Frederick at the church. I don't know where my father, my brother, or my baby sister are buried. Mama never spoke of it and I never asked. There are so many things I never asked her."

Mahkesîs nods.

"I have nothing of my father's to send with Mama. There are no photos of Mîstacakan and Okinîy on their wedding day, no keepsakes from their life together, no treasures they had traded or bartered for. That whole life is gone now. It will be buried with my mother next to the church."

Mahkesîs holds her mother in her arms and lets her weep.

∞

On the afternoon of December 31, 1892, the woman so many called Nohkum is laid in an expensive pine box that will be kept in the empty cold house until the ground thaws. In spring, she will be buried in the ground of the mission cemetery next to her second husband; her headstone will read "Angelique Letendre" and this is the name history will remember her by.

Right now, the coffin lies at the front of the packed Lac St. Anne chapel. Some people are here for the New Year's Eve Mass, but most are here to pay their respects to Angelique. Father Lizeé underestimated how many people would gather and he has stoked the wood stove so vigorously that people are sweating as if it was a July afternoon. He is wearing his black and purple robes.

"Requiem alternam dona eis, Domine . . ."

Virginié sobs in the front pew. Boots comforts her cousin with a robust hug.

Mahkesîs sits in a pew with her parents, Payesîs, Boots and George, and her quiet brother Francis. She wears her hair in one long braid and has deerskin leggings on underneath her plaid skirt. Virginié gave her Angelique's elk tooth necklace and Mahkesîs wears it with pride. Behind them sit Thomas and Ida with their four young children and baby Lucas. They arrive late and there is no time to greet one another. Mahkesîs wonders if this is deliberate.

"Requiem alternam dona eis, Domine: et lux perpetua luceat eis . . ."

The funeral is the first time Mahkesîs sees her son since coming back to Lac St. Anne, and she tries to steal glances every time Father Lizeé asks them to rise or sit. In her glimpses, she can see her son is healthy. He has a full head of light brown hair, prominent cheekbones, and bow-shaped lips. Mahkesîs is happy to see he looks like a Cardinal; he reminds her of Gabriel, but maybe only because she wishes she could see him too. The baby sits on Ida's lap while one of Thomas and Ida's older daughters, Mary, holds their baby Virginié, who is only a few months older than Lucas. *Lucas is a good boy*, Mahkesîs thinks. He doesn't fuss much and instead he babbles happily during the service. Just knowing her child is right behind her makes Mahkesîs feel light-headed with excitement and trepidation.

The priest stands at the pulpit and delivers the liturgy.

It is awkward for Mahkesîs to look behind her without everyone suspecting why she is doing so. Her return to Lac St. Anne has generated much gossip, resurrecting the old rumours from the summer and inspiring new ones. At her mother's request, she has not yet spoken to Thomas and Ida about reclaiming her son. She promised Virginié that she would wait until after today. Even so, her sister-in-law, Ida, avoids making eye contact with her in the church. Mahkesîs knows that her return cannot be easy for Thomas and Ida, Ida especially, and perhaps they suspect what she will do tomorrow. But she has to stay strong—she will be with her son. The baby is the reason she has returned to Lac St. Anne rather than heading west right away. Her whole body aches to hold him.

Father Lizeé pauses. He breaks protocol and ends the service in Cree. "Mrs. Letendre was a woman who was known to many and will be remembered fondly."

Father Lizeé sprinkles water on the simple coffin, made by Bertha's father, Albert Tourangeau, which has been covered in an off-white sheet stored at the mission just for this purpose. The priest walks to the side of the altar and lights incense.

After the service, Luc Cardinal makes an announcement

in church and invites everyone back to the cabin for the wake. Even though she wants nothing to do with her father's supposed hospitality to the community, Mahkesîs helped her mother prepare earlier today so they would have a table full of bannock and fried fish and meat pie and moose nose stew to serve to those who gather. Luc also has saskatoon wine and moonshine from Amos Yellowknee. Mahkesîs knows this has nothing to do with honouring her grandmother. And while she does not want to speak to or be in the cabin with her father, she is not angry with him. Mahkesîs has spent so many days and restless nights resenting and even hating Luc that she has nothing left in this regard. Even before his business with Barrett, viewing her as something to be traded, Mahkesîs recognized that her father's folly with drink and cards, his boastfulness, and his occasional cruelty to her mother made him a weak man. His decision to separate her from her baby is something she thought she would never forgive him for, and now that all seems irrelevant. She knows she will not change him or the past. Mahkesîs is focused on a new life, on a new possibility of happiness with her son and perhaps Marie.

Mahkesîs hopes that Thomas and Ida will come to the wake and bring baby Lucas just so she can see him, so she can sneak a glimpse. She knows this is not the time for the conversation she needs to have with them; she promised her mother. And she suspects that her sister-in-law left the church with baby Lucas before the service was over just to avoid Mahkesîs. Perhaps, then, it is for the best that only her brother Thomas comes to the Cardinals' cabin afterward where people gather. Mahkesîs keeps busy serving food and washing dishes so she can avoid talking to people. She finds it just as hot in the cabin as it was in the church and decides to get some snow for clean water from outside.

Boots follows Mahkesîs as she goes outside to dump a pot full of dirty water near the outhouse.

"Mahkesîs! You haven't stood still since I got here. I wanted to tell you, I am so sorry about your grandmother. I know how much you loved each other."

"Yes," says Mahkesîs, trying not to spill anything on her feet. "Thank you, Aunty. Thank you for coming. I know Mama is glad you are here."

"You know," says Boots, "I went to the store today to get some things, tea and some soap, for your mother, and someone was asking after you. He knows about your grandmother passing and thought you might be home." Boots smiles.

Mahkesîs feels as if she's been knocked to the ground. She tries to keep her voice calm. "Mr. Barrett?" She hasn't spoken his name in many weeks and the sound of it feels sharp on her tongue.

"No, no, no," says Boots. "Joseph Auger! He looks after the store when Barrett's away. Joseph's grown into himself, that one. Kind of handsome, if I do say so myself. Might be one to court."

"Aunty," Mahkesîs says, relieved that Barrett did not ask after her and is not on the settlement right now, "you and I both know why that would not work."

"Why not?" asks Boots. "Are you going back to the mission at St. Albert?"

"No," says Mahkesîs.

"Are you going to become a nun here?"

"No."

"Is there someone else?"

"No other man," Mahkesîs says.

"Well then, why not? What's wrong with Joseph? Not bad-looking. Has a job. Bet he wants children."

"I already have a child." Mahkesîs looks into Boots's eyes.

"Yes," the older woman says more seriously. "Payesîs told me about her visit to you. And I am sure Joseph has heard this rumour just like everyone else. And yet he still asks after you with longing and a twinkle in his eye. That's something, my girl."

Boots pauses. "Your grandmother would want you to be happy. She would want you to stop punishing yourself. That baby is fine with Thomas and Ida."

Mahkesîs bites her lip and nods.

"I wished for a handsome boy like Joseph to ask about my daughter Elin. Poor thing didn't get much for looks. But now she has a good husband. Take your chances while you can, girl! One day you will wake up and find an old woman in your place," Boots teases. "You could end up as wrinkly and ugly as a moose ass—look what happened to me!"

"Oh, Aunty!" Mahkesîs can't help but laugh.

"Brr. I'm going back inside. Too cold out here for an old woman like me!" She pulls her striped woollen jacket around her pink blouse with gaping buttons. "Besides, I can't let Payesîs hear better gossip than me. She loves to know something I don't. You coming?"

"In a minute," says Mahkesîs and points to the bucket. "I'll just rinse this out." She takes off her glove and lets the snow's soft whiteness cool the healing burn on her hand.

∞

Mahkesîs does not go to the dance at the hall to ring in the New Year. Instead, she sits outside. She can just hear the music emanating from the hall across the creek: her brothers Thomas and Francis are playing their fiddles, as they did last year, but without Gabriel of course. Luc has convinced Virginié to go with him to the party, saying there will be many people there who will want to pay their respects to Angelique, and Virginié agrees even though she is exhausted and grieving. Mahkesîs wonders how her mother manages and vows to never let a man control her ever again. Mahkesîs thinks about last year's celebrations: watching and listening to Gabriel play the fiddle, talking with Moira, trying to hide her belly, Georgina Barrett glaring at her, noticing the new and palpable desire hanging between her friend and her brother, feeling terrified about what was to come. Eighteen ninety-two was a terrible year. Tonight, out here in the cold darkness, Mahkesîs welcomes the chance to finish it and start anew.

Even though it took her the entire first night of sitting near the fire in the cabin to feel warm after her journey from St. Albert, Mahkesîs still does not want to sit in the cabin by herself right now. It is not so cold out that it feels sharp to breathe. Her eyelashes will not freeze. The young woman needs to be outside, see the sky, clear her head. Everything inside her family's home reminds her of her grandmother: the beaver pelt stretched on a frame, the jar of canned saskatoons on a shelf, a piece of deer hide with unfinished beading that sits untouched in a corner, the bouquets of white-yellow yarrow and faded magenta fireweed hanging to dry in upside-down clusters, the birchbark tea that Mahkesîs boiled into a foam to put on her burned hand the night she arrived.

Mahkesîs sits at the side of the cabin, on the tree stump used to chop wood. She holds a steaming cup of tea in a metal mug between her gloved hands. One of the grey-and-white sled dogs sniffs and whines and circles the woodpile. Mahkesîs calls it to come to her side; the dog rubs its snout against her woollen skirt and deerskin leggings.

"Sorry, I don't have anything for you, atim." She pats the dog's head and takes her glove off to give it a welcome scratch behind the ears. Mahkesîs recognizes the scar above the dog's eye and knows this is the mother of the brood. The bitch pants with pleasure as Mahkesîs gives her some attention.

"So, girl, where do you think Gabriel is right now? Hmm? What's your master up to tonight?"

The dog closes her eyes and lets her pink tongue fall out of its mouth as Mahkesîs runs her fingers through its wiry hair.

Mahkesîs hopes that wherever her brother and her friend are tonight they are warm. She remembers how, only a few weeks after Moira first arrived here, the Irish girl shivered and complained when the first frost came early one September morning. There were still yellow and green leaves on the poplar trees and the first snow fall was weeks away. Mahkesîs remembers teasing, and warning, her that that frost would seem "balmy" after a few dark months of temperatures so cold they would freeze her eyelashes in a clump and drifts so high they could encase the cabin in towering white snow. She made Moira come outside and help hang the sheets on the line. Mahkesîs knows Gabriel will take care of Moira; and, wherever they are, at least they have each other.

Mahkesîs thinks of Marie, at the mission, and wishes she were here with her now. She imagines Marie getting undressed for bed, taking off her headpiece and unpinning her hair, pulling her arm out of a grey woollen sleeve, stepping out of her simple dress and hanging it on a hook to ready it for tomorrow. Mahkesîs pushes down a gnawing anxiety that Marie will forget her or be made to in order to withstand Sister Ignatius's threats. Mahkesîs misses Marie's softness, her gentle hands, the way she smelled of fresh-baked bread and apples. Last night, to put herself to sleep, she imagined Marie touching her with her fingers, her open and generous mouth, her skin on her skin. Each encounter they shared dared to find a deeper kind of pleasure. Mahkesîs spent so many months ignoring how her body ached for her baby—the leaking breasts, broken tailbone, stretched-out hips—and Marie's touch made that ache retreat. With Marie, her body became a place of pleasure and not just shame. Marie made her feel a pulsing deep in the centre of her being; she built up a need in her that Mahkesîs hadn't known could exist. She knew others thought it was unnatural, and perhaps it was, but it felt right. Now her mouth and heart and centre miss Marie.

Mahkesîs misses the sense of possibility and release she felt when she was with Marie.

Marie told her once that she always knew she was going to be a nun, even as a little girl. Marie had said, "I was the quiet one of my five sisters. They were all pretty and precocious and loved attention. I knew that my life would be one devoted to God. That is the path for me." Mahkesîs knows that the devout life Marie imagined in a Quebec farming village does not exactly match the realities of life out West. Mahkesîs doesn't want to force Marie to be with her, but it is hard for her to understand why Marie stayed at the mission. Even if her father in Quebec is ill, there is little Marie can do for him while she is out West. But Mahkesîs has to focus now: she cannot cloud her mind with worries about Moira and Gabriel, or even longing for her beloved Marie. Tomorrow she will go and talk to Thomas and Ida about taking back her child. It will not be easy. She is not even sure she knows how to be a mother to baby Lucas. But she knows that, even though it may be selfish to take the little boy away from the family he knows, she has to try. *Will holding my son make me stop longing for Marie?* she wonders. *Can I replace one hole in my heart by healing another?*

Tonight, the sky is clear, as it often is this time of year. The stars form a blanket of light in the crisp, quiet winter darkness. There is no snow falling against the blue-black bowl of the sky at this moment. Mahkesîs savours her solitude. Travelling on her own, back home from St. Albert, gave her a taste of the freedom and independence she had long envied her brothers. She looks to the east and can see faint green and blue waves start to move across the black horizon. Angelique often told her favourite grandchildren, "There is a reason the whole sky separates people on the ground from the dancing ancestors who light up the night in the North. The living and the dead have two different worlds." The young woman would like to think that her grandmother is watching over her tonight, and that she will be with her tomorrow when she tries to reclaim her child. She strokes one of the elk teeth on her new necklace. The kîwetinohk kacakastek will get brighter late into the night.

The dog waits at her feet. Mahkesîs notices that beside the dog's tracks are other, smaller, tracks in the freshly fallen snow that look as if they were made by only one foot. *A fox*, she thinks, recognizing the four small imprints cupped by a chevron. She would ask her father if he has noticed a lair nearby, but then he would make it his mission to trap it. And Mahkesîs hasn't noticed that the three little hens in the coop are bothered, they are producing eggs normally. *This little fox is just trying to survive here too*, she thinks. And there are at least three more months of winter before spring can appear.

A gunshot rings out from across the creek and the dog barks into the sky. It must be midnight. The young woman tells the dog, "It's okay, atim," and gives it another scratch behind the ears. More shots follow.

Mahkesîs Cardinal welcomes the New Year at home.

⤫ *Journey* ⤫
JANUARY–MARCH 1893

After leaving Moira in her shallow, damp, and makeshift grave, Gabriel realizes that he and Trigger no longer have a destination. He thinks about the story of Christ wandering through the desert. *But there is no hot sun here, no sand, no warmth. This is a prairie in a deep-freeze of winter*, Gabriel thinks. Hoarfrost has become a permanent part of his thickening beard and lines the inside of his horse's ears. *It would be easier to survive forty days in the desert.* But Gabriel cannot rely on any angels to break his fall. *There are no mountains to climb here and it is too cold for even the devil. There are just endless miles of flat, ambivalent whiteness.* Gabriel wonders, *How would Christ himself fare on the winter prairie of the Northwest?*

Gabriel's mind whirs with regret. *What if I had come back from Athabasca Landing earlier?* In the fall, their journey east would not have been so demanding. *The snowdrifts would not have caused Trigger to falter, she wouldn't have needed so much rest, and we could have gone farther each short day.* He should have brought his dog team: they would have been slower, but hardier, and Moira could have ridden in a sled. That ride may not have hurt the baby. *What if I had been able to find help to stop the baby from coming, to stop Moira's bleeding? How could*

I have failed her so, after I promised I would take care of her?

Gabriel has a lot of time to think about what happened and what he has lost. He convinces himself that his main mistake was his belief that he could have something more. He wanted to provide for Moira what he thought she wanted: a home like Barrett's whitewashed, wooden-floored, china-filled Company house. He tries to remember. *Did Moira ever tell me that is what she wanted? Did I ever ask her?* What Gabriel does know for sure is that Moira had wanted him. She gave in to his advances and her own desires. She responded to his touch as if they had always been together. She had participated in love in a way neither of the other girls he had been with had allowed themselves to. *That must mean something*, he thinks. *She gave herself to me.* She gave herself to him in body and in soul and in all her hopes for the future. But Gabriel couldn't bring himself to give her that as he was—he didn't feel he was enough.

Gabriel's thoughts are the details of remorse. He needs to eat—and so does Trigger—but he knows he can't stop here in the middle of winter. Gabriel could hunt for some small game, maybe a young coyote on the prowl for food, but he would need to set up a better camp for that and have some sort of place to leave Trigger. And he doesn't want to use the few bullets he has for food in case he needs them for defence. Gabriel knows that to survive here, in order to not freeze to death, he and his horse must keep moving. Besides, the Mounted Police may still be looking for him. Gabriel knows he can survive; that was one of the gifts Nohkum gave him when she sent him away when he was twelve and told him to "Come back a man." And although that was during spring, that was also nine summers ago, and he knows so much more now. But not enough to protect Moira.

Gabriel remembers how, during that trial as a boy, he had snared a doe. He cut the deer's stomach from her still-warm body to eat: it was full of grass and leaves and sour bile, but the blood on his hands helped quench his thirst. Nohkum's people revered the moose stomach, and used the same word for it as they used to refer to the Bible, but a moose is hard for a boy to kill, so the deer stomach had to do at the time. The little doe he'd managed to snare with the sinew unlaced from his pack was small and had probably only lived two or three summers. Her death was not quick or easy: it began with a fall into last season's leaves, her hooves stepping in the makeshift snare, and ended with a boy hacking into her neck with a dull, dirty knife. Gabriel learned from that struggle. Sometimes, even now, when he got a moose or even a deer, he would remember that kill and make the present animal's death as quick and painless as he could. He remembers how her eyes looked up at him as he cut and stabbed into her smooth skin; he cannot forget her gurgling moans that sounded like a dog's or a child's. Gabriel became a better trapper, a better hunter, because of that small deer's terrible death. His boyhood died with that doe in the pile of snow-moulded leaves at the beginning of spring.

And now, as a broken man who has lost the woman he loves and their child, Gabriel finds himself thinking not only about that doe but also about the story of Saeve and Fionn that he and Moira spoke of the first time they kissed by the lake named for Christ's grandmother. He thinks about Fionn hunting in the woods of Ireland years after losing his wife and child. *I wonder if the woods in Ireland look similar to the forests that the Athabasca River runs through?* he asks himself. In stories at least, people manage to persevere through heart-wrenching loss. Gabriel thinks about Fionn, a broken, lonely king, finding a half-human, half-fawn creature that somehow, somehow, was his son. And his son grew up to be a great poet and warrior. Gabriel thinks of his little girl—a tiny babe who never took a first breath. *My daughter will not grow up to be a poet, a warrior, a wife, or a mother. Our child will not grow up.*

When he was a little boy, Gabriel knew winter as the time when even his father could afford to be kind, but this winter is anything but kind. Gabriel is used to being outside for days in the spring, the fall, and especially the summer, but not in these months of snow and ice and brutal stillness. He can survive, but that's all this is: surviving. It snows steadily, and some days Gabriel stays in his tipi. Some mornings, he barely musters up the energy to stoke the fire and melt some water for Trigger to have with the rapidly depleting supply of oats. It is good he has to take care of her, or he might just lie down and not wake up. Gabriel thinks of his body as a frame—his thigh bones, his ribs, his forearms, his cheekbones are like the first cross-pillars of a scow. His bones ache from days, weeks, of riding and being constantly cold.

Gabriel doesn't feel hungry, even though he is barely eating: he hears but does not feel his stomach churning and growling. When Gabriel realizes his pemmican will only last another week or so, he decides to take action out of necessity rather than hunger: he knows he needs to eat more or he could die. Gabriel leads Trigger to the edge of a small body of water. He takes his axe out of his pack. He walks out onto the frozen pond—probably not far enough for the water to be deep enough to catch anything that's edible, but he can't go too far from the shore when he is by himself. *The ice has to be shallow enough that I can chip away at it to make a hole.*

It takes Gabriel a few hours, maybe more, to carefully open a hole so he can try catching a fish. He thinks of Christ, walking on the ocean and bringing loaves and fishes to the feast, and almost considers praying to catch something before the sun sets into darkness. He thinks of Moira, crossing the ocean in a giant ship, journeying for weeks to get to a new place. *She never told me what the passage was like.* And he never thought to ask. *Why didn't I ask her more about her life, about what she knew, about where she came from?* Gabriel has never seen the ocean. The only kind of boat Gabriel has ever been in is a birchbark canoe. *Unless I count a scow, which is hardly a boat.*

As he tries to catch a fish through the small jagged opening in the ice, Gabriel thinks about standing in the Athabasca River on a summer's afternoon loading bales of fur on and off the scows. He can almost feel weight on his forearms. He remembers the relief of a gentle breeze and hears mosquitoes buzzing behind his ears. He can hear the river gurgle. He can see sunlight play off the water as the wind rustles through poplar leaves. He pretends that he is warm and that he will have plenty to eat tonight. He pictures Trigger at the Landing, swatting bugs away with her tail instead of shivering in the snow. Gabriel tells himself that he will spend the evening with a group of other men, telling stories and smoking a pipe, maybe someone will even share a flask of whiskey around the fire. Then, a tug on his line that dangles in the ice brings Gabriel back to the present. He pulls up empty.

Out here, on a prairie pond in the middle of winter, Gabriel decides that one day he will see the ocean. He imagines it to be as vast and deep as the night sky. He has seen some big lakes, paddled on them and fished them, and he thinks about how vast and deep the ocean must be in comparison. In the bright winter sunlight, the black water of the frozen pond sparkles like a sky full of stars. Gabriel can't see where his fishing line ends: it dangles in this pool with stillness. Nothing bites. Nothing moves. He waits in the calm. An hour or more after darkness falls, he gives up, fearing that he will fall asleep out on the pond and not wake up. Gabriel walks back to Trigger empty-handed. Even though she wouldn't eat fish, he apologizes. "Sorry, girl," and he strokes her muzzle.

The deeper into the bush he goes, the more alone Gabriel feels. When he sleeps, he dreams. Gabriel sometimes dreams he is a beaver, swimming along the bank of the Athabasca. His pelt glistens under the water moving with the current. He is single-minded, branch in his mouth, trying to finish building a dam. He keeps swimming, but the dam stays where it is: he never gets closer and he is always alone. He feels eyes he can't place watching him and danger under the river's surface. Gabriel tries not to read anything into these dreams: *it is the exhaustion, the hunger*, he thinks when he wakes.

The nightmares about Moira and the baby are the worst to wake up from. In his dreams, Moira is a rabbit being skinned by a beaten Bertha Tourangeau who bleeds from her eyes and nose as she holds the knife. Or Moira becomes Sutherland losing a leg to the *thump* of Muskwa's axe on the banks of the Athabasca. Sometimes Moira is the doe he killed and he is hacking into her neck with his knife as she moans. He dreams that he is holding his daughter, passing the little body to Moira, only to realize that his child is not a baby but a skinned weasel—pink and sinewy. Once, in his nightmares, Moira was floating in a pool of blood as big as Lac St. Anne and then she sank to the bottom. Gabriel awakes from these horrible visions in a cool sweat to find his dreams are both true and untrue.

It has now been weeks since Gabriel has eaten anything substantial. He has been diligently melting snow for him and Trigger to drink. He knows his mare is losing a dangerous amount of weight. For the past few days—he's lost count of how many as they all merge into one another in an endless state of loneliness—Gabriel has had to use the string of sinew that he lowered into the frozen pond to hold up his trousers. Gabriel knows that if he can find them something to eat, he and his horse will be able to travel farther and faster; he knows he has to find them something to eat soon or they will both fall asleep in a deep white snowbank and not wake up.

For the first time, Gabriel wonders if his grandmother's stories of weetigos are true. He has not lost his senses. He knows there are no half-man, half-monster creatures lurking in the trees waiting to eat the hearts of babies and elders. But he now understands how a man could turn into a monster. Gabriel has considered tying a rope around Trigger's throat but is not sure he has enough feeling left in his fingertips to do it quickly, or that he would have the strength to do it at all, or that after the initial feast he would have enough strength to walk through ice-crusted drifts of snow. He's never been fond of horsemeat and Trigger is getting thin too—he feels less of her every morning when he mounts her to start their journey. But Gabriel now understands how a man could consider eating one of his own.

Gabriel has never been so hungry—for food, for tobacco, for contact with other people. He fantasizes about his first real kill when he was a boy in the springtime woods—and how the doe's blood covered his hands—her blood the colour of wine in the chalice that Father Bourgine held to his lips as they confirmed him to be a Christian in that cold wooden church with the cast-iron stove. Blood has the same metallic aftertaste as wine. Perhaps it really was Christ's blood in the cup.

Gabriel knows that even if Moira's body is never found, the Mounted Police may accuse him of killing her—maybe even the baby if Georgina Barrett told anyone Moira was pregnant—but he is not sure he can wait it out or keep heading east or even survive out here alone until spring. He needs to go home to Lac St. Anne. He decides that he will have to face his fate eventually, even if that means swinging from a rope like Riel or those men at Frog Lake. Since his grandmother sent him into the woods as a boy, Gabriel has told himself that he is good at waiting, but that is not really true—he should have waited for Moira, he should not have convinced her to come to him on the beach of Lac St. Anne and then wait for him to come get her. *I should have married her right then, that after-noon I got back to the settlement and found her alone. I should have married her—in a church, a real wedding, not a country marriage, not a stolen night in the bush, not a mad chase into the snow and the wild toward . . . what? Maybe I should have married Bertha Tourangeau.* She was fit, with a simple face, round breasts, and hips that could bear children without trouble. *She's a good worker.* He would never have pursued Moira if he had been a married man when the Irish girl arrived at Lac St. Anne with all her pale beautiful difference. *I could have saved Bertha from Edward Castor's temper and fists. No wife of mine would have had to beg for a shopkeeper's charity to have flour to make bannock.* But these are useless imaginings. *What's been done is done.* Gabriel's biggest regret is that he did not wait until he had more, more to offer, more to give Moira than a few short weeks together, riding a small mare across the cold, flat, frozen prairie.

Gabriel is not sure he has much left to live for: it would be so easy to curl up under his blanket and fall into an endless sleep. He could use two of his remaining bullets: one for Trigger and one for himself. But he cannot go to the Creator knowing he would bring such pain, such shame, to his family. Not after what they have all survived. Maybe they are waiting for him to come back. Mahkesîs, his mother, maybe Nohkum, are the only people left in the world who give a damn about what happens to him. Gabriel has to get back to them to try to make sense of this. And he wants to survive long enough to give Moira a proper burial; he owes her that much. This is the part of being a man that Gabriel's father could never teach him: the love of a woman is what both tears you apart and makes you whole.

Gabriel decides he will do his best to live: for his mother, his sister, his Nohkum, but most of all for the promise he has made to Moira. He cannot risk her staying in that well for all eternity. He imagines someone finding her bones. He pictures someone trying to enjoy one of the last warm afternoons of a prairie autumn, and then, near the Indian paintbrushes and bear-berries, finding what is left of the mother of his child. They will not know Moira's story. *They will not know she came here on a steel ship from the Emerald Isle to start a new life. They will not know how her laugh made me feel better than any whiskey, how she loved to dance, how her green-grey eyes sparkled when she flirted with me, how she looked at me as we made love, how her blue-black hair sparkled like a magpie's feathers.* They will not know that she lost her life trying to give birth to his daughter. Gabriel is the only one who knows these things now.

Gabriel tries to reason with himself that he did the best he could in the moment. It could have been worse. If he had not found the well, Moira's corpse could have frozen in a snowbank. She could have had to listen to wheat stubble snap under a coyote's paws as the bitch comes to make a feast for her starving litter. Moira could have burned away to a skeleton under this big sky's July sun. *Instead, I found a makeshift grave that will keep her safe until spring, and until I can return for her.*

Gabriel thinks as he sees a familiar crow's nest in a barren poplar tree; he may be travelling in circles. Gabriel needs to survive to tell someone Moira's story. As his sister said to him as they watched the Northern Lights last New Year's Eve, "There is no such thing as just a story." Gabriel looks for the setting sun so he knows what direction west is, clicks his tongue, and pulls the reins to turn Trigger toward the darkening sky, toward home.

⇥ Redemption ⇤
MARCH 1893

By the time Gabriel finds his way back to his parents' cabin at Lac St. Anne, it's been months since anyone here has seen or heard from him. He's worn and thin, and his skin is burned leathery by the sun's reflection on the now-melting snow. Trigger is covered in mange, her ribs are visible through her once fine coat, and one of her eyes is swollen shut. The tips of her ears have turned black with frostbite; time will tell if they need to be severed. Gabriel dismounts. It is nearing the end of March—niskipîsim, the goose moon; but the geese have not yet returned and there is still a layer of ice on Lac St. Anne.

Gabriel sees a woman boiling water over an outside fire in front of the Cardinal cabin. He is sure it is a woman, although she is wearing men's trousers. The woman wears her hair in one long braid and her elk tooth necklace shimmies as she tends to a small child. For a confused moment, he thinks he is back at the lake that summer morning when he introduced Moira to his grandmother. But, no, this woman is not Nohkum: she is too young, too thin. He walks toward her, leading frail little Trigger, as if he is fog rising from the Athabasca River. Gabriel is a ghost of his former self.

Once he is closer, Gabriel recognizes his sister. Mahkesîs crouches near the fire, dressing a baby boy who is trying to stand: the little child wears moccasins beaded with tiny pink flowers and his hair is the colour of bull-rushes—like his mother's. He wiggles and squirms, then falls on his bum as Mahkesîs tries to coax his little arms into a tiny woollen jacket made out of a worn Company blanket.

"Lucas, it's too cold not to wear a coat. Be a good boy," she says. Mahkesîs gives his moss-filled diaper a final check and kisses him on the forehead.

"Mary, come get your cousin!" A little girl runs up to Mahkesîs and her son. The baby squeals with excitement as his older cousin scoops him up and runs with him toward a group of children playing nearby. The little girl also wears moccasins with a floral pattern designed by their grandmother Virginié. There is a thick layer of mud on the soles of her moose-hide shoes. The snow is melting and the ground is still damp.

Mahkesîs stands up to greet the stranger. When she recognizes the haggard, thin man walking toward them leading a skeletal horse, she whispers, "Gabriel."

When he is close enough to hear her, Mahkesîs exclaims, "Gabriel!" and she tries not to show her shock at his appearance. When she hugs him, she feels like she may crush his ribs. He smells of dampness and rot.

Gabriel tries to speak and ends up coughing.

Mahkesîs can hear phlegm bubble in Gabriel's chest. Mahkesîs thinks he may collapse.

The young woman says to her brother in Cree, "Come inside, I am just making some tea and we'll have something to eat . . ."

"Not yet."

"All right, then sit. I'll get you some tea and some bannock and bring it out here."

He nods.

Mahkesîs leads her brother to a tree stump by the fire. She grabs a blanket from the laundry line and wraps it around his slumped shoulders.

The young woman goes inside the cabin and returns to hand her brother a mug of tea. Gabriel's hands shake as he sips the bergamot-flavoured drink. His lips crack and bleed. Mahkesîs unwraps a parcel and hands some just-fried bannock to Gabriel. He takes it but does not eat it.

Neither of them speaks for several minutes.

Finally, Mahkesîs asks, "Where have you been?"

He thinks for a moment and says, "I don't really know. To the east and then back west and now I am here."

"I am so glad you are home." Mahkesîs tries to mask the growing concern in her voice.

"I found some people camped about a day east of here: they spoke Blackfoot, but they took me in for a few nights. People in the camp were sick."

Mahkesîs nods, fearing the worst.

Looking at the children playing nearby, Gabriel asks, "Is that your boy?"

"Yes, that's Lucas. I've had him the past few months and we're getting to know each other a little better every day. Thomas and Ida have their own children to feed and watch. I can look after my own. In fact, those are their children over there now—so I am looking after them in return!"

Now is not the time to speak of the rift that has risen among the Cardinals because of Mahkesîs's return, her father's offer to Thomas of a bigger share in the trap line in exchange for Ida's cooperation in returning the baby, or Virginié's uncharacteristically assertive demand that Thomas and Ida return Lucas to her youngest daughter because "the baby belongs with his mother."

"He looks like you," Gabriel says. His sister has changed since he saw her last. She's stronger, taller, and luminous. Under her man's trousers, Mahkesîs wears high moccasins with blue moose-tufted blooms. Gabriel's sister, who could have passed for white, looks Cree.

Mahkesîs says, "Funny that. Everyone says he looks like you."

"So, you're not a nun anymore?"

Mahkesîs doesn't correct her brother and explain that she was never a nun. Instead she says, "The mission wasn't the life for me. I'll tell you about it some other time." She pauses. "Gabriel, where did you go? Where's Moira? Why did you leave?"

Gabriel looks into his sister's face. He says in English, "Moira died having our baby during a snowstorm."

"Oh, Gabriel." Mahkesîs listens.

"It was too cold to bury either of them in the ground. I left Moira in a well. I need to go get her and bury her here at Lac St. Anne. I knew that I needed to stay away for a while. Away from Barrett and the Mounted Police. So I did. And I've been trying to find my way back. All winter."

Mahkesîs does not know what to say to her brother. She is sad, of course, to hear about her friend Moira, but it is clear he is not well—spiritually or physically—and this is what she needs to focus on. Mahkesîs puts her hand on his shoulder, and Gabriel crumples like an animal wounded by a bow or bullet. He spills some tea on the muddy frozen ground and Mahkesîs gently takes his metal mug from his shaking hands.

He starts weeping.

She lets him.

He starts to sob. The sobs turn into spasms that rack his body.

Gabriel pulls a filthy handkerchief out of his pocket and spits blood into it.

All Mahkesîs can do is reach out, softly rub her brother's back, and let him cry and struggle to breathe.

Gabriel gathers himself. "I won't be able to stay long. I can't get caught here. Barrett can't know I'm here. I'll leave first thing in the morning."

"The Barretts moved away," Mahkesîs said. She doesn't add "shortly after you and Moira disappeared."

"Gabriel, you are safe here. The Barretts cannot hurt anyone here anymore. You need to rest. You'll be safe here; this is your home."

"Taniwehkâk: Mama? Father?"

"Father's gone up north—he's guiding a group of Americans looking for gold. Mama went with him to cook. They are at Fort Chip now—had to get there before the ice melted—and they will make their way into the Dene territory. They won't be back until the end of summer."

"Nohkum?"

Mahkesîs lies and says, "Our grandmother went visiting with Boots and Payesîs, who are here from St. Albert for a week or so. You know what the aunties are like when they all get together. They could gossip for days on end."

Mahkesîs doesn't tell her brother that their grandmother passed away shortly after Christmas. She doesn't think he can take that kind of news at this moment. She hands him back his mug.

Gabriel takes a sip of tea. His hands still shake but not as violently.

"I am glad Barrett is gone. But I can still only stay a few days. I have to go back and find where I left Moira. I cannot leave her there all by herself. Now that the ground is thawing, I can make her a proper grave here, where she belongs."

"Gabriel, you should stay for a week or so at least—let us feed you, have a bath, gather some supplies, sleep in a bed before you head back out. Give Trigger a chance to eat something and rest a bit. It could still snow and storm," says Mahkesîs.

Gabriel nods.

They both know he will not be leaving in a few days.

∞

During the night, Gabriel's cough worsens. The next day, he sleeps, sweats with fever, and coughs bright red blood into a bucket Mahkesîs places beside his cot. Mahkesîs considers sending word for Dr. Horace but senses that it is too late for the old Scottish man to help her brother. And she knows that if she calls Dr. Horace, everyone in the settlement will know Gabriel is back and people will start coming to see him, to ask him questions, to find out where he was and if he brought the Irish girl back with him. Mahkesîs knows this will not help. When she sent Mary home to Thomas's with her older sister, Mahkesîs told Mary not to tell her mother and father that a strange man had come to visit. She knew she was burdening the little girl with a secret, but she needed some time to figure out what happens next.

Mahkesîs knows that Gabriel will soon leave again but worries it will be a different kind of journey: something has eaten him up and there is not enough of him left to start over. She needs to make him comfortable, and if she can't heal him, then she needs to help him find some peace with what has happened.

For two days, Mahkesîs sits with her brother and takes care of little Lucas. With her son on her knee, Mahkesîs tells them stories about foxes. She tells them stories from the Bible. She tries to remember the stories their grandmother would tell them when they were ill.

She asks Gabriel, "Do you remember the games we used to play? Voyageur—I hated that one because you would never let me steer the canoe. Trapper? Soldier? Farmer?"

Sometimes Gabriel answers her and sometimes his answers make sense.

Mahkesîs tells her brother as she wipes his sweating brow and cleans his hands, "In a few months the saskatoons will be ready and we will go to the place over the hill to pick buckets full of them. Babies love saskatoons. But I suppose Lucas will be a little boy by summer. You could take him fishing."

She looks at Lucas. "Would you like to go fishing with Uncle Gabriel? Wouldn't that be fun?"

The baby giggles at his mother's tone.

"We will all camp at Manito Sakahigan on the longest day of the year. Before the pilgrims come, before the beach is crowded with priests and nuns and all those people looking for miracles."

Mahkesîs makes Gabriel fireweed tea knowing that the right amount will quiet his coughing and too much could stop his heart. She wishes her grandmother were here to help her steep the herb. It is an ordeal to get Gabriel to sit up to drink the tea and Mahkesîs is not even sure enough water has passed his lips: he has stopped asking for water or the bedpan. She senses his body is shutting down. She settles her brother down again.

Mahkesîs is still recovering from losing her grandmother, and now it seems she will have to bury her brother. At least she will have the chance to say goodbye to Gabriel. And if being at the St. Albert Mission has taught Mahkesîs anything, it is resilience. She knows that she can survive; she survived James Barrett, Sister Ignatius, even Marie's fear and decision not to leave with her. And Mahkesîs has experienced great love, from Marie and for her son. In fact, Mahkesîs never would have thought she would have a chance to be a mother to her son: the shame she would bring on her family and the thought of seeing Barrett again and again kept her from thinking she could stay very long at Lac St. Anne. But she had to be somewhere where Marie could find her.

Despite the concessions that needed to be made to Thomas and Ida, Mahkesîs and her father have settled into a kind of tolerance of each other that facilitated her staying in Lac St. Anne. Luc can rationalize that they have already lost a son that winter with Gabriel disappearing, and now with Angelique's death, his wife might crumble apart if he turns their daughter away too. And with Barrett gone, Mahkesîs thought she could stay longer than the few months until Feast Day: the knowledge that she would not see him, that she could go to the store herself, that she did not have to hold her breath as she walked past the Manager's Quarters fearing he would walk out the door, kept the memories of the afternoon thunderstorm and the piercing pain firmly in the past. She could really move on. And she could allow herself to love her child knowing she would not be reminded of his father.

Mahkesîs knows now that she can start again and make a life based on what her grandmother taught her about the old ways, about the land and about the lake. Mahkesîs knows now that what she believes, at her core, is right and true. No church or punishment or trial lasts forever. After all she has been through, here she is, back at Lac St. Anne, a mother to her child. Manito Sakahigan is indeed a place of miracles. Now, Mahkesîs needs one for her brother.

∞

On the third night after his return, Mahkesîs tells Gabriel, "Early in the morning, we are going to go outside. We are going to the lake. We will watch the sun rise there. Our elders never waited until Feast Day to ask for a miracle and neither are we. We will go in the sled. The dogs need a good run."

Gabriel tries to sit up, but even that movement exhausts him. Mahkesîs decides to get him dressed for outside in spite of this. Baby Lucas is still sleeping and she will not wake him until she has Gabriel ready. As she tries to exchange her brother's sweat-soaked shirt for the last clean one that their father left behind in the cabin, Gabriel is wracked with more coughing and spasms. Mahkesîs lets him sink back down into the cot and wipes his forehead with a damp cloth.

She tells him, "This summer, after the Feast Day, I am going to convince Marie to stay here and she and I will head West. Where the old Jasper House used to be, people are starting to settle. There are no reserves there yet. The land hasn't been claimed. There are healing places deep in the mountains that I want to visit. There is even a place named Medicine Lake—the French call it Maligne. It has powers, like Calling Lake in the North, where you can hear the elders speak—and as much as people try to explain it by ice shifting or vapours deep in the bedrock, we know different. These are sacred places, special places, places like Manito Sakahigan was before they said we had to call it Lac St. Anne. Marie and Lucas and I are going to start a new life."

Gabriel's coughing subsides.

Mahkesîs says to her brother, "Gabriel, you can come with us. You will be well then."

Gabriel's generous lie has come back to him, full circle. He closes his eyes and sighs.

Even though she doubts her brother can hear her, Mahkesîs tells Gabriel, "When you are better, we will go find Moira and your baby and bury them here at Manito Sakihigan."

Mahkesîs thinks she sees a slight smile cross Gabriel's lips. She knows now that her brother has found his way home to her to die, and she wants to help him find some peace.

As little Lucas sleeps, Mahkesîs sits beside Gabriel and strokes his hair, as if he is her child, and listens to him struggle to breathe. After a while she feels his hand go limp. The rattle in his chest stops. She waits. Nothing happens. She knows she has lost him.

She kisses his forehead and whispers, "I hope you find her wherever you are now." Mahkesîs draws a faded woollen blanket over Gabriel's face and stands up.

"I will keep your story safe," she promises.

Mahkesîs goes to the stove and takes warm water from the kettle. She takes a clean rag and prepares Gabriel's body. She cleans the blood from his mouth and cracking lips. She gingerly wipes his eyelids and forms tiny circles as she traces his eyebrows, the bridge of his nose, and down to his cheekbones with the rag. She decides to shave off his patchy beard—*He probably would have anyway*, she thinks—being careful not to nick him with the straight razor although she knows it wouldn't matter now. *My brother looks better clean-shaven*, she thinks as she dips the silver into a wash basin to rinse off the hair and soap. *He looks like he did before I left for St. Albert*—except his face is much thinner and the skin where his beard was is lighter and smoother than the rest of his face. Mahkesîs wonders if her son will look like this when he is a man. Next, Mahkesîs cleans Gabriel's neck, his collarbone, and his wrists. She takes an eternity to make sure her brother's hands are clean, also between his fingers, even taking a small knife to clean underneath his fingernails. *People will see his face and his hands during the visitation.* She undresses him to wash his clothes and wraps him in a blanket. She places another blanket over him so that little Lucas will not have to see the body lying close to him when he wakes up. Mahkesîs goes to the wash basin and rinses the rag and the smell and Gabriel's fading warmth from her hands. She wipes her palms on her apron.

Mahkesîs grabs a woollen shawl that her grandmother used to wear and quietly opens and closes the door to go outside into the morning's half-darkness. She can feel the coldness of the earth through her deerskin moccasins. The settlement is quiet: no one is stoking a fire or fetching water or feeding horses or hanging clothes on a line just yet. It is early. Mahkesîs walks toward Trigger. The little mare seems excited to see her: she snorts and whinnies and lets Mahkesîs stroke her muzzle. Even yesterday morning, the horse shivered and seemed in danger of falling down dead when Mahkesîs brought her some fresh water and oats. *Maybe she can be brushed in a few more days*, Mahkesîs thinks, relieved the little horse will pull through.

Mahkesîs considers walking down to the water to see the sun rise but doesn't want her little one to wake up alone, so she goes back into the cabin.

She is taken aback at the sight of her brother's lifeless body next to the fireplace and has to turn away. Mahkesîs thinks about all she will have to do once the sun rises: ask Father Lizeé to help with Gabriel, arrange a funeral, tell her other brothers, write to her parents, and ask Joseph (who is managing the store until the Company appoints a replacement for Barrett) to mail the letter to the Fort Chippewan post office. The earth is not fully thawed, so maybe Gabriel and their grandmother can be laid in the ground at the same time. But Mahkesîs is not ready to do all this yet: she needs some time.

Her little boy is still sleeping soundly as Mahkesîs crawls into bed beside him. *Little Lucas is more beautiful than any painting of the Christ-child that Sister Ignatius showed the children at the mission*, she thinks. She strokes her son's soft brown hair, hoping she will not wake him. They are still getting used to each other, but Lucas seems to trust her a little more each day they spend together. Mahkesîs hopes he will always remember her as his mother; one day, she will tell him why she couldn't be with him those first few months. She will make sure he knows that she vows to be with him the rest of her days. Mahkesîs nuzzles into him and takes in his still-babylike smell. She gives him a gentle kiss and rubs her nose on his. Little Lucas instinctively puts his chubby hand on his mother's cheek and smiles in his sleep.

As she holds her son in her arms, Mahkesîs lets herself day-dream, just for a moment. She closes her eyes and pictures the lakeshore in high summer. She imagines Marie teaching her son to swim in the water of Lac St. Anne. The midday sun glistens on the surface of the lake. The green-grey sand lets the waves lap at its shore. Poplar leaves shimmer silver in a late-afternoon breeze.

Lucas splashes and spits water as Marie scolds him. Gabriel is nearby, carving a thick black-and-white poplar branch into a toy canoe for his nephew and his daughter to play with. He laughs at Lucas as the little boy splashes Marie. Moira is there too: she plops her baby on a red-and-black-striped blanket on the sand and makes sure the little one does not topple over. The baby squeals at Lucas's antics in the water and claps her chubby hands. Maybe they will all build a sand castle. Her grandmother is there too: Angelique fries up fresh fish for breakfast and teaches her great-grandchildren to say, "Manito Sakahigan."

In the quiet of the cabin at dawn, Mahkesîs gives herself this moment of imagined bliss, of an impossible miracle, before forcing herself to wake up, unwrap her arms from her little one, and start the day. She needs to collect more wood for a morning fire. The sun has risen. It has started snowing.

It is a week after St. Anne's Feast Day. I am standing at a shrine to Christ's grandmother on the edge of a lake named for her in northern Alberta. The grass is a lush green and freshly mowed. Pilgrims have left bunches of homegrown tiger lilies and blue hundreds-and-millions, branches of blue-purple saskatoon berries, collages of faded photos, and letters covered in plastic food wrap against the stone tower supporting the white statue. Tall, thin poplars create an enclave around the shrine, a nearby memorial, an outdoor amphitheatre, a small structure built to look like a tipi, a modern Catholic church, and a small parsonage; the green poplar leaves shimmer silver in the afternoon sunlight. Other than the mosquitoes that buzz around my head and bite exposed skin on my ankles, I am alone here.

It took me about an hour and a half to drive out here from my house in Edmonton. I've been to Lac St. Anne before, about three years ago, and I've recently been thinking a lot about this place. After all, my story takes place here, at an imagined Lac St. Anne settlement, in the 1890s. In *Pilgrimage*, Mahkesîs, Moira, Georgina, and Gabriel live in my fictionalized version of a real historical time and place.

This novel started as a response to a newspaper article about a woman's body found in a well in Saskatchewan. One early winter morning when I was on maternity leave, and my baby was having one of his two daily naps, I was drinking a cup of coffee and reading the *Edmonton Journal*. An article by Canwest News Service out of Saskatoon headlined WOMAN'S BODY STILL

UNIDENTIFIED caught my eye. It told how a woman's remains found in Sutherland, in an abandoned well, were estimated to be at least a century old. There was a necklace made out of European gold. There was an undisclosed injury, and it was believed she was dead before her body was dumped in the well. As if that wasn't tantalizing enough, the article said her body resembled a bog body, more typically found in Scandinavia or Ireland, rather than a prairie skeleton. My mind started racing: Who was she? Where did she come from? What did she expect out of life in the late nineteenth century on the prairies? And, of course, how did she end up in a well? Even though the body was found in Saskatchewan, I decided to write about Edmonton and the surrounding area because it is my home. Soon I was writing not only about my imagined lady-in-the-well, but also about the people she knew here: the people she loved, loathed, and those who shaped her life. Before I knew it, I had a novel—well, at least a draft of one.

I turned the Lac St. Anne setting of an early chapter from one of those drafts into the main place of the entire novel because it is a place so rich in its symbolism about motherhood and faith and the clash of cultures—and that is essentially what *Pilgrimage* is all about. *Pilgrimage* is a book about the lives of women and how pregnancy and motherhood shape, sustain, and betray. I have tried to show how difficult life might have been for women in northern Alberta in the 1890s, before birth control and legal abortion and criminal prosecution of rape and even the legal recognition of women as people in Canada. I also wanted to show the beauty of motherhood, so setting the story at a lake renamed for the patron saint of childbirth seemed fitting.

The Lac St. Anne settlement also embodies the tensions among European, Aboriginal, French, English, Cree, and Métis life in northern Alberta that I knew I would have to explore if I wrote a novel set in a late-1800s Alberta. So, *Pilgrimage* is also a book about race, class, and colonialism. I studied the history, poured through archives, loaded my arms with library books, and was a student of the Cree language long before I conceived of the story that would become this book. I have done my best to write characters who are first and foremost complex individuals navigating the realities of their world. I chose to tell my story from multiple perspectives, in the third person, for both artistic and personal reasons. I have tried, carefully, to show what racism might have looked like to people living at Lac St. Anne in 1890—and to people from different walks of life.

Pilgrimage is also a book about the North. And I have tried to find beauty in my imagined characters' lives, especially in the place they live, in their home, because the North is my home too. I spent my childhood summers picking saskatoons, catching bees in jars, listening to adults talk about crops and hailstorms and drought. As a married woman, I have camped at my family's trap line near Wabasca. I have tasted pemmican and moose jerky dried on a tripod of poplar branches. I wear moccasins made from an animal my father-in-law hunted. I know that place in *Pilgrimage* is complex. The northern setting in *Pilgrimage* is at times generous, ambivalent, and cruel—much like the people who try to survive it and, sometimes, dare to hope for miracles from a place they believe to be capable of delivering. I think this is still true about the North. At least it is for me.

And, at the end of the day, my own identity will matter to some readers. I am a white woman descended from European settlers writing a book with Aboriginal characters, and perhaps some readers will feel I don't have the right to write this story. I could debate appropriation and literary tradition and analyze this, but, at the end of the day, I myself am neither Cree nor Métis. I do not know what it is like to feel that my ancestry or the colour of my skin is an impediment to my ambitions or a provocation of hatred. I have tried to imagine this for some of my characters, but it remains an imagining.

Although I didn't realize it until this moment, this is why I have come to St. Anne today—I need to wrestle with this and I need to wrestle with this here. I take a deep breath and kneel at the statue of Christ's grandmother on the edge of this sacred lake. I don't even know if I believe in God anymore, but this feels right. I stay still for a moment, just to be and to be here. I feel the weight of anxiety on my chest, and my fingertips tingle. Historical fiction is a hybrid beast, and I feel responsibility as a writer who chooses to fictionalize lives. I created my characters at first from real life in a newspaper report, from history; then from parts of myself and people in my life; and then, as the writing took over and I learned by trial and fire how to draft a novel, I fleshed them out to drive the narrative in certain directions. But the rational, the intellectual, cannot diminish my body's physical reaction.

After some time, I stand up and walk back to my car, not free of the anxiety but at peace with it. I have been on a journey with *Pilgrimage*: I have learned and relearned much about writing and reading, about the history and present of the part of the world I choose to call home, about love and motherhood, and about myself. I hope *Pilgrimage* has created a journey of its own for you.

The inspiration for *Pilgrimage* came from a 2006 Canwest News Service newspaper report about the June 29, 2006, discovery of a woman's remains in a well in the Sutherland area of Saskatchewan. To my knowledge, this woman has never been identified, and the police estimate her remains to be at least a century old.

The heart of *Pilgrimage* came from my research on what Lac St. Anne, St. Albert, Athabasca Landing, and Edmonton may have been like in the late nineteenth century after the Riel rebellions and completion of the railroad to Edmonton. I have done my best to place Mahkesîs, Moira, Georgina, Gabriel, and the other characters in accurate situations and places relative to their identities and the time. I have used names befitting of the place and time, but the main characters in *Pilgrimage* are fictional. Some of the background characters are real historical people who lived at Lac St. Anne and in the surrounding area: Father Lizeé, Father Lacombe, and Factor Livestock, in particular. I have tried to be respectful of their work and of published memories of them.

The following publications were valuable to me during the writing process: E.O. Drouin's *Lac St-Anne Sakahigan*; Linda Goyette's *Edmonton in Our Own Words*; Pauline Jackson's article "Women in Nineteenth Century Irish Emigration" in the *International Migration Review*, Vol. 18, 4; Myrna Kostash's *The Frog Lake Reader*; Nancy LeClaire and George Cardinal's *Alberta Elders' Cree Dictionary*; Maureen K. Lux's *Medicine That Walks: Disease, Medicine, and Canadian Plains Native People,*

1880–1940; J.G. MacGregor's *Paddle Wheels to Bucket—Wheels on the Athabasca*; Patricia McCormack and Sarah Carter's anthology *Recollecting: Lives of Aboriginal Women of the Canadian Northwest and Borderlands* (especially Susan Berry's essay that mentions Lac St. Anne and Kristin Burnett's essay "Obscured Obstetrics"); Christine Miller and Patricia Chuchryk's collection *Women of the First Nations: Power, Wisdom, and Strength*; Oxford University Press's anthology of *Irish Writing: 1789–1939*; Brock Silversides's *Fort de Prairies: The Story of Fort Edmonton*; the St. Albert Historical Society's *The Black Robe's Vision: A History of St. Albert & District* (especially for the oral testimony and family history documented in its pages); Irene Ternier Gordon's *A People on the Move: The Métis of the Western Plains*; and W.B. Yeats's wacky collection of *Irish Folk and Fairy Tales*.

Trips to Fort Edmonton Park and the Ukrainian Heritage Village helped me picture what it might have been like to live in northern Alberta in the 1890s. We are fortunate to have these living museums in Alberta. I also consulted digital records of historical documents in *Our Future, Our Past: The Alberta Heritage Digitization Project*; the 1891 census in the Alberta Digital Archives; and copies of scrips available in the Government of Canada's Collections Canada archives.

In particular:

- E.O. Drouin's map in *Lac St-Anne Sakahigan* helped me place my characters in the settlement of the early 1890s.
- Bertha Tourangeau's job as a rabbit-skinner came from the historical document of Mrs. Victoria Calahoo's oral testimony, first published in the St. Albert newspaper and reprinted in Drouin's book.
- Diane P. Payment's essay "'La vie en rose'? Métis Women at Batoche, 1870 to 1920" in *Women of the First Nations* anthology for introducing me to the song Bertha Tourangeau sings in the chapter "New Year's Eve."

- Silversides's documentation of Gabriel LeBlanc's role in procuring medicine for women and children at Fort Edmonton was part of the inspiration for Gabriel's name, as I detail in "Summer Solstice." Of course, the angel Gabriel is connected to the Virgin Mary in Christian mythology: in Luke 1:26, Gabriel tells Mary, "Fear not: for thou hast found favor with God and thou shalt conceive in thy womb, and bring forth a son, and shalt call his name Jesus."
- Drouin records the testimony of Father Gabillon about the lake's healing powers that I depict in "St. Anne's Feast Day."
- The story of the curing fox and the weetigo that Mahkesîs tells Marie in "Missions" is based on a legend recorded by Norman Howard. He includes versions of this oral story in both his 1982 compilation, *Where the Chill Came From: Cree Windigo Tales and Journeys* (North Point Press), and his 1990 book, *Northern Tales: Traditional Stories of Eskimo and Indian Peoples* (Pantheon Books).

I adapted small turns-of-phrase from my creative nonfiction essay "Ahead of the Ice," published in *Alberta Views* in March 2012, to describe Mahkesîs giving birth to Lucas (in "Summer Solstice") and to describe Gabriel ice fishing (in "Journey").

ACKNOWLEDGMENTS

Thank you to Ruth Linka, Emily Shorthouse, Cailey Cavallin, and Pete Kohut, the amazing team at Brindle & Glass, for bringing this book into the world, and to Heather Sangster for her proofreading skills. Thank you to Leah Fowler for editorial expertise and attention, for loving these characters as much as I do, and for renaming our deadline a "birth-line."

Thank you to Linda Goyette, who told me I was a writer many years ago and, upon reading an embryonic draft of this book, offered the invaluable suggestion that I set the whole novel in Lac St. Anne. Thank you to Pauline Holdstock, who told me I was a writer, and to my colleagues at the Banff Centre "Writing with Style" 2010 workshop, who gave me feedback and encouraged me to write more—especially about Gabriel. Thank you to Thomas Trofimuk, who told me I was a writer (even and especially when I got rejected) and trusted me to read his work in turn.

Thank you to Heather Davidson and KJ MacAlister; both read early drafts and gave insightful feedback. Thank you to Kris Price and Jessica Kluthe and Paula Bissell-Molloy for making me celebrate. Thank you to my parents, John and Katja Davidson, for always supporting me and making books and reading a part of my daily life. Thank you to my mom-in-law, Shirley Bissell, for supporting me and, in particular, to my father-in-law, Robert Bissell, for sharing his trapping experiences with me as I attempted to give credibility to scenes and descriptions.

Thank you to my husband, Stan, a great editor who read many versions of this story, for always believing in me as a writer, and thank you to my son, Ewan, who makes me want to be a better person.

DIANA DAVIDSON lives in Edmonton, Alberta. Davidson's essay "Luminescence" was long-listed for CBC's Canada Writes creative nonfiction prize, and her piece "Ahead of the Ice" won the Writers Guild of Alberta Jon Whyte Memorial Essay Prize and appeared in *Alberta Views* magazine. She has published numerous academic articles, has a PHD in literature, and has taught at the University of Alberta and the University of York, UK. Her website and blog can be found at diana.davidson.org. *Pilgrimage* is Davidson's first novel.